Peter Watt has s[...], prawn trawler de[...]; real estate salesr[...] – geant and adviser to the [...] a Constabulary. He speaks, reads and writes Vietnamese and Pidgin. He now lives at Maclean, on the Clarence River in northern New South Wales. Fishing and the vast open spaces of outback Queensland are his main interests in life.

Peter Watt can be contacted at www.peterwatt.com

Excerpts from e-mails sent to Peter Watt:

'I heartily agree with the comments from readers that are printed in your books. I also have read Wilbur Smith and Bryce Courtenay and am very pleased to add you to the list of my favourite authors. Keep up the good work.'

'I have just read *The Stone Dragon* and I have to say that the first page made me smile so much because you resurrected a favourite character in John Wong. Then reading the story of Peking made me think about your recommendation of other books on this sad saga and I am now going to broaden my horizons on different countries. But I know you have many more stories to tell and I cannot wait.'

'I picked up *The Stone Dragon* at my local library in Western Australia, and after a couple of chapters am delighted to have found a new good author to add to my favourites. I'll be reading your other books and confidently pay for them at the bookshop.'

'Inside the cover you have emails sent to you and I would like to add my compliments. Thanks for many enjoyable hours of reading.'

Also by Peter Watt

THE
STONE
DRAGON

PETER
WATT

PAN
Pan Macmillan Australia

*For my mother, Elinor Therese Watt nee Duffy, who has
served her country in time of war and her community in
time of peace*

First published 2007 in Macmillan by Pan Macmillan Australia Pty Ltd
This Pan edition published in 2008 by Pan Macmillan Australia Pty Ltd
1 Market Street, Sydney

Reprinted 2009

National Library of Australia
Cataloguing-in-Publication data:

Watt, Peter, 1949–.

The stone dragon / Peter Watt.

ISBN 9780330423984 (pbk.).

A823.3

Set in Bembo by Post Pre-press Group
Printed in Australia by McPherson's Printing Group

Papers used by Pan Macmillan Australia Pty Ltd are natural,
recyclable products made from wood grown in sustainable forests.
The manufacturing processes conform to the environmental
regulations of the country of origin.

THE DRAGON
ASLEEP

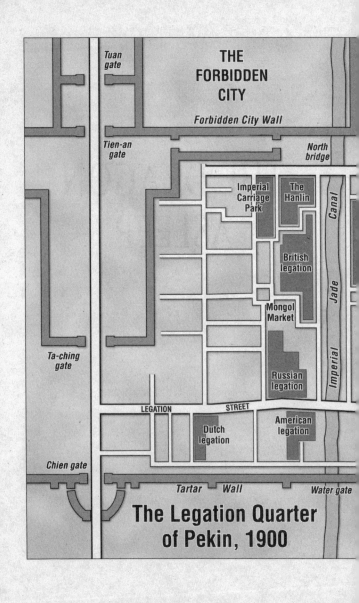

The Legation Quarter of Pekin, 1900

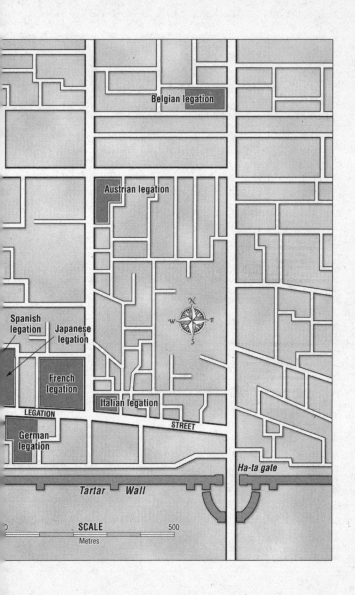

Late Spring, 1900
Chihli Province
North-east China

Sha! Sha! The chanting from hundreds of angry voices grew closer.

Dr Nathaniel Davies fought to control the terrible fear rising in his gullet. The American had been a Methodist missionary in China for a dozen years and his grasp of the Chinese language was excellent. *Kill! Kill!* The raised voices chanted as hundreds of native rebels surged through the streets and alleys of the village, moving inexorably towards his mission station.

Thank the Lord that he had evacuated his wife and two children, he thought as he stared at the open doorway to his office. His wife, Clarissa, had tearfully protested his decision to stay but he had no choice. He had a congregation of Chinese converts to protect from the mysterious members of the secret society he knew as the *Band of Righteous Harmony*. To many of the doctor's colleagues the same society was better known as the *Righteous Harmony Fists* – or simply, *Boxers* – a term derived from the practice of martial arts by adherents carried out before audiences of village peasants to impress them with their fighting prowess.

Now a more ominous sound mingled with the chanting. It was the sound of men, women and children screaming in terror as the Boxers advanced on the mud-bricked mission station at the centre of the village.

'Please, God, spare my children,' Dr Davies groaned.

Amid the sound of screaming was also that of death as broad-bladed swords hacked at those identified as Christian converts. It was only then that the brave missionary had any self-doubt as to the wisdom of remaining behind, instead of fleeing to the relative safety of Pekin, as it did not seem that he would be able to reason with the approaching rebels if they had now commenced slaughtering the helpless villagers. He sensed his own death was imminent and stared at the grapefruit-sized stone at the centre of his desk, lying next to a leather purse. If there was nothing else that he could do now for his congregation, he could at least do one service for science and all mankind.

Dr Davies reached for the unimpressive-looking, mostly rounded rock and turned it over in his hand to reveal the small but distinct fossil of an ancient dinosaur, many millions of years old. To even his experienced geologist's eye the stone was like many others that were being hewn from the earth in the hills of China – ancient reminders that the Earth once lived under the shadow of giant dragons, as his uneducated congregation would have called them for their reptilian shape.

The villagers to whom he ministered knew of his passion for rocks and stones. They might not have understood that Dr Davies had studied geology – a love grown out of his youth spent finding Indian arrowheads on his father's farm in Iowa. But they did understand that an unusual rock could please the mild-mannered missionary who would immediately pore over the specimen with a magnifying glass, muttering strange words.

This rock was different. The story of its discovery immediately piqued the curiosity of the geologist in Dr Davies. If his theory was correct, the tiny stone dragon encased in the rock was one of the most important finds in the history of science. But the stone required further examination by those even more educated in mineral classification than himself. At the least it was an interesting record of a fossil. At best . . .

'Dr Davies,' a voice pleaded from the doorway. 'You must flee now. They are almost upon us.'

The American glanced up at the young Chinese man standing in the doorway wringing his hands. 'I will not go, Chin,' he replied in a calm voice. 'It is too late. As a foreign devil I would not get far in the countryside. But you would – if you use that natural cunning of yours.'

The Chinese man was in his early twenties and in good health. He spoke reasonable English but always conversed with his friend, the American missionary, in Chinese.

'I have a red blouse,' Chin replied, lowering his eyes. 'I could pass as one of the Boxers in this time of madness.'

'Good.' Dr Davies smiled grimly. 'You must take this rock and the letter I have written to Pekin, and give it to the American consulate. It is important that you do this,' he continued, rising to his feet to stretch his tall, gaunt frame, attempting to prevent his assistant of the last five years from seeing how badly his hands trembled as he slipped the stone into the leather pouch. He secured the knot and passed the leather pouch to his assistant, who concealed it under his shirt. Chin did not attempt to further persuade his American friend to come with him. He knew that to do so would only bring death to them both. At least he hoped to survive and take this seemingly worthless rock to the Americans in Pekin. In discussing the implications of what Dr Davies suspected about the rock Chin had not understood his friend's philosophical ramblings in the doctor's own language, but he did know that the rock appeared as important to the missionary as the American's own faith in Jesus.

'Go, my young friend, and may the Lord be with you in your journey,' Dr Davies said as the sound of a wooden door shattering under the impact of heavy metal objects came to them. Both men knew that it was the gate to the mud-bricked wall surrounding the mission estate. The howling outside was chilling in its animal intensity and to the Methodist missionary it was not many human voices, but one snarling beast from a Christian hell.

Chin turned on his heel and slipped away to

change quickly into his disguise. He even had an old sword to go with his uniform of red blouse and white trousers. He planned to mingle with the Boxers when they burst into the Methodist missionary's office.

Dr Davies opened a drawer in his wooden desk and wrapped his hand around the butt of a .445 Webley revolver. Once he had been a young man wearing the blue uniform of a Maine regiment at the second battle of Gettysburg. With calm courage he had chosen not to turn the other cheek, but to go down fighting in a bid to distract the ever-advancing Boxer warriors. His last stand would distract them and allow his young Chinese assistant to merge into the melee.

'Dear Lord,' the minister prayed quietly. 'Forgive me my trespasses and forgive those . . .'

The snarling face of a Boxer appeared before him and the flash of a broad-bladed sword swirled through the air. Dr Davies fired, felling the first warrior who believed that he could not be killed by European firearms. A second stepped through the doorway taking his fallen comrade's place and the Methodist fired again. Davies kept firing until the hammer of the revolver clicked impotently. Then the swords hacked at him until he was a bloody, shredded mess.

Dr Davies was not the first missionary to die in the Boxer Rebellion. Nor would he be the last.

Chin heard the firing and slipped into the mass of warriors streaming into the compound. So intoxicated were they with the rapture of their mission that the Boxers paid little attention to the man who joined their ranks.

THE STONE DRAGON

1900
Cairns District
The Australian Colony
of Queensland

First Class Constable Stanley Ogden clambered cautiously along the bank of the wide river flanked by lush, tropical rainforest.

'Keep a sharp eye out,' he called over his shoulder to the Aboriginal tracker who was following, trailing his Martini Henry carbine. The Queensland policeman had good reason to be wary, as giant saltwater crocodiles lurked in the river.

It was the sickly stench that helped the policeman locate what had brought him in the course of his official duties to the banks of the north Queensland river.

'See 'im, boss,' the tracker said, squatting on his haunches with the rifle cradled in his arms. 'He bin die over there.' The young Aboriginal pointed to a shaded patch of evil-looking, black water in a gully leading into the river.

The policeman followed the direction and his eyes fell on the rapidly decomposing body, lying face down in the glue-like mud. He wondered how the big crocs had not already found the corpse and dragged it away.

Sweat poured down Ogden's face and trickled under the stiff collar of his blue serge blouse. He did not relish the idea of sliding down the bank into the mottled shadows cast by the surrounding rainforest.

'Give me the gun, Billy, and go down the gully. You drag the bugger up here,' the policeman said, reaching for his rifle.

Billy pulled a face. Handling dead bodies was not something he wanted to do. His culture had a reverence bordering on fear for the dead.

'Go on,' Ogden snapped, seeing the Aboriginal tracker's hesitation. 'Pull the bugger over here so we can get a better look at him.'

The tracker reluctantly obeyed, sliding cautiously down to the glutinous, black mud that immediately squelched up to his knees. With some difficulty he waded over to the body and gripped the cotton shirt. With a tug he attempted to dislodge the body but fell backwards into the mud, causing Ogden to burst into laughter.

Muttering fiercely, Billy made a second effort to reclaim the corpse. It came loose with a soft plopping sound and the tracker slid it across the gully to the bank. He was aided in his task by the body not being very large: hardly bigger than a child.

'Roll him over,' Ogden commanded, trying not

to breathe in the nauseous smell that was stifling in the hot, humid air around the lagoon.

Billy rolled the body over to reveal the barely recognisable, death-blackened face. From the information Ogden had received he had a fairly good idea that the dead man was a Chinese – although not a local member of the already established community of this part of north Queensland.

'Have a look to see if you can find anything on him,' Ogden said.

Reluctantly, Billy searched through the dead man's clothing. He found nothing and shrugged.

'Well,' the policeman sighed, standing to stretch his legs. 'We have the body, now all we have to do is find the culprit. You can leave him, Billy. With any luck the crocs will find him and save us the problem of transporting him back to town.'

Caked in drying mud, Billy scrambled up the bank to join his superior officer. The finding of the culprit was his job and far better than retrieving the body of what was, after all, only a murdered Chinee man, and therefore of no consequence.

Mounted on his horse, Ogden followed his tracker away from the riverbank into a maze of sugarcane clearings sprouting knee-high, bamboo-like stalks that slapped against the chest of the police officer's horse.

Billy was surprised how easy it was to track a quarry who had made no attempt to cover his trail away from the murder scene. He suspected that the man was also Chinese as the prints indicated a barefooted person who was not as large-framed as a whitefella. One thing puzzled Billy as he gazed at the almost invisible trail he was following. Whoever he was following walked with the stealth of a hunting animal.

It was mid-afternoon under a scorching tropical sun when the tracks led them to a copse of tropical forest left unfelled at the edge of a paddock. Billy stopped, looked up at Ogden and, with the thousands of years of accumulated skills of his people, declared softly, 'Chinee man we track in there.'

Ogden felt the short hair on the back of his neck bristle. Billy was never wrong and they were now only yards from their prey. Carefully, Ogden slid the carbine from its bucket and lowered himself from the horse. 'You take this,' he said quietly to Billy, handing him his police issue sidearm while he retained the hard-hitting carbine. Billy gratefully accepted the pistol. Something told him that the man they had pursued was different to others he had tracked. Billy gripped the pistol as both men inched forward towards the ominous clump of tall trees.

Tung Chi dozed lightly with his back against a large tree. It was hot and humid under the canopy of the small piece of jungle left by the Europeans who had cleared the rainforest to plant sugarcane. He was hungry, weary and alone in this foreign land far from his beloved Shantung province in China. But now it was time to search for the second man, and to do that he would need to make contact with the Chinese community in Queensland's north.

The slightest change in the air in the small clearing alerted him. Carefully, he eased himself away from the trunk and reached for the razor-sharp knife in his belt. Then he saw the uniformed policeman stalking through the shadows.

As lithely as a snake, Tung crawled to a better position to observe the heavy-footed European. It was obvious from the way the man moved that he was not aware of Tung's location. Tung knew this because he had spent many years hunting men himself and, although it was not within his orders to kill anyone not associated with the mission, the policeman presented an immediate threat. He would have to kill the barbarian as soon as he was within striking distance.

Ogden edged closer, totally unaware that he was being watched by a highly professional killer and was only seconds from death. Tung prepared to spring his ambush with a speed of a striking snake.

'You bin stick 'em up!' a voice challenged.

Startled, Tung swung to peer into the very black face of an Australian Aboriginal who had a revolver levelled at him. What was more frightening – and totally surprising – was that the Aboriginal was mere paces away. How had he done it? How had he been able to approach so silently to within striking range? Tung had been informed that the Aboriginal people would never really pose a threat to his mission. He had been briefed that they were now a broken people dispossessed across the land. But the young man he

15

was facing had the air about him of a warrior to be reckoned with.

'Chinee man, drop the knife,' Billy further ordered.

Tung obeyed.

Now that Ogden was upon Tung he realised just how close he had come to being ambushed by the Chinese man with the knife.

'You heathen bastard,' Ogden roared, using the butt of the carbine to club Tung to the ground. 'Try to kill a white man, would you?' he snarled, smashing the rifle once again down on Tung's head, drawing blood.

Semi-conscious, Tung slumped to the ground where Ogden manacled his hands and feet. It was a lot of trouble for one whose only crime had been to kill another Chinaman, Ogden mused, pulling the prisoner to his feet.

In his late forties, the Eurasian still had the body of a man twenty years younger. John Wong had the powerful frame of his Irish mother's family and the tanned skin of his father's Chinese ancestors. At first glance he appeared to be more European in his looks. A closer examination revealed the liquid, black eyes that seemed to conceal a dangerous man. His short-cropped hair was now almost all grey but he still held an appeal to women of all races with his fine looks.

Beside John stood a younger version of the Eurasian – although he appeared more Asian, thanks to a Chinese mother. Andrew's broad shoulders, however, were an inheritance from his long dead Irish grandmother's people on his father's side. He wore an expensive tailored suit with an elegance that bespoke his upper middle class position. Besides being the son of the colourful John Wong – whose exploits were part of north Queensland folklore – he would hopefully one day be known as Dr Andrew Wong. Andrew had escaped the cold sleet of his university campus during the term break to return to the warmer climes of Australia on extended leave. Soon he would go back to Scotland to finish his last term in the far off Edinburgh medical school before returning to the Australian colonies to practise medicine. Surgery was of particular interest to him.

Both men stood among barrels and bales of exotically scented articles in a roomy, corrugated shed gazing over the latest shipment of goods shipped from Hong Kong: spices, silks and pieces of Oriental artwork in vogue with Europeans.

'We need to reship the porcelain pieces down south to Sydney and Melbourne,' John said. 'Always a good market for them there.'

Andrew loved the big, tough man he called father. Standing in this newly opened place in the port of Cairns, he found himself reflecting on his family and the two precious women who were absent from his life.

With the premature death of his mother when Andrew was only five years old his father had steered his life with gentleness and discipline in equal amounts. But the discipline had not been applied to his little sister, Naomi, whom the big man spoiled beyond the comprehension of her older brother. Naomi was the princess, his father once explained, and he would have to be the gallant knight in the life ahead. It was only now that Andrew was older that he understood why his father had been seemingly hard at times. Being of mixed blood and living in a European world had not been easy. But Andrew had been blessed with a natural talent for sports and excelled at cricket, rugby, swimming, athletics and boxing. This had ensured a place in colonial society where such achievements were enough for many to turn a blind eye to his mixed blood – at least in social circles until the daughter, sister or even wife of a European associate vied for the handsome young man's attention.

Andrew treasured the short time he was home from his studies to be with his father who he proudly knew had led a colourful and dangerous life when his own age on the wild, lawless Queensland frontier of the 1870s. It had been rumoured that his father had once belonged to a Chinese secret society and that he had even ridden with the legendary Christie Palmerston, the explorer and adventurer who had opened up much of north Queensland. Even more intriguing had been his father's involvement with the infamous Michael Duffy – a man related to the well-known Duffy family of Sydney and linked to the gentry of the Macintosh dynasty. But his father never spoke of those times when he and Michael Duffy had disappeared into the Far East on mysterious missions. To the world John Wong was a prosperous man, well known in racing circles for the fine horses he bred on one of his many properties. The Wong financial empire also had offices in Brisbane, Sydney and Melbourne along with agencies in Hong Kong and mainland China. It had been the Wong contacts in China that had assisted in placing Naomi with one of the company's agencies in Pekin.

Andrew remembered the day he witnessed his father become truly angry with Naomi. She had approached John with the suggestion that she go to China to learn more about the family business. As she was a mere nineteen years old the idea was ludicrous. But his father also had argued that women did not have a place in commerce. It was his daughter's duty to meet the right man and settle down to a life as a wife and mother.

Even then, Andrew had known that beneath Naomi's female exterior beat the heart of a lion. He had come grudgingly to respect her and suspected that his father would lose the argument.

'Why in hell would you want to go to China?' his father had exploded.

Naomi had burst into tears. 'I would like to visit the land of my mother,' she replied in a humble voice, her eyes downcast.

Andrew had stood at the end of the verandah of their sprawling house and watched with just a touch of satisfaction. Finally his sister had not got her way. But he was startled to see his father throw his arms around her petite frame and draw her close to him. For a second Andrew swore that he saw an evil glint in his sister's tear-glistened eye – and even a smirk.

You little minx, Andrew had thought. You have

tricked him with your crocodile tears!

And Naomi had.

That had been two years ago and the only contact in that time had been her letters from Pekin to say how exciting the city was and just how much she was learning. Her father had to grudgingly admit that she was proving to be more astute in business than even he could have anticipated. She had an eye for obtaining the most valuable artefacts from village markets and shipping them back to Queensland.

Now, there was no doubt in John's mind that his son would be a medical doctor of great importance and that his financial empire would one day be ruled by his daughter – despite her defying all that he understood of a woman's role in Victorian times.

'I hope that she is all right,' John said softly, as if reading Andrew's thoughts.

'What?' Andrew replied, startled by his father's statement.

'Your sister,' John said softly, turning to his son. 'Reports being sent to me from Pekin indicate that there is bad trouble brewing over there. I would rather have her with us – away from it all.'

'You know Naomi,' Andrew tried to reassure his father. 'She is as tough as you. I am sure that if anything is happening in Pekin she will have taken measures to ensure that *Wong & Co* – as well as herself – are safe from any trouble.'

'Maybe you are right,' John said uneasily, placing his hand on his son's shoulder. 'When do you return to Scotland to complete your studies?'

Andrew was about to reply when a shadow filled

the entrance to the depot.

'Mr Wong?' a deep voice called, and both father and son turned to view the uniformed policeman striding towards them with the assuredness of one used to being obeyed.

'I don't mean to trouble you but I got a job you might be able to help us with,' he said. 'We picked up a Celestial . . .' The big policeman hesitated, aware that he was using a derogatory term in front of the important citizen of the north. 'Begging pardon from present company,' he continued in a more contrite tone.

'Sergeant Ogden,' John said, extending his hand to the dust- and sweat-coated policeman. 'I don't think you have met my son, Andrew.'

Andrew had flinched at the reference to Celestial and did not bother to extend his hand to the burly policeman. Instead, he gave a small nod of acknowledgment to the meeting.

'My son is studying medicine at Edinburgh,' John continued with noticeable pride in his voice. 'He will soon be in practice.'

'You going to work with them missions in China?' Ogden asked with what Andrew detected was just a note of contempt.

'I expect to practise medicine in Sydney,' Andrew replied coldly. 'I see that my father was wrong about your rank,' he continued. 'You are only a first class constable and not a sergeant.'

'I should be an acting sergeant,' Ogden answered defensively. 'But those in Brisbane have given us this other rank instead. But I am here to solicit your father's assistance in questioning a Chinee man we picked up on suspicion of murder of another Chinee man just south of here. We got tipped off yesterday by one of your own in Cairns.'

'You need my son's help,' John said. 'My knowledge of Chinese is a bit rusty and it will also depend on what dialect your prisoner speaks as to whether we can help you.'

'I thought all Chinee men spoke the same language,' the policeman replied.

'Depends on where in China he is from,' John answered. 'But my son is relatively fluent in Mandarin as well as having a working knowledge of other dialects.'

'Well, we will see,' Ogden grunted. 'Master Wong,' he continued. 'If you will please follow me outside.'

Andrew cast his father a questioning look. John nodded and followed both the police officer and Andrew into the scorching tropical sun.

On the almost deserted, dusty street they saw a badly beaten man sitting manacled on the dry earth. Blood had caked around his head and oozed down his face. Guarding the prisoner was an Aboriginal tracker with a rifle pointed at him. John thought this was unusual, as the police very rarely considered Chinese prisoners to be of much trouble.

'He has proven to be a very dangerous man,' Ogden commented as they approached the barely conscious prisoner. 'Already killed one man and tried to kill me.'

Andrew examined the prisoner and with his trained eye could see that one of the cuts in the scalp would require stitches.

Andrew straightened and addressed the police officer. 'If he does not get medical treatment then I suspect that he could die from his wounds.'

Ogden looked down at the ground for a moment. He was aware that the death of even a Celestial would mean a coroner looking into the matter and that always meant more paperwork to interfere with drinking time.

'No doctor available at the moment,' he answered. 'Maybe something you could do.'

Andrew considered the matter. He was not qualified but he had learned much in his studies and stitching was something he knew how to do, despite not having the right surgical equipment.

'Get him into the depot,' Andrew said. 'I am sure that my father will find something with which I can carry out first aid on your prisoner.'

Ogden hauled the man roughly to his feet and Andrew assisted the police officer to escort Tung inside the relatively cooler shed.

'What is your name?' Andrew asked softly in the Mandarin dialect.

Tung did not reply.

Late May 1900
Pekin
China

Naomi Wong was well away from the broad, shaded, avenues of the foreign legations where she had been visiting and now walked along streets where long lines of goods-laden camels from Mongolia plodded into the city vying with spring-less, wooden carts flanked by armed outriders. The rough and ready traders from the far-flung deserts of China shared the filth-strewn roads with Imperial mandarins clothed in long sable or silk coats in their human-propelled sedans. Pairs of weary mules with palanquins slung between them were accompanied by tough, sword-bearing men passing the stalls of barbers, scented Soochow prostitutes and roadside cooks from Canton.

The noise, dust and fetid smell all merged to become what Naomi had come to accept as the exotic, if not dubious fragrance of this crowded city of Far Eastern commerce surrounded by massive walls of stone.

At first impression, Naomi appeared to be one with the other Chinese women on the street, albeit she did not have her feet bound and her exotic beauty caused the male eye to linger. Because of her European dress she was given a wide berth by the water carriers jogging through the raucous crowds filling the marketplaces. The local Chinese peasants had come to learn that disrespect to a European could incur a savage reprisal from the barbarian occupiers of their city of a million people. Naomi had been closeted by her father's wealth and power while growing up in Queensland and any slurs there against her ancestry were not overt. She was aware of the tragic history of the land of her Chinese ancestors. The European powers, Japan and the United States of America, had insidiously occupied her country and split China into colonies. Although they allowed the Chinese to rule themselves under an imperial system it was the colonisers and their armed forces that actually dictated policy. Throughout the nineteenth century the Chinese had attempted to rise against this oppression in what was known as the Opium Wars. The Chinese had attempted to eradicate the opium forced on them, by the English in particular. But they had failed and now were acutely aware that they were subservient to Western rule. They knew their oppressors considered them sub-human, little more than a source of raw materials for the European markets. In return, the occupiers helped justify their presence with the excuse of bringing Christianity to the heathens, and missionary organisations of every denomination spread across China under the protection of Western firepower. As well-meaning as the missionaries were, they had in fact acted to erode traditional values established long before the birth of Christ in far-off Palestine.

As Naomi had been raised under a European educational system, she had been imbued with Western values and hardly thought of herself as Chinese. She was a British citizen of Chinese heritage and enjoyed the privileges afforded to one of her place of birth. But she did find living in Pekin had slowly made her aware of the Chinese plight although she still refused to seek any sympathy within herself for those around her who were not European. After all, she was in China to learn her father's business and profit from the status quo as established by Britain's powerful Royal Navy and civil service.

Naomi did not walk alone when she was away from the Pekin office of her father's company. The manager, Mr Soo Chow, insisted that she be accompanied by a tall, powerfully built Sikh bodyguard armed with a sword and revolver. His presence beside her as much as her European dress ensured that Naomi received free passage along the streets. The Sikh was totally devoted to her and it would have been a foolish bandit or would-be pickpocket who would attempt anything improper towards Miss Wong in his presence. He was an older man who carried the scars of his years fighting with the British army on the North-West Frontier of India. Naomi had grown fond of the taciturn giant with his dark eyes and skin and huge, bristling moustache. She had nick-named him Raj and now Raj found himself carrying the carefully wrapped parcels of precious and semi-precious ornaments Naomi had been able to procure from street hawkers for instalment in the *Wong & Co* inventory prior to shipment to Europe and the Americas via her father's depot in Queensland.

What had amazed Naomi in the last few days was the sudden appearance in the marketplaces of so many previously hard to obtain items. But she had soon learned from various sources she had cultivated that all was not well in the surrounding countryside. The word on the street was that the enigmatic Boxers were coming, sweeping all before them and forcing thousands to flee with all that they could carry, to barter for food and lodging. And now they were already within the walls of the city, brazenly demonstrating their martial skills with spear and sword while calling down the spirits of such deities as Pigsy, Sandy and Monkey to take over their bodies. In trance-like states the Boxer adherents would fall to the ground, snorting like a pig when the spirit of Pigsy possessed them or capering like a monkey when possessed by that spirit. As amusing as these ancient deities may have appeared to Westerners they were well-established gods to the Chinese.

'Miss Wong, are you sure that you should be on the streets in times such as these?'

Naomi turned to the man she was familiar with.

'Lieutenant Mumford,' she replied with a dazzling smile. 'You forget that I am Chinese.'

Within a pace Lieutenant Robert Mumford

stood facing Naomi in his spotless dress uniform of the British army. Naomi was pleased to see the handsome, blue-eyed, blond young officer around five years older than her. They had met a year earlier when she had been invited to an afternoon tea party at the British legation gardens in the city. The invitation had been extended to Chinese merchants considered friendly to British interests and Naomi had attended, representing her father's agency.

She had been chatting with the middle-aged, loud-voiced wife of a British colonel who had served in India and the woman proved to be an intelligent conversationalist with what were, Naomi considered, progressive opinions.

'If you would beg my pardon . . .' Overhearing the conversation, Lieutenant Mumford had introduced himself. Naomi turned to face him for the first time, causing the young officer a moment of shock. 'I'm sorry,' he blurted. 'I thought that you were English.'

'Because of my dress and that I speak English,' Naomi replied, seeing his discomfort clearly etched in his face.

'It is just that I heard your voice and . . .'

'And I have an English accent or rather, an Australian accent,' Naomi continued, enjoying seeing what she perceived as a typically pompous Englishman being put in his place. 'Actually, my father has informed me that I do sound more English than a colonial. I suppose that is because the good nuns who educated me insisted that a lady speak well.'

'I must beg your forgiveness,' Lieutenant Mumford stumbled in his speech. 'I did not mean to cast any aspersions upon your birth as your beauty surpasses all that ancient China has to offer.'

'You are forgiven for your mistake as to my identity.'

'Mr Mumford is not known for his charm,' the wife of the English officer laughed. 'He is better known as a soldier's soldier with little time left for us of the fairer sex. Mr Mumford is well known to me, having served in one of my husband's companies as a young ensign when George commanded a regiment in India. I suppose that I should introduce Robert to you,' she continued. 'Lieutenant Robert Mumford, this is Miss Naomi Wong whose father is the proprietor of *Wong & Co.* I think that you will find that Miss Wong is an extraordinary young woman.'

Robert Mumford gave a polite nod of his head and Naomi extended her gloved hand.

'I am sure that it is a pleasure to meet you, Mr Mumford,' she said sweetly.

'I know that it is a pleasure to meet you, Miss Wong,' Robert answered, reluctant to let go of her hand.

From that day on the English officer had vied for Naomi's company – at Embassy cocktail parties, afternoon teas, tennis parties and even the occasional picnic. Over the past year they had become close friends although neither had ever hinted of a mutual attraction. At least Naomi found Robert attractive and often found herself daydreaming of him holding her in his arms. She had grown to doubt that the feeling was mutual and strongly suspected that was because of the prejudices haunting the gulf between East and West. She was, after all, a Chinee woman and he a European. When they were together she could feel the powerful tension but interpreted the almost electric feeling as racial bias. So although friendship was acceptable their meetings never went any further. Naomi wondered deep down, however, whether the English officer's feelings for her were more carnal than spiritual. Was it that she was merely something exotic to him or did he really have strong feelings at some deeper level? Her feelings toward him would remain ambivalent until he demonstrated something else. Possibly he would even express love and propose marriage. Then she would know that his feelings went beyond racial bias.

Naomi was intimidating, Robert Mumford had often brooded whenever he thought about the beautiful Eurasian woman, which was often; beautiful beyond description, intelligent far above any man he had met and yet with an air about her of serenity that touched all she came into contact with. The son of a middle-class family which had fallen on bad times, he had enlisted in the army as a boy and earned his way towards a commission for his gallant and intelligent service on the wild and violent Indian frontier. He had loved the life of a regimental officer and had bridled at the liaison duties he had been assigned in Pekin. They meant being in command of nothing more than bits of paper, pandering to the whims of senior officers attached to the British foreign service departments of the international legation offices in the heart of the city. At least the existence of Miss

Naomi Wong had made the tedious life of a liaison officer more bearable.

'May I walk with you?' Robert asked now.

'That would be a pleasure, Mr Mumford,' Naomi said. 'We were returning to my father's office.'

The English officer fell into step and the three made their way along the wide street.

'You should consider leaving China and return to Queensland for a while,' Robert said with a frown. 'You must know from your contacts that the situation is deteriorating rapidly in the countryside and it is only a matter of time before we see trouble in the city. I know my opinions are not held by many in our legation who appear to have their heads buried in the sand but my soldier's instincts tell me that these damned Boxers are out to cause mischief.'

Naomi had heard the talk in the shops and stalls of the busy Pekin streets, as her fluency in Chinese opened many doors normally closed to Europeans. 'I agree with you about the situation but I also have faith that the Empress will use her army to protect us. After all, this is where she resides and she has a lot to lose if the Boxers attempt to stir up trouble with her people. You need not be concerned for my welfare, Mr Mumford.'

The English officer had strong doubts concerning the Empress. The seventy-year-old Dowager had been born to a minor court official and her beauty had caught the eye of the Emperor Hsien Feng. At sixteen she was taken as a minor concubine but she had been born with talents far beyond those the Chinese considered natural for a mere woman. A combination of innate cunning and ruthlessness was combined with luck when she bore the Emperor his first male heir. This event catapulted her to a position of great power in the royal court. It was ironic that she had a portrait of Queen Victoria prominently displayed in her quarters. She could greatly admire this other woman for the power that she wielded over her enemies. With the death of her debauched son the Dowager Empress appointed her nephew Kuang Hsu as Emperor but had him arrested when he attempted to bring reform to the outdated royal court bureaucracy. She assumed the throne once again and with ruthless efficiency purged all who had supported the reforms. Kuang Hsu found himself wandering the corridors of the palace devoid of power and supporters.

Robert Mumford did not trust the current ruler of China. He knew her capacity to be the supreme opportunist with a hatred for all things Western. The rise of the Boxer movement might well play into her hands and whenever he considered what she was capable of he felt real fear.

'Well, I am,' Robert growled. 'If anything should happen to you . . .'

Naomi stopped and placed her hand on his arm. She was a good head shorter than Robert and gazed up into his eyes. 'I am touched by your concern,' she said. 'And that means a lot to me.'

'I . . .' Robert did not finish expressing his deep thoughts to the woman before him. He wanted to tell her that his feelings were more than those based on a friendship between two people, but refrained as he had not properly thought out the consequences of doing so to his military career in the conservative British army.

'What, Mr Mumford?' Naomi urged gently, her hand lingering on his arm.

'It is nothing,' Robert replied, shrugging off any thoughts that might expose his true feelings for her. 'I just wish that you might consider leaving the city and return to your father for a little while until this matter with the Chinese rebels blows over.'

'I will consider it,' Naomi conceded, her hand slipping from his arm.

As they continued walking they were forced to step around a street butcher quartering a pig's carcass. Blood spattered the man's sweating torso and he ceased in his work to glare at the English officer. Catching Robert's eye, the butcher pulled himself erect and a tirade of angry words spilled from his mouth.

'What is that man saying?' Robert asked Naomi, whom he noticed had suddenly paled.

'It is nothing,' Naomi said and quickened her pace.

'Please, what was he saying?' Robert asked again.

'He was saying that you will be dead before the week is out. Death to all barbarians who have come to ravish China,' Naomi translated reluctantly. 'But his words are hollow.'

Robert did not think so. His information sources had already painted a picture of a situation about to explode around the European powers in the city. However, Naomi had not revealed all that the Chinese butcher had said as he had also included her in his tirade. It was the certainty in the butcher's voice that most chilled her. To him she was clearly no better than a whore to the barbarians and, when the time came, he would revel in her slow death at the hands of the Boxer warriors.

Late May 1900
Cairns

Without recourse to any anaesthetic or painkiller, Tung had not cried out when Andrew had expertly sewn his head wound. This had impressed Andrew, but not the police officer standing over his prisoner.

'Bloody heathens don't feel pain like us,' he grunted.

'I do,' John Wong said quietly.

'Present company excepted, Mr Wong,' Ogden added quickly.

'Your man needs to rest,' Andrew said.

'I don't have time to sit around here on my arse guarding him,' Ogden protested. 'He's got to be charged with slaying one of his own.'

'Leave him with us,' John suggested. 'I guarantee that you will not lose your man while he is in my son's care.'

Ogden chewed his bottom lip, staring down at the prisoner who did not appear to be in any physical condition to escape from custody. 'I know your reputation, Mr Wong,' he finally said. 'And I know that you are a man of his word. I will leave Billy with you while I get back to the station to do my report. When Master Andrew here thinks he is right to go, then Billy will escort the prisoner back to the lockup.'

'Probably only a few hours,' John said. 'We will give him some tucker in the meantime.'

Satisfied that he would not lose his prisoner with Billy standing guard, Ogden departed the shady depot to return to his station.

Billy found a comfortable bale of cloth and settled down with the carbine across his knees to watch his prisoner. The Aboriginal tracker still had a sense that this seemingly innocuous Chinese man harboured a dark and dangerous spirit.

Andrew sat by the wounded man, satisfied with what he had done, yet wondering why the man before him would be possibly responsible for the death of a fellow countryman. Andrew was intrigued. The wounded man was strongly built although not of a large physique. His hair was cut short in the European way and when Andrew caught the prisoner's eye he could see that an intelligence beyond the ordinary seemed to burn brightly. He calculated that Tung was in his mid-thirties and seemed to be at the peak of physical fitness. He was cleanshaven and had a handsome face. In all, Andrew mused, the man was out of place in the Chinese community of north Queensland.

'Thank you,' Tung said in a whisper that Andrew just caught. The words were spoken in Mandarin, which the young Australian understood. 'You and your father are not like the policeman.'

Andrew leaned close to the man, who stared at the floor. 'Who are you, and did you kill a man, as the policeman has said?'

'My name is of no consequence and I did kill one of my countrymen,' Tung replied quietly in Chinese. He slowly raised his head and could see the Aboriginal tracker watching him with dark eyes.

'Then you must answer to a charge of murder,' Andrew replied. 'I am sorry that I cannot do more than tend to your wounds.'

'It was not murder,' Tung said. 'I was forced to execute the man that I hunted, for the terrible crime he had committed against my country. The foolish man resisted me.'

The statement piqued Andrew's interest. 'What crime?' he asked.

'Treason,' Tung replied. 'He was a thief and traitor who betrayed my master, Emperor Kuang Hsu. I had no choice when I hunted down the man who had betrayed not only the Emperor but China's future.'

'From what I know,' Andrew frowned, 'China is ruled by the Empress Tzu Hsi – not any emperor.'

'Ha, how little you know of the country of your ancestor spirits,' Tung retorted. 'The real ruler of China should be the Emperor. It was his aunt Tzu Hsi who usurped him and had him removed from his rightful role. She is an evil woman, far more dangerous to the Western powers than you could know.

Even as I am a prisoner of the barbarians, my master is a prisoner of that evil woman, and I fear for his life.'

'I confess that I know little of the land of my ancestors,' Andrew said contritely. 'Tell me about your master.'

Uncharacteristically Tung stared into Andrew's face. It was a custom that he had learned of the barbarians. For some strange reason they considered looking directly at a person's face to be polite and forthright. In his own culture the same gesture would be seen as antagonistic and meant to demean. 'We have been crushed by the European powers for many years. We have had opium forced on us by the British and the drug has ruined my country. This could not be so if China did not supply its own self-interested classes of people to aid the foreigners. The ruling class of the Empress and her court – along with its evil eunuchs – conspires to keep China living in the past. This obedience to the old ways means that my country will never awake to its destiny. Then, one day, a ruler emerges who, despite his youth, learns about the West and attempts to modernise China so that it can resist barbarian occupation. But Kuang Hsu is no match for the deviousness of the court officials. He was forced to stand down and is now a prisoner.'

Andrew could see the fire burning in the man opposite him and felt the intense conviction in his words. He sensed that this man was no mere peasant from the rice paddies but someone of greater intellect. 'Tell me who you are.'

Tung lowered his eyes. 'If I tell you who I am will

you help me escape the bonds of the barbarians, so that I may complete my mission in this country?'

'I am an Australian,' Andrew replied quietly. 'I cannot be expected to break the law of my country.'

Tung glanced up at him with a hint of a smile. 'Are you really a barbarian?' he asked. 'To me you appear to be one of us.'

Andrew knew exactly what the man meant. Was he really an Australian when he knew well that he always had had to fight prejudice from the Europeans around him. They might be polite to his face because his family wielded political power through wealth, but he was also aware of the hurtful comments made behind his back. It did not matter that he had been born on the soil of this ancient, arid land. His appearance – and half his name – branded him Chinese. 'Tell me who you are and about your mission,' Andrew said. 'I will consider what you have told me and also consider whether I will help you.'

'If I do this,' Tung said, 'will you swear on the spirits of your ancestors that you will keep your promise to consider my plea for help?'

'I swear,' Andrew replied, casting Billy a quick glance. Andrew had never really thought about the importance of his ancestors before because he had been raised a Christian. Now, this enigmatic man was challenging him to look inward into his true soul.

'My name is Tung Chi and I was once a Shaolin priest. I was born in the Shantung province thirty-four years ago and came into the service of the true ruler of China two years ago. Before the Emperor was imprisoned he was able to give two men he thought he could trust a great wealth to be used in Europe and America to purchase Western technology. But instead of travelling to Europe and America they fled south to this place, with letters for the barbarian banks. Instead of travelling east and west they went south, thinking they could hide out here among others from China. Then, when all was forgotten, they would move on to spend the huge wealth they had at their disposal. They did not think that there would be people in this country who were followers of the Emperor and I was dispatched here to hunt them down, retrieve the papers and return to China. I found one of the men and after some persuasion he handed over his half of the papers. He then attempted to flee from me and I was forced to hunt him down. I returned to his campsite and concealed the papers before I was in turn hunted by the barbarian policeman and that black man over there. Sadly, I underestimated the black man and now I am unable to continue my mission to find the second traitor.'

'Truly an interesting story and if you are telling me the truth then you do not deserve to be tried by our courts,' Andrew said. ' How can you prove to me that you are telling the truth?'

'If I told you where I concealed the documents I recovered,' Tung said, 'then you might believe me.'

'Would you reveal that valuable information to a total stranger?' Andrew queried.

'You are not a total stranger,' Tung said. 'I can see into your soul and know that you are a good man. You have proved that already to me when you stepped in to protect me against the policeman. And besides, I have nothing to lose at the moment with these manacles holding me under the barrel of the black devil's gun.'

'If I find the evidence you say exists then I will help you escape,' Andrew said, realising the enormous decision that he had made.

'If you ride south of here you will come to a river,' Tung said. 'Follow the river west until you come to a bark shelter. It will be deserted and in a large log you will find a leather satchel inside that log.'

Andrew stood up, stretching his legs as he did. 'I will be gone for some time,' he said to Billy. 'Make sure that the Chinese man is treated well.

Billy nodded and Andrew went in search of his father.

'You are planning to do what?' John exploded as he sat at an old, battered desk poring through shipping papers for his exports and imports from Asia. He could hardly believe what Andrew was proposing.

'You are planning to ride out and go to the dead man's camp to find what sounds like rubbish? And *if* the prisoner's story proves to have merit, then return and assist the man to escape?' John rubbed his forehead as if he had a bad headache. He stood and his imposing size and obvious anger would have intimidated any other man than his son.

'Tung is not a criminal,' Andrew said calmly. 'He is little different to a soldier fighting for his country.'

John stared at his son in a new light. Growing up Andrew had been so stable and placid, he reflected.

Medicine had always been his choice and John had never really seen any of his son's wild, impetuous side before. Maybe he had been apart too long from Andrew, as the boy had grown up in boarding schools and then gone off to Scotland to study. It had been Naomi who had been closest to John, who at least had been able to blame his Irish ancestry for his yearning for excitement. But Andrew was more Chinese in his attitudes and looks.

'Father?' Andrew asked, observing John's reflective silence.

'You may as well go and verify the man's story,' John sighed. 'At least get your facts straight before you go off half-cocked on some foolhardy mission. You have too much to lose.'

'Thank you,' Andrew replied with a broad grin for the adventure ahead.

True to Tung's directions, Andrew located the deserted campsite. He dismounted and gazed around until he noticed a large log. Striding across to the fallen tree Andrew poked inside the hollow with a stick, aware as he was that such logs often harboured deadly snakes. Satisfied that the log did not conceal any snake, Andrew reached inside to retrieve a thick satchel.

He opened the leather case and pulled out a sheaf of papers.

'God almighty!' he swore as he perused the ornate paperwork with its impressive stamps embossed on the heavy sheets of paper. 'A bloody fortune!'

The papers were promissory notes drawn on a British bank in Pekin and valued at almost £50,000 sterling. Never before had Andrew seen a promise of fortune and for a moment he was almost paralysed by what he held in his hands. It was clear that Tung had not lied and this was only half of what was outstanding.

Placing the papers back in the leather satchel, Andrew returned to his horse which was grazing nearby. His hands trembled when he took hold of the reins and he understood why. He was about to commit himself to a new path in life – a path that would no doubt at best put his life in peril and at worst land him in prison. Bringing dishonour on his family was not something the young man took lightly. Death was preferable to that option.

With the sun sinking over the hills surrounding the village of Cairns, Andrew returned to his father's depot, where he reined his mount to a halt and stared at the police milling angrily before the big shed. Ogden was prominent in his rage, yelling curses upon the Aboriginal tracker, and for a moment Andrew thought that he might strike Billy with the butt of his service revolver.

Amidst the furore John stood calmly, smoking a cigar and watching the smoke curl away lazily on the still, tropical air. Ogden hardly noticed Andrew return.

'What is going on?' Andrew asked his father in a whisper.

'Tung escaped about an hour ago,' John replied with what Andrew thought was just a hint of a smile.

'He what?' Andrew gasped. 'How?'

'Well, it was like this,' John said, turning his back on the police officer who was still berating the tracker, and two young uniformed police accompanying him. 'I thought that your man should have some tucker and so I fed him. Just after that he seemed to have been able to release the chains on his ankles and wrists and sprang on poor old Billy, disarming him. Billy ended up in the manacles. It seems that Tung had a key and damned if I know how he got one. Now it seems that you are free of any obligation to help him escape,' John ended quietly in Chinese out of Ogden's hearing.

'You helped the bloody Celestial to escape, Mr Wong,' Ogden screamed, detaching himself from his confused men.

'Careful, First Class Constable Ogden,' John growled. 'That is a serious accusation and one that I might personally bring to the attention of your superintendent who just happens to a be a good friend of mine.'

Ogden came to a halt as if hit by a brick. He was aware that the Chinese entrepreneur and his superior officer were indeed friends, linked by a love of fast horses and good whisky.

'You don't frighten me with your threats, Mr Wong,' Ogden snarled. 'I promise you that when I recapture the prisoner he will talk and tell me of your conspiracy in his escape. Manacle keys do not just turn up in the possession of Celestials.'

44

'Maybe you dropped your keys,' John shrugged.

Ogden immediately slapped his pocket and smiled grimly. 'My keys are still in my pocket,' he sneered. 'And Billy did not have any keys on him.'

'Well, you know these Chinks,' John said, flipping away the stub of his cigar. 'They are very cunning and resourceful. Maybe he just picked the locks with a piece of straw.'

Ogden glared at John before finally turning his back and stomping back to his men.

'Saddle up. And Billy, get on the Celestial's trail,' Ogden roared as he gripped the reins of his mount. 'Just don't shoot the bastard out of hand,' he continued as he swung astride his police mount. 'He has some questions to answer before he goes to the gallows.'

Father and son stood alone in the rapidly gathering dusk in front of the big shed, watching the dust raised by the hooves of the departing horses float like gauze in the still air.

'Time we had something to eat, and you can tell me what you have in the leather satchel,' John said mildly.

Andrew suddenly became aware that he had been holding the satchel all the while the police had been milling about in their confusion. 'Do you think Tung will be able to elude Ogden?' he asked.

'He should – if he got aboard the boat I told him about,' John replied. 'It's headed south, so if he goes looking for any passengers of Chinese blood attempting to sail north Ogden will be thrown off the trail.'

Andrew had a great urge to put his arms around the big bear of a man who was his father.

Late May 1900
The British Legation
Pekin

It was Queen Victoria's eighty-first birthday and in true colonial style, an occasion for a grand celebration. As Britain's minister to China, Sir Claude MacDonald, the distinguished former soldier and tall, aristocratic Scot, was pleased to leave the organising of the dinner party to his wife, Lady Ethel MacDonald. Such things required a woman's touch and none were disappointed when the theatre in the British legation was transformed into a dining room. The lavish affair was attended by the who's who of British colonial society in Pekin.

Lady MacDonald, a dignified woman in her early forties, shone when she entered the dining room with the handsome Australian journalist George Morrison on one arm and Sir Robert Hart, the elderly inspector general of the Maritime Customs, on the other. When the dinner places had been cleared members of the other foreign delegations attended to share the free-flowing wine and some very good music. The latter was supplied by Sir Robert Hart's own band as they played on the edge of the tennis courts, bathed in the soft glow of Chinese lanterns that had been provided for the dancers, the ladies in neck to ankle dresses and the men in dinner suits or colourful military uniforms.

Lieutenant Robert Mumford also attended the affair, as was his duty as a liaison officer. He had received orders that the next day he was to travel down to Tientsin on the railway. He stood to one side of the improvised dance floor with a flute of champagne in one hand, gazing at the dancers swirling to the popular tunes of the day. Laughter, music and good wine combined to provide a festive air that Robert wished he could share with Naomi.

'Alone, old chap?'

Robert turned to see a tall, athletic, handsome figure whom he recognised as the London *Times* correspondent in China.

'Dr Morrison, how are you?'

George Morrison was an unusual man. Trained as a medical doctor, he chose instead to be a journalist and his colourful past well prepared him for life in China. As a younger man he had walked from one end of Australia to the other, he had been speared by natives in New Guinea on one exploration of that savage and wild country, and along the way found himself reporting for the prestigious newspaper. An intelligent and courageous young man, and single, he caught the eye of every young woman wherever he went.

Morrison stepped forward from the shadows. 'So, what do you think of the situation?' he asked the British officer.

'By that I presume you mean the Boxer troubles,' Robert replied.

'You are a man with his ear to the ground,' Morrison said, swirling the wine in his glass to catch the light. 'I seem to be getting mixed opinions from many of the distinguished guests here tonight.'

Robert liked the tall Australian. Had he not been a journalist or medical practitioner, Robert knew he could have also been a brilliant soldier. But then, Dr Morrison was capable of being anything he wanted – such was the character of the man. 'Are you asking on the record?' Robert asked guardedly.

'Not on the occasion of our Queen's birthday, God bless her,' the Australian said, raising his glass as a salute.

Robert raised his glass and echoed, 'God bless her and her heirs. Off the record, I think that there is trouble coming,' he continued, sipping his champagne.

'I have to agree with you,' Morrison commented gloomily. 'I have seen the Boxers drilling in the grounds of the Imperial barracks and yet many say that the Empress will not allow them to be unleashed on us. I have my suspicions that she says one thing but secretly hopes those dogs from hell will do her dirty work and drive us all from China.'

'I tend to agree,' Robert responded. 'My sources in the old city have passed on intelligence that the servants have been warned to leave our employment or risk death if they continue. Sadly, it seems that a lot of highly positioned people around here have their heads up their bums on any threat.'

'By your sources would you mean the beautiful young lady, Miss Naomi Wong?' Morrison asked with a twinkle in his eye.

'Er, yes, she and others,' Robert replied blushing. 'We tend to be a little cut off from the rank and file of the Chinese within the walls of the legations whereas Miss Wong is living out among those people.'

'So, old chap,' Morrison said, 'the question really is, would we be capable of defending ourselves if the worst comes to the worst?'

Robert glanced around at the guests at the party before replying. 'If we had sufficient warning then we may be able to bring in reinforcements to beat off any Boxer assault, but at the moment, I do not think that we would have a hope in hell of surviving a concerted attack.'

'Maybe we should ask our Yankee cousins their opinion of the situation,' Morrison said, noticing an American marine officer in his smart dress uniform escorting a matron from the dance floor.

'Harry, old chap, come and join us,' the Australian journalist shouted, catching the attention of Lieutenant Harold Simpson, United States Marine Corps. Sweat streamed down the American officer's face as he approached.

'Dr Morrison, Mr Mumford,' the straight-backed, steely-eyed young marine officer greeted, taking a flute of champagne from a passing Chinese waiter. 'What are you Limeys up to?'

'Only one Limey here,' Morrison replied. 'I'm an

Australian, but will accept the term on Her Majesty's birthday. How is it that you were not here earlier?'

'Goddamned matter of business at our offices held me up,' Simpson said, taking a long swig. 'Damned funny thing, a half-dead Chinese coolie turned up to see our minister, Mr Conger. He said that he was from one of our missionary stations where a massacre had occurred some days ago but we haven't had any confirmation on the matter as yet. Said he had posed as a Boxer and almost died in the process of getting here. All he had was a fossil rock and a letter he said was from the mission station. Mr Conger was busy and I got the job of sorting the matter out. I tried to read the letter but it had become drenched with water and the writing was unintelligible. By the time I sent the coolie off for a feed I missed a lift to your party. I had to wait around and now have a lot of catching up to do.'

'Why do you think that one of your missionaries would go to all the trouble of sending a fossil to you when he was in most dire peril?' Morrison asked, his journalist's curiosity piqued by the rock and its hazardous journey to Pekin.

'Goddamnedest reason that I would know of,' Lieutenant Simpson snorted. 'I've seen these rocks with fossils in them before and you can buy them in the Chinee markets as paperweights. Maybe the rock has some gold or something in it besides the stone dragon – though it looks more like a stone salamander to me. I should think about sending it to Tientsin to one of our mining engineers, Mr Herbert Hoover, who has pulled back his team saying that he fears for their safety out in the countryside. Maybe I can make arrangements to get the rock to him and see what all the fuss is about.'

'I am travelling by train to Tientsin tomorrow,' Robert said. 'I could do you Yankee Marines a favour and take it with me in my baggage.'

The American soldier glanced at Robert. 'All you have to do is get me a receipt from Hoover when you see him and I will buy you a bottle of the best Kentucky I know. It would save me a lot of trouble not having to go through our system. As the missionary was a good friend of Mr Conger's I know that he would probably insist that I provide a military escort. We don't consider you Limeys to be any real threat to our country right now, so I am sure my boss will approve of you conveying the rock to Tientsin.'

'Consider it done,' Robert said, extending his hand. 'A favour on behalf of Her Majesty's government to former rebels.'

Simpson smiled. It was only seventy-five years since Britain and the USA had exchanged angry shots in war.

The following morning, Robert reported to the United States legation and took possession of the stone dragon. On the train travelling to Tientsin he examined the rock, with its fossil bones clearly to be seen. Robert shook his head. Simpson had been right. There was nothing remarkable about either the rock or the fossil and it would no doubt end up in some museum or simply be used as an interesting paperweight. Why would a man facing probable death go to such drastic measures to have the sample sent to

Pekin? He mused on the question as the steam train rattled its way east towards the Chinese coast. The stone dragon was an apt name, Robert thought. This was China: a land where such spiritual creatures ruled the minds of the people. He once heard someone say that China itself was a sleeping dragon – and the way things were shaping up with the Boxers he prayed that the dragon would remain asleep.

Robert slipped the rock back into its cloth bag and placed it on the seat next to him. His mind was on other things – and foremost in his thoughts was Naomi Wong. The situation was growing worse by the day and he wished that he could be with her at this very moment, rather than travelling to Tientsin. At least he had the assurance that he would be returning to Pekin as soon as his mission was over.

Late May 1900
Cairns and District
Far North Queensland

Andrew Wong laid the bank documents on the table. 'What do I do?' he asked.

John fingered the papers by the light of a kerosene lantern. 'They are not ours,' he replied. 'I suppose we have to get them back to their rightful owner.'

'Easier said than done,' Andrew said, slumping into an old but sturdy chair in the corner of the compact office attached to the depot. Above his head a fat, almost translucent gecko screeched its challenge to others of his kind in the ceiling of exposed beams. The tiny crocodile-like creatures were fearsome in defence of their territory.

John frowned. He had struggled with a decision and now the parchment before him seemed to be a strange omen of where his life must lead him. 'I have something to tell you,' John said. 'I have decided that I should go to China to visit our office in Pekin.'

Andrew was not surprised. He sensed that his father was wasting away worrying about Naomi and he was not a man to wait for a reply to any letter he might send requesting that she return to Queensland. He would rather go and personally fetch her. After all, a letter could easily be lost in transit. 'I could take these papers back to China and somehow put them in the right hands.'

'Then I will come with you,' Andrew said quietly. 'You are not getting any younger, and your knowledge of our language is a bit rusty.'

'Our language?' John asked, arching his eyebrow. 'Our language is English.'

'You know what I mean,' Andrew hurried. 'My mother's language.' Andrew's mother could barely speak English when John married her and Andrew had spoken his first words in Chinese.

'I would rather you returned to Scotland to finish your studies,' John said. 'I can take care of myself as I have done in the past before you were even born.'

'I can always take a term off,' Andrew reasoned. 'And that would allow me to see the land of our ancestors.'

John stared at his son for some time, considering the request.

'Maybe that would be a good idea,' John finally relented. 'We can both bring back your sister.'

First Class Constable Stanley Ogden was not a stupid man. Despite any formal education he had that rare ability of a good police officer to sniff out those

54

who would attempt to break the law. He was a man hunter and to date no one had been able to elude him in the north.

Ogden had hardly departed the presence of John Wong when he turned to a young constable riding beside him. 'That bloody Chink has interests in shipping around here,' he said. 'I want you and the others to go to every ship that is about to leave and do a thorough search for the prisoner. He won't be hard to find – just look for the stitches in his head. Return to me when you either have the prisoner in custody or have news of him.'

The troop of three constables under Ogden's command spurred their mounts to the docks area, while Billy remained with Ogden, who wheeled his mount to take up a position in the shadows of the surrounding bushland to keep watch on the depot. Billy remained by his side. He was still seething about the way the Chinese man had sprung on him with a speed he could not have anticipated, and somehow struck him in the side of the head, immediately bringing the darkness that obliterated much of the memory of what had actually occurred. Should he get the chance, he would kill the Chinese man – that is, if he had the opportunity before his boss took that liberty. Either way, the Chinese man would die for escaping police custody.

Within the hour a constable quietly rode back to the depot and sidled up to Ogden. 'We missed him,' he sighed. 'We got a good report that he was seen boarding the *Nancy Smith* heading south to Brisbane. First stop being Townsville. It seems that he had money on him to purchase his passage.'

'He sure as hell had nothing when I searched him,' Ogden growled. 'Those bloody Celestials stick together. That bastard Wong must have given him the money when Tung laid out Billy.'

'What are we going to do?' the constable asked, shifting in his saddle.

'You and the others can return to your patrols,' Ogden said. 'Me and Billy are going to send a telegram to the station at Townsville to have a couple of the boys at the wharf with instructions to pick up Tung.'

The constable nodded and wheeled away to carry out his instructions. No matter what eventuated Tung would not escape the law.

Ogden's grim smile was not seen in the darkness of the tropical night. Well, Mr bloody Wong, he thought. You're not as smart as you think.

'C'mon Billy,' Ogden said, spurring his mount. 'We have a job to do.'

From his improvised bed in a corner of the depot Andrew heard the pounding of the horses galloping away.

'Looks like they have given up,' his father said softly from his own stretcher a few feet away. 'Your friend should be well out to sea by now.'

'I hope so,' Andrew replied, staring at the dark patches on the high ceiling. 'He is not a criminal but a man fighting for his country.'

'That's one interpretation,' John yawned.

'Father, why did you help Tung?' Andrew suddenly blurted. 'You could have got yourself into a lot of trouble.'

'Better me than you,' John replied, rolling over on his stretcher. 'You have a lot more at risk than I have.'

Andrew did not ask any other questions and dozed off with a fleeting thought for the small fortune at his feet in the leather satchel.

Andrew did not know how long he had been asleep but was awoken by an instinct for something sharing the space around him.

'Don't make a move,' he heard his father's voice growl. Andrew obeyed as the immediate area flared with a dull, yellow light as a kerosene lantern was lit. Startled, Andrew sat upright to find himself staring at a figure crouched by his bed and within an arm's length. He focused on Tung Chi, whose expression reflected something between annoyance and frustration.

'What in the blazes!' Andrew gasped, propped on his elbows and blinking at Tung.

'Your friend crept in about five minutes ago,' John said calmly. Andrew could see at the edge of the light his father holding a deadly Colt Dragoon cap and powder revolver which he had levelled on Tung.

'Your father is a dangerous man,' Tung said matter of factly to Andrew. 'I thought my training was enough to get past him to you but your father fooled me. He was never asleep, but on his guard. It is as if he and not I were a student of the arts that I learned in the temple.'

Andrew glanced at his father and back to Tung. 'I thought that you were on your way south,' he said.

'I paid the fare and boarded the steamer as your father suggested,' Tung said, sitting down to rest. 'But when it began to leave the shore I slipped over the side and swam ashore to make my way back to you. I had to wait until the police left here and waited some more in case they returned. But when I saw that they had not, I chose to enter and wake you. I had no intention of doing either of you any harm as you have already saved my life once and hopefully know by now that my story is true. I see that the satchel is here at your feet.'

'You can put down the pistol, Father,' Andrew said, acknowledging his father's rusty grasp of the Chinese language. 'Tung means us no harm.'

John lowered the gun to his lap. 'I could follow most of what Tung said to you,' he said. 'He is either the dumbest man alive or the smartest – depending on what you see as the priority.'

'I had to return,' Tung said, addressing John in good English and without much of an accent. 'I have yet to find the other half of the money to satisfy my oath to protect the son of heaven's trust in me and that meant remaining in this part of your country. Besides, if the police hunting me have learned that I took passage south it will distract their attention away from here.'

'I have a feeling that First Class Constable Ogden might have worked that out and is not going to be a happy man when he finds that you were not on the boat,' John said with a grin. 'At least you have bought yourself some time to finish what you came for.'

'Thank you, Mr Wong,' Tung said. 'It is of no surprise that the son is as honourable as the father. Your service to our cause will not be forgotten.'

'Do not mistake my help for service to China,' John warned. 'I am only assisting you to protect my son.'

'For whatever reason you are helping me you are also helping us fight for freedom,' Tung replied. 'Even now there is an uprising in China that will finally explode and sweep the barbarians from our land and lead us on the righteous path to becoming a nation once again. The money that I have been entrusted to safekeep will help us in our cause. The mission is more important than my humble life is worth.'

'Actually,' John said with a grim smile, 'I wasn't expecting you. I thought that Ogden might try something out of spite for me helping you. But now that you are here you may as well get a good night's rest and make your way out before first light. I will put some things together to help you finish what you set out to do.'

'Thank you,' Tung replied, bowing his head. 'Your kindness will never be forgotten. I owe you a great debt. I promise that I will be gone by first light.'

John shrugged off the grateful man's heartfelt thanks. He really wanted Tung away from his store and particularly away from his son. John smelled trouble in the two being together. In the fleeting time Andrew had known the former Shaolin priest he seemed to have changed in subtle ways that John found disturbing. The talk of China and its independence had struck a chord with Andrew. To John the scent of eucalyptus – and not lotus – was the very stuff that ran through his veins. The far north of the colony of Queensland was his true home, not the land of his father's ancestors.

True to his word Tung was gone by the time John and Andrew awoke. The small package of supplies John had put together and the leather satchel were also gone. Wherever Tung was by now John knew that he would have only one purpose and that would most probably result in a death. John had known men like Tung in his own past. He only hoped that his son would never know the danger and death John had seen at his age.

But for now John had his own mission. He would make arrangements for the business to be managed by a trusted friend in the Cairns Chinese community in his absence. Had not Tung mentioned that China was on the verge of exploding in rebellion? John prayed that he would be in time to spirit Naomi home to the land of her birth.

With the rising sun on his right, Tung walked swiftly north from Cairns. The information that he had picked up in the tropical town owed much of its existence to the influx of Chinese twenty years earlier. Tung's informant had placed the traitor as staying with a Chinese family that grew bananas along the banks of the picturesque Barron River. In China

Tung had been briefed that the men he hunted were most likely in the Cairns district of north Queensland because the town had a strong Chinese quarter. He had been impressed by the fact that a sugar mill he had passed was owned and operated by Chinese. Even one of the roads he had walked was named Hop Wah Road.

Sweat trickled down his face and Tung sought shade under a tree, He rifled through the supplies John had given him. The bank papers he had transferred to the canvas bag containing his supplies and then quickly buried the tell-tale leather satchel. To all he appeared as just another itinerant Chinese man wandering the tracks of the north looking for work. Tung found a slab of dried meat and bit into the tough, salty beef. It made him thirsty so he sought a supply of water in a pond not far from where he had stopped to eat.

His hunger and thirst slaked, Tung continued his trek north, praying to the spirits of his ancestors that he would find the man and the money together. At the back of his mind was a fear that the relentless policeman might soon discover Tung's deception and even now be using the black man to hunt him. Tung had been told that the family he sought were a good two days' walk from Cairns. He calculated that it would take at least that long for the police to discover that he was not aboard the ship. He would be able to reach the Barron but after that he knew he would once again be a hunted man.

Tung also recognised the Aboriginal tracker as a formidable foe. Never before had the Chinese warrior met such skills in hunting a man as those belonging to the black man whose roots were in the earth of this strange land.

Enraged after discovering that he had been tricked by a mere Chinee, Ogden rode to Cairns. Never before had the tough police officer been made to look so foolish, and he ached with a burning desire to set things right. He suspected that the constables working with him were laughing behind his back about how the Celestial made him look so stupid. But Ogden also had informants in the large Chinese community of Cairns and it was time to call in favours.

Before noon he had his answer; a strange Chinese man from the Shantung province had asked about a fellow Shantung man and as a result had left Cairns to travel north on foot to the Barron River two days earlier. Maybe he was the man that the policeman sought?

Ogden used the back of his sleeve to wipe the sweat from his forehead. The frightened Chinese trader had cringed away from the burly barbarian. He knew that the uniformed man represented the power and authority of his adopted land and it paid to keep in with the authorities.

'Billy,' Ogden said to the Aboriginal tracker patiently standing by the policeman's stirrup. 'You think that you could pick up any tracks north of here?'

Billy squinted against the sun. 'No trouble, boss,'

he replied. He too was desperate to find the man who had brought shame to him in his role of prisoner guardian.

Within an hour Billy proved true to his word. Squatting by the track out of Cairns he located the faint, two-day-old trail. Now all they had to do was follow and it would finally lead them to the elusive Chinee prisoner. At least the use of horses to hunt the man gave them an advantage in time. They were in a position to easily close the time gap in their pursuit of the elusive killer.

The information that Tung received in Cairns was accurate and he soon found himself concealed in a copse of trees on a small ridge overlooking a bark hut. Beside the hut was a small plantation of broad-leafed banana trees where a Chinese couple worked with hoes clearing between the trees. Running in and out of the trees were two small children.

Tung's eyesight was excellent and he focused in on the man. He was not the man that Tung hunted but the former Shaolin priest understood the value of patience.

As evening approached the family finished their chores in the small plantation and put away their gardening implements to return to the hut. Tung sighed. Had the man he hunted moved on?

The sun was setting across the jungle-covered mountains to the west and the air grew cooler by the minute. The sky was filled with giant bats winging their way in the late rays of sunshine in search of trees laden with fruit. Some of the fruit bats peeled off from the seemingly neverending stream and settled among the banana trees, where they screeched and squabbled with each other over the ripening fruit. A light flooded the area outside the doorway to the bark hut and two men appeared shouting Chinese curses on the bats.

Tung peered through the dim light and felt his heart skip a beat. There was the man he hunted! He had been in the hut all day and was now helping the Chinese farmer scare away the pests.

Tung felt for the short-bladed knife that John Wong had slipped into the bag of supplies. It slid into his hand and Tung waited. When the two men were satisfied that the bats had all gone one of the two returned to the hut. Tung was pleased to see that the man he hunted remained outside and had lit a cigarette. Obviously he was enjoying the coolness of the early evening after spending all day inside.

Tung left his hide and made his way down the ridge, careful not to make any sound as he stalked his unsuspecting prey. So far it had been easy and Tung was able to use the shadows to hide his movements. With the ease that came from his years of martial training, Tung was on the man with the knife at his throat. The man's cigarette spun into the air.

'Do not make a sound, traitor, or I will slit your throat,' Tung hissed into his ear. 'Walk to the trees.'

Feeling the knife biting against his throat, the terrified Chinese man obeyed without a sound, until they were away from the hut and in the trees at the bottom of the ridge.

'It is you, Tung Chi,' he finally gasped. 'I did not mean to keep the money.'

'Then you will return it to me so that it reaches the rightful hands,' Tung replied.

'I do not have the money,' the man said.

'Then I have no reason to keep you alive,' Tung retorted.

'Wait!' the man gasped. 'I can fetch it for you.'

'Then you will live, unlike your companion.'

'The money is in a satchel buried not far from here,' the man said. 'But you will have to let me go.'

'You know who I am, traitor,' Tung hissed. 'So you know that it would be foolish to attempt anything stupid.'

The man *did* know who Tung was. Although he himself was a thief, he was not a highly trained assassin like Tung.

Tung followed the man in the growing darkness back towards the hut until he stopped by a lone tree. He bent and began to dig with his hands until he hit the surface of a leather satchel. Tung stood warily over the man and was careful when he was handed the satchel.

'Li, the meal is ready,' a male voice called from the doorway of the hut.

Tung glanced away from the man bending by the small hole he had dug. Suddenly, Tung felt a sharp pain in his leg below the knee. A knife blade! Tung attempted to step away and swing back to confront the traitor, whom he could see rising up from the ground and wielding a long-bladed knife that must have been hidden nearby.

Recovering quickly, Tung swung his attention back to his attacker. For a thief the man had proven to be cunning. Tung balanced himself, ignoring the pain in the calf of his leg. No doubt giving up the fortune had unbalanced the stupid man's mind. Tung easily parried the next thrust at his chest and buried his own knife in the desperate man's throat. Hot blood immediately gushed forth, drenching Tung.

'Fool,' Tung hissed as the dying man's body went limp and fell to the warm earth. 'You might have lived if not for your greed.'

'Li!' the voice called again. The assault had happened so fast and almost in silence that the man calling from the bark hut was unaware of the drama unfolding only yards from where he stood.

Tung ran his hand down his throbbing leg and felt the blood running from the wound. He knew that he would live and scooped up the satchel, satisfied without looking inside that the money was intact. Why else would a man risk his life? As silently as he had slipped down the ridge, he clambered back. His mission was half complete. Now, all he had to do was return the money to the coffers of the Son of Heaven.

'No bloody doubt the Celestial did this,' Ogden said the following day.

He and Billy stood over Li's crumpled body. Ogden had ridden hard in pursuit of the man who had made him look like a fool, barely stopping for the overnight camp. His hard riding had paid off, swiftly closing the gap between hunter and hunted.

'Chinee man did this,' Billy said, bending to examine the earth disturbed by the short, sharp struggle. 'He go back up the hill.'

The Chinese husband and wife stood together with their children clinging to them, observing through wide eyes the scene of violent death. The man they knew as Li had paid generously for a place to stay and they had not questioned why he would want to be with them in such an isolated place on the banks of the Barron River. Whatever reason Li had for staying with them proved to be fatal and a thought of evil spirits living in the surrounding rainforest had crossed their minds.

Squatting, Billy peered hard at the story unfolding before him. 'Chinee man bin wounded,' he said, his eyes following a path to the ridge. 'Bin stabbed in leg last night.'

Ogden's face reflected a faint smile. 'Then he will be slowed down a bit.'

'Maybe,' Billy frowned. 'He bin a tough bastard.'

'No matter,' Ogden said, reining his horse around. 'We will follow him. I suspect that our man is attempting to get back to Cairns and hide among his fellow Celestials there.'

Tung was indeed retracing his path south to Cairns. His leg throbbed with pain and Tung feared that it might send him lame. He had made a walking stick from a tree branch and plodded through thickets of giant, green trees that bordered the meandering trail that he followed. He knew that he was going against all his training as a warrior to follow a road but his injury forced him to make up ground this way.

Tung knew that he must rest and check the bandage he had improvised from a torn piece of his shirt. He slumped to the earth beside the trail and carefully peeled back the blood-soaked bandage. The wound had stopped bleeding but the area around the puncture was swelling an angry red.

Tung took a deep breath to focus his thoughts. He gazed at the landscape around him and wondered at its beauty. Butterflies and birds filled the air while beautiful flowers he had never seen before added a dash of colour to the forest. For a moment he thought about his life. He did not like the killing but from his youth he had proved very capable of taking another's life. Denied the tender touch of a woman, his energy had been funnelled into countless hours of martial arts training and philosophical studies to achieve his role as a Shaolin priest. His mother had been forced to give him up when her husband had died in an accident and it had been her brother, a young Moslem soldier in the pay of the Imperial court, who had opted to place his nephew in the care of priests at a Shaolin temple. The young boy stood out from his contemporaries and found himself selected for the most rigorous of academic and martial learning. Tung had also learned the English language and this had opened a door to the knowledge of the Europeans who arrogantly occupied his country. It had been his choice to leave the priesthood to seek service with the Emperor.

But now the Emperor was a helpless prisoner of his ruthless aunt, the Empress, and the opportunity of modernising the nation and uniting it as one country had died with the Emperor's imprisonment. That had left Tung with only one other choice in his lifelong crusade to free China and the money he carried assured a supply of weapons to match the European powers in the coming rebellion. Tung was acutely aware that the very future of China lay in the canvas bag strapped to his body. No matter what it cost him personally, he knew that he must get the money back to China by any means his fertile mind could envisage.

A huge, blue-winged butterfly settled on a flower not far from where Tung rested. He wondered on the inane nature of mankind; why did famine, pestilence and war have to exist alongside such beauty in his own country?

With the help of his walking stick, Tung rose painfully to his feet. It was then that he heard the distant but distinct sound of horses' hooves. As he had not met anyone on his journey to the bark hut – nor on his way back – he could only conclude one thing: the enemies that were hunting him were closing in.

'Not far from here,' Billy said, peering at the earth.

Ogden shifted in his saddle and gazed into the shadows of the rainforest along the winding track. 'He bin sit down here and use walking stick,' Billy continued. 'He go that way,' the tracker said, pointing south.

'Better arm yourself,' Ogden said, slipping the carbine from its bucket by the saddle. Billy slipped the police issue revolver that Ogden had allowed him to continue carrying from his belt. With Ogden astride his horse and Billy on foot leading his horse, they continued to track the man. Suddenly Billy stopped and for a brief moment glanced either side of the track in confusion. Ogden was quick to notice the puzzlement on his trusted tracker's face.

'What, Billy?' he whispered. Billy's expression suddenly changed from puzzlement to alarm. He was about to tell his boss that the man they hunted had doubled back on them.

Tung sprang his ambush, leaping from a heavy branch just off the side of the track and falling on the mounted policeman, dragging him out of his saddle. They both fell heavily to the ground but Tung was on his feet before Ogden could recover from the shock of the unexpected attack.

Billy had brought the barrel of his pistol up and snapped off an un-aimed shot but Tung had suddenly disappeared from the line of fire in a blurring movement, to land on his feet beside the carbine. Billy swore and swivelled to snap off another shot.

'Do not shoot,' the Chinese man cried out, and Billy was aware that he had the rifle up to his shoulder pointed at him. The Aboriginal tracker froze, knowing the result of a heavy carbine bullet wound. 'Put your gun down,' Tung commanded.

Ogden clumsily rose to his feet, having realised that the commands were in English. Billy carefully placed the pistol on the ground.

'You heathen bastard,' Ogden swore. 'You will swing for this.'

'I am sorry,' Tung said. 'Do what I say and I will

not kill either of you. You will take the chains you have and chain yourself to a tree.'

'What!' Ogden exclaimed. 'You don't give me orders.'

'Chain yourself and the black man to the tree here,' Tung reiterated.

Ogden could see in the Chinese man's dark eyes a menace that backed his words. The policeman retrieved the shackles from his saddlebag and under the threat of the carbine secured himself, and Billy, opposite each other, around the trunk of a tree at the side of the track.

Tung went through the saddlebags and, satisfied that there was nothing to threaten him, dropped the bags by the policeman glaring up at him. 'There is food and water and I will tell someone where you are,' Tung said, hurling the rifle into the trees nearby. 'You will not come to harm.'

With that, Tung retrieved his walking stick and hobbled away, leaving the police mounts to graze contentedly by the chained men.

Ogden stared at the back of the man who had so easily ambushed him and then back at Billy sitting forlornly opposite. A mere Chinee had bettered him, a member of a superior race. 'You tell anyone how the Celestial bushwhacked us, and I will feed you to the crocs myself,' he growled.

Billy knew that he meant it.

All had been put in order with *Wong & Co*. John had secured passage for himself and his son on a cargo ship steaming for Hong Kong and then on to China. Meanwhile Andrew had put together a good supply of medical equipment. Although he was not yet a qualified doctor he had learned enough to be able to apply what knowledge and skills he had in emergencies.

They were scheduled to leave from Trinity Bay on the morning tide and spent the evening at the depot sharing a meal of corned meat with cabbage and boiled potatoes. Between them was a bottle of John's finest rum and Andrew hoped that a few tots of the fiery liquor might relax his father. The tension had been building over the days with his father's impatience to travel to China after reading the newspaper reports coming out of the troubled country.

They ate in relative silence, each man engrossed in his own private thoughts. Suddenly John pushed himself away from the table, reaching for the Colt revolver that lay a few paces away on his camp stretcher. Startled, Andrew froze between mouthfuls of his meal, to stare at his father who gestured him to remain silent.

'Come on out,' John ordered, pointing the pistol into the dark shadows.

A figure emerged, hobbling on a stick. John lowered the pistol and Andrew sprang to his feet. 'Tung!' he exclaimed. 'What in the hell are you doing here?'

As Tung hobbled forward on the stick, both men could see pain etched in his face. When he reached them he tried to raise a smile but it turned into a grimace.

Andrew saw the bloody bandage around Tung's

leg, just beneath the knee. 'Sit down and let me have a look at that,' he said, still holding his knife and fork.

Tung obeyed and John put his pistol back on the camp stretcher. 'Thought you might have been someone up to no good,' he grunted. 'But, come to think of it, your appearance here bodes no good anyway.'

Andrew unwrapped the improvised bandage to reveal a swollen wound festering with infection. His medical kit would now be used on his first unofficial patient.

'We have to take him with us,' Andrew pleaded as Tung slept fitfully a short distance away. 'He has all the money back and from what he has told us, he is a dead man if he falls into Ogden's hands.'

John slumped into his chair at the table and rubbed his face in his exasperation. 'Son, to do so is to put us on the wrong side of the law,' he said. 'No doubt, the first place Ogden will come looking for Tung will be here. I know Ogden has informants in the Chinese community. They are frightened of him and will betray Tung for nothing more than to get rid of the police.'

'All the more reason that we smuggle Tung with us,' Andrew said, sitting down opposite his father and leaning forward on the table.

'Smuggle?' John asked. 'How in hell do we smuggle a fully grown man aboard a ship?'

Andrew glanced over at the sleeping Tung. 'We could make a false bottom in my medical supply chest!' he exclaimed. 'We fit Tung in and take him aboard.'

John frowned but saw the merit of his son's plan. He wanted nothing to do with the man, whom he sensed was trouble, but he also knew that his son had taken on some kind of responsibility for him. To disagree with Andrew would only cause his son to go ahead with a plan that might put him in Ogden's hands, John considered. He would feel better if he could keep control of the situation.

'Okay,' he sighed. 'We get to work on your Trojan horse right away.'

An expression of happiness flared in his son's face. 'Thank you, Father,' Andrew said, rising to his feet with an impulse to hug the broad-shouldered man. But such an expression of love was not befitting a young man, and he simply thrust out his hand to grasp that of his father.

The following day a horse-drawn dray carried their baggage to the wharf. Tung lay hidden, curled up under a tray of medical supplies. It had been a tight fit but he had displayed a remarkable gymnastic ability to squeeze into the small space provided. As soon as they were out of Queensland waters and safe from the law John planned to pay for Tung. He would travel as a fellow passenger with them the rest of the way to China.

Late May to Early June
1900
Pekin and the
Western Hills

Naomi's room above the Pekin office of *Wong & Co* was not as spacious as her home in Townsville. But it did offer a view of the busy, narrow street below and privacy in a crowded city. Behind the office in a sprawling residence with a small courtyard lived Mr Soo Chow and his large family. Off the courtyard in a tiny room lived Raj, who also doubled as the security guard over the valuable goods stored in the shop.

At first, Naomi had found the smells, sounds and sights of the older quarter as alien to her as living on the moon. She had often regretted her decision to travel to China but after a couple of months the city became as familiar to her as her previous home. Her Chinese had improved considerably and because of that fluency she found herself very much at home haggling with traders and gossiping with the Chinese families living either side of the shop. Her links with Australia had allowed her an introduction into the European world of the legations only a half mile from where she lived and so she had been able to visit with the friends she had made in the British quarter to remind her of her roots in a European-settled country. Naomi was content to live between two worlds but had to admit to herself that she missed her father very much. There had been times when she considered taking passage back to Queensland just to feel his strong arms around her and smell the scent of tobacco that seemed always to surround him. She would remind herself that to give in to such yearnings might be interpreted by her father as her being a weak woman and so she was determined to wait one more year before returning.

Then there was Lieutenant Robert Mumford. Naomi lay on her bed and found her thoughts drifting to him. She knew that he would be in Tientsin by now and wished that she had gone with him. If she had made an excuse to visit Tientsin, Robert would not have objected to her accompanying him. Her consolation was that he would soon be returning and Naomi was determined to allow her deeper feelings to then show themselves. At the same time she was frightened. What if he did not feel the same way?

So attuned had the young woman become to her adopted environment that she was shaken from her thoughts about Robert by a subtle shift in the noise coming from the street below her window. Naomi rose from the bed, straightened her dress and went to the window. It was mid-afternoon and she was surprised to see how few people jostled each other for space. In fact, the street was almost deserted of the usual vendors and rickshaws.

Behind her she could hear the sound of footsteps on the wooden staircase to her room. 'Miss Wong!' the voice called from behind her closed door. 'Miss Wong!'

Naomi recognised the voice of her father's Pekin agent, Soo Chow, and also heard the breathless urgency in his voice.

Naomi left the window to open the door to the bald-headed man in his early forties. He wore a pair of cotton pants and a shirt covered in sweat and he puffed with the exertion of running up the narrow stairs.

'Mr Soo,' Naomi said. 'Is there something wrong?'

Soo Chow stood in the doorway, not attempting to enter. 'You must go with Raj to the British in the legation,' he gasped, regaining his breath. 'There is big trouble in the city. The Boxers are killing Christians. I think that they may have targeted you.'

'Why would I be a target?' Naomi frowned. 'I am a British citizen. They would not dare harm a British citizen.'

'I do not think they care if you are British,' Soo answered. 'I think that they are killing all foreigners and they may kill me and my family too. We have been identified as collaborating with foreigners.'

It was then that Naomi heard the sudden change

in the noises outside on the street and felt fear. The eerie silence was replaced by a chanting that was growing ever louder. Worst of all she recognised the words being chanted. '*Sha! Sha!*'

Her fear turned to terror. It was as if the voice of a giant was calling for her death and those of the family she lived with. But even in her panic she was quickly formulating a plan. 'Fetch Raj,' she said. 'Tell him to arm himself and we will make our way out the back and through the neighbouring houses. You gather your family together. Leave everything. We must move quickly.'

Soo nodded and fled down the staircase to herd his wife and five children together. His children ranged in age from a babe in arms to the eldest son, aged eight.

Naomi had hardly turned her back on the door when the giant Sikh bodyguard bounded up the stairs, passing Soo on the way down, and met her at the door. He had also heard the chanting and his years of living with danger as a soldier on the North-West Frontier caused him to spring into action.

He gripped Naomi's arm and yanked her from the room. 'Leave everything, Miss Wong,' he commanded. 'There is not time if we are to get away from here.'

Naomi felt some of the fear evaporate in the presence of her bodyguard. In his hand he held a big revolver and at his side swung his sword. He was a fearsome sight and Naomi knew it would take a brave or foolish man to attempt to impede their flight.

Following Raj downstairs they were met by Soo and his frightened family, all staring wide-eyed at them. Naomi could see the plea in Soo's eyes for her protection and she was suddenly aware of her responsibility as John Wong's daughter to protect his employees. The children clung to their parents, confused by the fear they could sense in the adults.

'Through the back,' Raj urged and the family fell into a single file following him. They passed through a wooden gate that separated the house behind from theirs and passed through its small garden. The next exit was similar and before long Raj led them to a lane that was deserted. On either side of the lane, doors were closed, the occupants inside no doubt praying that the trouble sweeping through the streets and lanes of the old city would pass them by.

Naomi breathed more easily when she could see that their escape towards the foreign legation quarter was unimpeded. All going well, they would be inside the safety of the legation's formidable stone walls within minutes. But her relief suddenly turned to the gut-wrenching terror. A dozen uniformed Boxers wearing red sashes spilled into the narrow roadway from a side street to block their escape. Raj stopped to confront the men wielding swords, spears and muskets.

He only had six shots and there were more than six enemy ahead. He raised his pistol and at the same time drew his old army sabre.

Naomi glanced over her shoulder, seeking another avenue of escape. She felt ill. Boxers were spilling into the lane behind them. They were hopelessly trapped.

As the Boxers broke into a sprint towards the trapped party Raj fired. He knew the Boxers believed that they were impervious to bullets but it must have been a couple whose faith was weak that fell to his pistol. Undeterred by his gunfire, the remaining rebels fell on Raj, slashing with swords and jabbing with spears. He parried as best he could, taking a step to the rear to back up against a wall in the alley. Sweat streamed down his face as he roared his defiance at the overwhelming odds stacked against him.

Naomi turned to see a second group advancing at a sprint at them. Before she could shout a warning the red-jacketed Boxers fell on her. The last thing she was aware of was seeing Mr Soo and his family being hacked to death. Their pitiful screams echoed in her consciousness before her world went dark after experiencing an explosive pain in her head from the shaft of a spear-wielding rebel. As she drifted into oblivion Naomi felt a great anguish for the fate of the Soo family yet, had she known what was to befall her, at that moment she would have chosen to follow them in death.

A lead musket ball from one of the few ancient guns carried by the Boxers struck Raj in the face, shattering bones and mincing flesh. He cried out as a spear point took him in the throat.

The courageous bodyguard died ringed by the bodies of the men he had felled with his sword. But his death had been in vain for the woman whom he had sworn to protect and the family she felt responsible for.

The last thing Naomi remembered was that she and Mr Soo's family had been attempting to flee to the safety of the legation compound. Her eyes were open and as she was conscious of her surroundings she became aware that her head throbbed and that her hands were bound behind her. First, she was assailed by the stench of decomposition and then the hum of voices. The hum became a quiet sobbing and Naomi struggled to sit up. Focusing on her surroundings she realised that she was in the enclosed yard of a wealthy Chinese family's home. But now the family members all lay around her as bloated bodies rotting under a searing summer sun. The crying she heard came from five other very young Chinese girls similarly bound to herself and, to Naomi's horror, they were naked and bearing the marks of brutal treatment.

'She is awake,' a male voice called from behind her.

Naomi painfully turned her head to see a Boxer soldier lounging a few paces away before an open door.

'Good,' a voice grunted from within the building and a pockmarked Boxer appeared to join the soldier standing guard. He was a well-built man and, under the terrible scarring caused by the dreaded smallpox, was what once had been a handsome face. Naomi attempted to avoid his appraisal but when she did look into his face what she briefly saw in his dark, serpent-like eyes was chilling. She felt she had just seen the devil, and at that moment was swamped by an even greater fear than that she had experienced during the vaguely remembered ambush. For what she read in those eyes was torture and death. Surrounded by Boxer warriors, her situation appeared hopeless. And what she saw in the courtyard was worse than anything she could have imagined. Naomi had no delusions as to her treatment at the hands of the Boxers. The involuntary shudder that racked her body was followed by a fervent prayer for a quick death.

In his house outside the legation compound, George Morrison listened in horror to the man who had stumbled into his presence. The man was on the verge of total exhaustion and said that he had escaped from Changsintien where he had been with the headquarters of a Belgian railway construction crew.

'They are tearing up the railway lines and bringing down the telegraph lines,' the man said as he was helped to a chair by Morrison, who gestured to one of his staff to fetch water for the man. 'The Fengtai railway station is ablaze and the Belgian families were besieged when I left them,' he said, gratefully accepting the jug from the servant.

Morrison stepped back to consider what he was hearing. What he had *feared* – and what had been ignored by the diplomatic staff of the other foreign delegations – had come to pass. The dragon was awake and breathing fire. The Australian journalist took a deep breath. It was time for action.

Hours later Morrison received written reports from his sources in Chowcow that the Boxers were massacring Chinese identified as Christian converts while the prettier female Christians were being spared for prostitution. It was time to resume his role as the *Times* representative and investigate the situation himself. He fetched two European companions and, arming themselves, Morrison and the two men rode out across the nearby racecourse to see the pillar of smoke rising in the hot air over the Fengtai railway station. Their horses were jostled by an endless stream of refugees passing them when suddenly an armed Boxer appeared in front of Morrison and his companions, fearlessly brandishing a sword and shouting threats of death. Despite being armed the mounted men chose to keep their distance.

'I think that you should return,' Morrison said, swivelling in his saddle to face his two companions. 'I have to go on to the western hills. I have friends up there who may need some help.'

His two companions gratefully bid Morrison their farewells, turned and rode back to the relative safety of the legation walls, leaving Morrison to ride on alone in dangerous territory through the crowds of terrified people streaming towards Pekin. His Yankee friend Herbert Squiers had sent his wife and children along with their governesses to the relative serenity and coolness of the hill country to escape the summer dust and heat of Pekin. Morrison also knew that a young lady from Boston, Polly Condit Smith, was with the Squiers family and although he was but one man he was at least armed. The fact that he was most likely outgunned and outnumbered did not factor in his consideration as he continued his journey. He only reflected on his duty to protect helpless women and children no matter the threat to his own life.

Of some slight reassurance was that Morrison knew a detachment of Chinese army soldiers had been assigned to escort the family to their mountain villa, a converted former Taoist temple. Not as reassuring was that the Chinese guard would be armed with little else than rusty spears. He also doubted that the Chinese army would stand up against the determined Boxer rebels – and at worst they might even join them.

Morrison pushed his little Chinese pony along the dusty valley, hoping that he would not be too late. But even as he approached the old temple he was not aware that he was being watched with great interest.

Lieutenant Robert Mumford had been fortunate, arriving safely in Pekin. He was back in the European legation after five days away, having seen at first hand the anarchy in the countryside as his train steamed back to the city. At Tientsin he had witnessed the masses of refugees desperately attempting to take passage on the train to Pekin. Fortunately for him, his uniform and side arm helped secure him a seat. In his possession were the documents quickly drafted by the diplomatic staff in Tientsin. Besides the leather satchel of government papers now in the officer's possession was a canvas bag containing the rock with the fossil. He had taken the stone to the American geological team under the management of Mr Herbert Hoover only to have a harassed young geologist – preoccupied by thoughts of his possible demise at the hands of the Boxer warriors – give it a cursory look and dismiss the stone as of no real importance to the American geological team.

'Had it been an anthracite sample I may have been more interested, Lieutenant Mumford,' he had said with his head down, packing papers and rocks into wooden crates for transport out of the city. 'Fossils are not of interest to Mr Hoover.'

Standing before the geologist, Robert had felt a little foolish.

'Keep it,' the American geologist said when he saw the expression on the English officer's face. 'Under the circumstances we have no room for unnecessary samples.'

And Robert did keep it. He did not know why but the rock and its little dragon seemed to be worth keeping – if only for sentimental reasons, or as a talisman. Maybe Naomi might like it as a paperweight, he had considered, slipping the rock into its bag and leaving the building flying the Stars and Stripes flag.

Upon his return to Pekin he had personally briefed Sir Claude MacDonald at the British legation offices about the situation developing in Tientsin. The aristocratic-looking British minister to Pekin had stood by a broad window, staring down at the parklands and listening with a grave expression, making little comment on what he was being told by the young liaison officer.

Robert understood why Sir Claude had said very little at his briefing; like so many other foreign delegations his own had been caught unawares when all the signs had shouted out that they would be attacked and besieged. An arrogant belief in the might of the British Empire had brought them to this current situation but the British Empire was somewhat overstretched with the disastrous war in far-off South Africa against the Dutch farmers. They all knew that they were on their own.

When Robert left the building he stood in the avenue of leafy trees which were drooping under a fierce summer sun. Now he was in a position to find Naomi and secure her a place within the strong walls of the foreign delegations. Around him were the signs of a city preparing for the worst. Missionaries and their Chinese converts poured into the relative safety of the legation grounds from the surrounding mission stations within Pekin. Mumford knew that he would not be a liaison officer for long. If nothing else his expertise as an infantry officer would be called on to assist in the defence of the legation. He had already made a cursory appreciation of the defences. The British compound was probably the best area for a defence as it had strong, high walls and was bordered on one side by the fetid, misnamed Jade River and the Imperial Carriage Park on the other. But to defend the compound would require seasoned troops and there were few of those from the German, Russian, American, Austrian, British, Japanese, Italian, French and Belgian diplomatic services within the European compound.

Robert asked staff members from the British diplomatic service if any of them had seen Miss Naomi Wong inside the legation. When he received a negative response Robert became worried, more so when a French missionary he knew informed him that the Boxers had already attacked foreigners on the streets.

Robert stood under the shade of one of the great,

sprawling green canopies and felt sick with apprehension. Surely Naomi would have sought safety here as she was a British subject? But he also knew that her father's offices were in a strongly Chinese quarter, and no doubt now under the influence of the Boxer movement. The situation did not look good and Robert wondered what he should do next.

Outside the sanctuary of the city George Morrison rode slowly towards the temple on the hill. His approach was being noted by Miss Polly Condit Smith from a stone verandah of the temple. Her eyesight was excellent and she easily could tell that the man riding towards them and trailing puffs of dust was a European. She alerted Mrs Squiers and they met Morrison with sighs of relief when he rode into the temple grounds.

Morrison glanced around and noticed the absence of any Chinese guards.

'I thought it my duty to ride here,' Morrison said grimly, dismounting. 'I am afraid that you are in the path of the advancing Boxers, Mrs Squiers.'

'I am hoping that my husband will be able to come to us,' Mrs Squiers answered. 'He may be able to bring armed men with him. Our guards have deserted us, leaving only the terrified servants and ourselves.'

'In the meantime I should examine how we can best defend the grounds,' Morrison said, appraising the temple for its best points of defence.

'You are a welcome visitor, Dr Morrison,' Polly

said, realising that she was blushing as she brushed away a strand of loose hair from her forehead. The handsome Australian was like an old-fashioned knight, arriving to rescue them. She found him very attractive and also knew that he was not married.

The Australian seemed to ignore her mild flirting as he strode away to begin his assessment of how they could defend the grounds against a Boxer attack. He was not optimistic but at least they would go down fighting and maybe even take a few of the attackers with them. He was carrying out his reconnaissance when he heard a joyous shout. Herbert Squiers had arrived, accompanied by an impressive-looking Russian Cossack in full uniform.

Morrison breathed a sigh of relief. If nothing else the arrival of the American and his Russian bodyguard, lent by the Russian minister in Pekin, De Giers, added arms and further protection to the party of helpless women, children and servants.

Between the three men they spent the night fortifying the temple and taking turns standing guard.

By dawn they were ready to move and a caravan of wooden carts, ponies, mules and donkeys accompanied by forty Chinese servants left the temple to cross the dusty plains for Pekin. To Polly, the journey was reminiscent of the stories she had read of the pioneers of her country travelling in hostile Indian country.

The three armed men acted as outriders to provide protection for the flanks of the train. Four of the Chinese servants were armed and trudged alongside the carts. They had been briefed to circle the carts in the event of an attack from either marauding Boxers or renegade Chinese troops set on looting foreigners.

It would take five hours to travel the fifteen miles to Pekin but for the entire time the long train wound its way through countryside ominously deserted apart from the caravans of coal-carrying camels in the distance.

Morrison rode with his eyes constantly scanning the country ahead and flanking him. His nerves were on edge, as were those of the others deep in this hostile landscape. Although heavily armed, he knew a concerted attack would most probably result in their massacre.

But by mid-morning they were within comparative safety and able to dismount in Legation Street to be met by European friends. As Morrison handed the reins of his pony to a Chinese servant and stretched his legs he recalled an old saying: out of the frying pan and into the fire.

The vicious rape had been expected and afterwards Naomi lay in the courtyard in a world of pain and despair. The pockmarked Boxer had been first and the most brutal. Naomi had expected that they might interrogate her beforehand seeing that she wore European clothing, but this did not seem to interest the brutal man she had heard called Commander Han. His only interest in her seemed to be to degrade her.

She now lay naked under the hot sun, staring up

at the blue skies and trying to forget the number of men who had taken their turn with her. None had understood what she had screamed when they ravished her. As the word 'father' had been in English it made no sense to them. Not that they cared, laughing at her pain. Naomi had not known a man before and as she lay alone on the stone slab courtyard in a daze, forcing her spirit to go beyond her physical self, she prayed for death. Her beloved father who had protected her for so many years had not come and only death could erase the shame she felt. Her despair-racked sobbing broke the silence after the Boxers had withdrawn into the shade of the house, leaving her with the other girls who appeared to have suffered the same fate.

'They did not kill you,' a female voice said nearby. 'You are still alive, so be pleased for that.'

Naomi was almost beyond hearing earthly words and stared with empty eyes at the sky, ignoring the blunt words from a less than sympathetic speaker.

'Come, drink some water,' the voice persisted and Naomi felt her head being lifted and a cup placed to her cracked lips. Despite her pain she sipped the water and her spirit was drawn once again to rejoin her body and she focused on the face hovering above her – a plain, broad face of a Chinese girl bearing bruises and a swollen eye.

'I am Meili,' the girl said. 'What is your name, foreign woman?'

'Naomi.'

'Are you a Christian?' Meili asked.

'I am,' Naomi answered.

'I am also a Christian,' Meili answered. 'That is why they took me from my family – after they killed my mother and father.'

Naomi struggled to sit up, realising that her hands were no longer bound. Meili passed Naomi the torn dress that had been stripped from her before the rape and Naomi struggled into it. Her nakedness covered and the water having helped, Naomi took stock of the reality of her situation. The pain remained as did the shame but Meili's company made her aware that she was not alone in her despair, although the other girls remained aloof from both herself and Meili. They sensed that the foreign woman had been singled out for a particularly brutal fate, one they did not wish to share.

'What will they do to us?' Naomi asked.

Meili shook her head. 'I do not know,' she answered. 'All I know is that they will keep us until they tire of us, and then I do not know.'

But both young women knew. They just did not want to answer their question. Naomi gave a silent prayer that at least their deaths would be quick and relatively painless.

Robert stood watching as the foreign contingents of soldiers marched into the legation grounds. American marines, tough and competent in their demeanour, contrasted with the young and cheerful British troops. The Americans were followed by the French, Russian and Italian soldiers.

Not enough troops to defend the legation, Robert

thought, and observed that a protracted battle for the European compound would be complicated by the fact that each army had its own calibre of firearms that was not compatible with the other.

Robert had great faith in the use of the new weapon to the battlefield, the machine gun, but he was also aware that the single .45 multi-barrelled Nordenfelt they possessed had a bad habit of jamming after around four shots. The Austrian contingent possessed a more deadly Maxim machine gun while the Americans had a light Colt 236. The only artillery was a small one-pounder and 120 shells owned by the Italians. The Russians brought the ammunition for something a little more effective but had left their twelve-pounder artillery gun at Tientsin railway station.

To the many civilians who greeted the arriving small contingents of troops, the artillery was proof that the Boxers would be suitably impressed and desist from any further threatening actions. But Robert only groaned his despair, for he understood the practicalities of defending such a large area of ground.

When the soldiers peeled off to their respective legations the welcoming crowd of men, women and children departed for parties where, over glasses of champagne and tumblers of whisky, they could thank God for their deliverance. The situation appeared to be under control and surely the Boxers would melt back into the countryside.

Turning on his heel, Robert walked back to the British legation to meet his fellow officers who had arrived with the British force. As he walked along the tree-lined avenue he thought about Naomi; she had not been seen or heard of in days and he considered rounding up a small force to sally into the Chinese quarter where she had resided. He knew a request for assistance would be frowned on as the legation needed every armed man to remain in place while the threat prevailed. If he could not gain assistance he would arm himself and go alone. He also knew taking leave would not be granted. It might have been different if Naomi had been a European, Robert thought bitterly.

'Mr Mumford,' a voice called from the street. Robert glanced over at a well-dressed man he knew as one of the civil servants working for Sir Claude MacDonald. 'Sir Claude has requested your presence at a meeting in his office.'

For the moment Robert dropped all thoughts of Naomi. If Sir Claude had summoned him then it must be important.

Robert was ushered into the office where the British minister for Pekin sat behind his desk.

'Please take a chair,' Sir Claude said, waving to a comfortable cane chair with a high back a short distance from his desk.

'Thank you, sir,' Robert replied after snapping his best salute. He could see from the worried expression on his normally impassive face that Britain's representative to China had much on his mind.

'I have been informed that you have been carrying out your duties in a very satisfactory manner, Mr

Mumford,' Sir Claude said, clearing his throat. 'As a former soldier myself I would have been pleased to have you on my staff back in Egypt.'

Robert wondered with some trepidation what was coming next. 'Thank you, sir,' he answered dutifully.

'I am satisfied that the arrival of the international force has impressed on those damned Boxers that we mean business and I am sure the situation will right itself. We now have a wholesome calm over the city with the further arrival of the Germans and Austrians from Tientsin and I am confident enough to support my views by sending my two young daughters to the Western Hills in the care of my sister-in-law, Miss Armstrong,' Sir Claude continued.

Robert hid his frown; what Sir Claude had failed to mention was that he had sent his two daughters, Stella and Ivy, with a British marine guard to the Western Hills. Robert knew of this as he had been partly involved in briefing the men before their departure. So, Sir Claude was not that confident after all.

'However, I also realise that the rebels have not left the city and the Empress seems to be vacillating in her loyalties towards us. I expect that it will be some time before the Boxer devils pack up and leave so I am giving you the mission of collecting intelligence on what these damned rebels are up to. In your task you will be able to requisition any persons you deem necessary to collect information to those ends, as you are acting directly on my behalf. You will submit a daily report to my secretary, young Hubert. Do you have any questions, Mr Mumford?'

'No, sir,' Robert replied without hesitation. Already he had calculated such a mission allowed him the scope to also search for Naomi – although Sir Claude did not know he had given his blessing to this.

'Well, if there is nothing else, Mr Mumford, you may take your leave,' Sir Claude said, concluding their brief meeting.

Robert rose to his feet, saluted Sir Claude and left the room.

He knew his first meeting would be with Dr George Morrison, who had opted to take up residence outside the grounds of the cloistered foreign delegations in a Chinese quarter of Pekin. As far as Robert was concerned what Morrison did not know about the situation they were currently in was not worth knowing. He would also call on the Australian for help in providing one of his Chinese staff as an interpreter and guide.

Robert was fortunate in finding Morrison at home and was ushered into his modest but comfortable residence by one of the servants. Morrison rose from a wicker chair to greet the British army officer.

'Ah, it is grand to see you, old chap,' he said, accepting Robert's extended hand.

'You, too, Dr Morrison,' Robert replied warmly. 'I have heard of your brave rescue of Mr Squiers' family.'

Morrison looked pleased but modestly waved off the compliment. 'No doubt Miss Condit Smith has embellished the escapade somewhat,' he said. 'A charming young lady, but a bit plump and gushing for my tastes.'

'I admit I did hear of the rescue from Miss Condit Smith when I was reporting to Lieutenant Simpson over at the Yankee legation on the fate of his stone dragon,' Robert said, removing his cap and placing it under his arm. 'It now seems that the fossil is mine. Mr Hoover's staff were in a bit of a hurry to leave Tientsin when I was there and had no interest in fossils. Ore samples were more in their line.'

'It's a bit early but would you like a drink?' Morrison offered. 'Gin? Whisky?'

'Your offer is tempting but I do not have a lot of time and have called on you with motives other than your largesse,' Robert said. 'I am currently working under Sir Claude's direct command and he has commissioned me to do a little bit of intelligence gathering.'

'So, we are both in the same business,' Morrison snorted in his amusement. 'But it will be wasted on a half-educated, unread former infantry major,' the Australian said, causing Robert to shift uneasily at the correspondent's views of the British Foreign Office appointment to Pekin. Although on speaking terms, neither Morrison nor Sir Claude liked the other.

'I have to confess, Dr Morrison, that my first priority is to locate the whereabouts of Miss Wong,' Robert said. 'Along the way I shall honour my commission to gather intelligence on the current situation.'

At the mention of Naomi's name, Morrison glanced away, avoiding Robert's gaze. 'I am afraid that information has come to me through my Chinese sources that in an incident about two days ago Miss Wong's Sikh bodyguard and the Chinese family she was staying with were found butchered in a street not far from the legation. It seems that they were attempting to reach safety when they were ambushed by the Boxers.'

Robert paled and for a moment felt as if he might faint. Quickly recovering, he asked, 'Was Miss Wong's body among those found?'

At this question Morrison looked even more troubled. 'It was not but I was further informed she was last seen being dragged away. It seems that she was not dead at the time otherwise the Boxers would have left her. If that is the case I am afraid her fate is sealed,' he said quietly, noticing the British officer's barely concealed distress. 'Let us hope her death was relatively quick and painless. I was under the impression that you already knew these facts before you came here. It is common talk among my sources.'

'You well know the blundering incompetence of our own diplomatic intelligence,' Robert replied bitterly. 'No doubt in a week they will make a report on her death as she was a British subject – despite being of the Chinese race. From what I knew of Miss Wong her father is a man of considerable influence in the colony of Queensland.'

'I am sorry, Robert,' George said gently. 'I did not wish to be the conveyor of such news to you, as I know of your great fondness for the young lady.'

'Still,' Robert said, lifting his chin, 'I will carry out my search for her. There may be a chance that she is still alive in the hands of the rebels. At worst, I shall endeavour to recover her body so that she may receive a funeral fit for a good Christian woman.'

'If there is anything I can do to help,' Morrison said, offering his hand, 'do not hesitate to ask.'

'Yes, there is something,' Robert answered. 'I could do with one of your people who can act as a translator and who knows the city.'

'Kai will be your man,' Morrison said. 'His grasp of English is excellent and he knows the city like the back of his hand. I will give him orders to accompany you. Is there anything else I can help you with?'

Robert shook his head, replaced his cap, thanked George Morrison and was led to meet Kai, a wiry Chinese man of indeterminate age although Robert guessed him to be in his forties. The long pigtail down his back was streaked with grey and his wizened face acorn-brown from a hard life.

Morrison instructed Kai that he was to provide all assistance to the English officer. The man nodded vigorously, following Robert from the Australian's house. All Robert had to do now was requisition a small contingent of well-armed Royal Marines to accompany him on his foray into the city in search of information but mostly in search of Naomi.

As the day drew on it seemed to Naomi the soldiers had lost interest in the pitiful huddle of young girls in the courtyard. From what she could glean of her captors she was in a transit place for the Boxers. The rebel she knew as Han appeared to be in command

and ensured that one of his men always stood guard over the cowering girls.

Meili remained by Naomi's side and nursed both her body and spirit throughout what seemed the longest day of Naomi's life.

'We should escape from here,' Meili whispered to Naomi, whose spirit had not yet recovered enough to consider such an attempt. 'The guards have not bound us and the darkness will be our friend.'

'Escape,' Naomi echoed in a dull voice. 'Where to?'

'Away from here is better than what they will eventually do to us,' Meili responded, staring at the young guard leaning against the wall of the courtyard and showing little interest in the distress of the captives. 'They will give us a little food and water soon,' she continued. 'They did before you were brought here.'

Naomi realised how thirsty and hungry she was. And while the pain had subsided to a dull ache, the shame of her terrible abuse remained, although she feebly attempted to dismiss what had happened as not her fault.

True to Meili's prediction a guard appeared with a pail of rice mixed with something that reeked so odiously Naomi felt her stomach churn.

Meili did not show the same revulsion as an empty bowl was thrust into her hands and the mixture slopped in the bowl. 'Take some,' she hissed at Naomi who stared blankly at the empty bowl in her hands. 'Or you will not have any strength.'

Naomi accepted the food. Meili lifted her bowl

and swallowed the contents and Naomi followed suit, without wanting to taste what she had consumed. It tasted as bad as it smelled and Naomi had to force herself to keep it down.

Water was brought in a large pottery jug and the captives fell on it without any thought for their sisters in a similar situation. Meili stepped in and used harsh words to force each of the girls to pause and take their turn. The girls obeyed her commands and Naomi marvelled at the young girl's natural abilities as a leader. She had always expected her own wishes and whims to be obeyed as she was a woman of wealth and education, but this girl from an impoverished village had a spirit of strength that Naomi envied.

'It is your turn,' Meili said to Naomi, who scrambled forward to drink from the communal jug.

Now fed and their thirsts slaked by the brackish water Naomi and Meili retreated to their corner of the courtyard away from the main huddle of girls.

'Why have you chosen me to go with you on your escape?' Naomi asked. 'Why not the other girls?'

'They are ignorant peasant girls,' Meili replied contemptuously. 'You are not like them.'

Naomi did not contradict the young woman by saying that from what she knew Meili was also a peasant. What mattered for now was that Meili was the only one who had expressed resistance at the circumstances Naomi was in. Yes, she would go with Meili when the time was right. That time she trusted to the young woman who watched her captors like a snake preparing to strike.

Early June 1900
Gulf of Chihli
East of Pekin

Off the coast of Queensland the money that
passed from John Wong's purse to the captain of the steamer had ensured Tung's passage from
Queensland to Hong Kong with the three men sharing a small cabin.

On the journey John had noticed that his son
spent many hours on deck with Tung discussing
many subjects but with one basis: China's future in
the modern world. John was not particularly interested in China, only getting his daughter out before
the troubles being reported by the papers overflowed
into blood. But Andrew seemed to be growing more
obsessed with the country of his ancestors and John
was irritated by his son's growing anti-imperialistic
stance which had led to an unspoken tension between
father and son on the voyage.

When they transferred in Hong Kong to a

Chinese coastal steamer they had learned the news which John had most dreaded. Sketchy reports filtering out of China pointed at massacres of Christian Chinese converts, and increasing large numbers of Boxers roaming the countryside, unrestrained by the Imperial troops of the Empress.

The rust-streaked, leaky steamer they had transferred to in Hong Kong was now off the Chinese coast of Taku in the Gulf of Chihli. Their voyage from Cairns to the Chinese waters had taken sixteen days and now the massive mud bar and Imperial Chinese fortress at the mouth of the Peiho River blocked the steamer's further progress.

The mud-brick fortresses guarding the entrance to the river were manned by Imperial troops touchy to any attempted intervention by the foreign powers. They had already faced off against two British warships some weeks earlier.

The three men stood sweating at the port side rail staring gloomily into the distance across a dirty brown sea that gave off little or no breeze to cool the clammy hot air.

'The captain has informed me that, due to the volatile situation ashore, he is not going to attempt to offload his cargo,' John said, leaning on the rails, gazing at the shore. 'We have to find some other way of getting up the Peiho River to Tientsin.'

'The captain is wise,' Tung said quietly. 'I know this province and I sense trouble ashore. It would be better that you both return home.'

'I have faced worse than this,' John snorted. 'All we have to do is get ashore and make our way up the river to Tientsin, and from there across to Pekin.'

'You would not get through the rebel lines,' Tung warned. 'From what I learned in Hong Kong the Boxers have torn up the railway tracks, cut the telegraph lines and they control the countryside of the province. You would stand out as foreigners and be executed.'

'Would I stand out as a foreigner?' Andrew asked.

Tung turned to gaze at the man he had befriended. 'You might,' Tung reflected. 'Unless you wore peasant clothes and stayed away from the Boxers.'

'Andrew is returning to Hong Kong,' John interjected. 'The situation has grown far too dangerous for him to attempt anything ashore.'

Andrew swung his attention on his father. 'What are you saying?' he flared. 'Are you saying that I have come this far with you to be told that it is too dangerous to go in search of my sister? She is just as precious to me as she is to you.'

'I was hoping that we would arrive before the trouble began,' John said. 'I cannot afford to have you risk your life in my mission. How do you think I would feel if I lost not only Naomi but you as well?'

'Sorry, Father,' Andrew snorted. 'But Naomi is my sister and you can't stop me going ashore. As Tung has said, I have more chance of passing as a local than you. Besides, I have already discussed the situation with Tung last night as to what we might encounter and he has agreed that he would help us get to Pekin if you insist.'

'I thought that we agreed to part ways on the

voyage when we reached Chinese shores,' John said, glaring at Tung. 'You have your mission to get the money back to its rightful owners.'

Tung's expression did not change under John's withering gaze. Tung was confused. He had *not* discussed with Andrew that he would help them and now the young man had put him in an awkward situation. Should he deny that he had spoken with Andrew about the situation they might encounter upon reaching China? 'I will help you both obtain passage to Pekin,' he replied without looking at Andrew.

'Just me,' John replied. 'Andrew returns to Hong Kong.'

'You need him,' Tung said bluntly. 'He can pass – but you are out of your depth here.'

'We need to get the captain to allow us to row ashore in one of his lifeboats,' John sighed, conceding Tung was right. 'I am sure for a good price that can be arranged. And when we get ashore we need to get hold of a sampan or similar to go up the river. The only arms we can carry will be concealed pistols and we will have to change from our European clothes into something like a coolie's garb.'

Andrew felt the tension leave him. The thought of putting ashore was more than just a mission to find his sister but also an opportunity to touch the earth of his ancestors. This was a spiritual aspect to his journey that he could not deny. China and its future had grown into an obsession for him and he could not tell his father about beliefs that he would not understand.

• • •

At first the captain of the coastal trader refused to ferry his three passengers ashore, until John produced a wad of English pounds. Feigning reluctance, the Indian mariner slipped the notes into his pocket and summoned his second-in-command to the bridge.

Dressed in peasant garb and concealing ready cash and revolvers, the three men were rowed ashore at night with the ingoing tide. No sooner had they stepped ashore than the boat pulled away lest it be detected by piquets of the Imperial Chinese army guarding the coastal forts. Such was the volatile nature of the current situation that Tung had warned John and Andrew to treat every Chinese they encountered as a potential enemy.

Tung had reassured his two companions that they were in territory that he was familiar with, and John realised he had to trust this enigmatic man.

'I am finally in the land of my ancestors,' Andrew whispered in awe.

'If we are not careful you might just join them,' John growled, still smarting that he had buckled to Andrew's wish to accompany himself and Tung ashore.

'There is a fishing village not far from here,' Tung said in a low voice. 'The people are poor so your English currency should buy us help. It seems the people of my country do not consider all things foreign as not desirable. Just keep your guard up,' he continued. 'There may be army patrols in the area.'

Silently, John and Andrew followed Tung as he easily walked through the night under the light of a half moon. John admired the man's ability to navigate at night. Tung had all the marks of a highly skilled warrior.

They trudged through grass-covered sand dunes in the night, using the shoreline as their guide. Eventually they arrived to see a cluster of timber and mud huts silhouetted against the starlit sky not far from the shore. There were no lights and John instinctively drew the pistol from inside his loose-fitting shirt.

'There will be no need of weapons,' Tung hissed. 'I will need some of your money and I will enter the houses to speak to the people inside.'

John shrugged and squatted in the hardy grasses. Andrew joined him and together they waited as Tung disappeared into the night.

After some minutes John was alerted to two figures appearing through the curtain of darkness.

'I have succeeded in hiring a sampan and supplies,' Tung said. Both John and Andrew peered curiously at the person who accompanied him. In the darkness they could make out a slim shape, shorter than Tung. 'The girl with me is Liling,' Tung added, sensing the two men's curiosity. 'She is the daughter of the head fisherman and part of the deal is that she will take us up as far as Tientsin. She knows how to handle a sampan in the river and knows the river itself.'

John nodded. It made sense.

Liling led them to a sampan big enough to carry them comfortably. The low-slung boat even had a shade cover, a sail as well as oars. Containers of water and dried fish were stowed inside. Before dawn they had launched the sampan and by first light Andrew was able to discern the young woman's appearance as she rowed the boat upriver. She was about sixteen years old, slim under her billowing trousers and shirt, and had a beautiful serene face with large, dark eyes. Andrew sat at the bow to observe her more fully as the blazing sun rose over the horizon. Liling had not said a word since joining them and shyly avoided their frank appraisals. It was not as if she appeared to be frightened by the three strangers so much as wary. It had not been her idea to accompany the strangers but the sight of the money produced to her father had won over the terrified man, who directed his eldest daughter to go with Tung.

Liling was aware of her unimportance to her father. It was not that he did not show great affection but she was a girl and not as crucial to her father and mother's future support as a son might be. At least by volunteering his daughter's services to guide the strangers she was contributing to the family income in a time of great uncertainty. When she did glance coyly at the young Chinese man in the bow of her family's sampan she noticed that he had a kind and handsome face. From his accent and the way he spoke in her language she realised that he was not from her part of the country. She knew Tung was, however, from the way he spoke and acted. Before long she had gleaned from listening to them that the older and younger of the two men were father and son. When she heard a foreign language spoken by them she realised that her suspicions were confirmed. The two men spoke in a language completely unintelligible to her. Now she wondered if she should be afraid of the situation she found herself in. But what she could see in the mysterious young man's face was not threatening. It was more like admiration and this made her feel more secure.

Liling continued to row and when the river breeze picked up Tung helped her to raise a bamboo-slatted sail. They passed flatlands of rice paddies where they could occasionally see a mule and a woman together hauling a plough, guided by a man. Liling noticed that the young man took in all he saw with an expression of great interest as they passed villages made of adobe brick and straw along the riverbanks.

'Liling,' Andrew said to her. 'That means "beautiful jade tinkle".'

Startled at being addressed, Liling turned to look directly at the young man. 'I do not know,' she replied. 'It is just a name.'

'My name is Andrew,' Andrew said gently. 'My father is called John.'

'I have never heard names like that before,' Liling said, drawn into conversation by this strange man. 'You do not live here.'

'No,' Andrew sighed. 'But I feel as if I have come home.'

Shy at being engaged by the young man, Liling dropped her eyes under the broad conical hat she wore. Tung had produced the same kind of headwear for himself and his companions before the rising of the sun, which was now a blazing ball of fire. They were lucky for the occasional breeze off the river.

'God almighty!' John swore softly, drawing the other three's attention to what had caused his blasphemy. From the shore a sampan filled with Imperial

Chinese soldiers was being directed their way and it was apparent that the water patrol was going to intercept them, with the intention most likely of searching their boat. Since the arms and money they carried would mark them for special attention, as Tung had warned, they would be viewed as potential enemy.

'What do we do?' Andrew asked, staring at the approaching sampan with seven soldiers aboard, all armed with modern rifles. 'They have us trapped.'

John's mind was racing. They had surprise on their side and could either attempt to shoot it out or try to bluff their way upriver. The latter option did not seem to be much of a choice as the soldiers would no doubt want to search their boat. The former option was not much better because it would attract attention from the shore where John could see many other soldiers gazing with curiosity at the unfolding scene on the river. In desperation he cast about the terrain as he calculated the other boat was still about five minutes away before it intercepted them. At this stage it did not appear the soldiers were alert to any danger as no doubt they were carrying out a routine inspection and considered their boat as what it appeared – just another sampan going upriver.

But John also knew he had only seconds to make a decision if he were to commit them to a timely course of action. The soldiers in the sampan were drawing closer.

'Dump the guns over the side,' John hissed. 'Tung will do all the talking.'

Surprised, Tung looked up at John. It was obvious that the tough bushman that he had come to learn about from Andrew was putting their lives in his hands. Turning away from the approaching boat, the three men slipped their revolvers into the river, their action unobserved by the soldiers on the patrol boat.

'Stay calm and say nothing,' Tung whispered as the sampan drew alongside.

'You people,' a soldier called. 'Where are you from and what is your business here?'

'We are poor fishermen from Taku,' Tung replied, standing and bowing respectfully. 'We are travelling to Tientsin to attend the funeral of an honourable uncle.'

The questioner was obviously in charge of the contingent in the army sampan. Tung thought that he noticed a frown on the man's face at his answer.

'We will come onto your boat,' the soldier said and gestured to a couple of his men to scramble aboard.

John and Andrew sat still, avoiding eye contact as peasants should in the presence of their superiors. The soldiers ogled Liling, who attempted to make herself look insignificant by looking down at the floor of the boat. At least their sampan smelled like a fishing boat.

Tung sat down while the two soldiers poked with the barrels of their rifles at their meagre stock of supplies. He was acutely aware that he had a fortune in banknotes in a leather purse tied to his waist under his shirt and that John and Andrew still had a substantial amount of gold and silver coins similarly concealed.

'Honourable master,' Liling suddenly said. 'We carry dried fish that you may use.' She pulled up a plank to reveal the strips of fish in a small hold. 'It is not much, but a gift to the Empress and her servants.'

The officer glanced at her and nodded his head to his two men who reached into the hold to take the fish. Andrew caught Liling's eye and she saw an expression of surprise mixed with respect. It pleased her.

'Be careful going to Tientsin,' the Chinese soldier said gruffly, addressing Liling as he eyed the welcome addition to his men's meagre diet. 'The countryside is full of Boxer rebels who would take you for their amusement, while the men they would take their time killing.'

Liling gave a short bow, her eyes downcast. The two soldiers scrambled aboard their own boat and it pulled away to return to the shore.

When it was a good way off John felt that he could breathe again. 'Phew, a close call, but thanks to Liling we made it.'

Tung also seemed to breathe a sigh of relief. 'You did well, girl,' he said to Liling.

'All are hungry in the land,' Liling dismissed. 'Food is more important than money when you are starving, and I could see that the soldiers were hungry.'

'Very observant,' Andrew mused. 'You may have saved our lives.'

Liling did not answer. The praise was more than

she had ever had before from any man and it was almost overwhelming. After all, she might only be a woman but she knew hers was a mind as sharp as any man's.

As they continued upriver towards Tientsin, John prayed that the remainder of their journey would be uneventful. They still had their money but with the loss of the revolvers they were now defenceless.

Early Summer, June 1900
Pekin

The guards were drinking and Naomi had hoped that they would forget their captives for a while but her hope was shattered when three Boxers staggered from the house adjoining the courtyard to drag two of the girls inside. When the courtyard was clear of guards, Meili pulled Naomi into the shadows, calculating that they might not be missed for the moment.

'We go now,' Meili whispered. 'It is our only hope.'

Naomi stood, stretching her legs, stiff from being forced by their guard to sit all day. Darkness was their friend as Meili had predicted and they made their way along the stone wall to a small gateway apparently unguarded. Cautiously, Meili peered around the open gate to focus on the narrow deserted laneway. She was pleased to see that there was no sign of any

Boxers and tugged Naomi's torn dress sleeve. 'Come,' she said with quiet urgency. 'We walk away now.'

Naomi followed and found herself walking beside Meili. Neither knew where they were in the city but Naomi prayed that they might stumble on a broader street she might recognise.

They had only gone a short distance from the place of their imprisonment when two figures loomed from the night. The men walking towards them were deep in conversation and Naomi felt her heart seemingly freeze in her breast when she recognised them as Boxers.

'Keep walking,' Meili hissed, taking Naomi by the elbow.

The distance between them and the Boxers was less than ten paces and at first the men appeared more interested in their own conversation.

'Good evening,' Meili bid the two men when they were within a couple of paces. The men stopped walking to focus on the two women who had loomed out of the dark.

'Where are you women from?' one of the men asked suspiciously.

'We are from the house commanded by Han,' Meili answered. 'He has sent us out to fetch food for the men.'

'Han has sent you?' the man continued.

'Yes, Han,' Meili replied calmly while Naomi fought to control the tremor attempting to rack her body. 'I am his number one woman.'

The questioner turned to his companion, shrugging his shoulders. 'Well, be quick,' he said, turning to Meili. 'Pox Face is not a patient man.'

'We will,' Meili answered, tugging at Naomi's sleeve.

With her parting words, Meili nudged Naomi down the laneway, leaving the two Boxers to continue on their walk.

'They are bound to speak to Han,' Meili said. 'We must hurry.'

They picked up their pace but avoided the almost overwhelming desire to run. Neither did they dare look back lest the two men had watched them disappear down the laneway. Within a couple of minutes they emerged onto a broader street and even in the dark Naomi recognised where they were.

'We are saved,' she said. 'This street is only a quarter-mile from the legation. If we turn right at the next street we will be able to seek sanctuary.'

Meili cast her companion a grateful look. She had chosen wisely to help this woman, she thought.

Picking up their pace they hurried along the eerily deserted street towards the intersection that would direct them to safety. They had only gone a few paces when Meili heard the noise. It was the sound of many sandalled feet slapping on the cobbled stones and it was coming in their direction.

'Run!' she shrieked.

Naomi hesitated, the food that she had consumed as a captive welling up in her throat to spill onto the roadway. The pain was crippling and she suddenly found that she had no strength to react to Meili's urgent order. Before she could follow Meili she felt herself gripped by rough hands.

Groaning in her sickness and despair, Naomi did not attempt to resist her captors before she was overcome with another bout of nausea and vomiting.

'You will pay for your resistance,' a voice snarled in her face. Naomi recognised Han's voice. 'When I have finished with you – you will pray to your god for death.'

In her current state Naomi was already begging for eternal release. Between bouts of vomiting she whispered one word over and over again: 'Father.'

She was dragged roughly back to the courtyard. The food poisoning gripped her and even her captors realised that they would have to stop to allow her to be sick or void her bowels. The way she felt she did not care if they killed her on the spot but Han seemed to want her alive, his threat echoing in Naomi's mind.

Dumped in the courtyard, Naomi curled up on the cobblestones and wept piteously. She was alone, gravely ill and shamed. Her prayers were being ignored and she wondered if God cared. Then a gentle hand touched her on the brow and Naomi sensed an angel had been sent from God to comfort her.

'Naomi, it is I, Meili,' the voice said, soothing her shattered spirit.

'Meili,' Naomi mumbled. 'Is it really you?'

'I was not able to get away,' Meili replied, stroking Naomi's matted hair. 'Han has promised to severely punish me for attempting to escape. Next time we must succeed – or die trying.'

Meili's presence and her indomitable spirit were the only tiny bright rays in Naomi's dark world. She was unaware that only a hundred yards from where she lay, Lieutenant Robert Mumford, accompanied by four heavily armed British marines and a Chinese interpreter, was even now searching for her.

Robert had chosen to sally out at night to begin his search. By day his presence in the Chinese quarter would have been more apparent, although his young and inexperienced soldiers were not keen on the idea of being out in the darkness, deep in territory that belonged to the Boxers. They had heard the stories of how the Boxers liked to torture those who fell into their hands and even the reassurances from their officers that the situation was under control did not help at the moment in the deserted streets and back alleys they patrolled.

Robert tacitly agreed with his men's uneasy comments concerning the lurking enemy. He had concluded that they were in the eye of the storm and that the Boxer movement was far from being impressed with the European show of force. He knew it was only a matter of time before the full fury of the rebellion would be seen and when it was he did not hold out much hope for their survival within the walls of the European legation. At least he could use the lull before the coming fiery storm to search for any sign of Naomi.

'This bad part,' Kai said quietly. 'Boxers have place here.'

'How do you know?' Robert queried the Chinese interpreter.

'My brother got shop here,' Kai replied. 'He tell me before he go with family to country.'

'Do you know anyone else around here?' Robert asked.

'Got cousin who live in house there,' Kai said, pointing to an ominously dark and silent house at the end of the alley.

'Then he would be in a good position to know what is going on,' Robert said, unholstering his service issue revolver. 'We will go in and speak to him.'

Kai appeared reluctant to carry out the task. The silence in the normally noisy streets was terrifying.

'Well, men, keep a sharp lookout,' Robert said, turning to the soldiers who were gripping their rifles and watching wide-eyed in every direction. 'I am going into the house at the end of the street with our interpreter.'

Satisfied that his contingent had taken up sentry posts in doorways covering the narrow alley, Robert followed Kai into the house through a narrow opening that served as a front door.

Inside, it was pitch black and Robert trusted in Kai's knowledge to lead them deeper into the house until they came to a small courtyard lit by a lantern slung from a rail on an overhanging verandah.

'Kwan,' Kai called softly. 'Kwan, are you here?'

A rustling from behind caused Robert to swing his pistol towards the source of the movement only to realise that it was a very large rat. When it squealed at the intruders, Robert realised how frightened he was and was glad that he had not fired, lest he frighten his highly strung troops outside and cause them to either flee or burst in shooting.

'Is it you, cousin Kai?' a voice whispered from behind a thick support post.

Both men turned in the direction of the voice. 'It is I,' Kai replied. Robert had not understood the exchange in Chinese. 'Cousin Kwan,' Kai said, turning to Robert. 'He will talk to us.'

A figure emerged from behind the big pole and Robert could see a man not unlike his interpreter in appearance.

'The British officer with me will not harm you,' Kai said. 'He merely seeks information.'

Kwan looked warily at Robert, who had lowered his pistol to appear less intimidating.

'Ask your cousin if there are groups of Boxers in the area,' Robert said.

Kai did so and replied, 'Cousin Kwan says many Boxers in street next to this one. They have already taken everything he owned but spared him because one of the Boxers was from our village and knew our family.'

'Ask him what the Boxers have been doing here in the city.'

A long conversation ensued and when it was over Kai turned to the British officer. 'He says that at first they put up notices and then they attacked all Chinese known to be Christians but did not attack any foreigners. They spared the pretty Chinese girls for their own use but killed all the others. Kwan says they have captured girls in a house in the next street.

He says that he does not know what the Boxers will do next but thinks that they will attack all foreigners at the legation.'

Robert nodded, satisfied that the Chinese cowering in the darkness of his house was confirming what he already strongly suspected. This was what Sir Claude had sent him out to ascertain but Robert wondered if his intelligence would be listened to. There was an arrogance among all in the foreign community that the Chinese rebels would not dare launch any attack on them. The death of a few European missionaries, however, was seen as almost routine; after all, was it not the role of a missionary to gain martyrdom in God's crusade to save heathen souls?

The information about the captive girls grabbed Robert's interest. Was it possible that Naomi may have been spared because she was young and beautiful?

'Thank your cousin,' Robert said. 'Tell him that he has done a service for Her Majesty.'

Kai frowned. 'My cousin would not care,' he said. 'He is Chinese and not a Christian. I think that if the rebels had not robbed him he would have been one of them.'

Cautiously, both men exited the house lest they be fired on by the nervous soldiers standing guard.

Robert signalled his men to gather to him. 'We are going to do a sweep of the street that runs parallel with this one,' he briefed. He did not tell them why but hoped that they might just get lucky and find the place Kai's cousin had told them about. It was a slim chance but at least worth taking if they were in the immediate area anyway.

Leading his men, Robert moved to the end of the street and down the next one, which proved to be wider with less crowded tenements. He could see that one of the houses in the street was lit by lanterns and could hear the raucous voices of men. Only Boxers would be celebrating right now, Robert told himself. With a wave of his hand he signalled in the dim light of the street for his small band of marines to extend into single line.

Although they were inexperienced the British marines were well trained and fell into their formation, rifles at the ready, for a sweep of the street. It appeared that the Boxers were not expecting foreign troops in the early hours of the morning so far into the territory they dominated. Surprise was on the British officer's side. Silently, they moved in on the house suspected of holding captives.

Robert did not see the dozing sentry until it was too late. He was leaning against a wall opposite the house that held Robert's attention and when the guard realised what had awoken him from his slumber the element of surprise was gone. He scrabbled for the rifle at his feet and shouted a hurried warning.

Robert swung his pistol across the street and fired wildly. His shot missed, causing the startled guard to scramble into an open doorway without his rifle.

'Go!' Robert roared at his men, signalling them to storm the house through an open gateway.

But they were brought to a stop when five armed Boxers spilled onto the street wielding swords and screaming their war cry. A small volley of shots from the soldiers with Robert felled one Boxer and forced the remaining men to retreat back into the gateway.

Naomi and Meili were torn from their despair by the sound of gunfire outside the wall and Naomi instantly recognised the voice calling orders loudly to his men. 'It is Robert!' she cried out in English, confusing Meili.

'What is it?' Meili asked as Naomi struggled to her feet, waving her arms.

'We will be rescued,' Naomi shouted, ignoring the Boxers who had poured into the yard with their motley collection of weapons, ranging from modern rifles to primitive spears. 'It is someone that I know come to rescue us.'

Meili rose to her feet, already acting on this information from the foreign woman of Chinese blood. If what she had said was true, this was their chance to make a break. But her spirits fell when she saw that the gateway was blocked by Boxers now firing around the corner at the would-be rescuers.

Naomi fought to ignore her feelings of nausea to stumble towards the gate but Meili grabbed her and pulled her down. 'We cannot escape yet,' she said. 'Not that way. We must pray to the ancestors that your friend is able to defeat Han and his men.'

Reluctantly, Naomi allowed herself to be pulled away. All she could do for the time being was pray.

Robert was surprised at the heavy volume of returning fire and any chance of storming the house was gone now as he could see that they were outnumbered and even outgunned. 'Fall back,' he yelled.

His companions withdrew in an orderly manner, shooting as they did. They were fortunate that the street was relatively wide and that the Boxers were firing into the dark. Without aiming, Robert emptied his pistol in the direction of the gate, as it was a matter of providing enough gunfire to suppress any counterattack.

The hammer of his pistol clicked on an empty chamber and he looked around to ensure his men were safe. Kai had already found shelter behind a low-set stone wall around the corner of the street that they had entered. Robert found him and the soldiers together.

'What do we do, sir?' one of the soldiers asked.

'We return to the legation,' Robert said, reloading his pistol. 'We have done what we were tasked to do.'

The soldiers looked relieved at their officer's decision. Warily, they moved out to return to the relative safety of the European compound. Robert led the way, brooding over his lack of success in storming the Boxer compound. It was not as if Naomi had been there, he attempted to reassure himself. It was just that it had been worth a try. He would report his findings and the skirmish with the Boxers to Sir Claude. At least he could try again at the first opportunity to gain information on her whereabouts.

The firing had tapered off and the Boxers were jubilant in their victory over the foreign soldiers who had dared intrude on their domain. The body of the dead Boxer outside the courtyard was dragged inside and his body stripped to provide a uniform and weapons for the next recruit. Han went among his men as any good commander would, congratulating them and hardly paid any attention to Meili and Naomi slumped in a dark corner of the compound.

Haggard and beyond caring, Naomi was barely aware that the sun was rising to bake with searing heat the plains and hills around Pekin. Robert's voice still echoed in her mind but she knew it was nothing more than that – an echo of hope smashed.

A shadow fell over her body curled into a foetal position. 'Look at me, foreign woman,' a voice commanded harshly and Naomi raised her eyes slowly to see the man she had come to hate more than any other creature on earth.

'Your attempt to escape me was foolish,' he said. 'As you will soon see I do not tolerate insubordination or incompetence from my men.'

Naomi was aware that a large copper tub suspended over a wooden fire had appeared in the courtyard, and that Han's man stood stony-faced beside it, holding a bound and pitifully naked man. The terror in the man's face caused Naomi to shudder and want to close her eyes.

'This man was supposed to stand sentry duty last night in the street. But from my questioning I have learned that he allowed the foreign devil soldiers to creep up on us,' Han said menacingly. 'Not only did he allow that to happen but he also left his rifle in the street and modern rifles are more valuable than the men who carry them.' Naomi closed her eyes as if to shut out the world.

'Open your eyes, foreign woman, or you will wish death could come quickly.'

Naomi realised the threat was real and once again opened her eyes. Meili, beside her, huddled away in an obvious state of terror.

'Now, look to the man who is about to be punished,' Han snarled.

The prisoner suddenly began screaming for mercy as the soldiers hoisted him to the edge of the tub. It was only then that Naomi realised the oily haze hovering above the rim originated from the tub's steaming contents.

Even before the struggling man was lowered feet first into the boiling oil, Naomi was vomiting the last of the bile in her system onto the stony courtyard. The doomed man's screams pierced the hot air like the sound of hell's doors opening. Mercy was the silence when he died under the oil now bubbling furiously over the brim and splashing onto the ground.

'I have been informed that you speak English,' Han said. 'I may have use of an interpreter and so for the moment you will be useful. What you have seen is a merciful death compared to the one that I have planned for you if you ever attempt to escape from me again. Do you understand?'

With her eyes down, Naomi nodded weakly. She felt her hair being grabbed as Han yanked her head up. 'Do you understand that I will not warn you again?' he spat into her face. 'You are nothing to me.

You are just a worthless cur of the foreign devils who has betrayed her own people. If I tell you to spread your legs, you will do so with a smile to express your pleasure. If I say to you to eat dog excrement, you will do so and tell me that it is the best thing you have ever eaten.'

Naomi was hardly aware of the agony in her scalp. All she knew now was that she would stay alive so that she could one day kill Han. Hatred and the desire for revenge had replaced all the physical pain she had ever experienced. She would feign obedience to the Boxer as he expected but she knew the pox-faced commander had underestimated the daughter of John Wong. Her father was with her now in spirit and she would gather his legendary prowess to her to overcome this terrible situation. Even the shame she felt over what had been inflicted on her was gone, and though she knew that she would be killed, it would not be before she removed from the earth this creature who belonged in hell.

'I understand, Master Han,' she said weakly through cracked lips. 'I am your servant to do as you wish.'

Han let go of her hair, turned and strode over to the pot to peer inside. He smiled grimly with satisfaction at the way he had delivered his message to his subordinates. They would need the utmost discipline when the time came to take on the European soldiers at the legation and only the Boxers' courage and superior numbers would overcome the firepower of the contemptible Europeans.

Early June 1900
The Peiho River
North-east China

Night was falling over the river as Liling guided the sampan into the shore.

Tung said that he knew the area and again assured his companions that their money would buy food and a place to stay.

As the boat was being nosed ashore not far from a small village John wished that he still had his revolver; old instincts told him that there was something ominous about the silence of the hot evening broken only by the sound of a barking dog and the crickets chirping in the dusty paddies, no longer under cultivation.

'You still have command,' John said quietly to Tung, reaffirming his right to make decisions on the river. 'We are still in your hands.'

Tung nodded before leading the way cautiously toward a mud–brick house where a dim light glowed from a doorway. They had almost reached the building when John froze. His nagging doubt about the village proved to be correct when a shadowy figure emerged from behind the building armed with a long spear.

The others followed John's example and remained still.

'Who enters the village?' the man challenged, holding his spear forward in a defensive manner.

'Tung Chi, a Shaolin priest,' Tung replied calmly. 'Are you of the Society of the Harmonious Fist?'

The sentry hesitated, turned and called behind him. Five other similarly armed men appeared in the half light.

'Come forward, Tung Chi,' one of the men commanded.

Tung turned to gesture to his companions to remain where they were as he went forward to meet the six armed men.

'Who are they?' Andrew whispered to his father.

'They are not regular troops,' John answered, surveying the garb and weapons of the men Tung approached. 'They are either bandits or Boxers. Either way I don't like our chances. Be ready to run back to the boat.'

The situation remained tense as Tung entered into a conversation with the armed men. One of the unknown men suddenly lifted his spear to Tung's throat and shouted. John felt adrenalin pumping through his body. As they were not in a position to fight then they would have to flee. But just as suddenly the man lowered his spear.

Tung turned back to John, Andrew and Liling. 'We are safe for the moment,' he said. 'They have agreed to allow us to stay over tonight and continue our journey in the morning.'

'Are they Boxers?' John asked bluntly.

'They are,' Tung replied calmly. 'They have been on a mission in the area, ripping up railway lines.'

'What did you tell them about us?' John asked.

'I said that you were under my protection and not to be harmed.'

'And they listened to you?' John asked incredulously. 'Four wandering strangers.'

'They are men fighting a war against the evil of European occupation – not bandits,' Tung replied. 'They could see that you are Chinese, albeit I had to explain that you were from Hong Kong to explain your part-European appearance.'

A nagging suspicion haunted John. How could Tung, seemingly a total stranger to the armed rebels, convince the Boxers that what he told them was the truth? 'Are you one of them?' he asked quietly.

'If you mean a rebel against the foreign destruction of my land, then I must answer yes,' Tung replied defiantly.

'Are you a Boxer?' John persisted.

'I promised to assist you to get to Pekin to find your daughter,' Tung said. 'Who or what I am is of no consequence. I have my own mission to go to the Son of Heaven and return what is rightfully his. Other than that, your question as to whether I am a member of the society is irrelevant.'

'Father,' Andrew interjected quietly, 'Tung has got

us safely this far, so I think that we are being less than gracious in questioning his motives.'

John did not take his eyes off Tung. 'I don't know whether I should trust you from now on,' he said. 'But my son is right. We do appreciate what you have done for us so far.'

Tung accepted the apology and realised that this man with equal amounts of European and Asian blood was not a man of compromise. But he was a tough and dangerous man who had proved himself many times in the past, according to Andrew. As for Andrew, he was also a good man but like many young people, an idealist searching for a cause rather than adopting his father's very practical outlook on life. But idealists could also be dangerous men when fanaticism was applied.

Tung led them to the hut where the Boxers stood, watching them with little interest. Whatever Tung had said, John thought as they passed them by, had worked well. The only real curiosity they showed was that of normal male admiration for the beautiful Liling.

Andrew was curious about the Boxers now he was actually in the presence of the warriors he had considered the enemy. They appeared to be disciplined young men of his own age, and from what he had been told by Tung, devoted to freeing China from the unwanted foreigners. They had sprung from the soil of China and without the backing of the Empress taken it into their own hands to put their lives on the line to gain freedom.

The newcomers remained aloof from the soldiers

who crowded into the hut to share a meal of rice and dried fish gruel. Tung was the only one to engage the Boxers in any talk and John noticed the deference they paid to him, heightening his suspicions.

Andrew observed how Liling kept close to him, eyeing the Boxers with great distrust. Occasionally their eyes met, but Liling would always quickly look away.

Finally the Boxer warriors found themselves a place to sleep on the earthen floor and fell into a sound sleep, with one of their number taking his turn to stand guard outside.

The newcomers found it hard to sleep. Fleas bit at them all night and Andrew hoped that none of the parasites was carrying the dreaded bubonic plague, currently causing great concern in the eastern colonies. Andrew marvelled at how easily his father had drifted into sleep and, as he scratched irritably, wished that he could be more like his father: tough and stoic.

When dawn finally came, after a stifling, uncomfortable night inside the hut the soldiers stirred to serve up the same food as the night before. The travellers joined the Boxers for the morning meal then bid them a good day to return to their sampan.

'Liling agrees with me that we are only about a day from Tientsin,' Tung said, when the sampan was shoved out from the shore. 'We should arrive after dark.'

John was pleased at the news. From there they could trek overland to Pekin and he would soon be united with his beloved daughter.

Andrew's reaction was a little more mixed. Arriving in Tientsin meant that Liling would return to her small village at the mouth of the river and he wanted to learn more about the young woman. Despite the fact that she was uneducated, could not speak English and had seen very little of the world, Andrew found her fascinating and attractive.

He gazed across the sluggishly flowing, muddy river at the shoreline and wondered at how different was the world he found himself in now to the dignified stone portals of his Scottish university, where he should be at this very moment continuing his studies.

The oil-like surface of the river glistened and flickered in the shadow of fires burning along the shoreline of Tientsin. The four travelling in the sampan watched in silence from the water, wondering at the situation ashore. Occasionally the muffled sound of an explosion reached them, along with voices raised in terror.

'It does not look good,' John said. He turned to Tung and added, 'Your friends seem to have beaten us here.'

'I will go ashore and see what the situation is,' Tung said. 'I will return in an hour. If I am not back you should continue up the river to Tungchow. The girl can be paid to take you further.' With these parting words, Tung slipped ashore and disappeared into the night. Liling poled the sampan away from the shore and anchored. All they could do was wait, watching and listening to a city being torn apart by revolution.

In less than thirty minutes Tung waved from the shoreline. Liling poled the sampan onto the river-bank to allow him aboard.

'We will have to continue up the river,' Tung said. 'The town is virtually under Boxer control, although the Europeans are gathered in their own area.'

Andrew felt almost relief at the news. Now it meant that Liling would have to remain with them until at least Tungchow.

'I will pay Liling for the journey,' John said, confirming Andrew's hopes.

'She has no choice,' Tung said bluntly. 'She is a woman and does what she is told.'

As the exchange between Tung and John was in English, Liling had not understood. But when Andrew explained in her own language that she would be required to continue upriver and be paid extra she did not mind. This was a grand adventure in the company of a young man she felt herself attracted to although she was realistic enough to understand the gulf that divided them. Liling thrust the pole into the muddy riverbed to propel them past Tientsin and deeper into the heart of China.

The tall stands of reeds at the water's edge were as still as the air around them and a fine mist hovered over the oily surface. The previous evening they had come ashore in a place Tung remembered was relatively scarce of people and set up camp. A small fire had been lit and a meal of boiled rice flavoured with fish was consumed.

John was dreaming about a large and juicy steak served up on a plate with fried eggs and potatoes. Despite his Asian ancestry he had never really acquired a taste for rice and fish and he missed the aroma of meat sizzling over a fire.

'Father,' a voice called and reluctantly John left his dreams behind and emerged into reality.

'Father,' Andrew said, shaking his father's shoulder. 'Tung has gone.'

John was now wide awake, silently cursing himself for being less vigilant. There was a time when his fine-honed instincts would have warned him but he knew he was getting older and less alert to the world around him.

'You sure?' he asked his son, rubbing sleep from his eyes to see a red ball creeping over the horizon of deserted paddy fields. 'He has not gone for a call of nature?'

'I have been awake for the last ten minutes and have seen no sign of him,' Andrew replied, squatting by the embers of the dead fire. 'Nor has Liling. It seems that Tung also took my money with him,' Andrew added gloomily.

John was on his feet, scanning the surrounding countryside. All he could see in the far distance was what appeared to be a farmer leading an emaciated water buffalo along a dusty, well-trod track. Overhead, the cloudless sky was a pale blue promising another searing day of heat. Only the sluggishly flowing river nearby held any promise of coolness in the drought-racked land.

'I would not have picked him for a thief. Maybe he has gone to join his comrades,' John said, squatting to poke at the grey embers of the campfire with a stick. 'Whatever he has done we will not be waiting for him. We eat and move on.'

Using their fingers they ate a breakfast of cold, gluey rice from bowls. Liling excused herself for a call of nature. When she was out of sight John turned to his son. 'You appear to be very captivated by the young lady,' he said. 'Just something an old man observes.'

Andrew ducked his head, avoiding his father's stare. 'She is very attractive but I know we are worlds apart,' he replied.

'You realise that when we find your sister we will be returning to Queensland and you will be going back to your medical studies.'

Andrew nodded. He had not thought about Liling in any light other than a young man's desire to explore the forbidden with a beautiful young woman.

When Liling rejoined them they cast off and John took over rowing the sampan upriver. Silence prevailed as the sampan glided past riverbanks devoid of the usual signs of habitation and industry. Now and then another sampan or river junk would pass them going downstream but they avoided contact.

Around mid-morning, when the sun was a blazing ball overhead, Andrew's attention was drawn to a tiny figure gesticulating to them from the shore some fifty yards away.

'Father,' Andrew called from the bow to John at the stern. 'Over there,' he said, pointing through the heat haze shimmering along the riverbank.

John looked in the direction his son had indicated and could see the figure waving his arms over his head. He shaded his eyes and peered as well as he could. 'Tung!' he exclaimed. 'What in hell is he up to?'

'Over here,' faintly drifted to the boat. 'Over here!'

'It is Tung,' Andrew confirmed. 'He seems to be calling to us.'

'I know,' John snorted, wiping his sweating brow with the back of his sleeve. 'I wonder what the thieving bastard wants? Maybe we should leave him.'

'I think we should pull ashore and see what he is up to,' Andrew replied. 'I am sure that he has a reasonable explanation for taking the money.'

Andrew's comment convinced John to pole ashore as he too had wondered why a man carrying a fortune would need to steal from them.

Upon reaching the shore Tung did not wait for them to beach the boat but leaped in, carrying a small bundle wrapped in dirty cotton cloth.

'Hope you have come back to return the money you took,' John snapped.

'No, but I used it to buy this for you,' Tung replied, opening the bundle to reveal a revolver and spare rounds of ammunition. 'I am surprised that you did not trust me. If I had intended to harm you I would have done so when we camped downriver with the Boxers.'

'You could have told me what you were up to,' John said, gazing at the revolver he recognised as a French army issue *Chamelot Delvigne* from his days as a soldier of fortune in French-controlled Cochin China. He had liked the gun; they had a good feel in the hand.

'You were all asleep and it was not far to a house I knew of,' Tung replied, handing the gun and ammunition to John. 'I thought I would be back before you had eaten. Your lack of trust in me causes me great shame.'

'I apologise for not trusting you,' John said gruffly. 'I appreciate the effort you must have gone to.'

'It once belonged to a French missionary,' Tung said. 'It was stolen and fell into the hands of a man I know here who deals in such expensive merchandise. Needless to say it did not come cheap. The gun is a necessity in these bandit lands.'

John slipped the chamber sideways and checked the load. It was good to be once again armed in this dangerous territory. 'Time we kept moving,' he said, placing the spare rounds of ammunition back in the cloth and securing it inside his trousers. At the same time he noticed a look of reproval from Andrew, whose sympathies seemed increasingly to be with Tung.

Fires lit the night sky over Tungchow city.

'It is the same everywhere,' John said, balancing himself on the deck of the sampan to gaze at the horizon. 'It does not bode well for Pekin, considering the city is only about ten miles to the west.'

'We will have to make our way across land from here,' Tung said. 'It will be dangerous. We no longer require the woman's services so she can be paid off to return to her family.'

'I wonder if that would be wise,' Andrew spoke up, 'considering the distance she has to travel back through areas we know are now under the guns of either the Imperial army or the rebels. I think that she should remain with us until the situation calms down a bit.'

Both Tung and John looked to Andrew, who was sitting near the stern with Liling.

'We don't need an extra person with us,' his father said. 'It is going to be dangerous enough for the three of us getting from Tungchow to Pekin. Liling would be better off taking her chances travelling home.'

Andrew rose. 'I disagree,' he said. 'I think that we owe her for getting us out of that trouble with the Chinese army. I think she should come with us.'

John could hear the determined edge in his son's voice. His son's attraction to Liling was clearly a big factor in Andrew's concern for her safety. But he also had to admit the girl was intelligent and had travelled with them without complaining of the dangers.

'The girl returns to her family,' Tung said bluntly. 'That was the contract I made with her father.'

'Maybe we should let the girl decide,' John said, turning to Liling and breaking into his bad Chinese to ask her what she would decide.

Liling looked to Andrew, then back to John. 'I would like to go with you to Pekin,' she said. 'I would feel safer.'

'Stupid woman,' Tung muttered. 'She does not know the dangers ahead.'

'It has all been dangerous,' Andrew said defensively. 'And she has proved her worth.'

Tung shrugged and turned his back to gaze across the river at the burning city. The girl was of no consequence to him and was free to die with them if she chose so. They would go ashore at night and attempt to bypass the city to reach the other side. Then, by following the main road out of the burning city, they would be guided into Pekin and his mission to deliver the money would be over.

'We should put ashore and use the night to avoid any rebels or Imperial troops,' Tung said.

John agreed. The sampan was guided to the riverbank and all the supplies that they would need taken from the boat. John felt elated knowing that he was probably only a night's forced march from his daughter and by morning he hoped to see the city walls of the ancient Chinese capital.

Early to Mid June 1900
Pekin

Despite his reassurances that the Boxer unrest would soon dissipate, Sir Claude MacDonald travelled outside the city intending to return with his two young daughters in the first week of the northern summer. He had previously called on the Imperial Chinese officials to protest the murder of two missionaries but was met with a hostile and insolent reception. He was informed that an edict issued by the Empress Dowager's court had absolved the Boxer movement from any involvement in the current troubles and even went further to say that the troubles were caused by unruly elements in the Chinese Christian community. Even if Sir Claude had to grudgingly admit that they could expect no protection from the Imperial armed forces in the event the Boxers launched an all-out assault on the European legation compound, he still maintained an optimistic official stance that the Boxer movement was little more than an undisciplined rabble that did not pose a threat. He was supported in his dithering by the American representative to China, Edwin Conger, who refused to send a telegram to Washington urging for greater forces to be deployed to Pekin. Surely President McKinley would show the flag, thought many outside the bureaucratic offices of the American representative, to impress on the Chinese the military might of the United States of America.

Robert was not surprised to find that his report concerning the skirmish with the Boxers four nights before had been lost in the system. Sweating profusely, he sat on the edge of his single bed in his cramped quarters attached to the British compound, staring blankly at the stone wall opposite. Since his foray into the Chinese quarter and the report that he had submitted concluding that the Boxers appeared to be a looming threat, Sir Claude had released him back to his liaison duties. Now his chance to go in further search of Naomi was taken from him.

'Bloody-minded idiots,' he muttered to a lizard clinging to the wooden beam above his head. 'A massacre is around the corner and the bloody fools will be caught sipping their gin and tonics while the Boxers hack them to death.'

Robert rose from the bed and slipped on his khaki uniform, adjusting the well-polished Sam Browne belt and attaching the holster of his service revolver. He had an appointment with his American counterpart at their legation and this time he was not going to be wearing his fancy dress uniform for the occasion. As far as Robert was concerned he was on a military footing, even if the British government in Pekin was not.

His foresight was soon to be confirmed to even the stubborn Sir Claude MacDonald.

The unrest in the streets of Pekin was becoming obvious even to Sir Claude MacDonald, who had hurried off a telegram to Vice Admiral Seymour of the British fleet standing off China requesting that a relief force be sent to their aid although only as a precaution. The Europeans had watched as a mass of armed Boxers streamed in from the countryside to swell the numbers of rebels already in the city.

In the second week of June a reply from the Vice Admiral assured Sir Claude that a force would be dispatched. Then the telegraph lines fell silent as the link was cut by the Boxers. This isolation from the rest of the world fell as an ominous pall over those in the European compound, heightening their awareness that they were truly trapped in a hostile sea of colourfully uniformed Chinese warriors.

Robert sat at his desk in his small office attached to the British government offices reading the intelligence report that had been compiled from the latest news. He had been scribbling notes on the Moslem Kansu fighters he had witnessed arriving in force from the north. The next item in a report on his desk caught his eye: the chancellor from the Japanese legation, Mr Sugiyama, had gone unarmed to the railway station and had been dragged from his pony cart to be disembowelled and shredded by Kansu troops who had accompanied the Empress back into Pekin. Dispassionately, Robert took note of the item and added to his report that from what he had seen of the Kansu fighters they were armed with the latest European rifles and should be considered a serious threat to the current forces in the legation compound.

A knock at his door was followed by the appearance of George Morrison.

'Hello, Mr Mumford. How is the intelligence gathering going?'

Robert placed his pen on the desk, blotted the ink on the page and stood to welcome Morrison. 'Have you heard about the attack on the Japanese chancellor?' he asked, accepting Morrison's extended hand.

'I reported it, old boy,' Morrison said, taking a seat in a wicker chair and crossing his legs with his hat in his lap. 'No one dares go out to recover the body and I heard that the Kansu cut out the Oriental's heart and sent it to a grateful Tung Fuhsiang as a gift. As we speak I have heard the local kids are in the street poking with sticks at what remains of Sugiyama.'

'Tung Fuhsiang is one of the Empress's generals,' Robert said, clasping his hands behind his back. 'The Chinese of the Imperial court have some nerve, considering what Chinese troops have done to the Japanese ambassador. Representatives of the Empress have actually gone to the Yankees to ask them not to send troops. At least the Yanks had the balls to dismiss the request. I notice that the Chinese merchants are closing up shop and leaving, along with what remains of the servants from the legation area.'

'My staff are staying put,' Morrison said. 'They have a false sense that we will protect them.'

'You don't sound very optimistic, Dr Morrison,' Robert said.

'Look at what we have,' Morrison replied. 'A handful of inexperienced and outnumbered troops from all over Europe here to protect not only ourselves but the thousands of Chinese converts flooding into the city and into the legation. Not only do we have to defend them but we also have to feed them. So if push comes to shove who do you think we will be defending – not the Chinese. On top of that, we have the outlying missionary compounds in the city that need defending and that means deploying troops into vulnerable pockets of defence. It is looking bloody hopeless.'

Robert silently agreed. They had left their run too late.

Days had passed and Naomi found that she was regaining her strength. Strangely, Han and his men had left her alone to recover and only Meili's company broke the boredom of her captivity. The Chinese girls who had been prisoner with them had been transferred to other Boxer outposts. Trembling, Naomi had stood up to Han and insisted that Meili remain with her.

Surprisingly, Han had consented. Meili could cook for his men, he said.

Naomi was given a minor task of sorting through and translating into Chinese any papers written in English that had fallen into the Boxers' hands. They were mostly personal letters taken from mission stations sacked and looted by the rebels and did not reveal anything that could be construed as important to the tactical situation of Han and his men, so Naomi was able to dismiss what she had read as being of no consequence. It amused her that she could have read state secrets and given the same answer and Han would not know if she were lying but, as it was, she had no reason to lie.

What Naomi did learn from reading the letters was that the situation was worsening for the European community around and in Pekin. Many of the letters had been written as if they would be the last words of the writer and dark bloodstains on one pile of letters written by a German missionary seemed to confirm her worst fears. Although she could not read German she suspected from the fine hand behind the pen that the letters must have been written by a woman.

'What do they say?' Han demanded from behind Naomi as she held the bloodstained letters.

'I do not understand German,' Naomi replied quietly, expecting a savage beating for her inability to translate the bloodied letters.

'All foreign devils are the same,' Han snorted. 'You must know the words on the paper.'

'It is like some Chinese speak Mandarin and

others Cantonese,' Naomi answered calmly. 'I only speak the English language of the foreign devils.'

She dared turn her head to glance at Han, who stood in the small room that had once stored spices for the wealthy Chinese family who had previously owned the stone and timber house. As he glared back at her, pondering her answer, Naomi realised that despite his seemingly intelligent mind Han was ignorant of the world beyond China. In the days that had passed during her captivity she had time to observe him organising and commanding them. He appeared to be competent – and even fair – in his dealings with his men but her hatred for him had not abated and she was careful to hide her feelings. And as she had not been molested since the initial stage of her capture, Naomi was grudgingly grateful to Han for at least that mercy.

Naomi now lived for two things: to kill Han and escape from the house. Meili, however, simply lived from day to day and Naomi was surprised at how the young Chinese girl had capitulated to her current situation of captivity. It was as if the fire of resistance was gone from her.

'You smell badly. You need to wash,' Han suddenly said, catching Naomi off guard, deep in her thoughts as she was.

Naomi did not thank Han but simply bowed her head dutifully. The Chinese Boxer leader turned and left the stifling little room to return to his duties, leaving Naomi with the wonderful thought of being able to bathe for the first time since she lived with Mr Soo's family.

Naomi found the tub located in a room where the Boxers slept at night and carried jugs of water to fill it. She was pleased to see that she had privacy and noted the Chinese pants and blouse set aside for her to change into. They were the clothes of a peasant but were clean and Naomi sighed with pleasure for the chance to recover some of her dignity. For now she found just a tiny beam of sunshine in her bleak world of despair. Being able to wash and put on clean clothes went a long way to mending the spirit.

Meili entered the room as Naomi slipped into the clothes. 'Han has been ordered to go to the walls of the foreign legation,' she whispered furtively. 'I overheard a conversation he had with a man from the Imperial court. His mission is important.'

Naomi glanced around them to ensure they were not overheard. 'Do you still wish to escape?' she asked.

Meili shied away with an expression of fear in her face. 'You have seen what they will do to us if we attempt to escape,' she replied. 'I do not have any desire to be killed in ways only these men can devise.'

Naomi accepted her friend's fear. When she closed her eyes she could still see the unfortunate Boxer soldier screaming his life away as the boiling oil slowly cooked him alive. 'I understand,' she said, placing her hand reassuringly on Meili's arm.

Meili slipped from the room to leave Naomi pondering as to why Han would be going to the walls of the European legation. What she could not imagine was that her captor was about to trigger the opening of the gates of hell for the Europeans trapped in the city.

Baron von Ketteler, the handsome, blue-eyed German minister to Pekin married to an American heiress, could not believe his eyes. And many others in Legation Street were similarly stunned. Sitting on the shaft of a small cart in direct view of all the Europeans was a brightly dressed Boxer casually sharpening a huge knife on his boot. The man was dressed with red ribbons around his wrists and ankles and a scarlet waist sash securing a white tunic. His hair was bound with a red scarf and the insolent expression on his pockmarked face spoke his contempt.

'He challenges us with his insolence,' von Ketteler snarled, rage turning his handsome face into a mask of fury. 'I will teach him to respect his betters.'

Before he could be stopped by one of his staff, the enraged German strode out into the street, waving a stick he had scooped up from the road.

Han saw the German hurrying towards him and hesitated in the act of stroking the large knife along the side of his boot. He had not expected the cowardly barbarians to accept his challenge and, in his hesitation, had allowed the German diplomat to descend on him. Von Ketteler struck Han savagely about the head with the stick. Han did not understand the guttural curses raining on him but did glean that if he attempted to retaliate he might easily be killed by one of the armed Europeans watching the show. The blows were painful but not as much as Han's sense of shame at losing face before the foreign devils. However, his instinct to live overcame his sense of shame and Han wisely fled to a nearby alleyway.

Von Ketteler might have followed but his attention was drawn to the interior of the cart where he saw a small, frightened boy huddling. The German diplomat hauled him by the scruff of his neck from the cart and began thrashing the terrified child with his stick.

As Han retreated he could hear the boy crying out his protests at the beating and the Boxer commander swore he would see the German dead.

Despite the protests of one of his staff, von Ketteler ordered that the boy be marched to the German quarters as a prisoner. 'It might not be a wise idea, sir,' an older and more China-wise civil servant warned. 'The heathens are watching every move we make here.'

'Nonsense,' von Ketteler snorted, shaking off his anger. 'They have had a demonstration that Germany does not tolerate insolence from mere savages.'

The civil servant nodded his obedience and escorted the battered and bruised boy away. But he had been right. Hell was unleashed by the spectacle. By late afternoon the exaggerated version of what had happened in Legation Street spread like wildfire to the Boxers throughout the city. Columns of smoke rose over the city marking a new outbreak of violence, and news came that even vaster numbers of armed Boxer reinforcements were streaming into the city. Any unguarded mission stations in the city were torched and any Chinese converts captured dealt with by the enraged Boxers. Any lucky captives were hacked to death but the unlucky ones were tortured in rebel camps and outposts before they died of their wounds.

Han was in a rage when he returned to his headquarters. The beating he had received from the European had been witnessed by many of his men watching from the open streets surrounding the European legation. He had never considered that his contemptuous bravado would be challenged. Rather, the barbarians were supposed to be terrified by his brazen act.

Naomi saw the blood splashes on his clothing and unfortunately caught his eye.

'Your foreign devil friends will pay for this,' he raged, his dark eyes bulging. 'You will pay for this.'

Naomi felt a chill of fear as Han strode towards her, grabbed her by the throat and smashed his fist into her face, splitting her upper lip. She did not resist but felt the blows striking her around the head until he let go and she fell to her hands and knees. In her dazed horror she realised that he was behind her and forcing her legs apart. The rape that came was savage and especially degrading in front of his men. When it was over he left her with a brutal kick in the ribs.

Naomi lay for a short time in a pool of blood and shame.

'You must get up and be somewhere Han cannot see you,' Meili said in a furtive whisper. 'If he returns he will see you and his anger is not yet spent.'

Hardly hearing the wise words, Naomi allowed

Meili to assist her into the courtyard to a corner shaded by a large tree under the stares of Boxer warriors idling in the courtyard.

'You have some cuts and your lip will bleed for some time,' Meili said softly. 'Do you feel pain inside your body?'

Naomi tried to focus on Meili's words but felt the dark despair return, blotting all else out.

'You must put this behind you,' Meili whispered. 'Do not live in the world of dark spirits that eat the soul.'

Meili's words sounded hollow but her gentle touch meant a great deal. 'I will get better,' Naomi responded hoarsely, bringing the faintest glimmer of a smile to Meili's face.

'And when you are better you will one day kill Han,' Meili said, causing Naomi to start.

'How did you know?' she asked.

'It is in your eyes,' Meili answered, applying a clean, damp rag to Naomi's wounds. 'I wish to live to see that occur.'

Naomi felt the rage returning. Yes, she would live to kill Han. For now that moment was not at hand but one day Han would drop his guard.

In the early evening Robert stood on the parapet overlooking the city and watched the myriad of dancing lights in the Chinese quarter. He knew they were torches and the now-common sound of '*Sha, sha*' drifted to him on the smoke of the burning missionary buildings. Below he could see a contingent of slouch-hatted American marines, shepherding a few lucky survivors of the afternoon's massacre into the safety of the walls of the legation.

Robert had seen enough. It was time to join the British troops and his fellow officers for a conference on the best way of defending the foreign legation. This was it, he thought as he walked down the stone steps to a large courtyard inside the walls. In the flickering shadows cast by the fires of the city he noticed Dr George Morrison. The correspondent looked tired and was covered in soot.

'Have you been out there?' Robert asked.

'Yes, and thank God I am here now,' Morrison replied wearily, wiping the grime from his forehead with the back of his hand. 'I saw some terrible things today,' he continued, staring bleakly into the flickering shadows. 'I saw men and women trussed up like cooking fowls, their eyes gouged out and their noses and ears cut off. I saw others that had been roasted alive on spits and luckier ones who had died from having their throats slit. I tell you, old boy, we are going to have to fight to the death if we do not wish to share their horrible fate.'

'It should never have come to this,' Robert responded bitterly. 'We saw it coming and those supposedly in charge left everything until too late.'

Morrison did not reply and both men stood silently for a moment, listening as the strangled screams for mercy from the continuing massacre of Chinese civilians drifted to them on the hot night air.

'I have matters to attend to,' Morrison finally

said, breaking the silence. 'With the help of Professor James from the Imperial University who acted as interpreter I was able to save a few Chinese converts and their families. Prince Su has agreed to my demands that they be given accommodation in his palace although he has chosen not to hang around.'

'Good for you, Dr Morrison,' Robert said. 'I should also be away to help form a defence. I hope all continues to go well for you.'

Morrison grinned from beneath the soot. 'How much worse could it get?'

'They are neither Boxers nor Imperial soldiers,' Tung hissed softly, crouching beside John, adjacent to an earth embankment. The campfire that the four heavily armed Chinese had built clearly silhouetted them as they sat together.

'We have to get past them,' John whispered.

'That would mean losing many hours of night,' Tung replied, carefully scanning the area beyond the light for any sign of others. 'I think that they are preparing to sleep.'

'Are you considering taking them on?' John asked. 'All we have is a single revolver between us.'

'I have a knife,' Tung responded. 'And we have surprise on our side. I do not sense any others with them.'

'A big gamble,' John said, peering at the region under the embankment. 'What if they have a sentry?'

'I will look,' Tung said. 'If they do not have any sentry then we will strike when they sleep.'

Both men snaked on their bellies to where Andrew and Liling lay together in the long, desiccated grass.

'Tung thinks the party ahead are bandits. They have one modern rifle between them while the others are armed with old muskets,' John briefed Andrew. 'Tung is going up the embankment to see if they have posted any lookouts.'

'Is he planning to find a way of bypassing them?' Andrew asked anxiously.

'Not exactly,' his father replied dryly. 'It appears that we are going to take on the party ahead when they retire for the night.' John did not see the shock in Andrew's face at his explanation.

Within the half hour Tung joined them.

'They do not have guards outside the camp,' he said. 'But they do have one man awake while the others retire to sleep away from the fire. They are not stupid and have made their beds in the dark. I have observed their locations and I think that we should strike in an hour.'

'What do you suggest we each do?' John asked.

'I will circle and with my knife take care of the one who is furthest from the others. I will then move on to the next not far from him and then the third man. You will place yourself within easy range of the man sitting just outside the firelight and shoot him when you hear me call to you,' Tung briefed them. 'It is a simple plan and will work.'

'I can help,' Liling said quietly, producing a small but deadly looking knife.

The three men glanced at her in surprise.

'It will not be necessary,' Tung rejected. 'You are a woman.'

'I have heard that the Boxers have women warriors in their ranks,' Liling said. 'I am no less capable.'

'Have you ever killed before?' Tung asked.

'No, but my village has fallen to bandits in my lifetime,' Liling replied. 'I have no love for such men and am prepared to kill them.'

Andrew was stunned by Liling's declaration. 'I think that you should stay out of this, Liling,' he said. 'Tung and my father can deal with such matters.'

Liling reluctantly slipped the knife back under her blouse.

'It is time,' Tung said, addressing Andrew. 'You and Liling are to remain here while we are away. You will know when we are successful.'

Tung's words caused Andrew a gripping fear. They were spoken so calmly that they did not hide the fact that things could go wrong. Andrew wanted to hug his father and tell him that he loved him, but to do so might imply they were embracing for the last time. Instead, Andrew reached over and touched his father on the arm. 'Be careful, old man,' he said with a forced smile.

'Old man,' John snorted. 'I will show you that your old man has not lost any of his skills in these matters.'

And then his father and Tung were swallowed by the night as they advanced on the unsuspecting bandit camp, leaving Andrew and Liling virtually defenceless. Andrew turned to reassure Liling that they would be safe but Liling was nowhere to be seen!

● ● ●

John had very carefully wriggled into a position opposite the shadowy figure of a short, stocky man holding a musket in his lap. Disturbed by his presence, chirping crickets occasionally ceased their song, and John would freeze as the sentry stirred to stand and look around him then sit down again.

The man was alert, John thought, holding the French military revolver out in front of himself. He was aware that he had to be very close to ensure that his first bullet found its target. Preferably no further than ten feet away in the dark, he calculated, from past experience on similar operations.

When the crickets resumed their song John would crawl slowly forward on his stomach until he was satisfied that he was within range. Now it was only a matter of waiting and wondering how good the former Shaolin priest was. John suspected that Tung was very good, judging how easily he had ambushed the police officer and his Aboriginal tracker back in Queensland.

Something crawled over John's hand and he was forced to stay his instinct to flick it off. He lay waiting, hoping that the heavy beating of his heart could not be heard by the sentry a stone's throw away. Then, everything went wrong.

The sentry suddenly rose, turned to one side and levelled his musket. A voice called to him and a fifth bandit was approaching from the dark. John could not see him but could hear the soft swishing of the grass beneath the man's feet and was suddenly aware the bandit would inadvertently step on him if he continued walking in the direction that he was. No signal had come from Tung and John had only seconds to decide what he should do.

He fired from his prone position, the sound exploding the still night air. The shot missed and the sentry swung in John's direction, bringing his musket to the shoulder. Cursing, John fired but missed once again. The unseen approaching man was on him before he could get to his feet and from the corner of his eye John saw the flickering light shimmer off a sword blade. He attempted to roll and bring his pistol up to bear on the second man, now shouting warnings to his comrades in the camp. Suddenly, the swordsman jerked backwards. Liling! The young woman was standing behind the swordsman, whose warning cries had turned to a gurgling sound.

A musket ball threw up dirt in John's face before he could leap to his feet. The bandit musketeer was also fighting for his life. It was not a long struggle, as Liling's knife had ripped through his throat, almost severing the man's head. The action had taken seconds but it felt like hours to John. The crickets were briefly silenced by the bloody hand-to-hand battle. John regained his feet and realised that his hands were trembling uncontrollably. He still held the pistol but realised that he would have had trouble aiming it if he had to.

'Liling,' he called. 'Are you hurt?'

Liling emerged from the darkness, her clothing stained a dark colour. 'I am unharmed,' she said in a shaky voice.

'They are all dead,' Tung said in a flat tone, joining them 'We had the ancestors on our side.'

In one hand he held a modern bolt-action rifle and a bandolier of ammunition that he had taken from one of the dead bandits. He held it out to John. 'You might be able to use this,' he said. 'It seems that you are not a very good shot with a pistol.'

John accepted the rifle. 'It was dark,' John defended himself, but he saw just a twinkle of mirth in the dark eyes of Tung.

'And you need a woman to protect you as well,' Tung continued, enjoying John's discomfort at his failure to kill the sentry as they had planned.

'Liling did well,' John complimented the young woman as she stood silently staring at the flames of the campfire.

Tung nodded his agreement. 'We must keep moving if we are to be near Pekin by dawn,' Tung said and called to Andrew, who stumbled out of the dark to join them. His eyes first fixed on Liling and John could see his son's great concern for her welfare but any anxiety was quickly replaced with astonishment when he saw the blood-soaked blouse she wore and the bloody knife in her hand.

'What happened?' he gasped, looking from his father to Tung.

'Liling will tell you when she is ready,' John said. He could see that the young woman was in a mild state of shock for what she had done only minutes before. 'Here, take this,' John continued, handing his son the revolver and spare rounds of ammunition. 'You might have better luck with it than I did.'

Andrew accepted the pistol, still staring at Liling in the flickering half light cast by the campfire.

Whatever she had done appeared to have gained respect from both his father and Tung. Their attitude to her was one of deference as they trekked away.

Just before dawn John called a halt. Their trek to Pekin had been slowed by the need to move cautiously in the dark, avoiding any parties of armed men. From time to time they had all smelled the stench of decomposing bodies wafting to them on the night air. And once they had stumbled over a group of bodies huddled together in death; a family, from what they could discern, that had died under the blades of swords.

'We need to rest,' John had said, although Tung did not appear to be tiring.

'We will rest,' Tung agreed without argument. 'I will stand guard.'

John was grateful and under the dim light of the disappearing stars they moved to a copse of spindly trees to seek sleep, which came easily to each of them after the night-long trek.

'Wake up,' a voice reached into John's troubled dreams. 'Dawn will be upon us very soon.'

John sat up, rubbing the sleep from his eyes to peer at a broad orange glow appearing all along the horizon to the east. A small fire was burning and Tung had already warmed the clumps of sticky rice in a small pot they had taken from the bandits' camp.

'The city is closer than we thought,' Tung said to John, handing him his share of the meagre meal. 'All going well we will be able to reach the outer walls by noon.'

'You realise that we will be crossing open plains in broad daylight,' John cautioned. 'I somehow think that we are going to stand out a bit.'

Tung gazed across the plains and reflected on the problem. In the distance they could see a small caravan of around fifty camels winding its way west. 'How much money do you have?' he asked.

'Enough to keep us going,' John replied.

'I think we can intercept one of the caravans and negotiate to travel with them to the city,' Tung said. 'They are men from Mongolia and have no interest in our affairs but do understand the value of British currency. By travelling with them we can pose as guards with the arms you and Andrew carry.'

John thought about the scheme. He sensed that he was so close to his daughter now that the idea was worth the risk. 'We will do it,' he said.

'We will wait here until one draws close and I will talk to them,' Tung said.

John agreed and passed on the plan to Andrew and Liling, who sat side by side on the other side of the fire.

By mid-morning the caravan had wended its way towards their position under the trees. Tung approached the leader, a short stocky man with a flat, broad face darkened by many years of exposure to the weather. John had ensured they remained hidden and trained his rifle on the leader in case things went wrong. It was a tense period of uncertainty until Tung turned to walk back to them.

'It is done,' he said and the three rose from their hide. 'They have agreed to allow us to travel with them into the city for ten English pounds. But keep a wary eye on all of them,' Tung continued. 'They are not to be trusted. The bandits we killed last night are of the same people as these.'

Warning in mind, they fell in with the caravan. By noon the mighty stone walls of Pekin loomed over the heat-baked plains. Above the walls columns of smoke could be seen rising to blot the pale blue skies.

'Pekin,' Andrew, walking beside Liling and his father, said with a touch of awe.

'Impressive,' John replied. 'The city of the Empress and her court – and a lot of Boxers. Now, all we have to do is find your sister and go home.' But even as John articulated the purpose of their hazardous mission, he knew that getting to the city was one thing and getting his beloved daughter home was another matter altogether. He brooded as they plodded towards the city that was already cut off from the rest of the world.

Despite Tung's suspicions concerning the honesty of the men from the sweeping deserts of the Gobi, they were able to smuggle him and his travelling companions into Pekin safely. The leader accepted the payment of British coins and left the foreigners to make their own way to wherever they planned within the city.

John gripped his rifle with his finger not far from

the trigger guard, gazing around at the almost deserted streets. A few brave merchants were continuing to ply their wares and there was some movement of wooden wheelbarrows being pushed by sinewy Chinese conveying their wares to the merchants' stalls. The dust and stench was almost overpowering after being on the river and crossing the hills and plains.

Andrew stood in awe of their surroundings. He had read much about the Orient and Pekin seemed to epitomise all he had imagined with the different Asian faces he saw on the streets: men from Mongolia, the taller Chinese from the north and the paler-skinned Cantonese from the south. Every now and then Andrew recognised the slightest whiff of a familiar incense or herb from his father's own store.

Liling also seemed to be in awe. She had only heard this city spoken of by more senior members of her fishing village who may at some time have visited Pekin.

'I will leave you now,' Tung said, cutting across their reflections on the mysterious city that held the forbidden palace of the Empress. 'My mission will be complete when I return the money to my master. You will need to travel in the direction of the Forbidden City along this road and next to it you will find the European legations. I suspect that under the current conditions your daughter will have sought refuge there. I thank you for your friendship that has helped me complete my mission and I pray that the Son of Heaven also hears of how you helped me. People you meet will direct you to the legation but try to avoid any soldiers. I have a written pass for you,' Tung continued, handing John a sheet of parchment. 'Should you encounter any soldiers or Boxer warriors show their leader this.'

John stared at the sheet of paper upon which were written Chinese characters. 'What does it say?' John asked.

'It states that you are under the protection of a general of the Empress and must be allowed safe passage. The general signed the paper for me but I have altered it to include your names as well.'

'But why will it work?' John asked.

'Because the general named in the pass is most powerful and he is also my uncle,' Tung replied with a faint smile at the surprise he saw in John's face. 'I doubt that any Imperial soldier or Boxer would dare take action without first ensuring the authenticity of the pass.'

John stared at Tung and wondered at this mysterious man. Who was he exactly? No matter who he was, his help had got them this far and now John was on the verge of finding his daughter. 'Thank you, Tung,' John said, holding out his hand in the Western tradition.

Tung accepted John's extended hand. 'It is I who should thank you,' he replied. 'Without probably knowing it, you have done a great service for my country. Soon, we will be a free and sovereign nation to rule ourselves and the rightful Emperor will usurp the court of the Empress, regaining his God-given role as head of our new nation.'

The words that rolled from Tung's tongue were laden with the same conviction that was reflected in his eyes. The former Shaolin priest was a man of action and John could believe that what he said could come about with men such as he to fight for their cause. But at what cost? John had no doubt that Tung was a revolutionary and most probably a Boxer warrior.

'I hope that we meet again,' John said, releasing the grip. 'In better times.'

'So do I, old warrior,' Tung replied with a grim smile. 'You are a worthy man whose Chinese blood is strong.'

Tung turned to Andrew and Liling. 'Andrew, remember all that I have spoken of,' he said. 'My country needs such men as you.'

Andrew nodded, stretching out his hand to his friend. 'And you, sister,' Tung said, addressing Liling. 'You are a true daughter of this land. You have proved that many times.'

Liling was overwhelmed by his words and looked down shyly, but her face was radiant with the praise she received from this man whose spiritual aura was so strong.

Tung turned and walked alone along the street.

John carefully folded the paper pass and placed it into his pocket. He was puzzled by Tung's comment to his son. When he had the opportunity he would ask Andrew what Tung meant. Hefting his rifle he turned to his son and Liling. 'Time to go,' he said and they commenced walking in the direction Tung had pointed out.

Very soon they would see the walls of the Forbidden City loom before them and they were fortunate that they were not accosted by the armed Boxers and soldiers they passed on their way to the compound. It was as if some of Tung's aura had rubbed off on them.

'What did Tung mean when he said China needed men like you?' John finally asked his son as they walked towards the barricades manned by soldiers John recognised as British.

'Nothing really,' Andrew replied evasively. 'Just an expression of his, I guess.'

Andrew's answer did not satisfy John but he had no further chance to question him as a nervous British soldier raised his rifle and called in English for them to halt. John carefully placed his rifle on the street, and raised his hands, replying loudly, 'Don't shoot me, you Pommy bastards, I'm an Australian.'

His broad accent and appearance that seemed at odds with it almost felled the young British soldier.

A British officer manning the barricade turned to the soldier who had issued the challenge. 'Don't shoot him, soldier,' he said in a commanding voice. 'He is a damned colonial from his accent, but probably deserves shooting all the same, for being cheeky.'

'Approach, old chap,' the officer called back. 'Just be careful where you point that rifle.'

John stooped to pick up the rifle and strode towards the barricade where the contingent of British soldiers gawked at the big broad-shouldered Chinese man who spoke English with a colonial accent striding confidently towards them.

'John Wong out of Queensland,' John said when he was allowed through the barricade and was standing before the British officer. 'This is my son, Andrew, and the young lady who speaks no English is Liling. I am here to meet with my daughter, Miss Naomi Wong.'

John wondered at the stricken expression that suddenly appeared on the British officer's face. Then unexpectedly the officer thrust out his hand. 'I am Lieutenant Robert Mumford,' he said. 'And I have news of your daughter that I wish could be better. Please accompany me back to our legation.'

John accepted the handshake but frowned at the young British officer's tone. A father's worst nightmare could be contained in the way the words had been expressed by the officer.

'My daughter?' John asked, hoping that his voice would not crack. 'What news do you have?'

'I think that we should return to the legation, Mr Wong. It is best that we get you and your son a cup of tea before speaking of your daughter.'

Shaken, John and Andrew, with Liling in tow, followed Robert. Liling had not understood the conversation but from the expression on Andrew's face she knew that something was terribly wrong.

Over the promised cup of tea Robert explained that Naomi was missing and told them what he knew of the circumstances behind her abduction. Considering the situation, he felt it wise not to add that he was in love with this fierce-looking man's daughter.

'Your daughter has spoken of your colourful past, Mr Wong,' Robert said, sipping his tea. 'Your added rifle and you will be a welcome addition to our defences. And your son's skills in medicine will be of great help at our hospital. I am sure that Dr Morrison, a fellow countryman of yours, will appreciate his assistance.'

'I am here to find my sister, Mr Mumford,' Andrew said. 'I doubt that my father and I will be remaining after we have found her.'

'If you find Miss Wong,' Robert replied, shifting uncomfortably in his chair, 'I do not think that it would be wise to attempt to travel under the current circumstances. Granted, your appearance gives you an advantage but the Boxers do discriminate between Chinese people and I suspect that neither of you would be able to completely pass as people born in this country. It would be better that you remained with us until we are relieved by our British naval forces.'

'I appreciate your concern, Mr Mumford,' John said. 'But we have already risked much just getting here and my only desire is to get my daughter out of this situation, as you call it.'

Robert put down his cup. He walked to the window of his quarters to gaze at the bedlam in the street. He had learned that around 4000 people now sought refuge within the walls of the legation compound. Of these, around 473 were civilians, an equal number were European or American soldiers, while the remainder were Chinese converts. Most of those from eighteen nations represented were crowded into the British legation quarter and shared the limited space with a flock of sheep, a cow and some

Chinese ponies and mules. Trunks of clothes, mattresses and bedding spilled over into the crowded street while harried British civil servants pointed the way to a recently refurbished chapel which would provide shelter for refugees of every denomination. Robert wondered how they would feed the refugees but dismissed the thought when he reminded himself that he was a soldier whose duty was to defend those same people. Feeding was someone else's problem.

'You are welcome to share my Spartan quarters,' Robert suddenly said, turning with his hands behind his back. 'Feel free to use my name if you need anything and I can ask Dr Morrison to provide quarters for your Chinese girl.'

Both John and Andrew looked at each other in surprise. This total stranger had offered to share his quarters with them.

'That is very generous, Mr Mumford,' Andrew thanked. 'But you hardly know us.'

'Let us say that I was – am – very fond of Miss Wong,' Robert struggled. 'Her welfare is primary among my non-military priorities. If there is any way I can assist you in finding her, be assured it will be done.'

John sensed that the British officer was struggling in relation to Naomi but he did not question the man immediately. Was it possible this man was courting his daughter? Strangely, Naomi had not mentioned his name in any of her letters home. 'Is it that my daughter holds a special interest to you, Mr Mumford?' he at length asked quietly.

Robert stared directly at John. 'It could be said

that I have a special interest in your daughter, sir,' he replied. 'I have already attempted to locate her, however without any success. But I will do so again when I am able.'

John did not press the matter. He suspected that his daughter's beauty crossed all barriers of race. He even felt sympathy for the young British officer who fought to keep his true feelings to himself. 'We will find her,' John assured him. 'I promise you that.'

'You may be able to provide us with valuable information on what you saw and encountered on your journey here,' Robert said, turning the conversation from the sensitive subject of Naomi. 'As you can see, we are somewhat besieged and any news from beyond the legation walls is greatly appreciated.'

John provided a brief outline of their trek from the coast to Pekin, being careful to mention Liling's invaluable role in assisting them with her family's sampan. He did not, however, mention Tung or his role in their journey. After all, Tung was a wanted man in the colony of Queensland and John thought it wise to keep the former Shaolin priest out of any report of their affairs.

Robert listened with interest. 'Tientsin appears to be cut off as well,' he sighed heavily. 'We were hoping to see a relief force come to our assistance by now.'

'We didn't see any signs of European troops,' John said.

'Well, I suppose that I should take you over to meet Dr Morrison,' Robert concluded. 'I am sure that your Chinese girl could do with some rest, as I suspect so could you.'

As much as John wanted to set out straightaway into the city in search of his daughter, he also realised just how exhausted they were from the arduous journey.

Dr George Morrison impressed Andrew from the very outset of their meeting and although dirt-stained and sweating, the tall, charismatic Australian carried the aura of a man in command.

'So you are from Queensland,' Morrison said, gripping Andrew's hand firmly. 'I have visited your colony.'

'Ah, Mr Wong,' Morrison said, turning to John. 'Your exploits are not unknown to me.'

John also fell under the journalist's spell and when he looked around him he could see a mass of Chinese men, women and children attempting to make a home for themselves in the cramped area.

Morrison noticed John's interest in the people around them – many he had personally rescued from certain death at the hands of the Boxers. 'Your linguistic skills will be invaluable to me here,' he said. 'At the moment my own grasp of the language is rudimentary at best. It appears, from what Mr Mumford has told me, you are fluent in Mandarin.'

'Not me,' John confessed. 'My son, Andrew, is the linguist. I just get by.'

When Morrison turned his attention to Liling, Andrew could see that the handsome journalist was admiring her. He even introduced himself to Liling in passable Chinese, to which Liling reacted with pleasure. Just for a moment Andrew experienced a pang of jealousy towards this accomplished man but quickly let that feeling go when Morrison immediately returned his attention to Andrew and his father.

'There has been some discussion that able-bodied civilian males will be armed and form a kind of militia to help boost the defences,' Morrison said. 'Knowing of your past I would expect you to join our little army, Mr Wong.'

Although John had not considered staying any longer than it took to find his daughter, under the gaze of Morrison he suddenly found it hard to say no. 'I suppose I could do that,' he replied.

'And you, Mr Wong,' Morrison said, addressing Andrew. 'I believe that you are a student of my old alma mater in Edinburgh. How far have you advanced?'

'Final year,' Andrew replied.

'Good, I will need assistance with the hospital when things warm up. Your skills will be invaluable. I hope that you can be of assistance. I can provide quarters for Miss Liling with my female servants as I believe Mr Mumford has provided you with accommodation.'

'Thank you, and it would be an honour to work in the hospital,' Andrew replied. 'I am sure that Liling could be trained by me to assist.'

'A good idea,' Morrison said with a broad smile. 'I am afraid my duties as a journalist will keep me away from any medical practices.'

Andrew was surprised that the Australian doctor

should choose journalism over medicine when he considered how difficult it was to study and qualify in that field. But then this man had struck him as intriguing from the moment they had met.

'Well, I must excuse myself to attend to administrative matters,' Morrison said. 'If you need to know anything you only have to ask Kai over there. He works for me.'

John and Andrew glanced across the busy yard crowded with refugees to see a wizened Chinese shouting orders at the confused and despondent men, women and children.

'Kai!' Morrison called. 'Come over here and meet these people.'

Kai desisted from ordering people around and walked over to them. 'You must look after these people,' Morrison said. 'And now I must bid you a good day but will meet with you both again very soon. We have a lot to talk about.'

As Morrison strode away Andrew introduced himself, his father and Liling in Chinese and the surly expression permanently set on Kai's face appeared to crack for a brief moment.

'You speak Mandarin with an accent,' he said. 'You are not from here.'

'A place in another country called Queensland,' Andrew replied.

'Is that near Canton?' Kai queried.

'No, it is nearer where Dr Morrison once lived.'

'Ah, the country of Victoria,' Kai answered, delighted at being able to demonstrate his knowledge of international geography to the strangers.

Andrew smiled. His answer was close enough.

'You have the same family name as the woman the lieutenant was searching for,' Kai continued. 'I was with him when we went into the city.'

At the mention of Robert's search for Naomi, both John and Andrew expressed surprise.

'Will you tell us about that?' Andrew asked.

When Kai gave a detailed account of the night patrol into the city John's perception of the English officer was greatly elevated. It was obvious that Robert Mumford had more than a passing interest in Naomi.

'Could you tell us where Lieutenant Mumford thought that there might be a chance of finding the woman he sought?' Andrew grilled.

'I could,' Kai replied. 'But it would be too dangerous to go there now.'

John gestured to Andrew to desist from asking any more questions. What he had learned to date could be added to by Mumford himself. Already matters were falling into place.

John left his son and Liling at the legation's hospital and returned to Robert's quarters where he selected a relatively quiet corner to bed down on the stone floor. Like the absence of any wind before a sudden summer storm John drifted into a deep and troubled sleep.

The distant but constant crash of gunfire ripped John from his sleep and he grabbed for the rifle beside him. Staggering to his feet, groggy from having his rest interrupted, John glanced at a large ticking clock on the officer's wall. It read 4 pm and he stumbled out of the room into the street.

A man wearing a white shirt and pants with a revolver strapped to his hip was running by the quarters. 'What's happening?' John shouted

'I don't know but keep your head down,' the man flung back over his shoulder.

John shrugged and returned to his temporary quarters.

He awoke the following morning before dawn, and went in search of something to eat and drink. He still had a good quantity of coins, as did Andrew, and expected that his money should be good.

On the street John saw a mass of confused people, mostly European but many Chinese refugees as well. He had decided to walk over to the area known as the Fu, which was designated for the Chinese converts, when he saw Morrison's servant, Kai, head down, hurrying along the street. When John stopped him Kai informed him that he had left Andrew and Liling at the Fu. Kai provided directions and John strode out to visit the former Chinese palace now commandeered for quarters. As John walked along the street, he noticed soldiers and civilians hurriedly piling bricks and sandbags in open spaces between the buildings as fortification against attack. Considering what he had gleaned about the obvious threat from the Boxers leading up to the siege, John wondered why this had not been done before.

His path carried him onto the broad street where the Russian legation sat opposite its American counterpart, then across a bridge spanning a canal that took him between the Japanese, German and French legation compounds until he turned north to continue his walk towards the former palace.

Eventually he reached the Fu, a beautiful and spacious building with ornate gardens, where he saw Andrew and Liling distributing cooked rice to lines of refugees.

'Hello, Father,' Andrew greeted cheerily, seeing John striding towards him. 'How did you sleep last night?'

'Very well,' John replied, propping his rifle against his hip. 'You wouldn't have a cup of tea and a bowl of rice for your old man, would you?'

Andrew spoke to Liling who produced a mug of hot green tea while Andrew filled a bowl with a meal of watery rice and meat.

John glanced at the food in his bowl. 'I trust the meat is pork,' he said.

'Horse meat tomorrow,' Andrew replied. 'It seems that we are lucky that the spring races are over and the horses available for consumption.'

John glanced around and could see a few Europeans tending to the health care of the Chinese. They were predominantly European women doing the aid work and John could hear the languages of Italy, Germany and France besides English being used to people who, although they understand none of them, did understand what the speakers were attempting to do.

'There appears to be no shortage of qualified medical staff here,' Andrew said, ladling a meal into a bowl being held by an old woman who thanked him before hobbling aside to allow a young mother with a child on her hip to fill her bowl. 'So, I have decided to join you in Dr Morrison's militia.'

'You don't know anything about soldiering,' John retorted. 'Stay here with Liling and help the medical staff.'

'I would rather be with you in case we get the opportunity to go into the city and find Naomi,' Andrew said, reminding his father of their primary mission. John had to cede to that point and said nothing further. The occasional popping sound of gunfire suddenly became more than a distant noise when an empty clay jar exploded on the table only inches from where Andrew was serving the rice. Andrew leaped aside, dropping his ladle. 'What the bloody hell was that?' he yelped, looking around him.

'That, son,' John answered calmly, 'is what a spent bullet can do. I suspect that the Boxers – or Imperial troops – are closing in on the Fu with sharpshooters.'

Andrew stared at his father who continued to sip his tea as if nothing had happened.

'I think I will look for Lieutenant Mumford and ask him about his search for Naomi,' John said, placing his mug back on the trestle and trailing his rifle. 'I will learn all that he has to tell me about where he suspects she may have been held, and from there we will discuss our own search for your sister. I will also find Dr Morrison and sign up for his militia.'

'Don't forget to sign me up as well,' Andrew said, picking up the ladle to resume his assigned duties. 'If nothing else I can shoot as well as you.'

'That's your opinion,' John grinned. 'Besides, these targets shoot back.'

Andrew had not fully considered the implications of his decision to volunteer until his father reminded him and now he thought about Tung. Was it possible he could become one of the targets in the Boxers' gunsights?

'What are you going to do with Liling?' John asked before he walked away.

'Liling remains beside me,' Andrew replied without any hesitation. 'But she can reside here at night. She has already met a woman from Taku who knows her family. She will not be totally alone among strangers.'

'Fair enough,' John said. As he walked away a ricocheting bullet exploded a fine film of dust in front of him, but he ignored the wayward shot and continued on his way.

It was early evening before John could speak to Robert, as upon returning to the officer's quarters he had found him fully clothed on his bed and in a deep sleep.

John decided to explore the grounds of the legation defences and familiarise himself with the layout. He gazed from the British legation grounds across the broad Imperial Carriage Park to the golden glitter of the tiles of the Imperial palace. It was strange, he thought. This country was so foreign to him although it had been the land of his father, and yet his own son was fascinated with all things Chinese. John turned away from the sight of the Imperial palace quarters to scan the area around the British buildings. Of solid stone, these looked more normal to him even if there was a hint of Oriental architecture in the structures.

The sporadic rifle shots echoing all around the legation did not cause him to flinch as it did those who had never come under fire before, but John was suddenly aware of another ominous sound in the hot, dry air of the city's summer. It was not a familiar sound and he cowered when an artillery shell exploded some distance off in the legation grounds. Artillery! The Chinese were shelling them! The stakes had been raised considerably, the Queenslander thought as he saw the dirty, grey dust from the explosion rise above the tiled rooftops of outbuildings not far from where he stood.

The thump of the exploding artillery round awoke Robert who rolled instinctively from his bed onto the floor. He kneeled for a moment attempting to gather his thoughts and finally rose to his feet when he ascertained that he was intact. Robert knew about artillery bombardments from his days soldiering on the North-West Frontier, and had seen at first hand the terrible wounds shrapnel could cause to the body.

'I see that you are awake, Mr Mumford,' John said, leaning his rifle against the wall. 'I need to discuss a matter with you.'

'Speak, Mr Wong,' Robert said, slipping his service pistol into the holster attached to his belt.

'Do you have any long-term intentions towards my daughter?' John asked, causing Robert to blink in his surprise at the man's forwardness.

'I have one regret, sir,' Robert replied. 'That I did not signal my love for your daughter before she was taken from us.'

John nodded. 'Then I can presume that you would do anything within your power to find her – as I have come to learn that you attempted in the past,' John said.

'I would, Mr Wong,' Robert answered. 'That is an oath on my word as an officer of Her Majesty.'

'I will hold you to your oath,' John said.

'Some weeks ago I was able to glean intelligence that Naomi may have been held in a house not far from here,' Robert told him. 'I made an attempt to storm the house but we were driven back by superior forces. Since then my duties have forced me to remain within the legation compound. But there is not a day that goes past that I don't pray for the opportunity to attempt another search for her.'

John could hear the sincerity in the young man's voice and did not doubt he would assist him find Naomi. Already a plan was forming in his mind how he would do that. It would require the assistance of Dr Morrison's servant, Kai, and faith in the pass Tung had given him when they parted. But, above all, it would require a lot of luck. He well understood that finding his daughter in a city teeming with hostile forces would be like finding a needle in a haystack.

'I would require information from you on where your intelligence suggests are the weakest points of the Boxers' perimeter around the legation,' John said. 'Do you have that information?'

'I will be coordinating such a plan,' Robert said. 'But, at the moment we are blind to what is happening beyond our defences. We do not have much idea of the enemy's strength, arms or disposition at the moment. Worse still, we are not exactly sure if the Imperial army of the Empress has allied itself to the Boxer forces besieging us.'

'I would suspect that the occasional artillery round passing overhead comes from the Imperial arsenal,' John said with a wry smile. 'And I don't have to be a soldier to guess that.'

Robert returned the smile. 'Had you chosen to be, I am sure you would have been a fine soldier. Your daughter proudly boasted to me of her father's colonial exploits.'

John was warming to the young English officer and wondered why his daughter had not thought it worth mentioning him in her letters. Maybe she was not in love with him, John thought. Or was she afraid to tell her father she was in love with an English officer, fearing that her father would disapprove of a man whom he might perceive to be one who might desert her because of her race? But then, what male understood the vastly complex workings of the female mind – even that of a daughter.

'Do you have something in mind?' Robert asked.

'I am hoping that by tomorrow morning you will be able to furnish me with enough information about the Boxer dispositions for me to plan a way into the city,' John replied. 'And as soon as the sun goes down I will attempt to make my way in with Dr Morrison's man to guide me back to that house where you suspect my daughter is being held.'

'My thoughts were a long shot, Mr Wong,' Robert said. 'And even if it had been where she was, I would guess that by now the Boxers might have moved themselves to somewhere else in the city. I think what you are planning is foolhardy. It would be better to wait until a relieving force arrives and then go in search of your daughter.'

'You don't even know if a relieving force is on its way,' John countered. 'If I don't find my daughter very soon, rescuing her will be a moot point if I remain to be massacred along with the rest of you inside the legation.'

Robert silently agreed with the Queenslander's summation of their position; cut off from the rest of the world, they had heard nothing of a relieving force coming to their aid. He was pragmatic enough to know it would only be a matter of time before they were eventually swamped by the sheer numbers of the enemy against them. It was not a thought he dared express openly but instead kept up an example of cheerful optimism in front of soldiers and civilians alike.

Robert rubbed his face with his hand. 'I would be with you, Mr Wong,' he said. 'But my duties here prevent that. Believe me when I say I would not hinder you in your foolish plan if it meant the slightest hope of finding Naomi.'

'I believe you, Mr Mumford,' John said. 'I am not

even telling my son what I plan to do and ask that you don't mention it to him either.'

'You have my word,' Robert replied. 'I pray that you succeed and I will help to the best of my ability.'

'If I don't make it,' John said quietly. 'I expect you to do all in your power to save my daughter.'

In the morning he would go to Morrison and request the help of Kai then, after the sun went down, he would find the best way through the defensive perimeter into the city. He had the pass and would exchange his rifle with Andrew for the use of the revolver, which could easily be concealed. As the English officer had said, it was a long shot. But anything was better than sitting out each day agonising over the fate of his beloved Naomi.

The following morning John walked over to the Fu for a meal and to meet with Morrison. He had hardly stepped onto the bridge spanning the Jade River canal when he stepped back to avoid being run down by a stampeding mass of panicked soldiers. As they passed him John could see the uniforms of German, Italian, French, Austrian, Japanese, Russian and American riflemen. He grabbed an American by the sleeve. 'What's happening?' he asked.

'Word has come down the line from that Austrian commander that the defences have been overrun,' he said, yanking away from John to continue his retreat towards the British compound.

John knew enough about the defences to realise that, if the Fu was being abandoned, they had just lost three-quarters of the area that they needed to hold the Boxers at bay. A cold chill swept over him. Andrew and Liling were in the Fu and if it had fallen then their lives were in great peril.

Pushing through the soldiers cramming the bridge, John forced his way onto a street leading to the former Chinese palace compound. His rifle was loaded and contained a full magazine of heavy rounds. He was running and came to a stop when he saw only civilians milling around the compound with expressions of confusion and concern.

With Liling at his side, Andrew saw his father and called to him.

'What in bloody hell is going on?' John gasped, fighting to catch his breath after the hard run from the bridge.

'From what I can gather,' Andrew growled, 'that stupid Austrian naval captain, von Thomann, heard a rumour that the American legation had been abandoned and without checking ordered a retreat back to the British legation. But as you can see we are now without any defence for the converts. As a matter of fact we are now wide open to an all-out attack.'

The words were hardly out of Andrew's mouth when their attention was drawn to the south-eastern horizon where a pillar of smoke was rising over the tops of the tiled roofs of the Fu.

'That's coming from the Italian area,' John said, remembering that the Italian legation stood at the outer edges of the defensive perimeter. 'It looks like the attack has started. Time you and Liling came back with me to the British compound.'

'Under the circumstances, I cannot leave these people to the mercy of the Boxers,' Andrew said, sweeping his hand to the crowd of frightened Chinese filling the open spaces of the former palace.

'Don't be stupid,' John snapped. 'You have to get out of here before the Boxers arrive. There is nothing you can do for these people.'

'I have my pistol,' Andrew said, touching the hand grip of the revolver in his belt. 'You take Liling with you and I will be all right.'

'You bloody fool,' John snarled, his patience stretched by his son's gallant but foolish gesture. 'You are no good to anyone staying here if you are going to get yourself killed.'

A bullet smacked into a stone column only feet from where they stood, and a tiny chip of stone struck Andrew in the face, causing him to flinch although no harm had come apart from a slight swelling that would turn to a bruise.

John was seriously considering dragging his son from the compound when Liling gripped John's arm.

'Soldiers are coming!' she shouted, pointing to the stream of armed men returning to defend the Fu.

'Someone has shown some sense,' John muttered, releasing his grip on the sleeve of his son's shirt. 'All we have to do is pray that the rebels haven't realised that we have dropped our defences.'

John's prayer was answered. For an unknown reason the Boxers had not pressed home an all-out attack on the fleeing soldiers.

• • •

'We will burn the barbarians out.'

Tung listened to the closing words of the impassioned speech by the commander of the Boxer contingent assembled in a deserted warehouse well back from the besieged quarters of the European powers. Dust filtered down onto the colourfully dressed armed warriors from the rafters where doves cooed.

Yung Lo was an impressive man. He was in fact a general of the Dowager Empress's Imperial army, and a battle-scarred veteran of campaigns waged against warlords in the name of the Imperial court. His voice echoed in the spacious building that once housed goods destined for Europe.

The situation of the siege needed to be resolved quickly as Tung, like many of his comrades, was aware that even now a multinational relief force under the command of a British admiral was fighting its way towards Pekin. Despite the logic in the proposed scheme Tung worried about his friends inside the legation compounds.

'Your commanders have been issued their orders and so you are dismissed to carry them out in the name of the divine Empress.'

Although Tung had been given command of his own contingent of Boxer warriors he had not as yet committed them to the fight against the Europeans. This would be his first action in Pekin for the cause. The cry of '*Sha! Sha!*' that rose from the voices of the five hundred Boxers assembled following the Chinese general's speech caused the doves to take flight and search for a more peaceful place to roost.

Commanders directed their men to assemble for the issuing of flammable materials to accomplish the task of setting the legation compounds ablaze and Tung prepared himself to issue his orders to his own men.

'Tung,' Yung Lo called out, walking with precise strides towards him. Tung turned to the military commander and waited obediently.

'Orders have been issued, but there is one very special task I am assigning you and your men, which I have not informed the other commanders of for reasons I think you will understand. I have assigned to your men the task of setting the Hanlin alight,' Yung Lo said, eyeing the former Shaolin priest square in the face.

'The Hanlin!' Tung replied, attempting to stifle his horror. 'But it is our most precious place of learning, honourable general.'

The Hanlin, a beautifully painted pavilion, housed the most ancient Chinese texts and was as much a university for the Chinese as Oxford was for the English. Filled with silk-covered volumes of writings by China's masters, its shelves contained the very heart and soul of China itself. The task given to Tung for his men to destroy such a place was almost beyond comprehension.

'It is also adjoining the British legation,' the general replied. 'We are at war and the Hanlin represents our past. What we do now is for the present and future. We must not look backwards. Besides, its burning will bring a lot of the Europeans out into our lines of fire when they attempt to put out the fire. If nothing else they have a sentimental if foolish desire to see that we keep our past. I suspect that this desire is motivated by the idea we are a backward people steeped in the knowledge of past glories.'

'Honourable general, I am as loyal to the cause as any man,' Tung attempted to protest. 'But will not the mandarins of the court themselves object to this task. After all, it is they who resist change to our old ways.'

The tough general glared icily at Tung, weighing up the young man's commitment to total war. 'Your uncle, General Tung, is a very old friend of mine,' he said quietly. 'We have shared many a campfire on the barren snow plains of this land fighting for the people. He has told me of your remarkable achievements in the recent past. But he and I suspect that you may be working for the imprisoned false emperor with his subversive ideas of progress. To complete this task will prove that you are totally committed to our revolution.'

Tung was trapped. It was true that he was committed to the cause of freeing China from the invaders, but it was also true that he was loyal to the rightful Emperor and his ideals of a nation freed by progressive ideas. Had not the Emperor, the Son of Heaven, predicted that this new European century would see the rise of China, to take its rightful place among the nations of the world. The general had set Tung a test of his loyalty. The burning of the Hanlin would not be popular with many of his own men.

'I will do it,' Tung finally ceded.

'Good,' the general said. He turned on his heel,

leaving the odious task to a man he would rather have beheaded, if it were not for loyalty to his old comrade-in-arms, General Tung.

The evening air was muggy and the flickering candlelight cast shadows on the sketched disposition of the legation laid out on the table. Robert had used his revolver to hold down one end of the curled-up sheet of paper while the candle stand kept down the other end.

John leaned over the map Robert had drawn and scanned for a weak point in what the English officer guessed, at best, were the Boxers' current siege lines.

'Since the debacle today our lines of defence have shrunk somewhat,' Robert said, pointing with the end of a long cigar at his map. 'That could be a good thing. We have abandoned the Dutch and Belgian legations and only have seven legations to defend. The Austrians and Italians stupidly lost their grounds and according to my calculations we are now defending a rectangular area approximately 700 by 750 yards. However, in our sector we are most vulnerable to an attack at these points,' Robert continued, pointing to the north of the British legation where the ancient Hanlin Academy connected with the legation. 'And here,' he indicated, shifting his cigar pointer to the south and west where lay the Imperial Carriage Park and the Mongol Market.

John examined the places on the map depicting the European legation compounds, and could see that the defended area included the American and Russian legations, overshadowed by the massive Tartar Wall at one end of Legation Street, while the French were at the opposite end. In the south lay the British legation and the continuation of the great Tartar Wall. At its centre were the German, Japanese and Spanish legations as well as the popular Hotel de Pekin and a mix of banks, shops and residential houses.

'Where do you suspect the rebels are weakest?' John asked, continuing to peer at the map under the flickering light.

'Nowhere,' Robert answered bluntly. 'At least that is my guess. We don't have enough intelligence to spot any breaks in their lines.'

John straightened his back and stood back from the table. 'I have to go tonight,' he said. 'My daughter has been long enough in the hands of those bastards.'

'Mr Wong, I would advise against any attempt to enter the city at this stage.'

'The longer I wait the less chance my daughter will be alive – if this relieving force of yours ever arrives at all,' John replied with a growl.

Robert sighed, smoke drifting on the humid evening air like a shroud around their heads. 'If you insist, all I can suggest is that you use this part of our defences to enter the city,' he said, pointing at a section of the defensive line. 'Reports that I have received indicate the least amount of sharpshooting and enemy activity at this point.'

'I will leave sometime after midnight,' John said.

'I will be at the barricade to ensure that you don't get shot by one of our own,' Robert offered. 'I pray with all my heart that you find Naomi. Good luck and good hunting, Mr Wong,' he said stiffly, offering his hand. 'I will still be on duty at the barricade when you return Naomi to us all.'

Robert picked up his revolver and holstered it to return to his post on the barricades, leaving John to snatch a little sleep before rising to fetch and brief Kai.

Together John and Kai made their way through the dark streets towards a burning lantern set at the barricades to provide illumination against any attempted sneak attack. Soldiers wearing the uniforms of many nations manned the improvised walls, some sleeping while others crouched awake behind the motley items used as sandbags.

Robert emerged from the shadows with a British NCO. 'Sergeant Higgins will brief you on the best possible route out of here,' Robert said, referring to the small but tough-looking British NCO beside him. John could see from the ribands on his uniform that the moustachioed sergeant was a veteran of many colonial campaigns.

'Yer best bet is to use the shadows over there,' the sergeant briefed, indicating a side of the street to their right. 'From there yer could chance duckin' into a 'ouse an makin' yer way back through the laneways. Does yer heathen friend know the city?' he asked, referring to Kai.

'He does, sergeant,' John replied.

'Good thing then,' the sergeant continued. 'Cos

all I could see today was that the only part of the street free of the heathens was where I said.'

'Thank you, sergeant,' John said.

'Very good, sah,' the British NCO answered and John could detect a slight note of contempt. No doubt he had observed John as being 'not quite a white man' and therefore not a gentleman that Mr Mumford should be assisting.

Without another word John moved away into the dark behind the barricades, followed by Kai and Robert. When they came to a small opening in the defences John and Kai pushed their way through into the vacant street beyond any illumination cast by the lanterns at the barrier. Only the vague silhouette of the buildings stood out against the starlit night.

Even with Kai very close by John suddenly felt very much alone. It was as if he had passed between the earth and the heavens but was in a place called limbo.

'This way,' Kai hissed, taking the lead as they encountered the first stone buildings on the street. 'House got yard.'

In the darkness John could barely make out Kai's back and his straining ears picked up the muffled sound of movement beyond the walls. Kai also heard the sound and froze. It seemed that they were only a wall width away from the enemy.

John was tempted to draw his revolver from under his shirt but knew his best chance, albeit a slim one, of breaking through the enemy lines was with Kai bluffing that they were sympathisers of the Boxer cause.

'No good,' Kai whispered in a frightened voice. 'We go back.'

'No,' John said in a low but forceful tone. 'We go on.'

Kai's expression of fear turned to terror when a figure emerged unexpectedly from the dark nearby and cried out a warning that was followed by the sharp report of a rifle firing.

John felt himself being flung back as if he had been punched in the chest by a giant. He was vaguely aware that Kai had already disappeared into the darkness.

'Shot,' John mumbled to himself. He was fighting to stay on his feet and fumbled for his revolver. Loud voices only feet away joined the confusion around him and he was aware that a burning brand of fire was spiralling through the night sky, landing in the street in a scattered blaze of embers and lighting up where he stood.

Three Boxers armed with rifles were standing only yards away and a volley of shots from the barricades felled one of them, just missing John with the ominous crack around his head.

'Run, old boy!' a distant voice called to John, who was fighting a battle with the numbing pain in his chest.

'Over here!'

John forgot about attempting to retrieve his pistol to fight it out with the now-disappearing Boxers falling back behind the buildings. Instead, he turned and stumbled towards the barricades.

Like a drunken man he staggered, fighting to keep his feet as he closed the distance between himself and the exposed faces of the defenders who were cheering him on to safety. While bullets whipped around him the defenders laid down fire to cover John's retreat from the enemy. But he did not make it. Within reach of the improvised sandbag wall, John pitched forward into oblivion.

Strong hands dragging him ... Nothing, then a lazy buzzing sound ... Nothing. Hard to breathe and now a low moaning sound mingled with a soothing voice of a woman, as if crooning to a baby ... Nothing again until the tickling but annoying sensation of very tiny feet on his face.

Thirst. John experienced a terrible thirst and croaked, 'Water.'

'Doctor,' the now familiar woman's voice called.

John opened his eyes to stare up at a fly-specked white ceiling. He was aware that he was lying on a stone floor and that flies buzzed around his head. The pain in his left side caught him when he attempted to sit up and he was restrained by a gentle hand of the woman kneeling beside him.

'I am Miss Condit Smith,' she said in an American accent. 'And you should remain still until Dr Poole has a chance to examine your wound.'

John did not reply but turned his head to see a tall, well-built, bearded man lying beside him in a pool of blood. John recognised his blood-soaked uniform as that of a Russian Cossack. The young soldier's face had a ghastly green tinge and his eyes were barely open.

'Poor man,' Polly said, observing John's gaze. 'He was shot through the chest yesterday and the staff do not expect him to live.'

'A hospital?' John whispered hoarsely.

'You are in a hospital,' Polly answered. 'You were brought in last night from the barricades.'

'Shot where?' John asked, suspecting that he too had a chest wound.

'The doctor will speak to you,' Polly evaded, returning her attention to the young soldier.

The doctor, accompanied by a young lady wearing a long, flowing dress, squatted beside John and grasped his wrist to check his pulse. John hardly took any notice of the doctor's examination but found himself staring into the beautiful, slightly sloping, green eyes of the young woman standing beside the doctor. She had a lustrous pile of chestnut hair framing a very pale face of flawless complexion and John guessed that she was in her early thirties.

'I doubt if your wound will take you the same way as our Russian friend,' the doctor said bluntly. 'The bullet smashed a couple of ribs but exited. All we have to do is avoid septus and you will be up on your feet in no time. Miss Gurevich will keep an eye on you, Mr Wong. Your son has been assisting us with our work here and tells me that you have had worse in the past,' he added with a smile.

'You can allow him to drink now, Miss Gurevich,' the doctor said, standing to speak to the young woman beside him. 'I will be back to examine you and change the dressing in around a couple of hours from now,' the doctor said in conclusion, leaving

John in the company of two young ladies and the dying Cossack.

'You must allow me to help you bend your head so that you may sip the water,' the Russian woman said. 'I am not a nurse, and this is new to me.'

John allowed the woman to place her hand under his head and help him half sit to swallow the warm, brackish water poured from a clay cup. The pain when he was moved caused John to wince, closing his eyes, but he did not cry out.

'You speak very good English,' John said through gritted teeth.

'I am a governess,' Miss Gurevich said, lowering John's head to the floor. 'My employers have always been Americans, Mr Wong. I have lived as long in America as I have in my own country.'

'So you are a nurse now,' John commented, attempting to ignore the racking pain in his chest.

'For the moment,' Miss Gurevich replied.

'Will you be caring for me,' John asked, 'as Miss Condit Smith seems to be doing for your countryman there?'

John's suggestion brought a scowl to the woman's beautiful features. 'He is a Cossack,' she said, dismissing the dying man without much sympathy.

For a moment John was puzzled about her dismissal of the man but suddenly he understood.

'You are a Jew,' he said, remembering how much suffering the Cossacks had inflicted on Jewish villages in Russia in their pogroms. The woman looked at him with an expression of surprise.

'How did you know that?' she asked, her mouth

slightly agape to reveal tiny but perfectly aligned teeth.

'One of my best friends in Queensland is Jewish,' John answered. 'He and his wife have told me of the purges the Tsar has launched against your people in Russia. My own daughter has an old Jewish name. I had her christened Naomi.'

'But you are not Jewish,' the Russian woman stated.

'How do you know that?' John replied with a weak smile.

'Because you had your daughter christened,' the woman replied, with her own trace of a faint smile. 'I think that you try to flirt with me, Mr Wong.'

'I would like it that you called me John. It would be nice to hear my name spoken by a beautiful woman in this hellhole of a hospital,' John said with a widening smile. 'If it is not forward I would like to know your given name.'

'It is Elizaveta,' the young woman said. 'My American friends call me Liza.'

'Well, I am a Queenslander,' John said with some pride. 'And I think Liza sounds like a beautiful name.'

'That is enough, Mr Wong, if you wish to have me remain to assist you in your recovery.'

'John, please call me John.'

'To do so would be forward of me,' Liza replied. 'I know nothing about you other than that you have a daughter called Naomi – and no doubt a wife.'

'No wife,' John replied with a note of sadness in his voice. 'She is dead a long time but left me with a wonderful son and daughter. Both are here in the city. My son Andrew is helping out your doctors and my daughter has been taken by the Boxers. I am here to get her back.'

Liza registered her surprise. 'I have met your son, Andrew, but he is Chinese . . . I am sorry, Mr Wong,' she said. 'I did not want you to think that I have a prejudice against Chinese people.'

'My Irish blood understands what you are saying,' John said, fighting the pain that talking caused him.

'I must visit other people,' Liza said, rising to her feet and brushing down her long skirt.

'You will return before I die?' John asked cheekily, eliciting a smile from the young woman.

'You will not die in this hospital, Mr Wong,' she replied, leaving John with a gentle smile and swish of her dress as she walked away from him.

John turned his head to see that the American woman had also left the Cossack, to attend to other duties. Now he was alone at the end of the make-shift ward with only the dying soldier and many flies buzzing in the hot air around his head.

John's next visitor was Andrew, who approached his father fighting back tears he hoped would be concealed in the dim light of the approaching evening.

'Mr Mumford came over to the Fu to inform me that you had been wounded,' he said, kneeling by his father. 'I came as soon as he told me.'

'Nothing to worry about,' John reassured his son who was feebly wiping his face to hide both his concern and his relief.

'You should have had me at your side,' Andrew chided.

'You have other concerns in your life now,' John replied, taking his son's hand in a strong grip of reassurance. 'Where is Liling?'

'She is at the Fu helping with the refugees,' Andrew answered. 'She is a marvellous woman.'

'I know,' John said with a sigh. 'She reminds me of your mother in many ways.'

'I also met with Kai who said that you were on a mission to find Naomi when you were shot.'

'That was the idea – except for getting shot,' John replied. 'All I have to do now is get out of here and try again.'

'Maybe we should wait for the relief force to arrive before we do so,' Andrew said. 'Mr Mumford is pretty sure they will come.'

'It may be too late for your sister,' John countered. He did not add *if she is still alive* because he refused to entertain that option. He was his beloved daughter's father and of all the men in the world it was his supreme duty to protect her. 'I am sure I will find a way to go back out.'

'If you do then I will be coming with you,' Andrew said firmly.

'No, I can't afford to lose you if anything happens,' John said, equally as firmly.

'Mr Wong,' a voice came from nearby.

'Ah, Liza, you have returned to see if I am still alive,' John said with a grin, recognising the young woman. 'I believe that you have already met Miss Gurevich,' John added, when Andrew stood up to greet the new arrival in the ward.

'We have met,' Andrew said, smiling at the young

woman holding a porcelain bowl filled with rice and cooked bully beef.

'I have come to feed your father,' Liza said. 'Or would you rather do that?'

Andrew glanced at his father and saw the expression of disapproval shadow his face. You old dog, Andrew thought with a start. It was obvious that his father preferred the Russian woman to tend to his needs. He had not thought of his father in that way before and it came as a shock after the many years he had known his father to shun the company of women for the sake of his mother's memory.

'I, ah, think that you would be best to look after my father,' Andrew said tactfully, 'as I must return to the Fu to look after the people there. I will visit again tomorrow morning,' he added in parting, leaving his father alone with the Russian woman.

'Your son is a fine young man,' Liza said, kneeling beside John to spoon him the meal. 'I believe he is training to be a doctor.'

'He is,' John replied when Liza had helped him into a sitting position against the wall. The pain had shot through his body at the movement but he only winced, gritting his teeth at the same time.

Liza noticed his unspoken agony. 'Are you well enough to sit?' she asked in a concerned voice and John nodded.

'I was able to obtain the meat and rice from Miss Condit Smith,' Liza said, spooning some of the food into John's mouth. 'She has the task of making up the American soldiers' meals for them and she ensured that I had a bowl for you, as you are an Australian.

Polly seems to have a great liking for Australians because of your Dr Morrison. I think that she is just a bit in love with the doctor.'

'Well, not hard to see why,' John said, savouring the hot meal. 'He's tall, mysterious, handsome and a doctor on top of all that.'

'What is it that you do, Mr Wong?' Liza asked.

'Normally I import and export goods from the East,' he answered. 'I also have a cattle property and a few good racehorses back in Queensland.'

'Then you are a fortunate man,' Liza said, scooping another spoonful of food.

'A fortunate man is one who is able to live to see his children have their own children,' John answered. 'At the moment that is not looking so clear.'

'You will get well and your life will get better,' Liza attempted to console the wounded man. 'I am sure that you will find your daughter and, God willing, we will all be able to leave this terrible place alive.'

'Tell me about you,' John said, turning the conversation. 'How is it that a beautiful young woman ends up in the middle of China. One who was born in Russia and lived most of her life in America.'

'There is not much to tell,' Liza answered with the hint of a blush. 'As for being beautiful, Mr Wong, that is in the eye of the beholder.'

'You are beautiful,' John said.

'I have come to learn that when men are helpless and in the care of a woman they seem to view that woman as beautiful so I will not take your words seriously.'

'I would say the same thing if we met for the first time on Legation Street – or in Townsville for that matter.'

Liza realised that she had finished feeding John and placed the bowl on the floor. 'We may be able to find you a bed tomorrow, Mr Wong,' she said. 'It will be a lot more comfortable.'

'I intend leaving here tomorrow,' John replied. 'I have a place at the British legation to recover.'

'I doubt that you will be well enough to do that,' Liza replied, but she realised from the look in the Eurasian's dark eyes that he was a man who did what he said.

There was something very interesting about Mr John Wong, she had to admit to herself. She guessed he was probably around ten to fifteen years older than her but he had the muscled body of a man half his age and the dark good looks that could only be inherited when East met West. From what she had come to learn about John from speaking with Lieutenant Mumford he was a man with a colourful past. Liza had to admit to herself that she could be seduced by the man's charm and animal magnetism. She had sensed that from the moment she had first looked into his dark eyes and his obvious attraction to her was more than flattering, although she would never allow herself to admit that to him.

'Miss Gurevich! We need a hand with two more casualties being brought in,' a male voice called from the end of the ward. 'Could you please spare us some of your time?'

'I have to help the doctors,' Liza said.

'I hope you will be here before ten in the morning,' John called after her. 'Because that is when I intend to be leaving here.'

Liza turned to acknowledge John's statement then hurried into the dimming light.

When John awoke in the early morning hours he turned his head to see that the young Cossack was dead. A blanket had been placed over the body until his comrades could come to fetch him. John sighed. He had a feeling that before much longer there would be many others lying with blankets covering their faces.

Mid to Late June 1900
The Besieged Legation

From the north-eastern corner of the legation quarter manned by the Austrians, Robert could hear the rapid firing of a Maxim machine gun in the night.

'Are they coming, sir?' a young British soldier clutching his rifle asked Robert.

'Not in our sector, private,' Robert answered. 'But keep a sharp lookout, it is only a matter of time before they probe our positions.'

From his position on the stone-walled parapet in the British compound, Robert continued his inspection of the guard placed to give the alert of any night attack on them and fumed at the inadequate force he now commanded as duty officer. They were too thin on the ground and all the men under his temporary command were inexperienced.

The probing attack did not eventuate and by

morning Robert was relieved by a fellow officer.

'Heard the damned Austrians fire off last night,' the relieving officer said to Robert on the handover. He was a fellow lieutenant but from a wealthy family in England and his aristocratic good looks coupled with his money had made him popular with the single young ladies in the legation. 'Buggers woke me from a good kip.'

'Did they kill any of the Boxers?' Robert asked, passing a completed roll book to his counterpart.

'I heard from the Yanks that the Austrians are flat out hitting the telegraph poles,' the lieutenant sniffed. 'They haven't learned to fire low at night and according to Simpson, over with the marines, not a body or drop of blood was spotted this morning. Bloody Austrians will make us the laughing stock of the Chinese, if you ask me. Better they hand over their Maxim to us so that we can show them how to fight a war.'

The handover completed, tired and strung out from being on duty all night, Robert made his way back to the British quarters for a breakfast prepared by Sir Claude's cooks. Then he would find time to take a short nap before resuming his military duties as a liaison officer. So far they had been lucky. The Chinese were simply probing the defences. But that was usually the prelude for an all-out assault and Robert wondered how long they would have to wait. It would not be long before he found out.

Robert met with his counterpart in the United States marines, Lieutenant Harold Simpson, at the western end barricades thrown up across Legation Street, manned by a contingent of Russian soldiers and United States marines.

'That goddamned German, von Ketteler, has been sniping from the top of the wall at Boxers drilling a couple of hundred yards away,' Simpson growled. 'If he is not careful he will agitate the rebels enough to launch a full-scale attack on us and we have nowhere near enough troops to hold them off.'

Robert agreed that the German diplomat was acting foolishly. There was hope that the silence from Pekin's legations would inspire a rescue mission from the combined forces of Europe and they had to avoid any full confrontation until those forces arrived.

'I have just been on a tour up to the eastern barricades,' Robert said as he stood beside the American, gazing over the hastily erected barricades at the mass of armed Boxers chanting their chilling war cry. 'The Italians and French are on stand-by there. They appear to have enough ammunition to hold off a substantial assault for at least a day.'

Simpson drew a long cigar from his pocket and lit up, watching the smoke curl slowly away on a slight breeze. At least the supply of cigars and champagne was not under threat of disappearing from the substantial stocks in the legation areas.

Sweat trickled down both men's faces as they shared a soldierly moment together watching their enemy watching them. 'You seem to know what is going on with all those pencil pushers,' he said. 'Is the Empress and her gang going to help us?'

'From what I have picked up over a cup of tea,'

Robert replied, accepting a cigar offered to him by his American counterpart, 'the Empress decrees, and then counters her decrees about forcing the rebels out of the city. It seems that her chief adviser, Prince Tuan, is on the side of the damned Boxers and he carries a lot of weight with the old lady. So, at this stage I presume that our diplomats are doing their best to buy time until someone comes to our aid. Our fate is in political hands.'

'I never put much stock in goddamned politicians,' Simpson snorted. 'When it all comes down to it the only language these blasted heathens understand is a gunboat sitting off their palaces. Wish those goddamned Chinks would do something and let my boys show them some good old Yankee lead.'

'Your first action, old chap?' Robert asked wryly, and Simpson looked just a little sheepish. The American officer was aware of his British counterpart's substantial record of active service prior to his posting to China. 'I would not be in any hurry to stand under the ragged remains of your stars and stripes. Glory does not help a man's career if he is not around to enjoy it,' Robert continued.

'I missed our war with Spain a couple of years ago,' Simpson said, puffing a blue smoke ring into the air. 'My brother in the navy got himself promoted for his service against the Spanish in the Philippines action. Promotion is almost non-existent in our military forces given the way Congress regards us as little more than a police force. If the politicians fail then it is a chance for me to prove worthy of advancement.'

'It is reassuring to see that our American cousins

suffer the same frustrations with the promotional system,' Robert chuckled. 'But I feel that even if we are forced to fight – and even possibly prevail – this place will be easily forgotten and become no more than a backwater for both our countries.'

'Maybe so,' Simpson reflected. 'About time I went and did an inspection of our outer perimeter piquets,' he said. 'I will see you around the defences.'

Robert watched as the American marine commanded a soldier to escort him on his tour of the men posted beyond the barricade on the fringes of the Chinese quarter. How long, Robert wondered, before the talking and skirmishing stopped and the war started? If only the promised re-inforcements would arrive and deter the Boxers who were growing more and more confident with each passing day. Robert also wondered about Naomi. No word had been heard of her since the reported abduction weeks earlier. If only he could mount another mission into the city he might be able to find more information on her fate – one way or another.

The chanting from the rebels only yards from the barricade continued as did the searing heat of the Chinese summer in Pekin.

To leave or remain in the city became the central argument among the diplomats. The royal court had issued a decree stating that the foreigners could depart and a meeting was convened in the legation. The American representative argued that they should consider leaving but Sir Claude MacDonald pondered on this choice as he still had memories of the promise offered during the Sepoy Rebellion in India at Cawnpore in 1857. 'One has to suspect the sincerity of Oriental promises,' he answered.

The German diplomat, von Ketteler, agreed with his British counterpart but pressure was mounted against Sir Claude's stance by his own diplomatic colleagues. In the early hours of the evening, Dr George Morrison emerged as the spokesman for the civilian population of those missionaries, bankers and engineers who also suspected the promises made by the royal court for their safe conduct out of Pekin.

At a meeting of the various European powers in Pekin, Morrison took the floor and in a clear statement said, 'The death of every man, woman and child in this huge unprotected convoy will be upon your heads, and your names will go through history forever as the wickedest, weakest and most pusillanimous cowards who ever lived.'

His words echoed around the room occupied by senior military representatives and diplomats.

'I agree with Dr Morrison,' came a voice from a senior British subject in the short silence following Morrison's impassioned oratory.

A Captain Poole also voiced his opinion. 'How are we to protect all these women and children during a long and perilous journey to Tientsin? I fear that we may be facing a repeat of what we saw at Cawnpore. The Chinese will slaughter us as soon as we leave the safety of our walled compound.'

For six hours until midnight the diplomats,

soldiers and civilians argued the matter. Finally, a resolution was passed and a message sent to the royal court stating that they had agreed to leave but wished to point out that the twenty-four hours ultimatum for their departure was far too short a time to organise an exodus.

The meeting was reconvened at 9 am but there was no answer from the Chinese government. They waited hours in the meeting room until the volatile German minister rose to his feet and exploded that he was waiting no longer. He would go to the Chinese government buildings and wait all night if necessary.

'It would be too dangerous,' the French minister countered. 'I say that we remain inside the legation, monsieur minister.'

De Giers, the Russian representative, now rose to his feet. The Russians had no intention of being outdone by their German neighbours in seizing the initiative.

'I say that we all go under an armed escort to the Chinese,' he said.

'*Gott in himmel*,' von Ketteler sniffed. 'Only yesterday I sent my secretary, Herr Cordes, to the Yamen to speak with their representatives. He returned unharmed to our legation.' The Yamen was located in the vicinity of the Empress's court and was the location of the local Chinese civil service offices.

'If that is so,' the Russian said, addressing von Ketteler, 'we should send him again.'

'I will,' von Ketteler replied, sitting down satisfied that he had kept the initiative to show his European and American counterparts that Germany would remain in charge of the talks. At least he had said that he would send his secretary.

But a short time later when the meeting had finally dispersed observers noticed two imposing sedan chairs, with red and green roofs denoting the occupants being people of great importance, leaving the German legation. The sedan chairs were escorted by finely dressed outriders and carried by Chinese servants. The diplomatic party moved through the silent streets now devoid of the usual throngs of noisy merchants, traders and street urchins. Inside one of the sedans, von Ketteler settled back with a book to read and a fine cigar to smoke in anticipation of the long wait he expected when he met with the Chinese bureaucrats at their headquarters in the city.

The sedans came into a wide street bordered by tile-roofed houses and tent-like stalls and unexpectedly came to a stop.

'What is it?' von Ketteler questioned, poking his head out from behind the sun shades to see a Chinese officer of the Imperial army in full uniform levelling a rifle at his head. After that the German diplomat saw nothing as the high-powered bullet exploded in his head.

Rifle fire erupted from a nearby contingent of Imperial soldiers, spraying the two sedan chairs, only ceasing when a large body of Chinese students from a nearby Methodist missionary compound intervened to force off the Imperial soldiers. They carried the badly wounded German secretary, Heinrich Cordes, who had been shot through the thighs, back to the missionary compound and delivered him into the care of the missionaries.

The news quickly spread to the legation and a unit of American marines, watched from a dangerously short distance by Imperial troops and a contingent of Boxers, was sent to escort the missionaries and their Chinese converts back to the relative safety of the legation compound.

The foreign diplomats had now seen at first hand what they might expect if they chose to make an attempt to leave the city. Not only were the Boxers ready to cut them down but they would probably be aided by the Imperial Chinese army under the command of the Dowager Empress. The city echoed to the muffled sounds of gunfire coming from the direction of the Catholic cathedral where over 3000 Chinese converts huddled and a handful of Italian and French marines held off the people who would slaughter them. The decision was made to pull back the armed piquets in the city to defend the legation compounds.

Han was in a jubilant mood; word had come to him that the foreigner who had caused him to lose face had died at the hands of the Empress's troops. He strutted around the courtyard giving speeches to his men that soon they would be enjoying the wages of a slaughter against the hated foreign devils. There would be plump white women to pleasure them while their menfolk watched helplessly, screaming their despair and pain under the various devious tortures that would be inflicted.

Naomi and Meili watched as Han addressed his men and his words chilled Naomi. From what she had been able to glean from overheard scraps of talk among the Boxer warriors the European legation was sealed off without any hope of relief from the outside. Ever since she had last heard Robert's voice – so close to rescuing her – she had entertained the hope that he might return with a mighty army to deliver her from this terrible captivity. But that hope was all but gone. The only hope she now harboured was that of eventually killing Han. She knew such an act would result in her own death but she no longer cared, as her desire for vengeance overrode any natural instinct to remain alive.

'We will be finally free of the foreigners,' Meili whispered.

Naomi looked askance at her. 'I am a foreigner,' she hissed back, causing Meili to look down at the stone paving in embarrassment.

'I did not mean you,' she mumbled. 'I meant the white devils. You are Chinese – like me.'

Naomi looked away angrily from the woman she had befriended but checked her anger when she considered how many times this young girl had risked her life to look after her. Why would Meili not have a desire to see her country free of foreign domination? She had never really thought of foreigners being in China as anything more than the rightful role of Western civilisation. But she was also of Chinese blood and aware of how, when growing up, she had borne the hateful whispers from her so-called friends of her being a Chink or Celestial. It was not easy looking like an Asian but thinking like a Caucasian, she brooded.

Late June to Mid July 1900
Pekin – The Siege

True to his word, John Wong informed the gruff doctor that he would be leaving the hospital. After all, the bullet had not actually penetrated his chest but simply smashed his ribs. Had not the doctor himself been pleased to see that none of the bone shards had pierced his lungs? The dressing wrapped around his chest would help heal the fractured bones, he argued, and the doctor finally conceded that his patient had a point.

John waited until near ten in the morning but Liza did not appear. Disappointed, he made his way back to Robert's quarters, passing groups of men sitting under shady verandahs chatting, smoking and sipping good wine as if there was no siege. It was a strange situation as bullets whacked into the grounds of the legation from rebels using the rooftops of the Mongol Market to pick their targets. Occasionally they were successful and the hospital staff were kept occupied with a steady flow of wounded men.

John reached the quarters and found the door open. He did not knock but went inside where he collapsed with a relieved sigh into a chair behind Robert's desk. The crack of rifle fire was now a constant in the hot summer air of the compound and little distraction. In the relative safety of the house with its sloping Chinese-style tiled roof, John stared at the opposite wall and then back to the desk where the strange lump of stone with its imprisoned little dragon lay. Idly, he picked up the fossil and stared at it, wondering what the world had been like when this creature was once alive. He had read that these fossils were most likely millions of years old and that the world had seen much change since they had become extinct. But all that was a vastly distant era. The reality was now, June 1900, in China. And tomorrow was another time as yet without substance.

Getting too philosophical, John smiled to himself, putting the stone back down on the desk.

'I thought that you might be here,' Andrew said, unslinging the rifle from his shoulder and leaning it against the wall.

'Good to see that you are still well,' John returned the greeting. 'And I want my rifle back.'

Andrew found a rickety old chair and sat down, wiping away sweat from his brow. 'Only if you promise me that you will not attempt any more forays into the city without me,' he said.

John offered his hand to seal the promise and

Andrew unslung the bandolier of precious ammunition for his father. 'No,' John said. 'I will join that mob of civilian militia Morrison belongs to, and take my place at the barricades.'

'We will get Naomi back,' Andrew said.

'I know we will,' John answered.

Both men found their attention unexpectedly distracted by a change in the routine noises from outside. The word 'fire' drifted to them and the sound of running feet outside emphasised some sudden urgency.

'You best remain here and rest up,' Andrew said, rising from his chair. 'I will go and see what is going on.'

John accepted his son's advice and watched him disappear through the door to see what alarm had been raised.

No sooner was he out of the building than Andrew came to a sudden halt. He could see a vast column of fire rising over the area he knew as the Chinese library. A faint scent of kerosene drifted to him on the pungent smell of burning timbers.

'Good God, no!' he exclaimed.

A stiff breeze was fanning the raging fire as it consumed the time-aged rafters and walls of the compound that covered a good four acres. The inferno had already condemned the pavilions and ornate courtyards to their fate. Equally as threatening was the way the wind shifted the tortuous column of fire down on the besiegers.

Andrew broke into a run, joining a steady stream of men, women and soldiers heading towards the scene of the fire. Among the volunteers were many Chinese refugees determined to save the site of their precious ancient heritage. A bucket brigade was already formed by the time Andrew reached the walls bordering the fire and he saw Liling among the volunteers, handing leather buckets of water down the line. He caught her eye as he moved to get closer to the source of the flames, passing through a hole that had earlier been knocked in the stone wall to assist movement of the multinational troops.

Inside the grounds of the Hanlin, Andrew was almost beaten down by the searing radiant heat of the furnace that completely engulfed the pavilions. Then he saw the Boxer riflemen manning the rooftops overlooking the fire and realised that they were pouring a steady volley of shots at the firefighters. Part of a ricocheting bullet struck him in the hand, causing a stinging sensation. A contingent of British marines were kneeling, returning the rifle fire to sweep the rooftops clear of their tormentors. Amid all this, the volunteer firefighters continued their futile attempt to put out the fire. If nothing else, they could fight to contain the flames destroying the Hanlin and not let them spread into the legation grounds.

Andrew could see one Boxer in particular standing defiantly on a roof and obviously directing both the arson and the rebel gunfire.

'God almighty!' Andrew swore when he recognised Tung's face. How could this be? How could such an intelligent man be involved in this act of wanton vandalism?

Transfixed by the sight of his former companion,

Andrew became aware that Tung had also sighted him. Tung suddenly ceased his bawling of directions to his men and stared down at Andrew. Whether by guilt or by commonsense, Tung opted to give up his exposed position and retreated down the rooftops to a place out of the line of fire.

Andrew flinched when a bullet cracked above his head. It was time for action. He moved forward to take the place of a woman in the bucket brigade who had been overcome by the heat and smoke. Coolies, missionaries, diplomats, soldiers and even older children had come together to fight this monster.

Some of the firefighters broke away from the bucket line to tear at the burning walls with shovels and rakes. Then, as if by a divine stroke of luck, the wind shifted, leaving the main library containing the most important of the ancient texts relatively intact.

The Boxer riflemen had retreated from the rooftops under the accurate fire from the Royal Marines. A small but important battle had been won by the defenders.

Weary, Andrew drifted out of the grounds of the Hanlin in search of Liling. He found her sitting in the shade of a tree by a house, her face was covered in soot and her dress filthy from the morning's effort.

'Liling,' Andrew said, sitting down beside her, 'are you hurt?'

Liling's eyes shifted to Andrew and he could see a strange happiness in her face. 'I am not hurt,' she said as Andrew touched her face with his fingers. 'I am just happy to share this time and place with you.'

Andrew drew the girl's slight frame to him in a

loving embrace. He knew then that he would never leave this uneducated daughter of a fisherman even though his choice would entail giving up the world that he had left outside the massive walls of the city.

'I saw Tung,' Andrew whispered as she clung to him. 'Damn him to hell. He appeared to be in charge of lighting the fire.'

Tung assembled his men under the protection of the high rooftops overshadowing the back alley. It was time to pull back and await further orders. He had lost five men to the well-aimed shots of the barbarians. But this did not matter, he rationalised. They had died fighting in a war to liberate their country. The memory of Andrew staring up at him with accusing eyes troubled Tung. He had wanted to discuss with the young man how such events did not matter if the price were ultimate freedom for his country. But what if they did not win? Already China had lost her glorious past.

'You did well,' the voice of the general drifted to Tung on the acrid air. 'Your loyalty to the Empress and the revolution have been cemented in what you have just done. I will tell your uncle of how you, Tung Chi, this day carried our war to the foreign devils.'

Tung looked wearily at the general who stood surrounded by his personal bodyguard. 'We must win if all this is to be worth it,' he replied bitterly.

At least good news had reached the Chinese court that the combined Allied force had been beaten back and were regrouping. In their arrogance the barbarians had underestimated the fighting resolve of their Chinese enemies. They were now defeated and any hope of a relief force reaching Pekin had been blown away. Tung knew that the besieged were living with a false hope of deliverance. It was only a matter of time before the inevitable storming of the puny force of defenders eventuated and the massacre of every man, woman and child would become a lesson to the Western powers.

As the weeks had passed Naomi no longer cowered from Han's many outbursts of rage. A strange understanding had developed between captor and captive. No longer were the brutal pack rapes inflicted, and from what Naomi had come to learn from Meili, Naomi had come to be known as Han's woman and as such was greeted with some respect by the Boxers under his command.

At times over her weeks in captivity Han would take Naomi in the most savage way and yet, strangely, he ensured that she was provided with good clothes and food. Often Naomi would catch the enigmatic man staring at her as if pondering a difficult question.

'You are a strange woman,' he said to her once after forcing himself on her. 'You are not beautiful like the other Chinese women I have had in the past. Your feet are not bound and you can read and write the barbarians' words. But you are useful until I tire of you and then you will most undoubtedly die at my whim.'

With these words, Han had rolled over and fallen into a deep sleep. As with other times when this occurred Naomi would force back her hate, biding her time to kill him and escape.

Now, as she sat in a corner of his gloomy room he ranted about the dishonour of not being given the task of burning the Hanlin.

'That bastard Tung only had the honour because he is the nephew of General Tung,' he spat. 'It should have been me. Even my own men are praising Tung's daring in destroying the symbol of our past.'

The name 'Tung' meant nothing to Naomi. Whoever this man was he had obviously attracted Han's hatred.

'It is rumoured that he has come back from the Land of the Golden Mountain,' Han continued, swigging at a jug of Chinese wine, and spilling much of it down his chest. 'Was it not I who single-handed went into the barbarians' territory, and challenged them with my presence there?'

The reference to the Land of the Golden Mountain caught Naomi's attention. She knew from growing up in Townsville that this was the name Chinese prospectors and miners had once given the area of Cooktown and the Palmer River goldfields. That meant this Boxer called Tung had visited northern Queensland and the reference made her tears suddenly well up. She felt a flicker of remembrance of being a little girl safe in her father's gentle love, and even the teasing of her brother was remembered with fondness. She recalled the smell of the dry earth under the first raindrops of the wet season and the sweet scent of the eucalypt trees in full blossom and felt her yearning for her past overwhelm her.

Han swung on her when he noticed her tears. 'Why do you cry, woman?' he asked savagely.

'It is nothing,' she replied, attempting to force back the emotion.

'Do you cry for the fate of your fellow barbarians in the legation?' he demanded. 'For they are already dead.'

'I do not weep for them,' Naomi answered. 'I am a mere woman and we sometimes cry for no reason, forgive me.'

Satisfied at the lie, Han grunted. After all, he knew much about revolution and waging war but women would always remain their own mystery. It was true that they would cry for no apparent reason. Had not his own mother done so when he was a small boy?

Han swilled at the wine and thought about the loss of face he had suffered because of Tung Chi. Perhaps one day he would have the opportunity to kill the man, he thought with some pleasure. He would have surprise on his side for, although Tung might well have powerful friends in the Empress's court, the man who was now Han's enemy did not know that he was marked for an untimely demise. It was only a matter of the right time and place to remove him.

Dr George Morrison stood in the twilight watching the vast, crimson glow of the smouldering ruins of the Hanlin. One of the great trees seemed to be standing out, glowing red without issuing flames. He was furious. The Chinese had wantonly destroyed their heritage and little was recoverable.

Andrew had been informed that the Australian journalist was at the scene of the fire and sought him out. 'Dr Morrison,' he greeted.

Morrison turned his face away from the fire. 'What can we think of a nation that sacrifices its most sacred edifice, the pride and glory of its country and learned men for hundreds of years, in order to have its revenge on foreigners,' he asked bitterly.

Andrew did not reply. He had no answer and even felt some guilt for the fact that his friend Tung appeared to have directed the operation that had brought about the fire. 'I was hoping to find you,' he said, distracting Morrison from his brooding thoughts. 'My father has left the hospital and insists on recovering at Mr Mumford's quarters. I was wondering if you could grant me a favour by dropping in to see him and examine his wound for any sign of infection.'

Morrison's hard expression softened at the request. 'I do not practise medicine, old chap,' he replied.

'Nor do I, but I have had to assist with the wounded and injured,' Andrew countered.

'Good point,' Morrison conceded. 'Then I will grant your request and drop in from time to time and look at your father's wound,' he said.

Andrew nodded. 'He still seeks my sister and it could get him killed.'

'Well, such a fine shot as your father is badly needed in our little band of civilian soldiers,' Morrison said, placing his hand on Andrew's shoulder.

'He intends to join them,' Andrew replied. 'A man in your position with contacts all over the city as well as in the legation must know if we have any hope of seeing a relief force soon.'

Morrison turned to gaze at the red glowing fiercely against the deep purple backdrop of the night sky. 'It is not the habit of the British Empire to allow another Cawnpore massacre,' he replied. 'The force will come. I just hope that we will be alive to greet them as they march up Legation Street with flags unfurled, bayonets fixed and bands playing.'

'Thank you, doctor,' Andrew said. 'I have faith in your observations. You seem like a rock in a stormy sea. Now I must return to my post in the Fu.'

'I have heard from my Chinese friends that the young lady with you is doing an admirable job assisting our defences,' Morrison said without turning away from the remnants of the fire.

Andrew was surprised by the remark but realised his fellow Australian made a living from knowing everything that happened within the legation and beyond into the city itself.

'She is,' Andrew replied. 'She certainly is.'

The three-inch artillery shell exploded in the ceiling of Robert Mumford's quarters, showering John with dust and plaster. For a moment he lost his hearing as he struggled to his feet, ignoring the pain in his chest from the sudden exertion.

'Bastards!' he swore and snatched the rifle propped against the wall.

Stumbling from the house, John was quickly aware that, once again, he had come very close to being killed. He quickly felt for any shrapnel wounds but found none.

'Mr Wong, you look like a ghost,' a shocked voice came from the darkness.

John turned to see Liza hurrying towards him and realised that the explosion had covered him in a film of grey dust. 'I missed you at the hospital,' he said with a smile.

'I was on my way over to bring you something to eat,' Liza said when she was closer to him. 'But, unfortunately I have spilled the meal.'

'I would rather see you,' John replied when he saw the worried expression on the Russian woman's face.

'I was annoyed that you actually left the hospital. I thought that you might have more sense than to do that,' Liza continued, as if chiding a child.

Without any warning, John wrapped his arm around her slim waist and drew her roughly to him. Before she could resist he had turned her face up to his. Feeling his lips upon hers sent an unexpected shiver through the startled woman. As rough as his embrace had been, his kiss was strong, sweet and tender.

'Just a thank you for caring,' John said, releasing Liza. 'Under the current circumstances I don't think the gesture would be considered forward.'

Catching her breath, Liza just stared at John, who stood with a slow smile on his face, challenging her to refute the statement.

'I have decided that it would be safer on the barricades tonight, shooting back,' John said. 'But I would invite you to join me for breakfast in the morning.'

John slung the rifle on his shoulder while Liza remained speechless. She was still transfixed when he walked off into the dark that was occasionally lit by the flash of an exploding artillery shell. A thousand thoughts swirled through her mind. The man was as brazen as any she had ever met but the kiss had been electrifying. She had not experienced such passion for many years. Although there had been men in her life who had attempted to court her, none had caught her fancy except one. When she remembered the young man she had loved with all her heart and soul Liza also thought about John's obvious desire for her. 'Never again,' she whispered to herself with bitterness for a lost love. John was too much like the man that she had once loved.

But John's kiss had reignited the possibility of intimacy in her life in a place where death was a constant companion. Elizaveta Gurevich had much to think about on her walk back to the hospital.

In the dark John found a section of the defences, a sandbagged barricade facing the Mongol Market pavilions, manned by a contingent of United States marines under the command of a tough young lieutenant.

'Came to add my rifle to your defences,' he said to the American officer. 'The name is John Wong,'

'Lieutenant Simpson,' the officer said without shaking hands. 'Had any military experience before?'

'In a roundabout way,' John answered.

'You much of a shot, Mr Wong?' the marine officer questioned him further.

'Reasonable,' John replied modestly.

'Well, you can take your place at the end of the section down there,' Simpson said, pointing in the dark to a vague outline of a raised wall of sandbags. 'Not much happening tonight,' he continued. 'They wait until first light before shooting at us directly. Had one little yellow bastard last evening almost get us and we are hoping he had a sleepover tonight. Hope to get a chance to send him to his Celestial heaven. You one of those Australians like Morrison?'

'I'm a Queenslander,' John said. 'Dr Morrison is a Victorian. There is a big difference in our country.'

'A bit like us with northerners and southerners,' Simpson replied with a chuckle.

'You could say that,' John answered. 'Back home they are talking about putting all our colonies under one government and calling Queensland a state. I don't think it will be the same when we lose our colonial identities.'

'Yeah, well, you need that before you can have secession and a civil war,' Simpson said with his lazy Texas drawl.

Even in the brief meeting with this Aussie, Simpson admired his manner. The unseen man with the name like a Chink had an easy confidence about him and Simpson liked that.

John groped his way to the end of the defences and settled down next to a young marine sleeping by his rifle. He laid the rifle against the sandbag wall, settling back to wait for dawn. He had time to think and was learning to cope with the sharp pain in his chest as if it were a natural thing in his life. His thoughts were of Liza and John cursed himself. He knew that he had acted like an oaf by forcing himself on the young woman but it was like he had said to her, time was measured in minutes in this place. Some things could not wait. The explanation helped ease his guilt at forcing himself on Liza. He would know the upshot of his actions in the morning. Would she still want to share his company?

Tung slid across the pavilion roof, dropped carefully down onto a stout wooden rafter and peered through a hole beside a young warrior gripping his rifle. Through a couple of tiles that had been removed Tung could see that dawn was nearly upon them. It was time to seek targets in the grounds of the legation. From where Tung was perched on the rafter he could see the flames of small fires flickering all over the area. None were blazing enough to immolate the buildings but a good wind might change that situation.

'Do not waste ammunition,' he said quietly to the sharpshooter he had assigned the evening before. 'I have seen your courage and good work. Today you will be successful and kill many foreign devil soldiers.'

The young man did not reply but was pleased at his commander's confidence in him. He had mastered the use of the rifle and had proved to be the best shot in his squad of Boxer warriors under the honourable Tung's command.

Unwittingly, John had allowed himself to doze off with his back to the sandbagged wall. He was torn from sleep by the yelp of a man down the line, followed almost immediately by the crack of a rifle shot.

'Goddamn!' Lieutenant Simpson swore at the top of his voice. 'Who did he get?'

'Corporal Gates,' came the reply from the centre of the defences. 'But he only nicked his elbow, sir.'

'Someone send that goddamned son of a bitch to hell,' Simpson roared. 'But only if you see him. Don't waste ammo. Anyone see where the shot came from?'

'No, sir,' the slightly wounded corporal replied. 'Not that we don't know he's on one of the rooftops out there.'

John rolled onto his stomach and saw a loophole in the sandbags that had been made from stockings and men's trousers sewn together. He had a good view of the Mongol Market and the pavilions and, easing his rifle forward to rest the barrel tip on the edge of the loophole, he scanned the curved, sloping rooftops of the buildings before him. Three hundred yards, he calculated, shifting the rear sight of his rifle to that distance. Slowly he swivelled the sights over the tiles but saw nothing. The young marine beside him was doing the same thing. Then John saw the slight movement of a tile in the distance. No wonder the gunman had been so elusive, he thought as he brought his sights onto the possible target. The sharpshooter was not on the roof but *in* it. He must have been there all the time.

The morning shadows had shown John the missing roof tiles although for someone scanning only the actual edge of a rooftop, they might have gone unseen.

Without taking his attention from the shadow he had in his sights John spoke softly to the young marine lying beside him, 'Lad, you see the second building from the right of that lone tree?'

The marine turned his head to glance at the man who had joined their defences only the night before. 'Yes, sir,' he replied.

'Look halfway down and you will see a shadow on the roof where there is a missing tile. You see it?'

After a short silence the marine answered. 'I see it,' he said, levelling his rifle on the point John had indicated.

'Just keep your eyes on that shadow,' John continued. 'I expect that we are going to see something interesting very soon.'

John had hardly spoken when two tiny figures appeared to fill the shadow. Then John saw the tip of a rifle barrel.

'You see that?' the young marine said excitedly.

'Don't shoot yet,' John cautioned. 'We will take one each and with any luck get them both. You take the one on the right and I will take the one on the left.'

'Yes, sir,' the marine replied, barely containing his

excitement. 'Should we tell the lieutenant?' he asked, holding his rifle steady.

'There won't be time,' John answered, quickly calculating the wind drift, distance and the remembered characteristics of the former French army rifle. The tiny white dots remained in their sights. 'I will count to three and on three, you fire,' John said. 'One, two . . .'

Tung knew it was not necessary to expose himself, but he wanted to get an idea of the layout of the defences this morning. From what he could see, little had changed – except that the barricade wall had been reinforced with more sandbags and rifle slits. His marksman's first shot had been aimed at a small space between the sandbags where he had seen movement. Whether he had been successful in hitting one of the defenders he did not know but at least the accurate shooting would keep the men behind the barricade pinned down.

Tung felt a searing pain along the side of his head as he and the young Boxer beside him were suddenly toppling off the rafter, to slam into the earthen floor ten feet below, where a party of Boxers were resting.

Tung lay winded for a moment. When he turned his head he realised there was a painful ringing in his ear, as if a bell would not stop clanging. He could see the bloodied face of the marksman staring at him with eyes wide open and his mouth agape, while his pulverised brains were spilled along the earth as a greasy slick.

One of the Boxers helped Tung to sit up. Moments earlier the young rebel had been sitting with his back to the wall, awaiting his turn to relieve the dead gunman.

'You have been wounded, honourable commander.'

Tung could feel the sticky flow of warm blood down the side of his face and when he reached up to feel for its source he winced. The ringing in his shredded ear was not abating and Tung reached for one of the scarfs attached to his clothing to use as a bandage. He had been lucky. A fraction more to one side and the Boxer who had assisted him would have been staring at his brains on the floor.

'You men can find another place to fire from,' Tung said, stemming the flow of blood from his torn ear. 'It seems the foreign devils know of this one.'

'Three!' John had said softly, squeezing the trigger of his rifle until it bucked in his shoulder while, at almost the same time, the young marine beside him also fired. A wisp of smoke curled from the barrels of both rifles and John rolled away from the loophole, lest he receive return fire.

'Who fired?' Simpson called down the line.

'I did, sir,' the young marine called back, remaining in position.

Simpson, mindful that ammunition required careful husbanding, stormed down the line until he reached John and his assistant's position.

'I think if you train your binoculars on a roof

over there you will see something of interest,' John said, sitting up to give relief to his chest wound.

Simpson lifted the binoculars strung around his neck and focused them on where John had indicated to see a rifle slowly sliding down the tiled rooftop.

'Goddamn!' he said under his breath. 'Mighty fine shooting.'

'Probably your young soldier here,' John said, causing the marine to puff out his chest. 'We think that there were two of them when we fired and I suspect that we got at least one of them.'

Simpson laid the binoculars against his chest to look at John, and a look of surprise swept across his face in the early morning light.

'Yeah, I have a touch of Celestial,' John said, putting the marine officer's unspoken thoughts into words. 'And also Irish.'

'Got nothing personal against Chinamen,' Simpson said with a grin. 'It's just the Irish I object to.' He extended his hand to John. 'Welcome aboard, Mr Wong. You are welcome anytime on my part of the line.'

John accepted the handshake. 'Thanks, Lieutenant, but I have a breakfast appointment so I will bid my goodbye for the moment.'

As John rose to walk away he heard a cheer from the marines on the line and was fiercely proud to have upheld the honour of Queensland in front of the Yanks.

In minutes he reached his quarters and when he entered saw Liza laying out a clean cloth on the desk. She had scrounged up two bowls of rice and hot meat for them and welcomed him with a warm smile.

'I did not know if I would see you this morning,' John said in a humble voice.

'I only came to ensure that your bandages were changed,' Liza lied. 'And that you had something to eat.'

John sat down at the desk and Liza took a spare chair to sit down opposite him.

'Thank you,' John said, reaching for a spoon beside the bowl. He was hungry and weary, and for the moment everything happening outside the building was forgotten. All John cared about was that he was alive and in the company of this extraordinary woman he wanted to learn more about. Somewhere in the compound a Chinese shell exploded as if to remind both that death was only yards away.

They came as a colourful swarm into the Fu, shouting their war cries, only to be mown down by the seemingly hopelessly outnumbered Japanese soldiers under the command of Colonel Shiba. Spent brass cartridges spun through the air behind the barricades where the Japanese soldiers ejected their rifles to reload and fire through the loopholes they had made.

Andrew snatched his revolver from within his waistband, seeking desperately for Liling. She stood frozen, mouth agape, watching the mass of Chinese soldiers attempting to storm the former palace of a Chinese prince.

'Liling, to me,' Andrew screamed above the ear-shattering din of continuous rifle fire.

Hearing his voice, Liling stumbled towards him. The Chinese troops were only a hundred yards out and closing the distance, but the Japanese soldiers' well-disciplined volleys continued to smash into the advancing ranks.

'We have to get the converts out,' Andrew yelled.

Liling nodded, her fear etched plainly in her face. She turned to see a Chinese woman holding a baby and with a toddler clasping her trouser leg. The woman was frozen with fear and the baby bawled in her arms. Liling went to her and spoke loudly to the woman, breaking her trance-like state. The woman immediately clasped her child's hand and dragged the small boy with her as she fled the Fu. Andrew similarly shouted orders to the terrified converts and they all began to flee the advancing rebels.

'You too!' Andrew said loudly to Liling, but she shook her head, standing her ground. Andrew dashed across and shook her roughly. 'You have to get out of here,' he said harshly.

'I will remain by your side,' she replied stubbornly.

Andrew was in a quandary. If he decided to remain and add his pistol to the firepower of the defenders he knew Liling would not part from him – even if it meant her death. To get her to leave required him to also desert the Fu.

Colonel Shiba had sent an urgent message by runner for reinforcements to stem the attack and a detachment of Germans and Americans fought their way along the strategically important Tartar Wall to relieve pressure on the Japanese flanks. Denying the Boxers and Chinese troops the wall meant keeping the enemy from being able to fire down into the legation area.

Andrew chose to fall back with the fleeing Chinese converts, deciding that his pride was not as important as Liling's life. As he did he could hear the firing from the barricades tapering off and when he turned to view the battleground he saw the multitude of dead and dying rebel Chinese scattered before the Japanese defences, their remaining comrades wisely choosing to retreat against the steady nerve of those they had intended to overwhelm with their numbers and firepower. Andrew's pistol had not been needed after all.

John worked the bolt on his rifle, pouring a steady fire into the advancing enemy soldiers. It was mid-afternoon and the new attacks had proved to be well orchestrated. He found himself back with the US marines under Simpson's command, along with many other civilian volunteers armed with a variety of weapons, ranging from target rifles to Colt revolvers.

John had found the young marine soldier who had worked with him to dispose of the sharpshooters that morning and the marine was glad to see him. He introduced himself as Larry Gilles, a former farm boy from Maine, and side by side behind their barricade the two kept up a furious volley of fire,

dropping their targets as if they had been on a shooting range.

Despite the withering fire from the barricades the
attackers reached the sandbagged walls and grappled
with the marines in vicious hand-to-hand fighting.
It was sword and spear against rifle and bayonet. John
was reaching frantically for more rounds to load his
rifle when a snarling face appeared above him. The
Boxer warrior was wielding a spear and instinctively
John swung his rifle like a bat to parry the weapon
thrust down at him. The wooden butt smashed against
the spear, jarring the wound in John's chest. Ignoring
his pain, he stood to counter his foe who had now
scrambled over the sandbags to thrust once again at
the Australian. The young marine beside him lunged
at John's attacker with his bayoneted rifle, wounding
the Boxer in the side. The rebel doubled over, col-
lapsing at John's feet. He smashed the butt of his rifle
down on the man's head, stunning him.

Both men turned to face their front where they
were relieved to see that the attack had spent itself
and Chinese soldiers and Boxer warriors were fleeing
back to the safety of their own lines.

John glanced down at the Boxer at his feet and
noticed the man was attempting to struggle to his
feet. Quickly, John placed a round in the breech and
slammed the bolt shut, loading the rifle. 'Don't move,'
he snarled in Chinese and the man obeyed.

'Shoot the bastard,' Larry said, swinging his rifle
on the man at their feet.

'No,' John commanded. 'He may be useful. He
can be questioned.'

The marine conceded that John was right and the prisoner was pulled to his feet to be taken by a corporal away to their military headquarters.

'I will need your expertise in the language,' Robert said to Andrew who had been fetched from the Fu.

Andrew glanced at two dejected, bound Boxer prisoners sitting on the ground outside the British legation building. A burly British marine stood over the two with fixed bayonet and pointing his rifle at the two prisoners. One of the prisoners had received a wound to the side but it had been a glancing blow that had not penetrated very deeply.

'What do you want me to ask them?'

Robert stood puffing on a cigar. 'Ask them who their commander is and how many men are under his command.'

Andrew relayed the question but only received a surly look of contempt from the prisoners.

'They aren't about to say anything,' Andrew said.

'Tough men,' Robert commented, turning to look at the soldier guarding the prisoners. 'Help them find their tongues, Private Owens,' he said, and the soldier slammed the rifle butt down on the head of one of the prisoners, who screamed in fear and pain.

'Ask them again,' Robert said calmly, puffing a circle of smoke into the sultry, hot air.

Andrew asked again but the prisoners remained mute. Although both men were terrified they remained defiant.

'I don't think that we should use brutal methods

to question them,' Andrew said quietly.

'Mr Wong,' Robert said, 'I detest the method I am forced to employ but I have no delusions as to the fate of the helpless men, women and children under my protection. Do you think that these same two men would not do worse if they were given the opportunity to overrun us?'

Andrew did not answer. He knew the British officer was right. They could expect no mercy at the hands of the Chinese should they breach the defences.

'I know that you are a man of civilised manners,' Robert consoled. 'But I have served on the Indian frontier and I know the depths of cruelty these people will stoop to when they have the upper hand. We need to know the strength and dispositions of our enemy.'

Andrew turned to the prisoners. 'It would be better that you answer truthfully the British officer's questions,' he said.

The wounded prisoner, a young man barely out of his teens, looked up and spat a gob of blood at Andrew's feet. 'We are already dead men,' he said through broken teeth. 'Just kill us now and be done with it.'

Andrew turned to Robert. 'I doubt all the beating you might inflict on them will get them to talk, Mr Mumford.'

Robert took the last draw on the dwindling cigar. 'I have already thought as much,' he said, flicking away the stub. 'Private Owen, fetch two men and organise a firing party,' he said. 'Take the prisoners to the wall behind the building and shoot them. I already have the warrants for their execution in my possession.'

'Very good, sah,' Private Owen replied, shouldering his rifle.

'Why not spare them?' Andrew asked.

'Under any other circumstances I would, Mr Wong. But we do not have the manpower to guard them – let alone the rations to feed enemy combatants. A quick death is more than I can promise they would do for us.'

Andrew looked down at the two men. 'You are to be given a quick death by firing squad.'

'I thank you,' the wounded prisoner responded quietly. 'I expected worse from the foreign devils.'

'I know that you may not have an answer to my next question and if you did, you may not tell me,' Andrew continued. 'But I seek a Chinese woman who was not born of this country. She has the foreign name of Naomi.'

'I know of her,' the young wounded prisoner replied. 'She is Han's woman.'

Stunned by the revelation, Andrew felt his mind whirl. He had not expected any answer to his question. 'Is she alive?' he asked, holding his breath.

'She was alive this morning,' the prisoner replied.

'Will you tell me where she is?' Andrew continued hopefully.

'That I cannot tell you,' the man answered. 'Is she of importance to you?'

'She is my sister,' Andrew said, forcing back tears of joy and sadness.

'I am sorry for your loss,' the young Boxer said. 'I also have a sister and she is very precious to me. I pray that she may be able to make offerings to our venerable ancestors over my body and feel pride for how I have died in the cause to free our country from the foreign devils.'

'I hope that you are granted your wish,' Andrew said sympathetically.

'I heard Naomi's name mentioned in your exchange,' Robert said. 'Does the man know anything?'

'He says that she is still alive but will not tell me where,' Andrew replied. 'At least I can thank God for that much information.'

Private Owen returned in no time with two soldiers of his platoon. Robert issued his orders and the soldiers pulled the prisoners to their feet.

'Come along, lads,' Private Owen said in an unexpectedly gentle tone. 'Time to meet your Celestial maker.'

Andrew did not want to look the prisoners in the eye as they passed him.

'Your sister is with Han at the merchant's old house in Lotus Street,' the young Boxer hissed as he passed Andrew. 'I do not like Han. He is a cruel and evil man and your sister would be better off dead than in his hands. I am about to die and so Han's eventual fate is not my concern.'

Andrew was stunned by the quietly delivered and unexpected information. He wanted to say or

241

do something but it was too late. The guards were already marching the men to their deaths. Lieutenant Mumford would supervise the execution and, if required, deliver any coup de grâce with his revolver. It was a matter already sanctioned by the military command of the defenders and it was concluded quickly. Andrew had remained in front of the building and heard two shots. In a matter of minutes Robert returned to where he stood.

'You might carry out the official inspection to validate that the two prisoners have been killed in accordance with military instructions,' Robert said, lighting another cigar.

'I'm not a doctor,' Andrew answered.

'And I am not normally an executioner,' Robert said, puffing the cigar into life. 'You have enough medical knowledge to determine whether they are dead.'

Andrew examined the two bodies that lay crumpled on the dusty earth, while the firing squad stood back watching him. Both men had been shot through the chest and Andrew could not feel any pulse. Later, the bodies would be tossed over the Tartar Wall to fall among the many other rapidly decomposing bodies of fallen Boxers and Chinese Imperial soldiers. The stench of decomposition was already becoming a problem to the defenders.

When Andrew returned to Liling at the reoccupied Fu his vacant expression caused the anxious girl to ask, 'Are you unwell?'

'It is nothing,' Andrew replied, taking Liling's hand. He was a long way from the hallowed halls of his medical school in Scotland where he had been training to be a saver of lives, indeed a long way from anything that he had once known as normal.

'Come with me,' Liling said, gripping Andrew's hand. 'I have obtained a room for us in the palace quarters. There we may be alone and safe for a while.'

Andrew let Liling lead him through the mass of refugees in the palace grounds along an ornately decorated corridor to a small room. There she drew him in and pulled him to a straw-filled mattress. Andrew lay beside Liling who cradled him in her arms. He did not know why he wanted to weep but staunchly resisted the impulse. Was it just the hopelessness of the situation they were in? Or was it that everything he experienced around him was contrary to how he had once thought life should be? The courage of the two Boxer prisoners in the face of torture and then death was in contrast to what he expected of their enemy. Examining men to ensure that they were dead – and not just wounded – was not within the scope of what he had trained for. Saving life rather than taking it would have been his preferred role.

And then there was Liling holding him to her. She was a woman born of China, a woman whose courage was inspiring in the face of the daily battle to live. Before Andrew realised it he was slipping Liling's shirt over her head and kissing her breasts. This was the first time he had allowed himself to be truly intimate with the young woman. Liling did not resist his advances and for a short time they were simply lovers. All around was carnage but for the moment nothing else mattered apart from the pleasure they partook in each other's embrace.

'It's impossible,' Robert said, standing under a great hole in the roof to his quarters, amid the wreckage of what had once been his neat and tidy bachelor's room. 'I cannot authorise a patrol to go out beyond the barricades to search for Naomi.'

'Just listen and you can see why,' Andrew countered.

Andrew and Liling had been fortunate to find the British officer attempting a short nap despite the continuous crash of rifle fire telling the story of how fierce the fighting was. The occasional crump of an exploding artillery shell added to the noise that was rapidly shredding the nerves of soldier and civilian alike, and the various commanders of the defences knew that their supply of ammunition was finite. It would only be a matter of time before the last round would be held back for the defenders to use on themselves, rather than be taken by the Chinese.

'You have been to Lotus Street,' Andrew persisted. 'You even guessed correctly that Naomi was being held there.'

'I'm sorry, Andrew,' Robert said, red-eyed and covered in grime from the days and nights of little sleep. 'I have to return to the wall.'

'Then I will make the effort to go to Lotus Street,' Andrew said. 'One way or the other.'

Robert was rifling through a drawer for a box of pistol cartridges and stopped to glance up at Andrew. 'You attempt to do that now and I guarantee your life expectancy will be around two seconds beyond the barricades.'

Andrew knew that the British officer was right. The battle for the legation raged all around them and they would be lucky if they saw the sun set that day. Mothers had made plans to shoot their children before shooting themselves and husbands promised wives that they would do the same for them when the Chinese eventually broke through. Andrew had considered his and Liling's fate and the thought that he may have to shoot her was something he could not face. That he had found love with this woman was something he had never entertained. Life had been simple up until now.

'You are right,' Andrew muttered grudgingly. 'I should join my father on the defences,' he said. 'Do you know where he is?'

'With our American cousins,' Robert replied, finding his last box of pistol rounds. 'My colleague from the US marines, Lieutenant Simpson, has informed me that your father's sterling service with them is greatly valued. The marines are holding out near the Tartar Wall but we cannot relieve them until dark as they are only a few yards from the Boxer positions. I am afraid the bastards have tightened their grip on us.'

Robert pocketed the box of pistol rounds, rubbed his eyes which were sore from the acrid smoke and dust. 'I still have faith in Admiral Seymour and a relief force eventually reaching us,' he said, placing his hand on Andrew's shoulder. 'Then we will go and find Naomi.'

Andrew accepted the reassuring words without much hope. He was about to reply when Robert suddenly frowned and looked alert.

'Do you hear that?' he asked, staring through the open doorway of his quarters.

Andrew also frowned. It was not that they could hear anything – except for a slackening in the crash of rifle fire – and even as they stood frozen by the change to the late afternoon air the rifle fire died away to just the occasional single shot. Both men sensed that something dramatic had just occurred and wondered what. Had the Boxers finally over-whelmed the defences?

'Son of a bitch!' Lieutenant Simpson swore. 'They're pulling back!'

Watching the enemy soldiers falling back and leaving their dead scattered across the stone-cobbled open space, John rubbed his red raw eyes with the back of his grimy hand. The silence was broken only by the muttering of the British and American marines spread along the barricade. The pain from his earlier wound returned to dog him, although when the fighting raged it was forgotten.

The situation had been so desperate that when the American diplomat Edwin Conger had met with Sir Claude MacDonald he had insisted that the American marines abandon their position. But the

Englishman had countered by sending a reserve force of British marines to reinforce the Americans. They had held their ground and beaten off the attacks.

John's supply of French-made ammunition had been exhausted and Simpson had tossed him a marine's rifle after the soldier had been evacuated suffering wounds. John had continued to carefully pick his targets and although he had not counted the number of men he had killed that day, he knew that it was many.

Private Larry Gilles was still beside him and turned his bloodshot eyes on John. 'What do you think is happening?' he asked.

'I don't know,' John replied, pulling himself into a sitting position with his back to the sandbags, his rifle propped between his legs. He could see the sun setting, flooding the pink walls of the Imperial city adjacent to their positions with a soft, yellow shade. In the distance John could hear the Chinese enemy blowing on their trumpets, a blaring sound that rose and fell on the evening breezes. It seemed a sad and ominous song, chilling John despite the warmth of the evening air.

On the north bridge, away from where John sat exhausted, a huge white placard had appeared displaying Chinese characters. Using binoculars the defenders – with the help of interpreters – read the message. It was an Imperial edict declaring that hostilities should cease immediately. The defenders immediately responded to the message by scribbling one of their own to say that they understood. The word soon reached John and the men around him.

'You think that Limey admiral is outside the city?' Larry asked. 'You think that is why the Chinks have pulled back?'

'I don't know,' John answered wearily, his thoughts drifting to a hot bath and a soft bed to sleep in.

'You, Mr Wong,' a US marine corporal said, standing over John. 'Lieutenant Simpson sends his compliments and wishes to see you.'

John nodded and wearily hoisted himself to his feet to go to the American officer currently huddling with his senior NCOs.

'Mr Wong,' Simpson said with a weak smile. 'Just wanted to say that I think you should have your rifle back and you return the property of the US to me.'

John accepted the French rifle, handing back the American issue carbine.

'I was able to secure some ammo from our French allies,' Simpson continued. 'So that you are able to rejoin us after you take some leave.'

'Thank you, Mr Simpson,' John said, accepting the bandolier of fresh rounds from the officer. 'I think I will do just that.'

Simpson returned to his senior NCOs. 'Use this time to reinforce our positions,' he said, taking a cigar from a pocket and lighting it with trembling hands. 'I can see that our Chink friends across the way are doing just that right now. Give every second man a stand down to catch some shut-eye and remain alert. I suspect that this bit of peace isn't going to last long.'

John left the line to return to the only place he could call his own piece of the city – Robert's shattered quarters. Whatever was happening did not matter as much as sleep.

With his head bandaged to cover his severed ear, Tung stood before the walls of the legation quarter under a setting sun. He and his men had not been committed to the attacks on the foreign devils that day and, when he glanced around, he could not help but be impressed by the spectacle: a vast sea of colour depicting the various uniforms of the infantry, artillery and cavalry. Imperial soldiers armed with everything from giant, two-handed swords, bows and arrows to modern rifles. The multitude of bright banners that hung limp in the hot evening air bore images of dragons and other exotic creatures. This was the might of China on display and Tung knew that some of the defenders who had climbed over the barricades had seen the spectacle. How could they not be impressed with what they saw?

'Commander Tung?' The soldier standing before Tung wore the insignia of his uncle's personal body-guard. 'You have been summoned by General Tung Fu-hsiang.'

Tung followed the uniformed messenger towards a dais surrounded by uniformed soldiers and flag-poles. On a chair in the centre of the raised platform was the grim-faced man who held the power of life and death over all he saw before him on the parade. Even though Tung recognised the man as his mother's brother, he still prostrated himself before the general as he would if before the Empress.

'Honourable General, I greet you with a humble request to forgive me for my tardy appearance.'

'I can see that you bear the badge of one wounded,' his uncle said, leaning forward. 'The money that you returned has been deposited in the Empress's treasury and she is grateful for your service, Commander Tung.'

Tung felt as if he had been kicked in the stomach. When he had turned over the banknotes to a court official he had been told he could trust, he was under the impression that they would be deposited in the imprisoned true Emperor's accounts. But having discovered this was not so Tung felt that he had risked his life for nothing in recovering the stolen money.

'Further still,' the general continued, 'it has been allocated to purchase artillery for the Imperial army so that we can better meet the foreign devils as they even now invade the Empress's kingdom. But I have summoned you here on other matters and we will speak alone.'

With a gesture of his hand the general indicated for Tung to follow him. Tung rose to his feet and followed his uncle into a building guarded by soldiers, some armed with long spears and others with modern carbines. Inside the room Tung could see that his uncle had staff gathered around a large map displaying the city. Small ivory pieces had been placed on the map, obviously indicating the disposition of the Imperial forces. Another map was affixed to the wall. It was of China itself. Coloured marks indicated what Tung guessed to be enemy forces and he was disturbed to see many marks around the city of Tientsin south-east of Pekin.

The soldiers in the room bowed respectfully when the general appeared among them. 'Continue your work,' he commanded, and the staff busied themselves around the maps.

'I can see that you have understood our current situation,' the general said, noting Tung's eyes scanning the map of China. 'I must complete the destruction of the Europeans in our city before Admiral Seymour gathers reinforcements to march on us.'

'Is it that bad?' Tung asked. It was only that the feared general was also his uncle that Tung would dare ask such a question.

'We have forced Seymour back,' the general answered quietly. 'In a similar situation as we have to here, we have the foreign devils of Tientsin besieged in their compounds. We need to eliminate the thorn that we have in Pekin so that I am able to deploy more forces to face the Admiral Seymour. That is why I have summoned you, honourable nephew.'

Tung glanced up at his uncle's normally dour face and saw the slightest hint of a smile. 'What is it that I can do in your esteemed service, uncle?' he replied, sensing that his mother's brother felt some warmth toward him.

'You are one of the very few men I know who has travelled much among the foreign devils and knows their language and ways. I have been informed of how you so resourcefully recovered the Empress's money and I need a man to command my intelligence service here in Pekin. You will hand over your present command to Commander Han, who has proved himself to be a capable member of the cause to free China. I have been informed that he already has a prisoner of some value to your future work. She is a Chinese woman who was born in the land that you have just returned from and knows the ways of our enemy. She needs to be interrogated vigorously as I believe Han has grown soft towards her. After you have gained as much from her as possible you may dispose of her.'

. . . a Chinese woman who was born in the land that you have returned from, echoed in Tung's mind. Naomi Wong was such a woman. Was it possible that she had fallen prisoner to the rebellion? If so, how?

'I will be honoured to accept the esteemed position as your intelligence commander,' Tung dutifully replied. But inwardly he was still seething at the suggestion he had returned the money to the Empress when it rightfully belonged to the true Emperor. Tung's loyalties were being severely tested. He was the imprisoned Emperor's man but found he was now reluctantly on the side of the usurper Empress working against the foreigners.

'Good,' the general said. 'Even now I am having Han summoned to brief him of the situation. You may take up quarters at the Empress's palace near mine and be at my disposal whenever I need to know what my enemy is thinking.'

'Yes, honourable general,' Tung said, bowing to formalise his new appointment.

Just as his uncle had promised Tung noticed a pockfaced man wearing the uniform of a Boxer commander enter the room with one of the general's aides. Han appeared apprehensive, glancing around the room and bowing deeply when his eyes came to rest on General Tung Fu-hsiang.

'Approach,' the general commanded and Han respectfully approached. 'This is my commander of intelligence,' the general said, introducing Han to Tung. For a second Tung thought he saw murder in the other man's eyes.

'Honourable general, I have heard much of Commander Tung's exploits,' Han said, not looking at Tung.

'You will be honoured by having Commander Tung's men join your command,' the general said. 'You will also send to Commander Tung the foreign woman I know you are holding captive.'

'Honourable General,' Han began, 'she is of no worth to our cause, other than as a common prostitute. I do not think that she could provide any more information on the enemy than I have already gained from her.'

The general frowned, contemplating the Boxer commander's words.

'What is the name of this woman that you hold captive?' Tung asked.

'She is known by her European name, Naomi Wong,' Han replied. 'She was captured in the days before we laid siege to the European legation.'

Naomi Wong! It was her, Tung thought with a start. 'I will still need her, honourable general,' Tung quietly insisted.

'I agree,' Han hurriedly said, having realised that

the man he had come to hate for upstaging his own exploits was also related to the feared general. 'Then, I would request that she be returned to me when Commander Tung has decided he no longer needs her services.'

'I consider your request reasonable,' the general replied. 'Commander Tung, you may have the woman for five days. In that time you will ascertain if she is of any worth to you and, if so, gain all the information you can from her by any means you wish to employ. After that time, she is to be returned to Commander Han as a reward for his excellent service to our cause. Five days is all you have with this foreign woman, Commander Tung.'

The Chinese general had managed to balance the exchange between his two commanders, knowing that he must appear to be impartial. The woman was of no consequence but the smooth operations of his many newly incorporated Boxer militia units were of importance to a final victory. To ensure that the Imperial troops and Boxer rebels could work together in the common cause of ousting the foreigners he needed harmony. Besides, he could not see why this woman would be of any real interest to his nephew other than for the intelligence she might be able to provide.

Tung was able to conceal his emotions and feigned indifference to the general's direction on the matter. 'It will be done as you have commanded, Honourable General,' he replied as if dismissing any further discussion of the matter.

But Tung's thoughts were in turmoil. Very soon

he would hold captive the woman his two friends had travelled so far to meet and return to her land. What was he to do in that valuable but short space of time? As it was it appeared the defenders on the other side of the barricades had little time left in their own lives. It was only a matter of a final push against them and they would all be inevitably slaughtered – every man, woman and child. Even as he stood in the room allocated as operational headquarters he could see preparations being made for the continuation of attacks on the European legations. According to his calculations there were at least five Imperial armies displayed on the map of Pekin and the area surrounding the city. Such force surely doomed the foreigners behind the barricades to their death.

As predicted by Simpson, around midnight John was wrenched from a deep sleep by crashing volleys of gunfire all around him and the shouts for men to fall in to their defensive positions.

Without even having to think John groped for his rifle, rushing to rejoin his American marine friends on the barricades. The fighting seemed without end and the battle had reached an even more vicious level to John's experienced ears. For whatever reason the Chinese had called a temporary ceasefire it was not because of any approaching relief force, John thought as he made his way in the dark, guided by now all too familiar landmarks, to rejoin the US marines on the barricades of the Tartar Wall.

Mid to Late July 1900
Pekin

From where Naomi lay on a straw-filled mattress she could hear the resumption of the fighting. At least the sound was reassuring, as it indicated to her that the defenders of the legation were still holding out. A lantern flared in the tiny room that she shared with Han.

'Get up, woman,' Han's voice commanded harshly. 'You are to be taken to the general's headquarters.'

Naomi rose to her feet to see Han standing with the lantern. With him were two of his men.

'What is happening?' she asked.

'You are to leave my company for five days,' Han replied without any show of emotion. 'You are to be interrogated by the general's nephew, Commander Tung. I doubt that he will show the same consideration to you as I have, and if he decides to let you live, you will be returned to me.'

Han's warning frightened Naomi. If you could call rape and beatings from Han considerate, what worse could lie ahead? Han's man stepped forward and seized her.

'Will Meili be going with me?' Naomi called to Han as the guards marched her from the room.

'She remains,' Han replied.

No further words were spoken as Naomi was marched through the courtyard. As terrifying as it had been in Han's company, she was even more afraid at what might lie ahead. She knew that she had nothing more to offer her Chinese captives and this is what she feared most. What if this Commander Tung decided that she was worthless to him? As she was led away, the sound of gunfire coming from the direction of the legation compound once more rocked the night.

As the sun rose John rested against the sandbagged wall to check his supply of ammunition. He was satisfied to see that he had spent very few rounds during the hours before sunrise; he and the other defenders had noticed the odd but satisfactory habit of the Chinese to fire high, which had kept down the number of casualties among the defenders. Looking around wearily he saw Simpson moving along the line of his men to speak with each one. When he reached John he greeted him.

'The young marine I have been with over the last few days,' John said. 'Where is he?'

'He was hit by a sharpshooter just after you left

us,' Simpson answered. 'I had him evacuated to the hospital. Though I don't think he will die. Those boys from Maine are a pretty tough lot.'

John was relieved to hear that the young man had not joined the ranks of the dead. The casualties had been mounting steadily and he had overheard that the number of soldier casualties of all defending forces was now thirty-eight killed and fifty-five seriously wounded. At that rate the dwindling numbers meant they were doomed unless a miracle happened. But since John was an atheist for him such occurrences did not exist.

'I think I will go and visit Private Gilles,' John said. 'That is, if you don't need me in the line for the moment.'

Simpson shrugged. 'You are a civilian, Mr Wong,' he replied. 'I am sure Private Gilles will be pleased to see you.'

John cautiously made his way from the barricades. He was hoping to see more than just the young man he had befriended on the barricades. With any luck Liza would be at her post in the hospital.

Even as John made his way through the shell-pocked streets of small craters and smashed masonry, Naomi was meeting for the first time the man she had been informed would be her interrogator in his quarters within the walls of the Forbidden City, the home of the Imperial court. She stood between two armed Boxers in a wide corridor that opened onto a large marbled room filled with priceless furniture and porcelain vases. Naomi noticed a man with his head bandaged conferring with uniformed officers of the Chinese army. She guessed that he was a relatively senior officer from the way he interacted with the Imperial officers but when she overheard his name mentioned, she realised that he was Commander Tung, her new captor. Having finished his conference with the officers, Tung turned to face Naomi.

Approaching her at the end of the hall, he ordered the guards away. Now Naomi was alone with the man she could see had a fine, intelligent face. For a short time Tung stood with his hands behind his back and appeared to be examining her as one would a target to be shot. No matter what it took she would not show fear under this man's relentless stare, Naomi told herself.

'I know your father and brother,' Tung said softly in English. 'I consider both of them good friends, Miss Wong.'

Naomi felt herself falling into a swirling space of empty air.

'I think that you should sit down,' Tung said gently, assisting Naomi to an ornately carved wooden chest.

'Is it really true that you know my father and brother?' she asked as Tung passed her a bowl of clean water.

'It is a long story that commences in your country,' Tung said quietly, still speaking in English. 'But I last saw your father and brother entering the city many days ago. They were well, and hopefully remain that way.'

'I prayed,' Naomi said, sipping the water, 'that my

father would come and take me away. But it did not happen and I despaired.'

'Your father and brother are good men and I regret very much that they should find themselves on the other side of the Tartar Wall.'

'Is it possible for you to deliver me to my father?' Naomi pleaded.

Tung took a deep breath and sighed. 'That is not possible for many reasons, Miss Wong,' he replied politely. 'I have sworn an oath to the cause of freeing my country of foreign invaders, and to do so would be construed as an act of treachery. But, I also fear that if I did so you may be slaughtered when the legation falls to our forces. I am sure that your father would wish you to remain under my protection with that eventuality a probability. Then, it may be possible to ensure you are able to safely return to the country of your birth.'

'I would risk my life to be with my father and brother,' Naomi persisted. 'I beg you to give me the opportunity to do so.'

'I am sorry, Miss Wong,' Tung said firmly, 'that is not possible. But I can promise that I will do all that is in my power to get a message to your father of your welfare.'

Naomi could see that pleading her cause was a waste of time, but was at least grateful for being in the company of a man who appeared to be very different to what Han had intimated.

'I must also caution you,' Tung continued, 'that what I have told you must not be spoken of to any-one. It could risk both our lives.'

'I understand,' Naomi replied. 'And I thank you for your kindness.'

'I will have to display a public face that you are nothing more to me than a prisoner,' Tung added. 'But I also promise you that no harm will befall you while you are under my protection.'

'Han has informed me that I will be returned to him in five days' time,' Naomi said. 'Are you able to prevent that happening?'

'I will do my best,' Tung answered. 'It will depend on the whim of my uncle, General Tung Fu-hsiang. In the meantime you will be given a room in this building and I will instruct the guard to ensure you are well fed and not molested in any way. Should you attempt to escape he has orders to kill you. Those are my orders.'

It was clear to Naomi that although this man appeared so caring towards her at the moment, he was also the enemy and would not hesitate to kill her in the name of the cause he fought for. It was a strange situation but still far better than being Han's prisoner. Naomi nodded that she understood and Tung called for the guard outside to escort her to her quarters.

John found Private Larry Gilles sitting on a palliasse with his back against the wall in the improvised ward for the enlisted men.

'Got it in the thigh,' he said cheerfully, exposing the bandaged leg for inspection. 'It just passed through without hitting the bone. The doctors say that I will be back with you all soon enough.'

John offered the young marine a big cigar he had been able to acquire from Robert Mumford's stock. Larry accepted the gift gratefully and John lit it for him, at the same time lighting one for himself.

'Don't be in any hurry to go back,' John said, puffing a cloud of blue smoke into the cloying, still air.

'Yeah, well I have to get back to my buddies,' Larry said. 'I don't want to die in this place, if the Chinks overrun us.'

The ward was filled with other soldiers of many nationalities; Italian, German, French, Flemish and English languages all blurred in the building that reeked of cigar smoke, blood and putrefaction.

John and Larry chatted for a short time until John slipped the marine an extra cigar before bidding him farewell to go in search of Liza. He found her accompanying a doctor on his rounds. Her long dress was covered in blood and wisps of her long hair hung down her face but when she saw John her face was lit with a weary smile of pleasure.

'It is good to see you,' she said, touching the loose wisps of hair. 'I have often thought about you.'

The doctor glanced at John, and then at Liza. 'How about you take some time off, Miss Gurevich,' he said, perceiving the change in her demeanour in the presence of the man who had approached them. 'You have not had a break in the last forty-eight hours.'

'Thank you, doctor,' Liza replied, and accepted John's hand to lead her away from this place of suffering.

'I am so weary,' she said when they had exited the building. 'I dream of a hot bath and clean sheets – even when I am awake.'

'Funny thing,' John grinned, still holding her hand, 'I dream the same things – except I see you sharing both.'

Liza pushed John's hand away and blushed. 'Mr Wong!' she exclaimed. 'That is a very brazen thing to say. I do not think that you are a gentleman.'

'I never said I was,' John answered with a cheeky grin. 'But I think that you are a true lady.'

Liza was too tired to challenge John any further. 'I think the way I feel right now your dream has a very slight appeal,' she sighed.

'I would not hold you to any promise,' he said softly, a bullet cracking overhead to remind them where they were. 'I truly think that you are a lady worth a man's life.'

As they reached a deserted, shady verandah, Liza turned to face John. 'Mr Wong . . . John, that is the nicest thing a man has said to me,' she said, taking his hand in her own. 'But you would think differently of me if we were not trapped in this terrible place.'

'No,' John said quietly. 'When my wife died I devoted all my time to raising my son and daughter in the best possible way I could. I allowed no woman to come into my life, but now that they are both adults, it is time to think about myself.'

Liza withdrew her hand and gazed at the court-yard strewn with the debris of war: spent cartridge cases, scattered balls of metal the size of grapes and chunks of masonry from buildings hit by high explosive artillery shells. 'You know nothing about me,' Liza said. 'We are strangers to each other.'

'I admit that I know very little about you,' John conceded. 'But what I know, and will never fully understand, is that I find you beautiful and desirable to the point that makes me want to learn more about you.'

'If God grants us that chance, John, we may do so.'

In the distance they could hear a bell tolling with an irritating clang, disturbing the precious moment they shared.

'Another attack,' John said wearily. 'I have to return to the barricades.'

Liza took a deep breath and sighed. 'I must return to the hospital,' she said. 'I am to help boil up rice water for our patients with dysentery.'

As they stood John reached out to touch her on the cheek. 'I meant what I said.'

'I know,' Liza replied, reaching up to touch his hand. 'I will admit that I do have some feelings for you as well but I am afraid.'

John did not ask Liza what she feared. He already knew that they would be lucky if they saw one more sunrise before they were killed. Without another word he turned and walked away.

For a day Liling had lain in a lather of sweat on the straw mattress. Andrew had known that it would be inevitable. Considering the crowded conditions and lack of hygiene in the Fu, there was bound to be an outbreak of virulent disease. He had ensured that he and Liling took precautions to avoid having the deadly fingers of disease grip them, but somehow Liling had taken sick. She had attempted to hide her growing illness as she tended to the mothers with children who were packed into the once spotless former palace. But eventually Andrew had noticed how ill she really was and forced her to lie down on their mattress in the privacy of their tiny room. It did not take long for the young woman to slip into a fever-induced state verging on a coma. Kneeling over her, Andrew held her wrist and felt her pulse beating weakly. Now and then she tossed her head, muttering incoherently, and Andrew forced back the tears. 'Dear God, please do not take this young woman,' he whispered.

Already he had seen the over-crowded mass of refugees coming down with smallpox, a disease that most often proved fatal.

Liling was at the edge of death and given the lack of medical supplies there was little Andrew could do for her but pray that she had not contracted the deadly sickness. Maybe she had scarlet fever, he tried to reassure himself. As dangerous as that disease was it was preferable to contracting smallpox.

'Take some water,' Andrew said soothingly, lifting a bowl to Liling's lips.

The water dribbled away and Andrew sat back on his legs in his despair. The stench all around was appalling but he had grown used to it. In the former palace the conditions were beyond insanitary but the besieged European community did not seem to care, preoccupied as they were with making sand-bags, rationing food and meeting the random attacks from the Chinese.

Shaking the ground with its explosive power, the blast of an artillery shell nearby shook dust down on Liling's face. Andrew threw his body over her to protect the seriously ill girl from possible shrapnel while terrified men, women and children huddled together, crying for deliverance from the Christian God they had accepted, forsaking the worship of their old gods and ancestors.

Andrew cringed when a second round burst even closer, hugging Liling to him.

Amid the screams and sobs of shrapnel victims, Andrew recognised the desperate cry for medical assistance and rose unsteadily to his feet. For the moment there was nothing else he could do for Liling. He stumbled into a wide hallway where refugees were huddled, gripping what little they owned. A man was crying for help. He lay on his stomach, attempting to crawl down the hallway on his elbows while trailing his pulverised legs behind him. Just beyond the dying man Andrew could see a woman holding what was left of her child's body, blood soaking the woman from her own wounds, and those of her headless baby. Andrew intercepted the woman stumbling in a daze towards him. Gently, he removed the lifeless body of the baby from the woman's arms and placed it on the ground. With soothing words he asked her to sit down and slid her blouse above her head to reveal the ugly black entry wounds of shrapnel balls in her breast. Even as he examined her, blood spewed from her mouth and she fell sideways.

Andrew squatted to examine the severely wounded man but knew that it was only a matter of time before he also died. The man looked at him with pleading eyes.

'I am sorry, old chap,' Andrew said in English. 'We do not have the means to amputate, and I doubt that would help anyway.'

As if understanding the foreign language the man lay face down on the dusty, tiled floor and cried softly.

Andrew rose to his feet just as another shell exploded somewhere in the maze of the palace corridors. People shrieked and Andrew felt the nervous tic at the corner of his eye. His world had already come apart and he wondered why he should continue to live.

Naomi had been isolated for half a day before Tung came to visit her. He brought a bowl of steaming noodles and vegetables as well as lychees and seasoned pork pieces and placed them on a solid timber table at the centre of the room.

'It was the best I could do,' he apologised. 'I wish it could be more.'

But to Naomi it was a rare feast. She accepted the food with an expression of gratitude and ate gingerly to ensure it went a long way to sating her hunger. While in Han's control she'd had very little to eat and had lost much weight. Her clothes hung loose on her thin frame and she often found herself remembering the large steaks her father loved to serve up. At the time, the slabs of meat had seemed to her almost obscene in their size and bloody texture. Now she would have given anything to be devouring one of those steaks with its accompanying fried potatoes and garden peas.

'I thank you for your kindness,' she said between mouthfuls of the delicious spicy food.

'I am going to attempt to get a message to your father,' Tung said, taking a seat on the single chair in the room as Naomi ate, sitting on her low bed of a timber frame and straw mattress. 'We have spies inside the legation.'

Naomi was not surprised to learn this. She knew there were many refugees and it only took one well-placed person to provide intelligence. She glanced up at Tung and noticed that the bandage he had been wearing around his head when she first met him was gone, revealing a large scab where his left ear should have been.

'You have been injured,' she said sympathetically.

'It is nothing,' Tung grimaced, 'I was luckier than the man beside me.'

Naomi did not question him further but resumed eating her meal. When she had finished the noodles she placed the empty bowl on the table. 'Will you tell me of events in the legation?' she asked.

'The foreign devils hold out with great tenacity,' Tung answered. 'Our leaders seem to be disorganised in their assessment of the tactical situation, launching probing attacks instead of an all-out assault.'

Good, Naomi thought. Not that she was not partially sympathetic to the rebel cause to free China but her Western upbringing had instilled in her a fierce pride for the might of the British Empire. 'You do not seem to be like the other Boxers I have met,' Naomi said.

'How do you mean?' Tung countered.

'I sense a wise and even gentle side to you,' Naomi responded, without having to think of the appropriate reply. 'You appear to be a very intelligent man.'

Tung shifted and Naomi could see that her words had touched a nerve. 'I am a man whose life has been dedicated to seeing China become a free and progressive nation. To that end who you may perceive me to be is of little matter.'

'Have you always been a revolutionary?' Naomi asked, finding that she had a genuine interest in her captor for more reasons than that he had shown only kindness and courtesy towards her.

'I was once a Shaolin priest,' Tung said, finding it easy to talk to this pretty young woman. 'I had a desire to learn and from my travels in the country I saw that we are a people who deserve to regain our past glory. To that end I learned English along with practising my martial skills. Eventually I fell in with people who followed the Son of Heaven. They shared our dream of a non-violent means to modernising China and eventually freeing us of the destructive foreigners. Sadly, my lord is now a prisoner of the Empress and the only option left to me was to take a command with the Boxer movement.'

'As a former man of religion how can you justify

the terrible things the Boxers do to Christian converts?' Naomi asked.

'I do not agree with all that my comrades do,' Tung sighed. 'But they are uneducated and ignorant men steeped in superstition. I pray that when we win our war things will change under a good leader. But who that will be I do not know. For the moment it is the Empress. I pray that she will see that the people of China, who are sacrificing so much in the war against the foreign powers, need benign leadership.'

'Do you believe she will?' Naomi asked pointedly.

Tung did not answer but rose to his feet. 'I will return to my duties,' he said. 'But I will visit you as often as I can. After all, I am using the most vigorous means at my disposal to extract any information you may still have of use to our cause.'

Naomi thought that she saw a shadow of a smile on Tung's face and knew she would be looking forward to seeing this enigmatic man again – if only for the fact that in his presence she felt safe.

Twenty-eight-year-old Captain Jack Myers, USMC, had been on the Tartar Wall for a week and the lack of sleep and constant danger were taking their toll on his mental and physical stamina. As commander of the crucial defensive position he had guessed that the Chinese opponents were placing their best sharpshooters up against his positions and the well-aimed, deadly fire was proving to him that this was true. Other national legation forces defending the compound were certainly not on the receiving end of such attacks.

In his growing despair he had sent a note to Edwin Conger, the overall senior American representative in the city. *It is slow death to remain here . . . The men all feel that they are in a trap and simply await the hour of execution.*

The response from the senior commanders of the defence was a simple answer from non-military men. Myers was to lead a sortie along the wall to capture a position held by the enemy, relieving the pressure on his own defences.

'You have seen it,' Captain Myers said to Lieutenant Simpson, huddled beside his commander. Both peered cautiously through a narrow slit in the sandbags. 'The little yellow bastards have pushed the construction of their wall to reach the left-hand flank of our breastworks.'

Even as they sat back from their observation post they could hear the cheerful laughter of the enemy at work, carefully piling up more bricks to reinforce what was becoming a fort from which they could eventually look down into the US marines' position.

'I hear that you have a man who speaks their language,' Myers said.

'A civilian, Mr Wong, he is part Chinese,' Simpson replied. 'Kind of attached himself to us and we kind of made him an honorary marine on account of his shooting prowess. He is an Aussie.'

'Maybe he could come up here and tell us what the hell those little Celestial friends of his are jabbering about,' Myers suggested.

Simpson turned to a marine crouching nearby and gave orders to fetch the Australian civilian and a short time later John joined the American officers. Simpson introduced them.

'You understand what they are saying over there?' Myers asked bluntly.

John strained forward and listened to the words. 'You don't really want to know, Captain Myers,' he said with a frown.

'Spit it out, Mr Wong,' Myers said.

'They are saying it won't be long before they are in a position to overrun us, and that they will take their time torturing to death each and every defender who falls into their hands alive. They are even suggesting the best ways of keeping a man alive in prolonged agony. One idea is to . . .'

'I've heard enough,' Myers cut John short. 'Simpson has informed me that you have been doing commendable work alongside his boys, Mr Wong.'

'Just what I can do,' John shrugged modestly. 'As has Private Larry Gilles.'

'Gilles?' Myers asked, looking to Simpson.

'One of my men,' Simpson answered. 'Currently laid up with a wound.'

'He should get a medal,' John added. 'I am sure that a few days back he took out that marksman who was causing your boys a bit of grief.'

Myers grinned. 'I will look into writing up something,' he said, taking John's hint. 'Thank you, Mr Wong. You can return to your position.'

John slipped away, staying in a low crouch to ensure none of his big frame was exposed at any point on his way back to his position on the line.

'We have no choice,' Myers said. 'Or tomorrow those Chinks will be putting into practice what Mr Wong has said they are planning for us. Organise a force of whatever you can get together of our allies, Mr Simpson. We are to assemble at 3 am at the bell tower. These are my orders for an assault on the enemy positions to our front.'

He passed Simpson a sheet of paper on which he had pencilled a sketch of their location marking the enemy defences as well as instructions as to how he envisaged the attack to be carried out.

'Can I attach Mr Wong to our contribution, sir?' Simpson asked, causing Myers to frown.

'Mr Wong is a foreign national and a civilian,' Myers answered.

'But my men feel he is lucky,' Simpson countered.

'I suppose,' Myers accepted.

Simpson slipped away to liaise with his Russian and British opposites, and to inform John that he would be joining the group selected for the early morning attack.

The single candle flickered in the room. Andrew's whole being was racked with his grief. Sobbing, he kneeled by Liling's lifeless body, holding her in his arms and spilling tears down her now strangely serene face. Her death had come with a convulsion and there had been nothing he could do to save the courageous girl to whom he had sworn his love only hours earlier. When she had a brief moment of lucid recognition before slipping back into her fevered coma, he had promised her that when she finally got well they would always be together. Liling had smiled, hearing his words.

Now she was dead. Andrew's tears were bitter when he remembered how he had gone to the European hospital to ask for medicines but had been refused the precious supplies when the doctor had learned the young Australian wanted the medicine for a Chinese patient. 'Sorry, old chap,' the doctor had dismissed Andrew. 'But I must keep our supplies for the European sick.'

An old Chinese man whose back was bent with age shuffled over to Andrew. 'She is with her ancestors,' he said, gently touching the young man on the shoulder. 'She has flown from this terrible place to one far better.'

Andrew looked up at the old man. 'She was not a Christian,' he said.

'She was an angel,' the old man replied. 'Liling helped so many of us as an angel from God would. Now she flies with the other angels the missionaries have told us about.'

Andrew gripped Liling's slight body to his own as if to never let it go.

'Thank you, honourable uncle, for your words,' Andrew said, seeing the sad pain of loss on the old man's face. 'You are right in what you have said. Liling is now with God and His angels.'

Andrew lowered Liling's body onto the dusty floor and rose unsteadily to his feet. All he could do for her now was ensure that she be buried rather than disposed of over the wall like unwanted refuse.

'Please watch over Liling,' Andrew asked the old man. 'I will return to have her buried.'

The old man nodded. 'It is she who now watches over us,' he said. 'But I will stay by her side until you return.'

Andrew turned and walked away, wiping the remaining traces of tears from his face.

John had left the line to get some sleep in Robert's quarters before the planned night assault on the Chinese barricades. Sitting with his back against the wall, he stared up through the hole in the roof at a cluster of stars, thinking about many things. His mind drifted over the fate of his two children, the feelings he had for Liza and the fear he felt for the ominously close hour of the dangerous attack on the enemy. As weary as he was, John decided to write a letter. He groped around until he found the stub of a candle which he lit. Its weak light provided just enough illumination for him to locate the desk drawer where he knew Robert kept his stationery.

On top of the desk, which was splintered in places from the impact of shrapnel balls, was the little stone dragon encased in its protective shell. John paused in his search to gaze at the object. It bore the recent scar of a shrapnel ball that had glanced off it, chipping away a very small fragment from the outer shell of the rock. John took the stone in his hand and drew it close to his face to examine the tiny traces of the long extinct creature's feet. He did not know why but he found himself quietly swearing an oath. 'I swear to the spirit of this rock and its dragon that I will protect my son, Andrew, my daughter, Naomi, and also Liza and Liling from all harm that may attempt to come upon them.'

Self-consciously, he placed the rock down and laughed softly. His oath had been such a pagan thing to do. But then John was a self-declared non-believer in the Christian ways. In his youth he had been influenced by the Aboriginal people with whom he had come into contact in Queensland's most isolated places, far from the white man's world. Those people had believed in the practicality of the things of their world: of spirits that lived in rocks, trees, waterholes and up in the sky. Death was accepted as another part of life and the tangible world of the living very much in contact with the world of the dead. So it had been with this rock and its fossil, John thought. Although it was a long dead creature, it was still visible to him in this present time.

John forgot about writing the letters. Sleep overwhelmed him and he slipped sideways onto the floor of the room. The candle beside him flickered and died, leaving the room under a starlit night sky where the red planet, Mars the god of war, reigned supreme in the heavens.

A few hours later, Andrew found his father assembling with the small force of Russian, American and British troops at the Bell Tower. In all, sixty men formed the force under the command of the US marine captain, Jack Myers.

Fear was something that each man attempted to contain in front of his comrades and John was only too aware of his own. Between snatching brief naps and manning the barricades he had not had the opportunity to seek out Liza who he knew worked equally long hours assisting in the hospital. Now, he regretted not writing the letters for his son, daughter and Liza.

'Father,' Andrew called to him in the dark. John recognised his son's voice and sought him out.

Seeing his father emerge from the dark, rifle slung on his shoulder, Andrew immediately clasped him in a rib-crushing hug. 'She is gone,' he sobbed, the pain of loss overwhelming him once again. 'Liling, she is dead. A fever has taken her life.'

John extracted himself from his son's desperate embrace and clasped his shoulders. 'I am sorry, son,' he said. 'I know how much you loved her. She was as fine a young lady as any I have had the privilege to meet.'

Andrew forced back what remained of his tears and glanced around him. He could see the armed soldiers talking quietly, smoking cigarettes and standing close to each other in the light cast by a bonfire.

'I have heard about the attack to be launched on the wall,' Andrew said. 'I pray that you are not to be part of it.'

John felt uncomfortable. 'I am,' he said. 'I can't let down the Yanks.'

'It is a soldiers' fight,' Andrew chided. 'You do not have to go with them.'

'I am sorry for your loss,' John said gently. 'But we

277

are fighting with our backs to the wall and every gun counts. Fighting is something I am good at.'

'But you still have your wound,' Andrew attempted to rationalise.

'I hardly feel it now,' John lied. 'It only hurts when I laugh and I have not had much chance to do that lately.'

'I have lost the woman I swore my eternal love to, and now I face losing you within the next few hours,' Andrew pleaded. 'We have to remain alive to find Naomi.'

'I would expect you to do that, Andrew,' John answered, 'if something might happen to me.'

'Ready, men,' a voice called. 'Prepare to move out.'

'Father,' Andrew said, clasping John by the shirt sleeve. 'Remain behind. You don't have to go.'

'I have to go, Andrew,' he said gruffly. 'I will see you when the sun rises on the morrow.' With these last words, John walked briskly to the huddle of US marines forming up in their ranks, passing Robert Mumford who was with a contingent of British marines.

'I see that you have deserted the British Empire, Mr Wong,' Robert joked.

'The Yankee marines have nicer uniforms,' John retorted, joining the rear section of the contingent.

'Good luck then, old chap,' Robert said.

'You too, Mr Mumford,' John responded, not daring to look back to where he had left his grieving son. Why was it that he felt such a feeling of dread?

But his dread was heightened when the half mad

Norwegian missionary, Nestergaard, suddenly loomed from the night, waving his arms and howling accusations at the men ready to move out, shouting that his name was being sullied by all and that King Oscar of Norway would grant him justice. The soldiers' attention was focused on the tall, gaunt man whose appearance in his long, black cassock reminded John of what he had read about the ancient Celtic Druids.

'Get that man and gag him,' Robert ordered, seeing the superstitious fear that the missionary was evoking in the men waiting to face battle. 'Get him away from here, now.'

Two soldiers immediately stepped forward to grapple with the Norwegian, who was still babbling about justice for his good name. They stuffed a rag in his mouth and, holding his flailing arms down, frogmarched him off into the night to place him in custody, thus bringing relief to all waiting to move out. John had wondered about the sudden appearance of the man and shook his head. He was growing superstitious, he chided himself. Not a good thing at this moment.

The soldiers moved in a silence only broken by the never-ending sporadic rifle fire that rained down on different sections of the legation defences. Soon they were all assembled behind their lines on the great Tartar Wall.

John unslung his rifle and waited. He was not the only civilian volunteer, he realised, recognising one or two British men with the Royal Marines. Light rain fell on the assembled force of soldiers and civilian militia preparing to launch the attack.

'We are about to embark on a desperate enterprise,' Captain Myers spoke, addressing the assault force. 'It is one that I have advised against but the orders have been given and we must do it – or lose every man in the attempt. We will line up on the wall and rush the covering wall, then follow up that covering wall till we get to the back of the Chinese barricade. If there is anyone whose heart is not in the business he had better say so and clear out.'

A silence followed, and only one man excused himself on account of an injured arm. Dying was bad, John thought. But being seen to be a coward was a lifelong slow death.

'Go!'

The order shouted by Myers galvanised the waiting men into action. They scrambled over their barricade to tumble ten feet to the wall below. The light patter of raindrops had turned into a torrential downpour as the Americans erupted, yelling like Indian warriors. John found himself yelling alongside them as they charged forward into a hail of bullets from the Chinese.

All thoughts left John apart from reaching the barricade. He hurled himself at the outline of the wall in front of him and slung his rifle before clambering over the stone fortification, aware that others were doing likewise, while continuing to yell like demons out of hell.

Then John found himself on the other side and a figure loomed up to meet him. It was a Boxer whose predominantly white uniform stood out in the dark. John fired from the hip, felling the figure before him and then felt something jab him in the arm. He swung, using the rifle barrel to parry the point of a bayonet and followed up by swinging the butt of his rifle, smashing into a Chinese soldier's head. Around him he could hear men grunting, cursing and screaming. The heavy scent of unwashed bodies mixed with the coppery smell of spilled blood while an occasional shot sounded as soldiers on both sides freed themselves from the melee to reload. The hand-to-hand fighting asked no quarter – nor gave any. Surrender was futile and the men stabbed, bit and gouged at their foe. John chambered a round just as another enemy figure lunged at him with a spear. John was so close that he rammed the rifle barrel in the man's stomach and fired. Then, as suddenly and savagely as it had begun, the desperate fighting ceased.

'Hold your ground, lads. Form a skirmish line,' Robert bellowed. 'Report casualties.'

John edged his way into the skirmish line and kneeled on one knee, facing down the wall where he and his comrades remained until the sun began to cast its first light on their position, revealing the carnage all around them. John counted at least sixty dead Chinese, and heard that they had sustained three dead, six wounded. He did not count the deep cut to his upper arm as a wound even though it was bleeding profusely. He did not think any major artery or vein had been severed and had already applied a clean rag to stem the blood flow.

Against the odds they had swept the enemy from this vital part of the wall and among the wounded was Jack Myers, who had slipped on a spear in the dark, sustaining a deep thigh wound. By mid-morning a relief force came to take possession of the new defences, now popularly known as Fort Myers, in honour of the courage of the US marine who had led the almost suicidal attack against the Chinese.

Exhausted, John made his way down the wall to seek sleep. He collapsed on the mattress at his temporary home in Robert's quarters. The ever-present stench of rotting flesh pervaded the room but John was beyond caring as he slipped into a troubled sleep filled with nightmares.

A new problem had emerged for the defenders.

Robert stood at the back of Sir Claude MacDonald's spacious office, surrounded by the uniformed officers of the Russian, American and Italian military contingents. All his fellow officers were red-eyed and covered in dust that stained their uniforms a dark colour when combined with the sweat of the Chinese summer.

'Those confounded Germans gave up the wall without a damned shot being fired,' Captain Poole, a British officer raged, 'forcing our American friends to leave their posts a couple of a hundred yards away when their rear was exposed to an attack.'

Robert had witnessed the debacle when the Chinese had crept up a ramp to take possession of the broad ramparts of the Tartar Wall. The massive wall was the key point to the defence of the legation and its loss would mean certain defeat. He had tried to rally the fleeing German soldiers, but to no avail. One vital observation Robert had made was that the Chinese now occupying the ramparts had not followed up with reinforcements.

'Do I have any suggestions, gentlemen?' Sir Claude asked quietly, stilling the fuming British officer's verbal attack on the German troops and their officers' lack of courage.

'I think that we can clear the Chinese from the ramparts, sir,' Robert said. 'A sizeable force could sweep them back but I doubt we would have enough force to reoccupy the positions the Germans lost.'

I agree,' Captain Poole concurred. 'Because if we don't succeed, then we are all doomed.'

'Major Tolsky,' Sir Claude said, turning to a Russian officer whose uniform was spattered with dried bloodstains. 'Do you think that you could assemble a contingent of your men for an assault on the wall?'

'Da, I can do that,' the Russian answered with a growl, befitting his bear-like appearance.

'We will muster troops,' the American officer present volunteered.

'That leaves you, Mr Mumford, to arrange soldiers from Captain Poole's command to join with our American and Russian friends. The overall command of the attack will be given to Major Tolsky as the senior officer present. Are there any questions?'

Heads shook and Robert was already thinking about how he would organise his contingent of seconded troops to integrate in the attack to sweep the Chinese from the wall.

'Very good, gentlemen,' Sir Claude concluded.

'I trust in God and the might of European arms to achieve your mission.'

After attending a briefing from the Russian commander, Robert assembled his men and double-marched them to join the American and Russian contingents. He had twenty men assigned to him and each and every one of his soldiers already bore the sign of constant battle – the long, staring look of a man who had seen too much and sought something beyond the hell of possible sudden death, or worse, a lingering death from a severe wound.

'Fix bayonets!' Robert commanded and the click of bayonet rings being connected to the end of rifle barrels had the ominous sound of men preparing to fight so close to their enemy that each man would see the other's agonised expression when the long blade was plunged into his stomach, chest or throat.

'Advance!' Robert said, drawing his revolver and stepping in front of his men.

The sun was midway on the horizon and the American and Russian forces beside them were also advancing with fixed bayonets. The troops of the Chinese army gaped with surprise at the sudden appearance of the advancing Europeans. They were under the delusion that their foreign enemy, once swept from the ramparts, would be too weak to mount a counterattack. Most turned and fled and those braver Chinese soldiers who did not found themselves fighting hand to hand with the professionals from Europe and America. Within bloody minutes Robert and his multinational comrades had cleared the wall and secured it against a possible Chinese counterattack. It was a small victory but a vital one.

Late July to Early August 1900 Pekin

Who was he, and where was he? The light returned to John's world. He was confused and had little memory of either who he was or where he had found himself.

'He is waking,' a distant voice said from what seemed to be miles away.

It was a female voice, one he vaguely remembered, but his peaceful world was rudely shaken by the sound of scattered rifle fire followed by the crump of something exploding. The sounds and stench he was becoming aware of brought back vague but unpleasant memories.

'Pekin,' he whispered hoarsely through dry and cracked lips. He felt a cool cloth on his brow.

'Do not try to sit up,' the soothing voice said as John slowly opened his eyes. 'I will give you water to drink.'

John flinched when the light came back into his world and illuminated a face hovering over his.

'Who are you?' he asked, staring at the pretty young woman. 'I think that I know you.'

'I am Elizaveta,' she said with an expression of concern.

'Where am I?' John asked, accepting the water being dribbled into his mouth. He felt so weak that he had trouble swallowing.

'You were brought to the hospital when Lieutenant Mumford found you,' Liza said. 'Your wounds were infected and you have been delirious. I thought that you might die.'

'When was I brought here?' John asked, slowly remembering parts of nightmares and dreams that must have been real events in his life.

'You have been here eight days,' Liza answered.

Despite her protests John struggled to sit up in the hospital bed and lean against the wall behind him. When he gazed around he saw many soldiers and from their bandages realised they were casualties of a war.

'I am in Pekin, China,' John said softly. 'There is something happening and I have met you before,' he continued.

Liza nodded. 'Have you lost some memories?'

'I think so,' John replied, turning his attention to the woman tending him. 'How did we meet?'

'We met here,' Liza replied sadly. 'When you were first wounded. You do not remember our meeting?'

'I wish I could,' John answered, shaking his head sadly. 'Do you know why I am here? I vaguely recall that this place is not home.'

'You came to Pekin with your son, Andrew, to find your daughter, Naomi,' Liza replied.

'My son and daughter,' John repeated. 'Where are they now?'

'I think that you should rest and take some soup before you wear yourself out,' Liza said. 'I will inform the doctor that you have regained consciousness and that your fever has broken.'

Liza turned her back on her patient and walked away, forcing back the tears. How could she tell this man who was fortunate to be alive that his son had been reported missing just hours before John had regained consciousness? How could she tell this man she had strong feelings for, that he had lost a daughter, and now his son? Liza had learned that a Chinese convert had informed Dr Morrison that he had seen the young man – well known to them for his dedicated service to the sick and injured – slip beyond the defensive barricades and disappear into the Boxer-held territory beyond. In Morrison's opinion, to do so had been suicidal.

'Please, God, help me,' she prayed as she went in search of the overworked doctor on duty that day.

Blood streamed down Andrew's forehead into his eyes as he attempted to rise from the hard earth but felt the butt of a rifle drive him down again.

'I have a pass,' he groaned. 'I have a pass from your general.'

The bashing ceased and Andrew became aware of what seemed to be a sea of legs all around him in the dimly lit room, smelling of sweat, urine and rotting bodies. They had snatched him from the street in the dark and dragged him into a building before he could even explain that he was in possession of a pass. The beating had commenced at once and Andrew knew that a mere scrap of parchment was the only thing between him and a painful death.

'Rice bowl Christian,' a voice snarled. 'You expect us to believe you when you do not even sound like a true son of the soil. Soon, when we have tired of hurting you, we will take your head and collect our reward. You were seen coming from the foreign devil's compound.'

Andrew removed the pass, holding it out to his tormentor who snatched it from his hand.

'What does it say?' he heard the voice of his chief torturer ask, handing the pass now blotted with Andrew's blood to another Boxer warrior who could obviously read.

'It is a pass granted by the general,' the man said with just a touch of awe.

'How do I know that you are not lying?' the man snarled. 'How do I know that you did not steal this pass from someone else?'

Andrew lifted his head, and staring up at his tormentor saw a pockmarked face scarcely concealing a deep cruelty. 'There is one of you who can vouch for the authenticity of the pass,' Andrew said, aware that the eyes boring into him were those of the devil himself. 'His name is Tung Chi, a former Shaolin priest who I believe is of some standing in your cause.'

'Tung Chi,' the man said. 'You claim to know him?'

'I do,' Andrew replied, knowing that his life hung in the balance.

He was cursing himself for his foolish, impulsive act of leaving the barricades to go in search of his sister. But the grief of losing Liling and learning of his father being hospitalised had made Andrew consider the situation. In the balance it appeared they were most likely to be overrun, as there had been no indication of a relief force coming to their rescue, and Andrew had decided to at least take the risk of using the pass to find Naomi. After all, that is why he and his father had risked their lives. Now, it seemed that once too often he had gambled against the odds on succeeding.

'Honourable commander Han,' a warrior said. 'This man has the same family name as the woman you kept, according to what is written on the pass.'

Andrew thought that he saw the man called Han blink, but he did not take his attention from him.

'You have the same accent as woman called Naomi Wong,' Han said. 'Are you her husband?'

At the mention of Naomi's name, Andrew experienced a fleeting moment of happiness.

'I am her brother,' he replied softly.

'Then you are an enemy of the people,' Han said with a satisfied smirk. 'You can expect no mercy.'

'Honourable Commander Han,' the soldier who held the pass said. 'I think that it would be wise to inform Commander Tung that we have this man as a prisoner.'

Han turned slowly to stare at the warrior who had dared suggest a course of action to him, contemplating the option of slowly killing the man at his feet. It was possible that having this man in his custody might assist in bringing the former Shaolin priest down. All he had to do was think of an angle to approach the challenge of disgracing Tung. Han returned his attention to Andrew and the Boxer adviser breathed once again; it did not help one's life expectancy to upset Commander Han.

'Why did you risk your life leaving your defences?' Han asked. 'Did you come to spy?'

'No,' Andrew answered. 'I had hoped to see my sister, Honourable Commander.'

'I know your sister,' Han said with a cruel smirk. 'She has been of great assistance to the morale of my men on many occasions.'

Andrew felt a sudden rage grip him. Oh, how he wished that he had kept the pistol and could now ram it into that pockmarked face and pull the trigger. But he also knew his only hope of surviving the next few minutes was to kowtow to his captor's whims.

'It is good that she is of service,' Andrew replied, forcing back the rising bile in his throat. 'Is there a chance that I may see my sister?'

'I would grant you that wish, dog,' Han hissed. 'But she is the prisoner of the Shaolin priest you say you know.'

Andrew heard Han's words and felt a hope rise to wash away the bile. If what Han said was true then maybe Naomi was in safe hands after all. 'I beg you to let me live to see my sister, Honourable Commander,' Andrew said, feigning subservience. 'I can see that you are a man much respected by your men.'

Han knew that his captive's words were motivated

by fear rather than any respect for him, but this did not matter. He still held the foreigner's life in his hands. 'It is possible that I will grant you time to see your sister before I execute you,' Han said. 'I will take you to Commander Tung on one condition only. To refuse me will mean a slow death without ever seeing your sister again.'

'I will do whatever you say,' Andrew answered, sensing that his life would be spared.

Han turned to his adviser and spoke to him while Andrew remained on the ground. He remained thus for some minutes until Han ordered him to his feet, directing him to a small table.

'Sit down and sign this paper,' Han said, thrusting a sheet of paper in front of him.

Andrew perused the freshly written document. Although it was in Chinese he could follow the script and paled under the blood streaming down his face. 'This is not true,' he said softly.

Han leaned forward into Andrew's face. 'It is true, if you sign it,' he said with a stony face. 'The choice is either your signature or your death in a way that will have you screaming to be killed quickly.'

A quill dipped in ink was placed before him. Andrew stared for a moment at the pen. He may as well have picked up a knife or gun for what he was being asked to do.

'You will not be killed if you sign,' Han said. 'After all, I will need you to corroborate your story before the general.'

Andrew reached for the quill and held it above the parchment. He knew that by signing he was sentencing Tung to death but the memory of the great Chinese library burning helped him decide although he knew that he was being forced to choose between his former friend and his sister. As Andrew applied the ink to the paper he thought he saw the slightest glimmer of a smile on Han's face.

'Now you will see your sister,' Han said, slipping the signed document from the table. 'And I will make an appointment with the Honourable General. I am sure that he will be unpleasantly surprised to see what you have told us about the Honourable Commander Tung's treachery.'

Andrew suddenly felt violently sick and could not prevent himself from vomiting on the floor.

'The boys was wonderin' when you was returning,' Private Larry Gilles said.

'Er, as soon as possible,' John dutifully replied, to humour the tall, broad-shouldered young soldier standing by his bed.

'The Lootenant agrees with the boys that you are lucky for our section,' Private Gilles continued. 'We have been takin' a hammering on the line. But I should let you get some rest so I will see you soon, Mr Wong.' John took the young soldier's hand and felt his strong grip. 'So long, Mr Wong. Be seeing you soon.'

'I obviously know him,' John said to Liza, who had returned to his side at every possible opportunity since he had regained his senses three days earlier. She had told him how he had lapsed in and out of his fever, drinking and taking a little food, seemingly oblivious to all around him. And it was only when the fever fully abated that he appeared to be conscious of the world around him, but without any real memory of the past.

John's next visitor was his compatriot Dr Morrison, who seemed to accept John's lack of memory.

'Our Chinese converts found an old artillery piece,' Morrison said, sitting by John's bed and briefing him on events since his admission to the hospital. 'Sergeant Mitchell from the US contingent has been able to get it working and we recovered the Russian shells from a well where they had been dumped. The calibre was just about right and the old gun has caused the Chinese a few headaches. We do not understand why the Chinese army has not brought up his best gunners and guns to finish us off and I suspect that they are deployed to stop any reinforcements reaching us. But the Imperial troops and Boxers are continuing to build barricades further each day and many of our converts are trying to flee, poor devils. They usually end up as mutilated corpses floating in the river. Our Japanese allies have been fighting superbly,' Morrison continued. 'Of all our contingents I think they have suffered the hardest blows. Their Colonel Shiba is a remarkable man.'

'I have a son, Dr Morrison,' John said, cutting the informal briefing short. 'Do you know him?'

Morrison sat back in his chair and cleared his throat. 'Your son, Andrew, is a fine young man who has provided sterling service in the last week or so tending to the Chinese in the Fu.'

'Could you get a message to my son that I would like to see him?' John asked.

Morrison looked uncomfortable. 'I am afraid that your son was last seen slipping out of the legation yesterday, in the late evening hours,' Morrison answered.

'Would not that be extremely dangerous?' John asked.

Morrison looked away. 'I cannot answer that question, Mr Wong. Nothing has come to me through my sources to report his death.'

'I must find him and my daughter, who I have been told is also a captive of the Chinese,' John said, staring at the fly-specked ceiling of the improvised ward he shared with many other wounded soldiers.

'Well, Mr Wong, Miss Gurevich has informed me that you are getting well very quickly,' Morrison said, rising to his feet.

'Why is it that I do not remember so much?'

Morrison paused. 'I have heard a theory that the constant stress of facing death, coupled with a severe illness, can cause a block to our memory,' he said. 'But, with good food, treatment and rest I am sure your memory will return, Mr Wong.'

'Thank you, doctor,' Liza said, taking over. 'I will ensure that he receives all three.'

Morrison picked up his rifle. 'I know he is in good hands,' Morrison said and walked away leaving John alone with Liza.

'You should sleep,' she said gently.

John closed his eyes. When he next opened them it was dark and humid and he realised that he had slipped into a deep, dreamless sleep. When he turned his head he could see Liza sitting in a chair by his bed, her eyes closed.

'Liza,' John called softly.

She woke with a start. 'What is it?' she asked, bending over him.

John suddenly pulled Liza's face down to his, and kissed her with a passion that came from the heart. 'I remember,' he said with a broad smile. 'I remember the kiss.'

Liza gasped, attempting to pull away, but he drew her down onto the bed where he kissed her again. She did not resist, surrendering to her feelings. Then, straightening up, she brushed down her dress, pleased that the ward was so dimly lit.

'It is obvious that your memory has returned,' she said with her own gentle smile.

'I remember everything,' John said softly. 'And I know why I am here. Tomorrow, I am leaving the hospital.'

Robert sat at his battered desk in what was left of his quarters. Sweat dripped onto the sheets of paper laid out on the desk. The last thing he wanted to do was write a report for Sir Claude when he would rather have accepted an invitation to dinner with the American Conger family. But an unexpected truce had been called by the Chinese, and Sir Claude wanted a report on the situation as it stood for the defenders. Robert, like many others, was at a loss to understand why the Chinese would want a truce. Was it possible that advancing European forces had forced the Empress and her army to reconsider their situation? But one never knew with the Chinese mind, Robert thought, shaking his head. They were not as predictable as many of the European community had presumed.

Glossy black flies crawled over his exposed flesh and the British officer was only too aware of why they were so fat. He brushed them away with a sense of disgust and leaned back in the chair, attempting to dismiss the ever-constant stench of rotting bodies that pervaded the hot, summer air. Two mines buried under the French legation buildings by Chinese sappers had exploded earlier in the week, forcing the French soldiers to give up two-thirds of their territory. The defences were shrinking every day, with no sign of help from the outside world.

The tough and courageous Japanese soldiers had been forced to pull out of the line for badly needed rest and, while they were recovering, the defences were vulnerable.

The damned, demented Nestergaard had succeeded in going over to the enemy lines, where he was welcomed. It seemed that the Chinese had a respect for mad men. After a hearty meal supplied by the enemy, the missionary had informed the Chinese soldiers that they were firing too high, along with providing them with the latest information on the layout of the defences. The Chinese marksmen had since rectified that situation and the casualties mounted behind the barricades. Many in the legation wanted Nestergaard shot as a traitor when he was returned unharmed, but Robert had joined those defending him, saying that it was not cricket to shoot a mad man.

Robert glanced at the loose sheets of papers submitted to him from the hospital. It was the casualty list and two names on it made the British officer sigh. Both were men he knew well. One was young Henry Warren, a British student interpreter with the civil service who had been hit in the face by shrapnel from an exploding artillery shell while serving alongside the Japanese in the Fu. Robert had heard how the doctors had fought to save his life on the operating table but a bone from his shattered face had slipped into his throat and even a tracheotomy had not been successful. Polly Condit Smith would miss him, Robert mused, remembering how many times before the siege he had seen the two dancing together under the Chinese lanterns.

A fellow officer, Captain Strouts, was listed as killed in action. Below his name was that of Dr George Morrison with the initials WIA – wounded in action. Again, it was a situation Robert knew about from eye witnesses. Strouts and Morrison had accompanied the British relief force to replace the Japanese in the Fu and while returning with the Japanese commander, Colonel Shiba, had run into a hail of enemy rifle fire. A bullet had ripped into Morrison's thigh, shattering his thigh bone, while Strouts fell mortally wounded into the Japanese officer's arms. A bullet tearing the artery in his thigh caused Strouts to bleed to death three hours later in the hospital, where he had been carried by a stretcher party under heavy fire.

Robert neatly drew up columns on a sheet of paper and added each man's name as either military or civilian, officer or enlisted man, dead or wounded.

When his report was completed, there was little time to reflect on finding a meal and getting some badly needed sleep before accepting the American diplomat's invitation. At least Robert knew that he would be eating something other than horse meat at the Congers' table. They had their own cache of tinned food and with any luck Robert might get to eat tinned fruit.

Despite his pass from General Tung Fu-hsiang, Andrew was treated as a hostile prisoner by Han. He was force-marched along darkened streets through Chinese military formations until they reached the Forbidden City, the palaces of the Empress. He was taken through lavish, ornate gardens until they reached a building surrounded by heavily armed guards who challenged Han and his warriors.

After a discussion with the guards, Han was admitted alone into the building that Andrew guessed, from the activity he observed around him, was being used as a military headquarters. His head throbbed from the rifle butt blows but the blood had dried forming a scab on his scalp.

A short time later Han returned, gesturing to Andrew to follow him inside and, although he was not bound, Andrew realised that escape was impossible in the streets teeming with Imperial troops and Boxers. He followed Han through avenues of armed guards until they reached an anteroom decorated with murals of Chinese rural scenes. The room was lit with braziers that cast eerie, flickering shadows in the corners.

'Get down on your knees,' Han hissed, prostrating himself at the same time.

Andrew obeyed, ensuring that his eyes were fixed on the marble floor. Then, the feared Chinese general entered the room and Han's plot to have his hated opponent removed was set in motion.

'This is the man who has sworn the statement that Commander Tung is a traitor to our cause?' the general asked.

'Yes, most Honourable General,' Han replied, kowtowing respectfully. 'My unit captured him attempting to make contact with Commander Tung. He carried a pass purporting to be granted by you.'

'Let me see the pass.'

Han quickly produced the now crumpled piece of paper and handed it to one of the general's staff. It was in turn passed to the general, who had now sat himself in an ornate chair raised on a small dais.

'I know of this pass,' the general said. 'But why is it that this foreigner should confess to a statement condemning Commander Tung as a traitor?' he asked in a menacing tone.

Han suddenly felt a chill of fear. Had he overstepped his mark in getting the captured man to lie? After all, he was attempting to discredit one of the general's own blood. Now, he wished that he could retrieve the statement and simply do away with the captured man for the price the Empress had secretly put on all captured and killed defenders from the legation.

'I admit that I applied more than persuasive means to extract the confession from this man called Andrew Wong,' Han said quickly, attempting to find a way out of a situation that was turning dangerously against him. Sweat had broken out on his brow despite the coolness of the marbled room. 'I also thought it was a lie and that this unworthy dog was attempting to smear the good name of the honourable Tung Chi.'

The Chinese general stared hard at the Boxer commander. Trouble was breaking out between the Imperial troops of the Chinese army and the rebel Boxer units and such a rift could cause serious problems. Besides being a tactical soldier, the general was also a good politician. He suspected that the man before him had a deadly grudge against his nephew but at the same time he could not be seen to be playing favourites.

'Does not Commander Tung currently hold a foreign woman in his care that you were forced to hand over?' he now asked in a menacing tone that frightened the already terrified Boxer commander even more.

'He does, most Honourable General,' Han confirmed. 'She is to be returned to me at first light tomorrow.'

'You, prisoner,' the General said, turning his attention to Andrew. 'I have been told that this woman is your sister.'

'She is, most Honourable General,' Andrew

replied, his eyes still downcast. 'I was only attempting to find her.'

'How do you explain this statement condemning Commander Tung?' the general asked, waving the statement of written lies in the air.

'Commander Han was so enthusiastic in his interrogation of me when I was first captured that I thought I would not see my sister so I made up the lies,' Andrew said, knowing that for some reason he had to extract the odious Chinese captor out of this difficult situation for both their sakes. 'The Honourable Commander Han is most obviously dedicated to the cause of freeing China and I bitterly regret saying those things when I consider Commander Tung a friend.'

'A friend,' the general growled. 'How is it that my nephew knows you?'

'My father and I assisted Commander Tung when he was in the Land of the Golden Mountain.'

'He spoke of your help,' the general said. 'He said that you were a Western-trained doctor of medicine.'

Andrew did not think it wise to correct the feared Chinese general about his qualifications. A final year medical student was not a registered doctor. 'I am,' he lied once again.

'I have need of medical men to treat my sick and wounded,' the general said. 'As a prisoner of the Empress, you will be supplied with medical supplies that we have captured from the missionary stations and go about the work of treating my men.'

'Most Honourable General,' Han said, attempting to hold onto the last scraps of whatever he could retrieve from the dangerous situation that he had put himself in. 'The woman is to be returned to me.'

The general glowered at Han. 'She remains with Commander Tung, and the prisoner will also be placed in his custody. You are dismissed, Commander Han, to return to your post on the lines.'

Kowtowing again, Han retreated from the room but as he passed Andrew he cast him a look that spelled death and Andrew had no doubt that he would have to protect his back at all times from this man.

'Dr Wong,' the general said when Han was out of the room, 'you are now a prisoner, but will be treated with courtesy, so long as you comply with my wishes and directions from Commander Tung. He has told me how you risked much in your country to protect him and, more importantly, how you aided his mission. You will meet with your sister.'

Andrew could hardly believe how his fortunes had changed in a matter of minutes. He also realised that if not for his relationship with his former friend, Tung Chi, he would have been dead.

'I thank you, most Honourable General,' Andrew replied, kowtowing. 'I promise on my life that I will carry out my sacred mission to assist the sick and wounded.'

'Take Dr Wong to Commander Tung,' the general said, turning to one of the aides standing by his elbow. 'Make sure that he is kept safe at all times.'

The general left the room, followed by his staff of uniformed army officers. How strange it was, Andrew thought, that he could not hate all these people who were seen by the Europeans at the besieged legation as being little more than barbaric savages. That he was granted the respect of a healer meant a lot to Andrew, and he had no concern that he would be treating the sick and wounded of a people considered the enemy. He was, after all, a doctor in their eyes.

But as he was being escorted from the palace to meet with Tung, Andrew felt more nervous than frightened. Soon Tung would come to learn of his betrayal. How would he react?

A huge, well-fed dog nosed among the scattered bones in front of the legation barricades. It snatched a thigh bone and scuttled away to enjoy the feast that the Europeans had provided in the vicious fighting.

Robert had joined many others who now dared raise their heads and scramble onto the top of the sandbags to survey the silent scene before them. The truce seemed to be holding, he mused, as many of the former enemy approached their positions without any sign of malice. When he looked back from his new perspective of the legation he noticed that many of the old, familiar landmarks were now little more than rubble. He spotted Kai, formerly Dr Morrison's servant, approaching the lines and wearing the colourful uniform of a Boxer. He could see that the man, who had mysteriously disappeared during the fighting weeks earlier, had been wounded. Dried blood discoloured his uniform.

'Kai,' Robert called. 'You old rascal. What are you doing in the uniform of our enemies?'

The old Chinese man, his face a mask of misery, looked up at the British officer.

'Sir, it is good to see you,' he replied.

'Why is it that you are wearing the uniform of our enemy?' Robert repeated.

'I went to see my cousin in the city,' Kai answered. 'I thought that he might have food but he turned me over to the Boxers and they made me fight with them. But now I want to return to my master, Dr Morrison.'

'Dr Morrison has been seriously wounded,' Robert chided. 'Because you were not there to defend him.'

Kai's face crumpled. 'I, too, have been wounded,' the old man whined. 'I must go to my master.'

'You would not do that, you old scoundrel,' Robert said. 'Unless you knew something of importance.'

Kai screwed up his wizened face. 'The Boxers and the army are sick of fighting, and we have heard that great battles have been fought from the Taku forts to Tientsin. Many are being sent to fight there.'

The news caused Robert to take a deep breath. From what the old servant had said it appeared a force was indeed fighting its way towards them and, for an instant, he felt no need to punish the old man for his treachery; he had relayed the best news he had received in all the time of the siege. The vital intelligence had been unwittingly relayed. 'You can enter and go to Dr Morrison,' Robert said gruffly.

It was time to pass on the valuable information to Sir Claude MacDonald. Robert had already calculated that their siege was far from over but now there was hope – so long as they held out in the legation and wisely ignored the pleas of the enemy to leave.

Sitting with his back to a tree inside the legation, John leaned on his rifle, staring blankly at the soldiers and civilians who passed by. He was tired and despondent. The killing never ceased and he doubted that the truce would last. Andrew was missing – just as Naomi was – somewhere in the city. At least with the truce he had the opportunity to plan a way of resuming his search.

'John.'

He snapped from his reverie to focus on Liza. From the weary expression and dark circles under her eyes he could see the siege was taking its toll on her. 'Liza,' he said with a faint smile. 'Would you like to sit down with me and share the shade?'

Liza sat beside John on the dry earth under the bullet-pocked tree. 'I have heard about Andrew and Liling,' she said. 'I am sorry for your loss.'

'If I know my son,' John said, 'he is still alive, having talked his way out of any trouble, and in time will rejoin us.'

'Why did he leave?' Liza asked, turning to gaze at the profile of the man who seemed to occupy her thoughts more and more each day.

'He was searching for his sister,' John sighed, leaning back against the substantial trunk of the tree. 'It is funny how much they used to fight when they were young, but he was the most protective brother any sister could have.'

'I have read a notice on the board at the Bell Tower that a combined force of 11,000 troops are on their way to relieve us,' she said. 'Colonel Shiba was able to get a messenger through to Tientsin and back with the good news. It will not be long before we will be relieved and you will be able to go in search of your son and daughter.'

'I will not wait that long,' John said softly. 'I am only here for one purpose.' He ceased speaking when he noticed the look of hurt cross Liza's face. 'But I would like you to leave with us when we return to Queensland.'

'I could not do that,' Liza said, looking away from John.

'Why not?' John asked. 'What is holding you back?'

'It is something that you would not understand,' Liza replied, not daring to look at him.

'I love you,' John said, grasping Liza by the shoulders. 'I would like to share the rest of my life with you.'

Liza shook off John's hands and stood up. He could see tears streaming down her face which she attempted to wipe away with the back of her sleeve. 'I must return to the hospital,' she said. 'And you must pursue your foolish idea of going in search of your son and daughter when the situation is still so dangerous.'

Liza walked away. Was she so unimportant that this man who professed to love her would risk getting himself killed and still expect her to believe he *really* loved her? The memory of another young man from a time not so long ago flooded her thoughts. He had chosen to enlist and fight in Cuba against the Spanish. Had he not promised to return and wed her? But all he found in his choice was a grave on foreign soil. She was no longer a young girl but a mature woman and had learned that men such as her former fiancé, and now John Wong, were men who chose to face death without much thought for those whom they loved and left behind.

John watched Liza walk away and was confused. He cursed himself. What had he said that could cause Liza to doubt his love for her? 'Talk to her, you bloody fool,' he muttered to himself, and was just about to follow when he was surprised to see Kai at the end of the street. 'Kai!' he called.

The servant stopped walking and turned to face John who had caught up with him. 'Mr Wong, it is good to see that you are well,' Kai said, bowing respectfully.

'Have you been in the city all the time that you were missing from here?' John asked.

'Yes, Mr Wong,' Kai replied. 'And I have seen your daughter, who is well, but I could not speak to her.'

'You have seen my daughter!' John gasped, grasping the little man by the shoulders. 'When?'

'Yesterday,' Kai replied. 'She is a prisoner of Commander Tung, but he treats her well.'

Tung! John knew that the name was held by many Chinese. And as far as he knew, his former travelling companion was also a high-ranking Boxer.

'What do you know of this Commander Tung?' John asked.

'He is the general's nephew and was once a revered Shaolin priest who speaks your language and has travelled beyond our lands.'

It had to be the same man, John exalted. If so, he must have discovered Naomi's identity.

'What of Master Andrew?' John asked, but Kai shook his head. 'Where did you see Miss Wong?'

'She is being held by Commander Tung on the Street of Dragons,' Kai answered. 'But I think she may not be there now as the general has been ordered to take his troops to fight at Tientsin. Commander Tung will probably go with him and if so he will take Miss Wong also.'

'Has the general left yet?' John asked, holding his breath for the answer.

'He left this morning when the truce was called,' Kai said, noticing the expression of bitter disappointment sweep across the big Eurasian's face. 'But he might have left his prisoners behind,' he hurried to add.

Andrew knew something was very wrong. On the way out of the general's headquarters one of Han's bodyguard had intercepted his escort. A heated discussion occurred that Andrew could not hear but the Boxer from Han's bodyguard turned to the men escorting Andrew and barked, 'Bind the prisoner.'

The guards immediately fell on him, securing his hands tightly behind his back with rope.

'Am I to be taken to Commander Tung?' Andrew asked Han's man as he was pushed forward at the end of a bayonet.

'It seems that the general is to leave the city for the front at Tientsin,' Han's bodyguard sneered triumphantly. 'His influence is not so well established with the Boxer command here, and you are now Commander Han's to dispose of. You can forget ever seeing your sister again.'

Andrew was propelled forward to slam into the hard earth.

'Get up, dog of the barbarians,' his guard snarled. 'The Honourable Commander Han has a fate for you that will make you wish I had killed you with my bayonet.'

Struggling to his feet, Andrew felt the total despair of a man standing on the scaffold staring at the noose to be placed around his neck. Although he suspected hanging would have been a merciful death compared to what Han might have planned for him.

'First, I will smash your knees,' Andrew's guard said with a cruel smile. 'Then I will smash your elbows, before slinging you over a pot of boiling water, where I will lower you slowly into the pot. You will scream to be killed but I will ensure that you stay alive to feel the flesh peel from your bones before death eventually comes to you.'

Bound and helpless in the stifling heat of the room, Andrew broke into a sweat and fought to control his bowels lest they let go in his terror. He had already seen the large metal pot being set over timber and overheard the guards laying bets as to how long he would live when lowered into the boiling water.

'Please, God, grant me mercy,' Andrew prayed softly as his guard stood over him, stinking of sweat and fish.

Han had not appreciated his efforts to protect him before the general, Andrew thought bitterly. What kind of demon had his sister been forced to endure?

'When?' Andrew rasped.

'When do I get to execute you for the Honourable Commander Tung?' the guard asked. 'As soon as the water boils.'

Andrew dared not look again through the narrow door at the pot being tended by Han's soldiers in the courtyard littered with the rubbish of occupation. All he could do was to continue praying for a quick death.

'Bring the prisoner,' Han's voice called from the courtyard.

The guard grabbed Andrew by the hair, pulling him to his feet. There was no point resisting, Andrew knew.

'I can walk on my own,' Andrew said to his guard.

He walked from the room into the blazing sunshine to see around twenty Boxers standing in a semi-circle around the pot, keen to observe the puppet of the foreign devils die a slow and agonising death. A solidly built Chinese soldier, stripped to the waist, swung a length of hard timber while two uniformed soldiers left the semi-circle, advancing on Andrew. When they reached him they untied his ropes and seized him by the arms. The Boxer with the length of timber approached and it was obvious that he was going to smash Andrew's limbs. Casting desperately around him, Andrew sought a miracle to save his life, but all he saw was Han's impassive face staring back at him. Andrew promised himself that he would not cry out for mercy, as that would be futile.

The two soldiers forced Andrew to the ground on his back and two more Boxers joined them to grip Andrew's ankles, while the Boxer with the timber raised above his head loomed over him.

'This is the death we grant those who would come to invade our sacred lands,' Han orated to the assembled Boxers. 'This man is of our blood, and like those dogs who accept the religion of the foreign devils among us, he will experience the death due to those who would sacrifice our children and drink their blood.'

A short silence followed and Andrew closed his eyes, preparing for the searing pain he knew would come when the timber connected with his knees. He could feel the vomit already rising in his throat.

The blow did not eventuate and Andrew opened his eyes. Rolling his head to the side, he could see through the legs of his guards many other legs on the other side of the courtyard. A heated conversation was underway between Han and an intruder backed by many men.

'Get him to his feet,' Andrew's guard growled.

Andrew was hoisted grudgingly to his feet. The sun was in his eyes and he shaded his eyes to try to see the newcomers.

'Bring the prisoner to me,' a voice he recognised commanded.

Andrew wanted to cry with joy. He was propelled roughly forward, stumbling, his legs still devoid of strength as he recovered psychologically from how close he had come to an agonising death. Tung was dressed in a uniform of black and scarlet and on either side of his saviour were men similarly dressed and armed with modern rifles casually pointed at Han's warriors.

'He is my prisoner,' Han spat at Tung's feet. 'I have deemed that he die in an appropriate manner befitting his crimes.'

'He is my prisoner, on the directions of General Tung Fu-hsiang,' Tung said. 'I have come to claim him in the name of the Honourable General.'

'The general is no longer in the city,' Han sneered. 'And you are a commander in the Boxer cause and not under the direct command of the Empress. You carry no more authority than me in these matters.'

'You speak treachery, Commander Han,' Tung said menacingly. 'It is her will that we fight alongside our brothers in her army and the General is one of the Empress's favourites. Would you dare question her authority?'

Han reddened to the point that Andrew thought the man might suffer a heart attack. Clearly Tung's quiet authority was causing his opposite to lose face. That and the many guns facing Han's warriors in the courtyard.

'Take the man,' Han finally relented, turning his back as if the matter was not really of any great importance.

Andrew was left standing alone. Without further

ado, Tung ordered his men to take him with them. As they edged away from the confrontation with Han and his men, Tung appeared to ignore Andrew and continued to do so as they marched along the street. Andrew accepted being ignored. He was simply grateful that his former friend had saved his life.

Early August 1900
Pekin

The stone splinters smacked John Wong in the cheek and he instinctively flung himself to the floor of Robert's quarters. The so-called truce had done little to stop sharpshooters seeking targets of opportunity, and John realised that the stone dragon had been directly in line with his head when the bullet entered the ruins of the room.

Warily, he sat up and rubbed his cheek, at the same time lining up the direction of the shot to see a Chinese soldier slither away from a rooftop at the edge of the defences.

John eased himself over to the table and picked the rock up. A small chunk had been bitten out of the rock by the bullet, taking a section of the delicate fossilised bone of the little dragon's rear leg. 'Better your leg than my head,' John muttered, turning the rock over in his hand. It had saved his life and he suddenly felt a strange sense of gratitude. The dragon was now his talisman and John wrapped the rock in an old, worn shirt to protect it from stray bullets or shrapnel. On second thoughts he dug a hole and buried the rock in a corner of the quarters. Satisfied with this added protection, he slung his rifle and went in search of Robert to propose a plan.

'I understand your need to go in search of your daughter, Mr Wong,' Robert said. 'But this so-called truce is as shaky as anything could be. They have already indicated the truce is all but over.'

John sucked on a cigar as both men stood behind a loop-holed barricade with a view of the golden-topped Forbidden City, seemingly rising out of a sea of green.

'Surely you could convince your superiors to launch a raid into the city to collect intelligence,' John replied. 'I have seen the Japanese buying rifles and ammo from Chinese soldiers and bartering for eggs.'

'It is not that simple,' Robert sighed. 'That happens only from the safety of our defences and we have a good idea that the enemy is still in great strength in the city. You know that I care for Naomi very much and if it were up to me I would not hesitate to go out alone in search of her. But we know that she is safe for the moment and I advise that we wait until a relief force arrives.'

'I have looked around the legation area and can see that by night the canal is a way to get out of here,' John said.

'We need every gun we can muster to man the defences, Mr Wong,' Robert said. 'I cannot order you to remain, but would beg you consider what I have advised.'

John took another puff on the cigar and watched the blue smoke curl away over the top of the sandbags. Swayed by the British officer's logic, he would give the relief force another week and if by then they had not arrived, it was most likely the rapidly reinforced Chinese army would overwhelm them. That would put the Chinese in a position to bargain with the Western powers allied against them.

John might have had information concerning his daughter but he had heard nothing about Andrew and it was this absence of news that worried him most. He gazed around and could see the pitiful state of the defenders living on meagre rations of rice and horse meat. Starvation might beat the Chinese to a victory, he thought. Despite the rumours of a relief force, the reality was that the Chinese were mustering for an all-out attack. Maybe the British officer was right. Every man toting a gun was needed on the lines. Besides his son and daughter, John now had one other to consider protecting – Liza.

Tung had provided Naomi with new quarters adjoining the palaces of the Empress and even a young servant girl to look after her needs. Fresh food arrived at her spacious rooms with their marbled floors and walls decorated with bright murals. Water was available and Naomi had a chance to bathe and change into clean clothes, albeit still the simple coolie outfit of trousers and long-sleeved flowing shirt. Despite her seeming freedom she was aware that she was still a prisoner and did not doubt Tung would have her executed, should she dare attempt an escape.

Her imprisonment took a turn when Meili found her way to an utterly surprised and overjoyed Naomi.

'I was able to slip away from Han and his men,' she said, as the two women sat in a shady garden by a water fountain holding hands. 'He has been in a terrible rage, swearing to kill Commander Tung. His rage has been so fierce that he was not aware of my existence, so I slipped away one night to go to Commander Tung and plead with him to be allowed to join you.'

'Why is it that Han wishes to kill Commander Tung?' Naomi asked.

'He is jealous of Commander Tung, but with a man like Han I think a demon worm crawls through his head. He does not have to have a reason to want to kill anyone,' Meili answered. 'Commander Tung must be very aware that Han will not rest until he has his head before his feet.'

Naomi thought about the threat to Tung. She surprised herself with her thoughts of concern, as the man was also her captor, promising her death should she attempt to escape. But despite this threat she had many opportunities to be in his company and share his conversation.

In the evenings Tung would retreat to her quarters and share his evening meal with her while his men stood guard outside. Never once had the Boxer leader attempted to force his attentions on her. Naomi was aware, as only a woman can be, that this mysterious man was interested in her as a woman of beauty and intellect.

Their conversations – shared over good wine and cool watermelon in the evenings – ranged from Tung's vision of a new China – where the people lived under a benign leader with rights before the law – to his reflections on the life he had experienced in his past as a Shaolin priest.

Sometimes he laughed at a joke, and Naomi was aware of how his normally serious expression lit up with a warmth that he could not conceal. Sometimes she had to remind herself that there was a man waiting for her on the other side of the barricades – a young British officer who had been on the verge of openly declaring his lifelong love for her. One thing Naomi had to concede was that the former Shaolin priest was a very attractive and desirable man.

Her unspoken reflections concerning Tung and Robert were suddenly interrupted when she paled and buckled to vomit. The sickness had started a week earlier and Meili cast her a worried look. 'You are with child,' she said bluntly.

'I cannot be,' Naomi gasped, wiping her mouth with cool, clear water from the fountain.

'It is something I have seen before,' Meili said. 'Have you missed your time?'

Naomi looked at Meili with an expression of fear and nodded.

'Then you are carrying a child,' Meili said.

Naomi had attempted to deny to herself something she had suspected for a week. The signs were there and if she were pregnant then the chances were that she was carrying the baby of the man she hated most in the world – Han.

'Oh please, God, no,' Naomi whispered in English, causing Meili to question her with a look. 'It is nothing,' Naomi replied in Chinese and bent over to be sick again, the retching this time brought on by the terrible realisation that she might one day give birth to a child conceived by a monster.

That evening Tung brought Andrew to meet with his sister. Andrew and Naomi fell into each other's arms, weeping and hugging as Tung discreetly left the room to leave brother and sister together for the night, as they had much to discuss.

For hours until the morning's first light they exchanged all they knew, catching up on events to the present moment. The only matter Naomi did not mention was that she thought she might be pregnant.

'I have not had a chance to speak with Tung,' Andrew said. 'He has been very distant with me. I guess he cannot be seen to be friendly with a man considered the enemy of the Boxer movement.'

'I worry about Father,' Naomi said. 'What will happen to him if the Imperial troops and the Boxers overrun the legation?'

Andrew did not have an answer, and at first light a guard came to take him away.

• • •

Tung brooded over the map of the city. The former governor of Shantung province, Li Peng-heng, had arrived to take command of the northern armies. Tung knew of the man's extreme hatred of foreigners; already high-ranking officials in the Empress's court who had advised a more moderate approach to dealing with the Europeans had been executed. As a favourite of the Empress, Li Peng-heng had promised that he would escalate the attacks on the legation and the warriors of the Boxer movement had been heartened by his arrival and rallied strongly behind him.

Tung already knew from his intelligence sources that the European forces slowly advancing on Pekin would defeat them with sheer force of arms and it had only been his clever organisation of intelligence that had helped save Andrew Wong's life. Tung had even recruited a favoured bodyguard of his uncle, without the general's knowledge, to pass on any information from the Imperial army headquarters. It had been through that source that Tung had learned of Andrew's capture and Han's treachery, and with his loyal contingent of warriors, Tung had been able to rescue Andrew from a terrible death.

The most disturbing matter to arise was that Tung had learned that Han was the favoured man of the new commander, and would already be currying favour with him to Tung's mortal danger. It was not just himself that he had to protect, but also the lives of Andrew and Naomi. Would it be wise to assist Naomi and Andrew to rejoin their father in the legation? He agonised. Considering the new commander it was very possible for the legation to fall, despite the advance of relief forces, and then all within the legation would be slaughtered.

Tung walked away from the map on his table and gazed out the open door of his office, surveying the sea of colourfully uniformed warriors and soldiers mustering. They were still a formidable force, as the advancing troops from the allied European armies had discovered to their woe, suffering heavy casualties in the process. Tung's intelligence had informed him that naval brigades from the colonies of Australia were among the advancing troops. This was to be expected when he considered the colonies as lackeys of the British lion. As Tung was not a gambling man, he could not throw a dice to choose which option was best. He drew a deep breath and sighed. Was it that he wanted to keep Naomi close because he was drawn to her? For the moment he thought it would be best to see what the new army commander would do. After that, he would be in a better position to decide their fates.

The Chinese soldier, armed with a rifle, moved cautiously between the piles of rubble. John lifted his rifle and rested the stock on the loophole made of bricks. Fifty yards, he calculated, as the enemy rifleman disappeared behind a scrap heap of masonry.

'You reckon you can pick him off, Mr Wong?' Private Larry Gilles whispered.

John nodded, waited and calculated where the Chinese sharpshooter would take a shot at them from.

He and the US marine occupied a forward position to give early warning to the barricades behind them. It had once been a Chinese position but now lay in no-man's-land between the lines. Lieutenant Simpson had recognised that his soldier and the Australian civilian made a good team and had already accounted for many rebels. Both had crept in under the cover of darkness to take up their positions and would remain until night came again for their retreat from the improvised hide. By then it would have been identified by the Chinese sharpshooters, whose accuracy was to be respected.

John took a deep breath and then breathed out slowly, allowing the foresight to settle on a section of the masonry from where he suspected the Chinese marksman would emerge to observe the barricades. He winced at a sharp, stabbing pain as his chest still hurt but the wound was healing remarkably well. His guess was correct; he could see the top of the soldier's head appearing slowly above the rubble.

The rifle bucked in John's hands, at the same time as he saw a tiny red film rise above the rubble. The Chinese marksman had disappeared with a short-lived scream.

'Got him!' Larry exclaimed, observing the fall of shot.

John settled back, sliding the bolt on his rifle to eject the spent cartridge and chamber a fresh round. He took no satisfaction from his skill but, at the same time, felt nothing for the man he had just killed. 'You take the next one,' he said softly to the marine beside him.

Larry lifted his rifle to seek out any other foolish Chinese soldier seeking a position to snipe at them. A shower of incoming bullets plucked the dirt and stones around their position, showering them with dust and rock chips. It had not taken the enemy long to identify where their man had been shot from and John doubted that Larry would find another target. More importantly, they would have to be alert to a possible sudden charge against them by the numerous enemy troops on the other side of the improvised wall of bricks they had constructed to edge closer to the legation defences.

John had time to reflect on his life while he waited for the darkness to come, and for them to pull out. His thoughts drifted from his children to Liza and back to whether he would live long enough to embrace any of them again. He was experiencing that terrible darkness that comes to men constantly in combat, the sense that he had used up his life already and it was only a matter of time before a rifle round found him. It had only been the existence of the little stone dragon that had saved his life earlier and now that was buried in Robert's quarters. Superstition was something John normally dismissed as the prerogative of the ignorant. But in this place and time he wondered why he had ever thought that. The siege seemed to have no end.

Andrew clamped his hands down on the Chinese soldier's leg to stem the blood spouting into the air in time to the beat of the man's heart. The Chinese soldier did not scream but moaned his despair. So many, Andrew thought, amid the wounded brought to him from the Chinese barricades. He had been able to obtain a few rudimentary medical instruments and a small amount of medicine to treat the men he once considered the enemy. Tung had helped set him up in a section of the buildings that had been crudely improvised as a hospital.

By Andrew's side kneeled the Chinese girl, Meili, who now was rapidly learning the business of nursing battle-wounded men.

'Here, hold down with both hands,' he said, turning to Meili with a blood-soaked face. She obeyed and Andrew sought for metal clamps among the surgical instruments but when he turned back he could see Meili squatting on her ankles with her bloody hands in her lap. Their patient no longer moaned and blood no longer pulsed from the leg where the vital artery had been severed. 'He is dead,' she said bluntly.

Andrew reached over her to feel for a pulse. 'He is dead,' he concurred. 'How did you know?' he asked the girl.

'I could not feel his blood moving and he was not breathing,' she replied, wiping her hands on her trousers.

'Impressive,' Andrew said in English, respecting the girl's commonsense.

Without wasting time, Andrew stood and moved to examine the next soldier lying on the stone paved floor. The young Chinese soldier stared up at Andrew. The man was clutching his ripped stomach and Andrew gently moved his hands away. 'Scissors,' he said, reaching behind him and feeling the implement placed in his hand. He cut the shirt to see the soldier's stomach had been torn open, exposing his intestines. Andrew passed the scissors back to Meili and searched among the medical supplies for a needle and cotton.

'This is going to hurt,' he said as gently as he could to the young soldier, whose face was pale with shock.

Andrew carefully stuffed the protruding intestines back into the man's stomach cavity and began to sew the skin together, sealing in the internal organs. There was a slight chance that he might save this one, Andrew thought, and felt like laughing at himself. He was not a qualified doctor and under any other circumstances such treatment might have had him before a legal court for malpractice. But his training had been advanced enough for him to know what he was doing, and in the situation he found himself he was the nearest thing to a doctor they would ever have, and Meili the closest thing to a nurse.

He was not aware that Tung had entered the room and stood watching as Andrew focused on his work of saving lives.

'You are doing good work with our wounded,' Tung said.

Andrew turned to look up at the Boxer commander. 'I wish I could do more,' he said, finishing the last stitch. 'But I am not really a doctor.'

'That soldier you are sewing up will probably live,' Tung countered. 'Is that not what a doctor does?'

Andrew rose to his feet and faced Tung. 'You have

not given me the opportunity to thank you for saving my life,' Andrew said. 'And for the kindness you have shown to my sister.'

'We are not all like Commander Han,' Tung replied. 'I do not apologise for trying to kill those in the legation, as they are the occupiers of my country. But I do not condone the methods used by men like Han.'

'I saw you burning the library,' Andrew said. 'Is not that a barbaric act by a man such as yourself?'

A pained expression clouded Tung's face. 'I did not want to carry out that order, but if I did not I would have been seen as disloyal to the cause. As it is I am aware that my life may be measured in hours or days, now that I have lost the patronage of my uncle. Han has a powerful friend in our new commander and I have no doubt that even now he is plotting my demise.'

'What will you do?' Andrew asked, knowing the answer also had to include the fate of himself and his sister.

'I do not know,' Tung sighed. 'If I thought that it would be safe for you and your sister to return to your father in the legation I would arrange for you to do so. But I fear with the zeal of the new commander the legation will be overrun and all within slaughtered.'

Andrew understood the dilemma Tung faced and could feel no animosity to him. The memories of their many conversations before arriving in Pekin returned to him. Ironically, Andrew mused, he was now fighting to save the lives of men wounded in the cause to free China and his loyalty was now being tested. He found that he had a deep sympathy for what Tung was attempting to do.

'Even if you choose to return us to the legation,' Andrew said, 'I will choose to remain here to tend the wounded. My sister may have other ideas.'

Tung was startled. 'To choose to remain with us would make you an enemy of your people,' he cautioned.

'My people,' Andrew replied. 'I had no choice in where I was born, but I can choose where I die. My people are here,' he said, indicating the room of wounded with a sweeping gesture. 'I am Chinese. The woman that I loved and lost was a poor peasant girl who would not have died if the European community behind the legation walls really cared about us. No matter what I might achieve in a European society I will always remain a Chink, as they call us. Here, I can be of value to a people who deserve some kind of peace in their lives after centuries of suffering at the hands of war lords and invaders. I have come to believe that we can be a strong and great nation in this century and by swearing my allegiance to your cause I can remain to carry out the work I was destined to do.'

At first Tung frowned, then he stepped forward to clasp Andrew by the elbow. 'You are welcome and I will call you brother but you will lose much in choosing to join our cause. You may even lose your life.'

Andrew shook his head. 'At first I blamed you and all those who stood with you for the death of

Liling, but I have come to see that if she had been European then she would have been granted the best treatment possible. I tried to get help but was turned down by the Europeans. They will call me a traitor, I know that, but I do not feel like a traitor.'

The two men were approached by a Boxer warrior Tung immediately recognised as one of Han's men. He stepped back.

'Most Honourable Commander Tung,' the man said respectfully, bowing at the waist, 'I carry a decree from our new commander that the woman known as Naomi Wong is to be immediately placed in the custody of the most honourable Commander Han.'

The messenger thrust a scroll into Tung's hands.

'This cannot happen!' Andrew gasped.

Tung's grim expression told Andrew that it could, and that he was powerless to stop Han from reclaiming her.

Naomi's protest had proved futile when Han's personal bodyguard came to fetch her. As she was roughly manhandled she realised that, if the rumours she had heard of Han being favoured by the new commander were right, then there would be dire consequences not only for her but also Tung.

Han was waiting for her and she was shoved into his presence.

'You can forget Commander Tung,' he snarled. 'You have been returned to me by the order of the honourable leader.'

Naomi attempted to display defiance by staring

Han in the face. He stepped forward and she felt a crashing blow to her head from his closed fist. Stunned, Naomi collapsed to the ground, tasting the coppery blood that filled her mouth. She tried to recover her feet but was battered by a rain of blows until she could take no more and fainted.

When she regained consciousness Han was on top of her, grunting like a pig as he carried out the rape in the presence of his men. Naomi's hatred for the man rose up as a fire that could not be quenched, and she sank her teeth into his shoulder, biting so hard that his scream echoed through the hallways of the building. Naomi could taste his blood until a savage blow to the side of her head returned her to the blackness. Maybe she was dying, Naomi thought sadly, carrying the last thoughts of her father's smiling face with her.

But she was not dying. She did not know how long she had been unconscious and had little memory of what had happened prior to waking up. As she focused her eyes she became aware of her head throbbing and the pain was intense. When her eyesight cleared she could see Han staring down at her with such hatred that no words were really necessary. Blood had dried on his blouse top and he grimaced when he moved.

'I will kill you,' he hissed, leaning forward into her face. 'I will kill you for being with Tung.'

'No you won't,' Naomi croaked, spitting blood from her mouth.

'Why not?' Han sneered, amused by her bravado.

'Because I carry your child,' Naomi laughed bitterly.

The look of surprise on Han's face was also an expression of confusion. But Naomi was not sure if the statement she had made would have any effect on him. Was it possible for a demon to have human feelings? The answer to that question would mean the difference between her living and dying.

'I cannot allow my sister to go back to Han,' Andrew had said.

'Nor can I,' Tung replied quietly. 'She is a woman worth dying for.'

Andrew glanced at Tung, registering surprise at the man's answer. 'You like my sister,' he said.

Tung did not reply but looked away, lest he show any embarrassment at displaying his feelings in public. Composing himself, Tung turned to Andrew. 'I will go to Han and return Naomi to you,' he said.

'How will you do that?' Andrew asked, knowing Tung had lost support when his uncle had left to oppose the allied forces slowly advancing on Pekin. Andrew was increasingly aware of the delicate nature of shifting allegiances in Chinese politics and, at the moment, Tung had no support in the city.

'My men are loyal to me,' Tung replied confidently, but a quiet voice warned him not to take their loyalty for granted. 'I will speak to them.'

'I will stand by you,' Andrew said. 'No matter what should eventuate we are brothers and this is now my land.'

• • •

Days had passed and John had not seen Liza. He had eventually been relieved from his place on the barricades and chose to go in search, finding her at her post in the hospital feeding the wounded with the monotonous but essential stew of horse meat and coarse rice. She glanced up at John standing at the end of the ward with his rifle slung on his shoulder, and put down the bowl she was holding to feed an Italian soldier shot in the hip.

'You look wonderful,' John said awkwardly when Liza approached him. 'I am sorry that I was not able to meet with you in the last few days.'

Liza looked tired but John noticed that her eyes registered pleasure in seeing him. 'You did not risk your life going out in search of your son and daughter,' she said. 'I am very happy to see that you are still here.'

'You know that I must search for them,' he said. 'But I must be getting old because I have listened to wise advice to wait for the right time before I do so.'

Liza smiled. 'I am glad you did,' she said.

John frowned. Was it that she was frightened that he might be killed? It was not a question he would have asked himself until now.

'Being out there on the barricades I have had time to think about many things. You have always been among my thoughts. When this is all over I would like you to return to Queensland with me – as my wife.'

Liza was stunned by his proposal. 'We hardly know each other,' she protested.

'Under the circumstances I would say that fifty days here is worth fifty years outside the legation walls,' he replied with a warm smile. 'All I know is that from the very first moment that I saw you, I was bewitched. I know that we have not had the opportunity to court each other but I also know I have met the woman I want to spend the rest of my life with. I am not a poor man, Liza. I have all the means to take care of you.'

Liza's expression reflected her confusion, doubt and at the same time barely concealed love for the man standing before her with his gentle smile.

'I am Jewish,' she said. 'I do not even know what faith you hold.'

'I have never thought about religion,' John said awkwardly. 'I guess my beliefs are a bit like those of the blackfellas of my country. I see life in everything around me – the rocks, trees, billabongs and the stars above. I guess I have thought of all of them as having a spirit.'

Liza reached up to touch his grimy face with the tips of her fingers. 'You have a soul, John, but you do not know it.'

Her gentle touch warmed John in a way he had not felt for a long time and he even felt moisture in the corner of his eyes. The moment had taken him outside the besieged city to another place where his soul lived.

'I smell gum trees,' he said, taking her hand.

'What does that mean?' Liza asked, puzzled by his statement.

'If you choose to marry me,' he replied, 'then you will understand.'

'I will think about your offer,' Liza said.

'Have you heard the news?' a voice called from the end of the ward. Both John and Liza were distracted by the British soldier who had hobbled into the dormitory on crutches. His excited voice had caught the attention of all within hearing.

'News from a General Gaselee who is leading the relief force has reached us that they are on their way. A Japanese general has also sent a message to say that they should be here around the thirteenth or fourteenth of the month.'

His announcement brought a cheer from the wounded men in the ward and John turned to Liza. 'I hope the news does not change your mind about marrying me,' he said, with a broad smile.

'I have not accepted your offer,' Liza replied, but from the smile on her face John felt confident.

'What day is it?' John suddenly asked, realising that he had not kept track of days, let alone months, since he had arrived in Pekin.

'It is the eleventh day of August,' Liza replied.

Two to three days before the relief forces would arrive, John calculated. He would have to act before then, otherwise there was a chance a retreating Chinese army might execute their prisoners.

Robert scanned the newly arrived Chinese troops, planting their black and yellow banners a mere thirty yards from the barricades. 'What do they say?' he asked the young English civil servant interpreter beside him.

'They declare the names of generals I have not heard of,' the interpreter replied, lowering the binoculars.

'Not good,' Robert mumbled.

As if to confirm his worst fears the air was suddenly rent with the crack of bullets and the blast of artillery showering down on their positions. Robert had guessed the Chinese would make one last effort to crack their defences before any forces could arrive to save them. Short on ammunition and low on food supplies as the defenders were, he knew that the Chinese just might succeed.

Both men ducked behind the sandbags as an explosive artillery shell found its mark, blasting a hole in the barricade. And then, with everything they had, the Chinese poured death and destruction into the legation.

'Yu Hsien, the governor of Shansi, has promised to take the legation in five days,' Tung said to Andrew after he had returned from a briefing. 'One of his generals has stated that he will not leave any fowl or dog alive.'

'Any news of Naomi?' Andrew asked. He now wore the Boxer uniform Tung had given him. Wearing the uniform allowed Andrew to move freely in the city.

'I saw Han at the briefing, but we did not talk,' Tung said. 'I think if he had harmed your sister he would have boasted to me of the fact. He did not look well.'

'Do you have a plan to rescue Naomi?' Andrew asked.

'I would go to Han's headquarters and seize her myself if I could,' Tung replied. 'But I have been relieved of my post as intelligence officer, to return with my men to the forward lines. We know that a force of Japanese, Russian, British, American and French bolstered with troops from Italy, Austria and Germany are advancing on the city. It appears we must defeat the legation defenders before they arrive and so I have been ordered back to the front. I cannot do anything at this stage but pray that Han is also too busy with his command to care about Naomi. I am going to send Meili to his headquarters to report for me, as the girl knows where to go. You should prepare for the wounded we expect from our attacks on the legation.'

Andrew was frustrated by Tung's answer, although he knew that he was right. To attempt to snatch Naomi from Han's quarters would be suicidal. All he could do was pray that Tung was right about Han being too busy and that Meili would get through to his sister and be able to report back to them.

John wished he had a bayonet. His bruised shoulder ached with each shot and he knew his ammunition was running low. A bayonet would have turned his rifle into a weapon when his ammunition ran out and he could take at least a few of the enemy with him to hell. The pitch black of the night was torn constantly by flashes of lightning drowned in the sheets of rain beating down on the desperate defenders. Rolls of thunder all around them were in turn drowned by the crash of rifle and artillery shells exploding around the three flags hanging limply on their staffs atop the Tartar Wall. The British, American and Russian flags had been hoisted earlier that day to show the advancing allied troops that they were still alive and fighting.

As a desperate final act the Imperial Chinese army and its Boxer allies had launched an all-out attack on every point of the defences and now John found himself leaning against the sandbags next to Private Larry Gilles, snapping off shots at any figures that might appear in the flash of a lightning strike.

In the Fu, the Japanese commander, Colonel Shiba, had his men banging pots and pans to give the illusion that their numbers were greater than they actually were. At last light the Chinese had wheeled up a modern, quick-firing two-inch Krupp gun to a high point on the wall to blast with deadly accuracy the defenders' positions. It wreaked havoc until its crew were wiped out by the defenders' Colt machine gun while waves of Chinese soldiers threw themselves at the barricades adjoining the Mongol Market, and the fighting in many places came down to hand-to-hand combat.

'Are we gonna die?' the marine private shouted to John in the dark as he chambered another round.

'I don't know,' John answered, feeling along his bandolier for rounds left. His fingers found nine rounds and he knew he would fall back, deserting the defences, when he was down to one round. He would find Liza, and if the Chinese overran them, shoot her with his last bullet rather than allow her to fall into the hands of the Chinese. It was not something he had ever spoken of to her but he also knew that she kept a small calibre revolver as her own insurance not to be taken alive.

Suddenly, a part of the sandbags defence collapsed on John and a figure loomed above him on the wall. An attacker had got through. Instinctively John swung the barrel of his rifle up to thrust into the enemy soldier's stomach. The blast ripped through the Chinese soldier who screamed in his shock and pain, falling on top of John. Private Gilles immediately thrust his bayonet into the body, narrowly missing John under the now fatally wounded Chinese soldier. John extricated himself and groped around for the dead soldier's weapon. He found it, recognising the rifle as a modern, German-manufactured Mannlicher carbine. He also found a full bandolier of ammunition. If nothing else, the prize had extended his time on the barricades, guaranteeing the death of many more of the attacking Chinese soldiers.

'Listen!' Private Gilles yelled above the din of gunfire. 'You hear that?'

'I hear it,' John replied. 'It's not the Chinese guns.'

In the distance, beyond the current crash of rifle and artillery fire originating from the Chinese forces, a deep booming could be heard. The crash of Chinese artillery and rifle fire suddenly died away as did that of the defenders. In the lull separating both sides European and Asian listened.

• • •

Sitting by a dying German soldier in the hospital, Liza also heard the distant boom.

'They are coming,' a voice shouted from outside the hospital.

Liza rose from her chair to go outside into the shell-blasted street where she saw men, women and children cheering, crying, laughing, hugging each other and some even dancing in the dim light thrown up by fires burning from the rubble. Liza sighed as an English woman she knew from her work in the hospital clasped her to her ample bosom, crying with joy as she did. 'We are saved,' she sobbed. 'They are coming.'

Relief might be at hand, Liza mused. But men were still fighting a desperate defence on the barricades. Her thoughts were with John, whom she now had not seen in three days.

'If I die then my men have orders to kill you,' Han said to Naomi, who was curled on the bed. 'I would have by now but for the news you have concerning the baby. For all I know it could be the child of one of my men who first had you,' he continued. 'When it is born I will know, and your fate will rest on that day.'

Naomi did not know for sure whose baby she carried. It could well have been conceived by one of the many men who had first raped her, but for some strange reason she felt it was Han's child.

Han strapped on a broad sword and reached to touch the inflamed wound close to his neck. Although it felt hot and the reddening had increased, he thought it would heal. After all, the woman had only broken the skin and he had suffered worse wounds in the past from enemy swords and spears. For now his only concern was the bullets of the foreign devils when he joined his men preparing to make a final assault on the barricades opposite the Mongol Market.

'Pray that I return in the morning,' he sneered at Naomi as he left.

Naomi prayed instead that Tung would come for her as he had for her brother before the sun rose.

The number of wounded being returned to Andrew was overwhelming. He worked under the dim light of lanterns, treating each casualty who was laid out on the large wooden slab Andrew had been able to convert into an operating table. The wounds were mostly from bullets but towards dawn he noticed many of the soldiers and Boxers being brought to him were suffering the terrible wounds associated with shrapnel from artillery shells.

Andrew knew that they could not have been inflicted by the legation's single gun and when he questioned the soldiers acting as stretcher bearers, they informed him that the Chinese defensive lines on the eastern side of the city were being shelled by the advancing forces of the foreign devils.

So they were finally coming, Andrew thought, wiping his blood-soaked hands on the legs of his trousers. What would his old medical instructors say if they saw him doing that? But hygiene hardly mattered to most of his patients whose only hope of recovery mostly lay with their own will to live. He did not have any real medical supplies or equipment at hand and was barely providing first aid for the least critically wounded. But still his endeavours were appreciated by the wounded soldiers whose pain was at least the concern of another human being.

'Honourable doctor,' a young Chinese soldier whose face was smeared with blood said, 'we have brought another of the wounded to you.'

Weary from his non-stop attempts at treating the wounded, Andrew hardly looked up from the patient, whose shrapnel-shattered leg he was sawing off below the knee. Two of the wounded man's comrades held the screaming man down as the saw bit into raw nerves, flesh and bone.

'Place him on the ground,' Andrew said through gritted teeth as the saw broke through and he reached for a sharp knife to cut the flesh holding the severed leg in place. It was not until then that Andrew glanced down at the next wounded man he was to treat and saw Tung's pale face staring up at him. Andrew suddenly felt sick, fighting to stay on his feet. His friend was covered in blood.

Meili had no trouble talking her way into Han's headquarters, as the few soldiers remaining behind recognised her.

'Where have you been?' one growled, lifting his lantern as she walked into the courtyard.

'I went to visit my mother,' Meili lied. 'I have

always meant to return to the Honourable Commander Han.'

'We have missed your cooking,' the Boxer said in a more friendly tone.

Meili waited until the remaining Boxers were distracted and edged her way inside the building where she knew Han had his private quarters.

'Naomi,' she called softly, her heart pounding with fear, expecting at any moment for Han to step forward and strike her down.

'Meili?'

'Have you been hurt?' Meili asked, seeing Naomi curled on the bed.

Naomi rose and rushed to her friend to embrace her. 'Oh, Meili, my sister, I thought that I might not see you again.'

'I have been sent by Commander Tung to see that you are still alive,' Meili said, extracting herself from the embrace. 'Your brother is safe and well,' she added.

'I cannot remain here,' Naomi whispered, despite the din of gunfire and exploding artillery shells in the distance. 'If Han is killed I will be executed, and if he returns, I think I would rather kill myself than ever feel his stinking breath on my cheek again. Oh, Meili, please help me.'

Meili frowned. She had been instructed to ascertain Naomi's welfare and report back, but had no further instructions. Suddenly they both became aware of a strange silence that descended on the city. The firing died away to be replaced with a continuous rolling boom.

'What is that?' Meili asked. 'What is that other sound?'

Naomi realised immediately what the distant booming meant. 'It is our guns,' she said. 'It means that the siege will soon be over. When the European troops arrive, we will be saved.'

'We will be slaughtered,' Meili cautioned. 'The foreign devils will hunt us all down, and avenge themselves on us.'

Hearing her grimly delivered statement, Naomi meant to reassure her friend this would not be so, but realised that she might well be right. The European soldiers would view all Chinese as less than human. It was their way and men like Tung would be considered less than criminals for being Boxers. 'If Tung cannot come for me, I shall go to him,' Naomi said. 'If I stay, I am surely dead.'

'You cannot walk out of here,' Meili said, gripping Naomi's arm. 'The guards will kill you.'

'I would rather risk leaving now,' Naomi replied. 'It is the only chance I have if the relief force is almost in the city. I am a British citizen and the British respect that regardless of my skin colour. It seems that the Boxers and the Imperial troops will have more to worry about than a lone Chinese girl wandering the streets.'

'I have a plan,' Meili said. 'I know the soldiers who guard you and they appear to accept that I have returned of my own free will. I will promise my body to them and while I have lured them away from guarding the gate you will slip out.'

'You cannot do that,' Naomi said in a shocked voice.

343

'Why not?' Meili shrugged. 'It is not a matter of great importance to me anymore.'

Naomi stared at the young girl and could see that she was telling the truth. Their worlds were so far apart, Naomi thought, but she loved Meili for her selfless gesture.

'What will you do when you are finished with the men?' she asked.

'I will demand that they pay me money!' Meili grinned. 'But I know they will not. Then I will leave in my disgust at their meanness, and catch up with you.'

Naomi hugged Meili to her and the Chinese girl pushed her away, embarrassed that the foreign-born Chinese girl should think she was doing anything very special.

'Kwan Lee,' Meili called to the guard at the gate. 'You are so big and strong and I would like to go to the storeroom with you.'

The guard could hardly believe his luck. Looking quickly around to see if he was being observed by any of the other men and seeing that the coast was clear, Kwan Lee left his post by the gate to follow Meili into the dark.

Naomi braced herself, and when Meili and the guard had disappeared into a room off the courtyard, she slipped across the stones to disappear through the gate into the narrow street now filled with armed soldiers moving up to join their comrades in the human wave attacks being launched against the lega-tion defences. In the dark she was hardly noticed among the milling troops and made her way towards the Forbidden City where she knew she would find Tung and her brother.

Lieutenant Simpson moved along the line of his marine defenders, encouraging each soldier with promises that they would soon see the stars and stripes leading the allied relief force into Pekin – at least he hoped it would be an American force. The sun was rising and first light was a dangerous time. It was the time Chinese sharpshooters could find targets among the defenders.

'Keep your head down, sir,' a marine cautioned as the bullets continued to tear the air around them.

He reached the end of the line, where he knew his civilian attachment and the contingent's good luck talisman would be. He found John Wong sitting with his back to the sandbags. Blood soaked his once white shirt and his eyes stared blankly at the sky. As if asleep, in his lap lay Private Larry Gilles.

Simpson froze. How could this happen? They had been so close to being saved. The marine officer stepped up to the rampart.

'I didn't even see it happen,' John said. 'I only realised at first light that the young fella was dead.'

Lieutenant Simpson picked up the dead marine's Krag rifle and bandolier of ammunition. This was no time for sentimentality. Every rifle and round was desperately needed if they were to survive until the relief force fought its way into the city.

'We will give him a Christian burial,' Simpson said in a sympathetic voice. 'He was a good marine and did his duty.'

A marine sergeant and private retrieved the body of Private Larry Gilles, leaving John alone at the end of the line. He positioned himself at the loophole facing the direction of the enemy attacks and surveyed a scene of carnage. Bodies of Chinese soldiers and Boxers lay heaped where they had been shot down. Black flies were already settling on the freshly killed bodies as here and there a body twitched, indicating a man moaning in his pain. John felt nothing for the wounded Chinese soldiers. The constant fighting had numbed his soul.

Andrew had sewn the flaps of skin together, where a bayonet had torn through Tung's side. It had not been a fatal wound but would be subject to infection if not cared for properly. It was mid-morning and the day hot and steamy as Andrew squatted by Tung, lying on his back, recovering from the secondary wound of a severe blow to the head, that had actually put him out of the fight with the Japanese troops at the Fu during the night.

'How do you feel?' Andrew asked.

'I have a bad headache and my vision is blurred,' Tung rasped, licking his dry lips. 'Do you have any water?'

Andrew produced a beaker of water and held it to Tung's mouth. Around them lay the bodies of the wounded and dead while blood dried in sticky puddles and the flies buzzed with their irritating song of death. Most noticeable was the silence, broken only by the moaning of the wounded, the occasional rifle shot and the constant, distant thud of artillery.

Tung drank down the water and licked his lips. 'We have lost,' he said to Andrew. 'It is time that we must leave.'

Andrew sat back on his haunches. 'Where would we go?' he asked.

'China is a big country,' Tung replied. 'I think that we should flee north.'

'I cannot leave without finding my sister, and I must ensure that my father is safe,' Andrew replied.

'I understand,' Tung said. 'I too must find Naomi. Your sister trusted me to protect her and I have let her down.'

Andrew gripped Tung's hand. 'It is not your fault Han took her,' he said. 'All I can do is pray that she is safe.'

Tung struggled to his feet. His shirt had been removed and he winced when he raised his arm. 'We need to get rid of these clothes,' he said. 'We need to find the clothing of a coolie if we are to break out of here.'

When Andrew assisted Tung to the door of the building that had been his first aid station, both men froze in their shock. Walking towards them were Meili and Naomi.

They saw each other at the same time and Naomi broke into a run to fall into Andrew's arms. She was weeping as Tung stood by, relief clearly reflected in his face.

Naomi then turned to Tung. 'Commander Tung,' she asked in a concerned voice, 'is your wound severe?'

'Your brother has cared for me,' Tung replied. 'But I am no longer a commander. I fear that we have lost and I am now just Tung Chi.'

'Is it all over?' Naomi asked.

'The relief force is already at the gates of the city,' Tung said. 'It is only a matter of time before the siege is lifted and you can rejoin the Europeans safely. I am sure that your father will be overjoyed to see you.'

Naomi turned to Andrew but his silence disturbed her. 'Do you hear that?' she asked. 'We will be able to seek out Father and go home.'

'I am home,' Andrew said quietly.

Stunned, Naomi stared at her brother. 'What do you mean?' she asked.

'I am staying with Tung,' Andrew answered calmly. 'This is now my country and I can do more good for the people by remaining here. I may not be a doctor but I have enough knowledge to help many who might otherwise die. I am Chinese – not a Chink or Celestial as I am viewed in European society.'

'You were born in Queensland,' Naomi attempted to reason. 'You only have another year of medical training before you can practise.'

'I did not need the final year to treat the wounded that were brought to me,' her brother answered. 'I can train people like Meili to work as nurses in the villages. There is so much I can do here, my beloved sister, to help China become an independent nation.'

Naomi fell silent. She could see the fire of conviction burning in her brother's eyes and knew that he was as stubborn as their father. Instead, she embraced her brother and whispered in his ear. 'I will always love you and include you in my prayers every day.'

Andrew laughed. 'When did you ever pray every day, little sister?' he said, yet feeling a deep affection for her. 'Better that you send me medical supplies from time to time.'

'I should make my way to the legation,' Naomi said.

'That would not be wise until it is certain that the legation is secured by the invading forces,' Tung said. 'It would be better that you remain with us until we have news the legation is relieved.'

Naomi could see the sense in Tung's argument. But did her ready acquiescence mean that she was reluctant to leave Tung?

Mid August 1900
Pekin

The armed forces of Britain, Japan, France, America and Russia were poised to launch the all-out assault on the city. Under the command of General Gaselee, the British moved up two artillery pieces to batter the main gate to the Shawomen section of the outer walls, and the guns did their job, as the Chinese defending the gate fled. The way was open, but Gaselee was concerned that his American and French allies might turn their artillery on his British troops, so the Union Jack was flown from a Chinese pike above the wall where, on the other side of the imposing wall, the British came across a sea of little tents deserted by the Chinese. Cooking utensils and military equipment lay about among the tents and not a soul was to be seen when the British troops burst into the city through the captured gateway.

Gaselee followed the rapid entry with detachments

being dispatched to seize critical strategic points while he commanded the main force to advance parallel with the Tartar Wall. Their advance was not hindered by Chinese troops and the silence was only broken by the crashing of doors closed after the still-fleeing Chinese troops. It was only when Gaselee turned north to seek out the sluice gates on the canal running through the legation area that his soldiers ran into any opposition. Rifle shots met his men and return fire suppressed the Chinese marksmen on the wall.

The flags of Russia, America and Britain were seen hanging limply on their masts above the wall in the still, oppressive heat of the day. Gaselee halted his force, as a rumour had swept through the ranks that the city had fallen to the Chinese. As the British gazed up at the wall the lone figure of an American marine appeared, waving a flag and signalling in morse, *Come in quickly by the sluice gate*. A rousing cheer greeted his message and the troops swept towards the gate. US marines tugged frantically at the perpendicular timber bars used to block the entrance, even as bullets whipped through the ranks of the advancing British soldiers and a small artillery shell exploded before them. Not all the resistance was gone from the Chinese army.

But the British surged forward to pass through the battered American legation to reach the British legation lawns, where they were met by Captain Wray of the Royal Marines who, in turn, introduced to Lady MacDonald the sweating and filthy British officer clutching a flag.

'I have no idea who you are, young man,' Lady

MacDonald said in her most patrician voice, 'but I am simply delighted to see you.'

Robert Mumford had joined a party of volunteers to sally forth into the Fu on a reconnaissance mission. Former positions occupied by the enemy were now deserted and when he and the party he was with continued they broke into an adjoining street littered with bricks, broken and rusted weapons, piles of spent brass cartridges, and the bones of many Chinese, some with tufts of pigtails still adhering to the skulls. Fat crows cawed their protests at having their feasting disturbed, and fully fed dogs slunk away from what remained of those corpses still retaining any flesh.

At the edge of what had been the original grounds of the legation they came across bowls of rice ready to eat and cooking fires still smouldering. The reconnaissance party did not stop but continued their advance, seeing Chinese soldiers fleeing ahead of them, flinging off uniforms and leggings so that they could run faster. They were at the pink-tinged walls of the Forbidden City of the Empress when they had a view of long columns of Chinese infantry marching rapidly north, while their cavalry galloped as hard as they could alongside the footslogging infantry. Robert realised that he was witnessing an army in full retreat and knew then that the fighting was finally over.

John stood with many of the tired and gaunt defenders, now buoyed by the magnificent sight of the dashing

Indian Lancers and cavalry mounted on their war horses parading before them. The fierce-eyed, bearded, dark-skinned men of the British army were a magnificent sight with their tall red turbans, and the Indian mounted troops were followed by British infantry.

John found himself cheering with those either side of him. That he had survived almost two months of constant combat was not enough for him. Now he was in a position to go in search of his children and he cheered for this thought alone.

'It is finally over,' Liza said, slipping her hand into his.

John had not heard her approach and was surprised by her gentle and loving gesture.

'The fighting is over,' John said. 'But my mission is about to be resumed.'

'We have to leave now,' Tung said to Andrew.

They could see the city emptying of Tung's former comrades and had obtained coolie clothing for themselves, to merge with the columns of refugees fleeing the city now re-occupied by the foreign devils. Meili had even scrounged some rice and dried fish for them and only Naomi stood aside. Tung looked to her.

'I will go to the legation and assure myself that Father is safe,' she said. 'I have a duty to him.'

Andrew stepped forward to clasp his sister in a warm embrace. 'It is the right thing to do,' he said.

'What do I tell him of your decision to remain in China?' Naomi asked.

Andrew shook his head sadly. 'It might be better if he thought I had been killed. I don't think Father would understand my decision to give up my studies and join the cause to free China.'

'I cannot lie about your decision,' Naomi answered. 'Father has a right to know his only son's fate.'

'Hurry,' Tung prompted, cutting across the temptation for brother and sister to prolong what might be the last time they would ever see each other. 'We can use this time to slip away. One of my men has told me that there is still fighting along the Tartar Wall where the Russian Cossacks are attempting to force their entry.'

Andrew withdrew from the embrace of his sister. 'I know you will find a way to explain my decision,' he said, turning to join Tung and Meili.

Naomi watched them slip away. It was time to go and find her father.

The danger was not over. A few braver Chinese troops remained behind in the city to snipe at the soldiers of the relief force, and casualties occurred among civilians and soldiers alike. Naomi moved cautiously along the litter-strewn streets. She could see the Tartar Wall looming ahead, and questioned her wisdom not to wait a little longer before attempting to enter the besieged compound. But the sight of a tall Sikh soldier standing guard at a gate into the legation compound cheered her.

She began to walk towards him when suddenly

the crack of a bullet brought the soldier down. Naomi froze. Even now with safety in sight she was unable to proceed without the danger of a Chinese marksman targeting her. She turned and began to walk back along the street, seeking sanctuary until she could be sure of a safe entry.

'You have returned to me,' a voice snarled from a doorway.

Naomi felt sick. How could she have been so close to safety and now have to confront the man she most feared and hated? She wanted to run, preferring the chance of being shot at the gate where the wounded Sikh soldier lay, but her choice was snatched from her when Han stepped out of the building with two of his bodyguards.

'Seize her,' he ordered and strong hands gripped her by the arms, dragging her inside the building. Over her shoulder Naomi could see a group of rescuers dragging the wounded Sikh inside the gate. She had been so close to being saved.

Han stared at her with feverish eyes. 'Never again try to leave me,' he said, following his threat with a stinging slap across her face. 'I have not finished with you.'

Naomi bent her head so that Han could not see the tears welling up in her eyes. She did not shed them for her situation so much as frustration at seeing this hated man still alive.

'You can see that I am sick,' Han said and Naomi could indeed see that he was very ill. His eyes were staring with the fever of the wound she had inflicted. 'These dogs of men are only waiting for me to die so

355

that they can flee with the rest of the cowards.' The two heavily armed bodyguards looked away lest their reluctance to remain be seen by their feared commander. 'Well, they may not have to wait long and I thank the ancestors for delivering you to me so that I may kill you just before I die.'

Han stumbled to a corner of the room and slumped into a chair. The bodyguards seized Naomi and bound her hands with rope. She was forced down onto her knees as Han slid a sword from his waistband.

'When I feel that the time has come I will cut you many times. Each cut will inflict pain, but will not kill you. That will come when I have grown tired of hearing your screams.'

Naomi knew that begging for mercy was useless. She could only pray that the infection she had unwittingly inflicted with her bite would kill him before he could carry out his threat. But when she stared up at Han she doubted that would happen. His imminent death would be painful but it would also be slow.

Sporadic fighting still tied down various international forces throughout the city but already looting was occurring. Troops not tied down by the fighting were going from house to house in search of valuable items and treating any Chinese civilians they found as Boxers. Killing and rape accompanied the looting and the reports Robert was hearing from soldiers worried him. If Naomi was still alive in the city she could suffer rape and death at the hands of European soldiers as easily as at the hands of the Boxers.

'Corporal Kent,' he called to the NCO acting as a clerk collating reports in the room next to Robert's new office at the British legation building.

'Sir!' the NCO replied dutifully, leaving his desk to go to his senior officer, crashing to a halt and snapping off a salute.

'I want you to locate a Mr John Wong immediately and inform him that I am extending an invitation for him to report to my office on a matter critical to us both.'

'Sir,' the corporal replied. 'Where will I find the gentleman?'

'Either at my old quarters, with the Yank marines or at the hospital where a Miss Gurevich may be able to assist you,' Robert replied.

'Will do, sir,' the corporal said, snapping another smart salute before turning on his heel to go in search of Mr Wong.

Robert rose from his desk and took down the Sam Browne belt from a wooden peg in the wall. The leather shoulder strap and waist belt were much lacking in shine from their constant wear under fire. He slid his revolver from the holster attached, checking the rounds in the chamber. Slipping a box of rounds into a trouser pocket, he gazed out the window of his office to see the thin, pale survivors of the siege pass by wearing the best of the clothes they had been able to stash away. The ladies in particular took great pride in their appearance, Robert noted. He knew that he was organising his search for Naomi on his own authority, and knew that he would get away with it. He would report that he was carrying out a reconnaissance of the city. Whether Sir Claude would accept that he was doing this alone was another matter, but considering his own valuable role in assisting the British diplomat during the siege, Robert also reckoned that the worst he would get would be a mild rebuke for risking his life in a city still not pacified, since small bands of armed Chinese soldiers and Boxers still lurked in the narrow streets and alleyways.

Robert did not have to wait long, as John was already on his way to his new office when intercepted by the British corporal.

'We are going to find your daughter, Mr Wong,' Robert greeted John as he entered the office. 'You and I.'

John smiled grimly. He was still in possession of the Chinese rifle he had taken possession of at the barricades and had plenty of ammunition. 'My son, too,' he added.

'I think that we begin our search where it ended. The house in Lotus Street.'

Andrew was at the edge of the city with Tung and Meili when he stopped walking, to turn and stare back at the smoke rising behind them from the many buildings still smouldering from the effects of the shelling. 'I have to go back and face my father,' Andrew said quietly.

'You will be killed if you attempt to return,' Tung

cautioned. 'If I know the foreign devils they will be in the mood for vengeance, and anyone who looks Chinese will probably be shot on sight.'

'I have no choice,' Andrew replied. 'I could not live with myself if I had not assured myself that my father was unhurt. It is up to me to explain my decision to remain – and not up to my sister to do so.'

Tung sighed. 'When you have done so, you will have to make your own way to Kalgan.'

'I will go with Andrew,' Meili said. 'I know the road.'

'What is at Kalgan?' Andrew asked.

'The Empress, and my master, the Son of Heaven will be there,' Tung replied. Tung had been informed by his men still faithful to him that the Empress had disguised herself as a peasant woman, to flee from the Forbidden City during the night. She had clipped her long nails and taken on the rough, blue clothing of an old peasant woman and travelled in an ox-cart from the city's walls. The true ruler of China had been forced to accompany his ruthless aunt.

'I will rejoin you in a few days,' Andrew said. 'The ancestors willing.'

Tung nodded and walked away towards the great, treeless plain outside the city walls. He was not alone, but part of a great caravan of Chinese civilians and soldiers fleeing the wrath of the European powers who had once again conquered them.

With his rifle in his hands, John stood in the deserted courtyard of the house on Lotus Street. The signs of occupation were everywhere, as were the scattered skeletons picked clean by the numerous scavenging dogs.

'It has been some time since anyone was here,' Robert said, revolver in hand.

'Where now?' John asked.

Robert rubbed the sweat from his face with the back of his sleeve. 'I don't know,' he answered with a sigh. 'It is like looking for a grain of sand on a beach.'

John slung his rifle over his shoulder and took out the cigar he had been hoarding and sucked in the smoke to steady his nerves. Was he too late? He realised that his hands still shook even though the main fighting was over. Why this should occur was a mystery to him.

'I think that we should return to the legation,' Robert suggested. 'It is possible that we may be able to glean intelligence from any captured Chinese we have as to Naomi's whereabouts.'

'Not much chance of getting information from a dead man,' John sneered, knowing that the soldiers were rarely taking any Chinese clearly identified as former soldiers or Boxers alive. 'To do that we would have to capture one ourselves.'

Robert tended to agree with the Australian. He did not want to admit to himself that he might no longer have the opportunity of seeing the beautiful young woman again, but the possibility was there. Why would a retreating army keep a foreign woman alive?

'We will continue searching,' Robert said, but with little conviction.

Until dusk the two men moved cautiously through the city, intercepting patrols of allied soldiers and questioning them about whether they had come across a Chinese woman claiming to be a British subject. None could help and finally even John accepted that they must return to the legation, where he would reassess the search for his daughter.

The two trudged wearily through the gates now guarded by soldiers of the relief force and John bid Robert a good night to return to his old quarters. He had barely arrived when Corporal Kent appeared breathless at the front door.

'You got to go over to the hospital, Mr Wong,' he said. 'Mr Mumford sends his regards and says that the matter is one of urgency. That is all I can tell you.'

John snatched up his rifle and hurried into the night. When he reached the hospital his mind raced with the thought that something had happened to Liza. Why else would Robert send him there?

He entered the building and was met by one of the European doctors who had treated him.

'Ah, Mr Wong,' the man beamed mysteriously. 'I think you will find Miss Gurevich in the dispensary.'

John thanked the man and hurried to a room that had been set aside to store the legation's precious supply of medical supplies. The door was open and John could see that the room was lit by a lantern. The dim light revealed a sight that caused him to freeze in his tracks. He stared in disbelief. Sitting in a chair was his daughter, and standing beside her was Liza.

John felt that his legs would buckle. Naomi glanced up at him and, sobbing, flung herself from

361

the chair to embrace her father, crying over and over again the words he had only dreamed of throughout the siege: 'Father'.

Liza quietly left the room to leave father and daughter alone.

'She was brought to the hospital by a British patrol,' Liza said. 'I immediately recognised who she was.'

John stood outside a room in a building that had been used by Liza for accommodation. It was near the hospital and had thick mud walls that had kept her safe from stray rounds and shrapnel during the siege. Inside the room, Naomi slept with the help of a sleeping draught.

'How is she?' John asked, the worry etched in his face.

'She has suffered terrible physical and mental privation,' Liza replied. 'And she is with child.'

The latter statement caused John to gasp. How could that be possible? He did not want to believe the most probable answer.

Liza could see the pain in John's face and gently took his hand. 'It is not a bad thing,' she attempted to console him. 'Your daughter is young and with good care will be able to take the pregnancy to full term.'

John nodded, words eluding him lest he break into tears. But Liza's gentle touch compensated for the pain he was feeling for his daughter's suffering.

'I should have been strong and not allowed her to come to China,' he whispered hoarsely. 'It is my fault that she has suffered so much.'

'It is not your fault,' Liza said softly. 'Women have always known the suffering caused by men. But we have a strength that allows us to endure. Your daughter is very much like her father.'

John folded Liza into his arms, tears splashing her hair. The tough, grizzled old warrior, who had lived a life occasionally interrupted by moments of killing, had reached breaking point. What was important to Liza was that she was with him to provide the comfort he needed at such a time and it sealed in her mind the place she would find in this extraordinary man's company.

Throughout the night John sat by his daughter's bed as she slept, and when she whimpered and trembled he stroked her head, whispering soothing words. Naomi awoke in the early hours of the morning to see her father's tired face staring down at her and reached up to take his hand.

'I had almost lost hope that I would ever see you again,' she said. 'There is much that I must tell you.'

'Only when you feel that it is the right time to do so,' John replied soothingly.

'I want to tell you everything,' Naomi said, choking back tears.

John sat and listened without interrupting as his daughter related all that had befallen her since the moment that she had been captured on the street weeks earlier. But it was the last part of her story that struck him most.

'I should be dead,' Naomi said with a deep sigh.

'Han had promised to kill me and I knew he would. But, as he grew sicker, he seemed to change. He gave orders for his bodyguards to leave and it was then that I thought he would kill me. He was near delirious, waving the sword and staring at me with his feverish eyes. Then, he suddenly changed. He started to talk about the child I carry being born to carry his memory forward. He even forgave me for the wound that was killing him. I did not know if he was just taunting me – allowing me to take hope that I would live – but he did not touch me. After a time he slumped into a kind of dazed state and the sword fell from his hands. I lay bound, helpless to attempt any escape, when I heard English voices. A patrol of British soldiers in the street heard my cries of distress and burst inside the room. They saw Han sitting in the chair and one of the soldiers drove a bayonet through his chest. They released me and brought me to the hospital.'

'Is the child you carry Han's?' John asked awkwardly.

'I believe so,' Naomi replied, turning her head away.

'There are ways to dispose of it,' John said and Naomi turned on her father with an angry look.

'That is my decision,' she flared, surprising him.

John shrank back under his daughter's withering look, understanding that she was a woman with her own ideas and beliefs. 'I am sorry,' he said apologetically. 'I just thought, considering the circumstances ...'

'I think that I should sleep again,' Naomi said and turned her head into the pillow. She had not told her father of Andrew's decision to remain in China, as that was something she believed only her brother could do in person. When he asked her about Andrew, Naomi shied away from being specific and replied that her brother would eventually meet with his father to tell him of his situation, although in her heart Naomi was not certain this would eventuate. When John pressed her further she continued to be evasive, leaving John with a sick feeling. But grilling his daughter was not an option considering what she had so recently been through.

John rose from his chair to leave the room. The sun would be rising soon on another hot and humid day. He had one child back safe – if not sound. Now, all he had to do was find his son, and return them both to Queensland. When Liza came to join him he took her in his arms. His siege was not yet over.

It was against Meili's better judgment to return to the city and Meili felt afraid. But despite her apprehension she chose to accompany this remarkable young man who brought life and not death to her people and now Andrew walked beside her, clutching a cloth in which he had retained a few precious medical supplies. They were unarmed, but Andrew was confident that any troops from the European powers they might encounter would not fire when he identified himself as a British subject. Meili was not so sure, considering the chaos all around them.

When they passed through the city gates Meili noticed the ominous lack of people. On the streets were only the decomposing bodies of the dead and the ever-present dogs of the city. As they continued their journey towards the legation area, passing shops and stalls long smashed by looters, she wished that she had Andrew's courage.

Meili jumped when she heard a volley of gunshots ahead of them. Andrew paused. It was something about the controlled rate of fire that caused him to wonder where he had heard a similar sound before.

'Execution, firing squad,' Andrew said quietly in English, causing Meili to stare at him questioningly. 'It is nothing to fear,' he said, answering her unspoken question in Chinese.

Clutching the medical equipment, Andrew continued walking, with Meili following.

They had only gone a short distance when the steady clop-clop sound of shod horse hooves interrupted the dogs feasting on a human carcass at an intersection of the broad street. The pack of snarling dogs quickly scattered, and Meili suddenly felt a greater fear than before. She knew that it had not been their presence that had frightened off the dogs. And then they both saw the reason for the dogs skulking away.

'Cossacks,' Andrew said, recognising the colourful uniforms as the mounted squadron of fierce-looking men advanced in disciplined ranks along the street with their lances raised to the sky. 'They are Europeans. I can request them to escort us to the British legation,' he said, confidently turning to Meili. He raised his hands, still clutching his package of medical supplies. 'British,' he called in a loud voice. 'I am a British citizen.'

The squadron came to a stop to observe the Chinese man and woman standing at the centre of the intersection. Suddenly one of the horsemen spurred his horse into a gallop. Meili could see the deadly tip of the lance come down, pointing directly at them as the Cossack charged, yelling a Russian war cry.

'Run!' Meili screamed, turning on her heel and sprinting towards the empty stalls without looking back. Panting, she ducked down behind a stall, crawling on her hands and knees into a small space hidden from view.

With sickening certainty, Andrew realised that he would have to stand his ground, distracting the Cossack from possibly going after Meili, if she were to have a chance to live. That this was an extreme act of courage was not something the young man had time to reflect on before the charging Russian cavalryman was on him.

From her concealed position Meili could see down the street to where they had been attacked. She burst into a deep sobbing, hardly caring that the mounted foreign devils would find her. A Cossack on his horse was pinning Andrew's body to the ground with his long lance. Why had he not attempted to flee? The question screamed in her mind. Why had Andrew stood his ground in the face of certain death?

Meili remained hidden as the mounted Russian troops continued their advance along the street, searching for Chinese. After all, any Chinese who had not been inside the legation quarter during the siege could logically be seen as enemy combatants.

When the patrol had clattered away, Meili cautiously returned to where Andrew lay on his back, his eyes staring blankly at the sky. She could see the ghastly wound to his chest that had been inflicted by the point of the lance and she kneeled, rocking as she sobbed her despair at losing this remarkable man, who had carried in his hands the means to heal her people. When she could mourn no longer, Meili reverently picked up the blood-soaked package and continued towards the legation. If nothing else she would complete the mission that Andrew had set out on and meet with his father.

John found Robert leaving Sir Claude MacDonald's offices. The young officer emerged wearing a new uniform with a spit-polished Sam Browne belt across his chest. He turned to hurry along the rubble-strewn street where teams of Chinese coolies were working to clear the debris away as if intent on returning the legation compound to its former state.

'Mr Mumford,' John said when he had caught up with Robert.

The British officer's face crumpled at seeing him.

'Mr Wong,' Robert said, 'no doubt you have seen Naomi by now.'

'I have,' John replied, eyeing the young man's face and seeing the edginess of guilt in his expression. 'I was wondering why you have not paid a visit to my daughter?'

Robert wanted to look away. He shifted his gaze

across John's shoulder. 'I ah . . .' he uttered, as if clearing his throat. 'I have been rather busy.'

'I take it that you will continue to remain very busy then, Mr Mumford,' John replied, knowing that everything in the man's demeanour spelled avoidance.

Robert glanced down at the ground like a guilty school boy. 'I think that you must appreciate how the last few weeks have changed everything,' Robert answered. 'The damned rebellion and all that.'

'You mean what has happened to my daughter,' John growled. 'Not good for the old image, what,' he added, imitating an English aristocrat. 'Not good for future prospects of advancement, old chap.'

Robert glared at John. 'You do not seem to appreciate that we live in a world that is very judgmental, Mr Wong,' he said. 'I do not have to justify my actions to you.'

'Never consider travelling to Queensland,' John said, turning on his heel. 'Because I will be there and you won't want to meet me on my own turf.'

Robert felt his hands trembling as John strode away. It was not through fear but shame for the confrontation he had been forced to endure. He had fought too hard to get where he was now in this class-ridden society that did not accept mixed relations. No matter how strongly he might feel about Naomi, he was a soldier first and foremost and the sacrifice he made was not taken lightly. But how could he stand tall in the Officers' Mess with his brother officers if it was known that his wife was a Chinese girl who had been with many men?

Especially Chinese men. Robert was not a man to moralise on his choices because that was simply the way things stood in his tight, socially driven class. When at length he was able to bring his hands under control, he turned and continued to march along the street to join an impromptu afternoon tea being thrown for European guests only.

Liza had been able to obtain nourishing food for Naomi from her American friend, Polly Condit Smith. Dr George Morrison had also made himself known to the daughter of John Wong, and immediately enlisted her assistance with the care of the Chinese survivors at the Fu. Their medical treatment had not been a priority for the European community during the siege, although many had helped build the barricades and carried out vital tasks in the defence.

Naomi was puzzled that Robert had not attempted to contact her, considering what she had perceived as his strong feelings for her. She understood that facing the man she had once had strong feelings for would be an awkward moment as so much had changed in her life in the last two months. But the work of assisting Dr Morrison took her brooding thoughts off meeting Robert again. She had been acting as Morrison's interpreter, going among the Christian converts, who were pitifully malnourished and ill. Particularly hard for Naomi was dealing with the mothers of children only hours from death, as in her present state of pregnancy she found herself identifying with them.

She was feeding a tiny, skeletal-like baby with canned milk dripped from a rag when she looked up to see her father watching her. The sadness in his expression was apparent.

'Hello, Father. What is it?' she greeted.

John stepped forward, removing his broad-brimmed hat.

'I don't know how to tell you this,' he said. 'But I don't think you will be seeing Lieutenant Mumford in the future.'

'Has Robert been injured or killed?' Naomi asked in a dull voice.

'Neither,' John answered, looking past his daughter to a line of Chinese men, women and children patiently waiting to receive medical assistance from a doctor who was sitting at an improvised table made from wooden crates. The medical man had been persuaded by Morrison to go to the Fu and assess the physical condition of the Chinese survivors. 'I spoke to Mr Mumford just after I saw you in the hospital and I think your young man has had a change of mind.' John stared down at the ground with an abject look of misery for what he had done, expecting a bitter rebuke from his daughter.

'So be it,' Naomi sighed and returned her attention to feeding the baby.

'You are not angry with me for telling Mumford of your condition?' John asked, surprised by his daughter's calm response to the news.

'What else would I expect from a European,' Naomi snapped, fire blazing in her eyes. 'I am carrying the bastard child of some Chink. Do you think that an ambitious officer of the Queen would go far in the service hooked to a Chinese girl, let alone one carrying a Chink bastard? I may have had strong feelings for Robert once, but times have changed and I am a different person to who I was two months ago.'

John was taken aback by his daughter's outburst. 'But he was always attempting to find a way to go in search of you,' John attempted, defending the man he had once liked and respected.

'It was not he who hurried to see me when I was brought in by the patrol,' Naomi retorted. 'I have no doubts that Robert may have had my rescue in mind, but that was obviously driven by his sense of being an officer rather than his feelings for me. I am, after all, a British subject, despite also being Chinese. Love can fade with time, but this country around us remains constant in its centuries of suffering under tyrants. But . . .' Naomi suddenly ceased her tirade against Robert, remembering something. How could she tell her father about one man she had met who appeared to be as constant as the mighty Yellow River flowing to the sea – a man of courage, wisdom and gentleness.

'But what?' John gently prompted.

'Nothing,' Naomi said, shaking her head.

For a moment Naomi envied her brother for being in the company of Tung Chi and now it was as if her thought had conjured Meili from the throng of Chinese around her in the Fu. She had just passed the baby back to its mother when she saw Meili standing at a distance, staring at her and holding a dirty-coloured bundle in her arms.

'It is Meili!' Naomi exclaimed, leaping to her feet as her father followed her gaze to the young peasant girl standing at the edge of the crowd. Naomi walked quickly towards Meili but froze when she was only feet away.

'Oh my God!' Naomi gasped, seeing the stricken expression on Meili's tired face. 'Who?' she asked.

'Your brother,' Meili answered. 'These are his instruments of life,' she said, offering the bundle of surgical tools to Naomi.

John caught his daughter in a strong embrace as she swooned under the sweltering, mid-morning sun. He had understood every word that had passed between the two women. He may have found his daughter but he had now lost his son.

September 1900
Off the East Coast of
Queensland

Weeks had passed since John had last seen his daughter and buried his son. The engine of the coastal steamer throbbed beneath his feet as he stood on the deck gazing forward from the stern at the flat outline of Queensland's northern coast. He was almost home and the fluffy, white clouds billowing into thunderheads over the horizon promised a tropical storm.

From his pocket John withdrew the letter he had carried with him from the legation at Pekin. It had been written in his daughter's neat hand and explained that she had chosen to leave with Meili in search of the former Shaolin priest, Tung Chi, taking with her only the medical instruments Andrew had once possessed.

She had written that China was now her home; it was not that she did not love her father but the rebellion had changed her life forever in ways that she could never have envisaged.

Grief-stricken, John had attempted to find his daughter in the city. The rebellion had taken from him the two most precious things from his life – his children.

'It is as hot as China,' Liza said, slipping her arm through John's. 'But the air smells clean. I feel that you are thinking about Naomi and Andrew,' she continued softly.

'I was,' John sighed. 'They should be with us now. I failed them.'

'No,' Liza replied. 'Andrew found his identity and your daughter will do great things in her new land, I just know that. It is a new century and the world is changing. I think Naomi will help that change in China for the good of all the people there.'

'A big task for just one young woman,' John said.

'Not for the daughter of John Wong,' Liza answered, squeezing his arm affectionately.

John held the letter over the blue-green sea that was hissing softly against the hull of the ship as it ploughed south through the tropical waters. It fluttered from his hand to skip over the wash from the boat and bob on the small waves.

'Make China a free nation,' John whispered. 'Then one day, come home to me.'

The wind washed away his words, but not his hope.

THE DRAGON
AWAKE

1967
Beijing

'*Sha! Sha!*'
     Comrade Professor Tung Li stood at the window of his cramped office with geological samples strewn in every nook and cranny of the tiny room. The distant chanting chilled him as he gazed down on the crowd of blue-jacketed students milling in the snow-swept university courtyard below. As they stared up at him with glazed expressions of hate, the professor of geology recognised many of those calling for blood as his students. The Great Leader had mobilised China's youth for his cultural revolution to hold on to power and now the youth of China was tearing down what little the nation had managed to build.

     Professor Tung Li shook his head and walked away from the window. He gazed at the rock on his desk. It had been delivered to him months earlier when a labourer toiling on the old legation site had unearthed the stone, wrapped in a rotting rag. That it was one of the most valuable finds the world had ever known had been confirmed that morning when one half of the puzzle as to the rock's origin had been confirmed by colleagues from the West. Sadly, his liaison with the geological department in Paris had been another strike against the sixty-six-year-old teacher, whose fine features reflected the blood he had inherited from his mother, Naomi Wong and his father, Tung Chi.

Soon they would come for him and he knew that he would be berated for his revisionist, counter-revolutionary ideas. At best they might wave their copies of Mao's thoughts in his face, and force him to confess his sins. At worst, he would be dragged from the office and executed in public. Tung Li had already lost friends in that manner to the insane hysteria that had gripped his country. The Great Leap Forward had failed miserably and scapegoats had to be rooted out and sacrificed. Who better than the intellectuals and scientists of the newly emerged nation free of foreign domination to blame for the Great Leader's failure? Millions had starved to death and the purge had begun the year before. Tung Li had known that sending a fragment of the rock to a friend he had met years earlier studying geology in France was dangerous. But his whole life's work as a geologist had centred on the small stone dragon discovered in the old foreign legation ruins and it would be worth it if his theory proved to be correct.

As a door below crashed open the geologist could

hear the heavy clatter of boots on the stairs leading to the floor of his department. Wisely, the rest of the academic staff had already fled but Tung Li knew he must remain to protect the stone dragon.

Then it was his door that was being smashed down, spilling the young, blue-jacketed former students into his cramped office.

'He is here!' a girl cried to her comrades as Tung Li felt hands seize him, forcing him to kneel on the cold floor of his office.

'We have the counter-revolutionary criminal,' the girl called back to the mob, who cheered at her news.

Tung Li kept his head bowed, hoping that they might deliver little more then some rough handling and berating for his contacts with the Imperialist West, but when he chose to glance up at the girl who led the mob he could see no pity in her eyes. She was probably only seventeen years old and he vaguely remembered her as a student in one of his classes on the chemical composition of igneous rocks. He could not remember her name; she had been but one of many hundreds he had taught over the years at the Beijing University.

She reached forward and gripped the professor by the hair, wrenching his face up.

'You are Comrade Professor Tung Li,' she stated, rather than asking.

'I am, but you know that,' Tung Li answered, seeing the flame of a fanatic in her dark eyes.

'You have been accused of harbouring old ideas and communicating with the enemies of the revolution,' she spat. 'It is useless to deny the charges, Comrade Professor.'

Tung Li felt the numbing fear begin to overwhelm him. It did not feel as if he would be just rough-handled and then let go. He sensed that his contact with the French university's geological department had become public knowledge, and something as simple as having his results confirmed would be interpreted in political terms as subversion. Logic no longer prevailed in the new revolution unleashed on China. He knew it was better to remain silent and hoped that his dignity might impress some of his old students, now hanging back in the mob crushed into his office.

'You have no need to answer the charges,' the girl screamed in his face. 'They are already proven.'

She let go her grip on his hair and glanced at the table where the stone dragon lay. With a strange smile on her face she picked up a large, metal hammer.

'No!' Tung Li yelled, realising what the girl was about to do.

'Was this the rock that you used as an excuse to contact the foreign devils?' she asked.

Tung Li attempted to rise to his feet but was forced down by the mob. Without waiting for an answer the former student brought the hammer down, pulverising the rock. Again and again the hammer fell until all that remained was a fine powder and a few minuscule chips. The little stone dragon, which had lived safely in his rock case for millions of years, ceased to exist.

Still brandishing the hammer, the girl called on her comrades to drag the counter-revolutionary criminal down the stairs to the courtyard, where he would be executed in the name of the Great Leader's revolution.

The tears that flowed from the old geologist's eyes were not for himself – but for the death of the stone dragon. 'You fools,' he roared above the calls to kill him. 'You have just destroyed mankind's greatest find.'

But his tirade against the insanity of what was happening in his country was lost in the hysteria of a youth out of control. Tung Li fell and was kicked but fought to regain his feet and by the time they had dragged him to the snow-swept courtyard he was on his feet, battered and bruised.

The girl still held the geological hammer and waved it over her head.

'It is the judgment of the people that you be executed here and now,' she said, stepping forward. 'Hold him down,' she shouted.

'You will not execute him,' a deep voice roared above the murmuring of the young students ringed around their battered former teacher.

The students fell silent, turning their angry attention on a high-ranking officer of the People's Liberation Army, accompanied by a large contingent of armed soldiers holding their bayonet-tipped rifles at the high port across their chests. Many in the mob recognised the feared soldier and fell back to allow the representative of China's formidable army to stride forward to where the girl stood over Tung Li with her hammer raised.

'This man is my prisoner and you will hand him over to me immediately,' the officer commanded.

Tung Li looked to the girl and saw a fury in her eyes at having been usurped by the senior officer of the PLA.

'Comrade General,' the girl said angrily, 'you do not have the authority to interfere in the deliverance of the people's justice.'

With blurring speed, the general raised his pistol and fired point blank into the girl's face. A fine mist of red stained the snowdrifts as the girl toppled, still gripping the hammer.

'This man will come with me,' the general said, reaching down to assist Tung Li to his feet.

The shock of the girl being killed still hung in the air and, without any attempt to interfere, the crowd parted to allow the general and Tung Li through, with the general's escort falling in protectively as they made their way from the university grounds.

'Brother,' Tung Li said when they were a safe distance from the mob of students, 'I thought that you were stationed on the Manchurian border.'

'I was,' Tung Han replied. 'But the Great Leader requested that I return to Beijing to keep control of his revolutionary guards.'

Tung Han was a year older than Tung Li, and had chosen the life of a soldier, whereas Tung Li the life of a man of science. Despite their different paths the two men had remained as close as any two half-brothers could. Tung Han had been told of his different blood by his mother on her deathbed. That he was the son of a man who had fought the foreign devils at the turn of the century had helped the young man choose the life of a soldier, and he had wisely chosen to fight with the young Chinese poet who would lead them on the historic Long March, and eventually into nationhood. The Great Leader had purged many of those who previously had been faithful to him but with luck and good judgment Tung Han had survived and was known to many as a close confidant of the Great Leader and a man to be feared.

'Will the incident at the university have repercussions for you?' Tung Li asked as they walked.

'I was exercising my right to control the crowd,' Tung Han replied bluntly. 'Nothing more.'

Tung Li knew that his brother had risked much in rescuing him. In many circles of the Party he was considered suspect on account of his Western contacts and that was not good for his half-brother's career. 'What will you do with me?' Tung Li asked.

'You will be sent to a little village in the north of the country until this insanity abates,' Tung Han answered. 'There, you will work as a stonemason until it is safe for you to return. I cannot understand why you did not comply with my earlier suggestions to flee.'

'It was the stone dragon,' Tung Li said. 'I had to wait for the results to be confirmed. And now it has all been a waste of time. The evidence has been completely obliterated.'

'What was so important about the rock?' Tung Han asked.

'It was confirmed as coming from the planet Mars, and thus the fossil had to be a creature originating from that world. It would have answered one of mankind's most asked questions, about whether life existed beyond our own world.'

Tung Han ceased walking and turned to his brother. 'I am sorry that you have lost the stone dragon,' he said sympathetically. 'But you are alive, as I swore to our mother to protect you. I cannot mourn for your loss, as I am a soldier who has fought for my country. We need to find peace among ourselves before we find the answer to mankind's philosophical questions. It will pass.'

Tung Li gazed down the cold street. Maybe his brother was right, he mused. What good was the answer to the question of life on other worlds when on his own there was no peace. Ah, but at least he'd had the opportunity to gaze upon the little stone dragon and, for a brief moment, wondered who else had seen the creature from another world. That was a question to which he would not have an answer. For now his country was a sleeping dragon, awakening to make the world tremble.

Author's Notes

I had originally set out to write of the Australian colonial involvement in the Boxer Rebellion but soon learned that, as with the Suakin Campaign of 1885, Australian forces arrived just a little too late to see the bulk of the military action in the advance to Peking.

However, in the list of pre-Federation wars that saw Australians committed to fighting in foreign disputes, the Boxer rebellion is counted among our ventures. At least we did make an impression on some observers once our various naval brigades arrived. A British officer remarked in passing upon the arrival of the American soldiers: 'the men of the American Army were equalled in physique only by the Austral-ian Contingent and our Royal Horse Artillery.'

Bob Nicholls has comprehensively detailed our service in China in his excellent book, *Bluejackets and Boxers: Australia's Naval Expedition to the Boxer Uprising* (Allen & Unwin, Sydney, 1986). However, as the main source of information for this novel I was fortunate to come across Diana Preston's *The Boxer Rebellion* (Walker & Co., New York, 1999). Never before had I read such an interesting account of any historical event as I did in the pages of her book and I am indebted to her, as she has provided the canvas upon which I have detailed the fictional story of John Wong and his family. I would thoroughly recommend her book to any reader with an interest in history as it details so many interesting incidents I did not have the room to include in my story. Her account is a page turner to those with even a mild interest in such historical matters.

The Boxer Rebellion in the middle of 1900 also included the siege of the European legations in the city of Tientsin and the advance of the allied army and naval forces fighting their way towards Peking. Never before or since in modern history did so many European nations combine to attack a single nation. German, British, Austrian, Italian, French, Dutch, Belgian, Russian, Japanese and American marines stood shoulder to shoulder against the Boxers and Imperial Chinese land and naval forces. Fourteen years later these same nations would be split into two warring camps. And again, forty-two years later, American marines would find themselves fighting Japanese marines in bloody campaigns in the Pacific.

The Boxer Rebellion was a complex saga with so many events and plots unfolding that my fictional account has only explored one, comparatively small aspect. It was not within the scope of this novel to describe the engagements between the Chinese navy and the Allied navies, nor the vicious battles fought on the advance to free Tientsin and Peking. Again, I would recommend Diana Preston's work on the subject to learn more of what occurred during the Rebellion and after the Chinese were crushed.

Needless to say, today the nation of China is the emerging world superpower and Australia's foreign relations with that nation are of great importance to our economy.

This novel is so closely woven with factual events that I was almost tempted to give up on the adventures of John Wong as he was overshadowed by the real life adventures of men such as Dr George Morrison. Most of the events described in my novel concerning the larger than life Australian were real, such as the rescue of Polly Condit Smith (who, it appears, had a crush on Dr Morrison, although the feelings were not mutual, according to what was recorded in their respective journals).

Morrison's impact following the Boxer Rebellion on Chinese politics still echoes today in China. Tall, handsome and charismatic, his life is the stuff of Hollywood sagas. For further information on the man Cyril Pearl's *Morrison of Peking* (Penguin, 1967) provides a comprehensive description of his colourful life. He is, in my opinion, one of the greatest Australians we have ever been able to claim.

Herbert Hoover is also mentioned and it is interesting that the future thirty-first president of the United States was besieged with his wife, Lou, in the city of Tientsin. As a young mining engineer, Hoover was sent in 1897 to Western Australia to assist develop the gold mine at a little place known as Gwalia. The residence where he stayed is now a bed and breakfast for the intrepid tourist. From Gwalia he was transferred to China and his personal bravery was demonstrated in an incident when he rescued many Chinese children. His wife, Lou, worked in the hospital during the siege and suffered the same dangers with her husband.

I have used the spelling 'Pekin' throughout, rather than 'Peking'. From my research, the spelling that appears in the novel was used extensively by the real historical characters I have written about.

Finally, on a more personal note, the story of the Boxer Rebellion touches on my own life. My partner Naomi Howard-Smith's great grandparents, Thomas and Mary Howard, who were members of the London Bible Society, lost a young daughter, Dorothy, at the end of the siege in Peking, as did many other Australians. I hope this small part of our history with China will be remembered.

Acknowledgments

My gratitude and thanks for the production of this book go to my publisher, Cate Paterson, who has listened to my ideas for almost a decade. Cate has had the capable support of Catherine Day, who has done wonderful work editing this novel. Not to be forgotten is the work of Janet Hutchinson, who has had the tedious task of working through every word and sentence to correct grammatical errors. Special thanks to Jane Novak, my publicist, who has stood by me as long as I have been with Pan Macmillan. I would also like to express my thanks to Julie Crisp, whose editing work on my previous novel, *The Silent Frontier*, was remarkable. I wish her well in her new job in the UK.

My particular thanks go to my agent, Geoffrey Radford, who is always there for me. Thanks, mate.

I have recently moved to Maclean in northern

New South Wales from the beautiful village of Finch Hatton in Queensland. While living in the Pioneer Valley I worked as a volunteer emergency driver for the Queensland Ambulance Service. In my eighteen months with that organisation I was fortunate to work alongside some of Australia's finest people, sharing the sometimes heartbreaking situations as well as the occasional highs they experience. To all of you whom I have worked with, my very special thanks for your camaraderie and professionalism.

My thanks also go to so many people of the Pioneer Valley whom I had the chance to befriend. They are too numerous to mention but know who they are. However, a special thanks to Mel and Alice Lowth and all the family; you will not be forgotten. I would also like to extend a special mention to the wonderful ladies at the Mirani Library who ensured that my supply of research material for this novel was there for me.

It is here that I also have the opportunity to thank a few friends who have consistently supported me in my work. They are Virginia and Garie Wolfe from Tweed Heads and my old Yankee mate Larry Gilles, who served his country in Vietnam with the USMC. Larry's comments on aspects of the ongoing manuscript were invaluable. A special thank you to my old mate Kevin Jones and his wife Maureen who have both helped Naomi and me settle into the town. Many years ago Kevin and I served together in the NSW Police and the Army Reserve.

To my readers who enjoy this style of story, I would strongly recommend fellow Aussie author

Tony Park, whose books *Far Horizon*, *Zambezi*, *African Sky* and the soon-to-be-released *Safari* are well and truly in the tradition of that great author Wilbur Smith.

Last but not least I want to thank Naomi Howard-Smith for the love and support she has given me over the years in the good and bad times and through the publication of eight books. It is Naomi who points out that romance is essential in any story.

ALSO BY PETER WATT

'a rousing and revealing yarn'
WEEKEND AUSTRALIAN

CRY OF THE CURLEW

PETER WATT

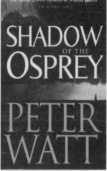

'the home grown version of Wilbur Smith'
THE SUNDAY AGE

SHADOW OF THE OSPREY

PETER WATT

'the historical detail brings the 19th century
sites to rip-roaring life' THE AUSTRALIAN

FLIGHT OF THE EAGLE

PETER WATT

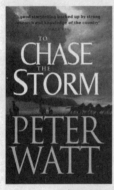

'good storytelling backed up by strong
research and knowledge of the country'
COURIER-MAIL

TO CHASE THE STORM

PETER WATT

PETER WATT

'the home-grown version
of Wilbur Smith'
THE SUNDAY AGE

PAPUA

EDEN

PETER WATT

THE SILENT FRONTIER

PETER WATT

THE STONE DRAGON

PETER WATT